I0653664

The Way the Future Was:
An Anthology of Science Fiction Fables

By

Pierre V. Comtois

Interior illustrations by
C. George Porter
Gregorio Montejo

Cover illustration by
Stephen Ralls

This book is a work of fiction. Any resemblance to actual events or persons, living or dead, is entirely coincidental.

"The Way the Future Was," by Pierre Comtois. ISBN 978-1-60264-241-6.

Published 2008 by Virtualbookworm.com Publishing Inc., P.O. Box 9949, College Station, TX 77842, US. ©2008, Pierre Comtois. All rights reserved. No part of this publication may be reproduced, stored in a retrieval system, or transmitted in any form or by any means, electronic, mechanical, recording or otherwise, without the prior written permission of Pierre Comtois.

Manufactured in the United States of America.

Contents

Introduction

THIS VOLUME IS DEDICATED to two groups of people: all of us in our 50s and 60s for whom the future was to have arrived in the year 2000 and that could not come soon enough and to the rising generation for whom it might yet arrive in 2100. I use the word "might" because the future that was scheduled to have arrived in the year 2000 never came.

Let me explain.

When I was a boy growing up in the 1960s, the year 2000 was still far off; far enough in the dim future to retain a mythic meaning to my friends and I. Fueled by vistas of cloud cities and flying cars seen in such television shows as *Lost in Space*, *Star Trek* or *Jonny Quest* and in countless books and stories by such classic SF authors as Isaac Asimov, John Campbell, Edmund Hamilton, Murray Leinster, C.M. Kornbluth, Frederik Pohl, Eric Frank Russell, and Stanley G. Weinbaum, we dreamed of a future that would be exciting simply to spend our day to day lives in.

As it was, the SF stories we spent summer afternoons devouring, described futures made up of bubble domed cities, moving slidewalks, regular space travel service between the planets, and personal jet packs. And though many of the futures dreamed up were of the dystopian variety, that never took away from the background toys that we believed could be possible in any future. But of all the writers detailing the future in those days, none captured the awe and wonder of what could be better than Ray Bradbury. His stories of rocket ships and alien worlds were less about what could go wrong in the future, than what could go right and were more often than not populated by families: mothers and fathers and especially children. The future, in Bradbury's stories, was one that most matched the one my friends and I expected down the long years to the 21st century which seemed so far away when we were 12 years old!

So imagine our disappointment to find that when the future arrived in 2000, it was not at all what we had expected. Instead of artificial gravity hovercars and overhead flight patterns, personal transportation was still earthbound and still based on the hundred year old internal combustion engine. Instead of cloud cities and bubble shaped domiciles, there were still drab apartment complexes and colonial style homes reminiscent more of the 19th century than the 21st. Instead of a sleek monorail system or frictionless trains, public transportation still consisted of subways and busses that continued to spout foul smelling exhaust into the air and even the space program, which had begun with such promise, had retreated from the moon and withered to almost nothing. Finally, the 21st century was dominated by a society that, for the most part, had devolved from that of the more civilized 1950s.

With those disappointments in mind, the stories in this collection were written. They are meant to recapture that spirit of optimism young people had for the future at a time when World War II was not that far removed from living memory. When the can do attitude of the United States in particular following its great victory over two powerful foes still dominated American pop culture. When American heroes were square jawed soldiers, brave policemen, or God fearing scientists who were as comfortable in the cockpit of a jet plane as they were in a laboratory.

My hope in writing the following stories has been to recapture the sense of optimism in the future that most young people once had; the ones for whom the year 2000 was to have been the tripwire beyond which everyone would be living in the superfuture. Here, in these tales, I hope to have revived some of that spirit and hope that any members of the younger generation reading them can be uplifted and find that the world of the future need not consist of limited expectations and the dead hand of political correctness.

Mars Needs People

DEXTER SNOW PAUSED AS he pushed the magno-sweeper down the long corridor of the admin building.

The low thrum began slowly. Imperceptible at first; something that was sensed before it was actually felt. Gradually, however, it built to such a pitch that anyone not as attuned to it as Dexter was, could feel the vibrations in the floor. Across the hall, a picture frame holding a print of a tri-D landscape of Venus swayed and dipped just off kilter. With the familiar excitement growing inside him, Dexter abandoned the magno-sweeper where it hovered and ran down the corridor to the exit membrane as fast as he could.

Outside, the sun was shining in the kind of summer day he remembered as a child when he and his friends used to race their frictionless bikes through the hover ways, heedless of descending flyers, madly making their way through the remnants of the old suburbs into the countryside. And the countryside in those days meant only one thing to a boy with any kind of imagination: rockets! The big, blue liners that took sightseers out to the asteroids and back again; the sleek, two man cruisers that shuttled the hop, skip, and jump run to the moon and back in a single day; the supply hulks that lifted off in thick clouds of steam to lumber the spaceways on their way to outlying survey parties on the moons of Jupiter; and the shiny science vessels, their holds crammed with equipment and stocks of condensed foods and their specially trained teams of scientists going bravely off to explore new worlds. All of them carried payloads of men and dreams and the imaginations of every boy who ever thrilled to the sight of a rocket's blast or the sound of its fins screeching into the sky or simply the look of it as its metallic surface gleamed in the summer sun.

Among his friends, the lure of exploring new worlds, of braving the hostile environments of methane seas, frozen atmospheres and gravities ten times that of Earth's was always at the forefront of their youthful ambitions, but for Dexter, none of those compared with Mars. Dull, red Mars, his friends used to call it. Thoroughly explored with over ten thousand colonists scattered in a half dozen domed towns whose environments made daily living easy. No danger on Mars at all! And all that sand! Red sand and pink skies! No greens or blues, even the sun shone a dark pink in the heavens. No, the action was all on the outlying planets these days! In all their discussions and speculations, Dexter never argued with his friends over the relative merits of life on Mars compared to the other planets. After all, his friends were right. There was no more excitement on Mars.

But there was beauty; beauty in abundance!

Whenever he could, Dexter would buy holo-discs on Mars, ask for photocomps of Mars for his birthday or Christmas, would save his money to buy the latest pop-bio of someone who had lived and worked on Mars. Early on, he fell in love with those red vistas, the sandy pink plains that seemed to stretch on forever, the rocky plateaus that suddenly dipped into vast craters, the mountains and the dry polar caps that had once held ice. He yearned to step out of a dome town and breath in the thin atmosphere whose oxygen content had only recently allowed humans to walk under the Martian sun without the protection of an environment suit. What that must feel like!

Pushing through the membrane of the admin building, Dexter stepped out into the warm sunlight only to have its intensity remind him that he was after all, not on Mars, but on Earth, not two miles from where he grew up. In the distance, he could plainly see the glassite towers of Canaveral, all pastels of blue and green and yellow, the bright gleams of moving levitators inside catching the sunlight as they moved passengers up and down. Tiny dots indicated flyer activity in the hover ways around the towers and although he couldn't make them out from this far, he knew pedestrians would be traveling along peoplewalks, mothers with their children mostly at this time of a work day. Closer in, the ruins of the suburbs he used to ride his 'bike through when he was a boy were mostly gone, plowed over to make room for parks and orchards. Overhead, not a cloud marred the blue perfection of the sky and Dexter breathed deep of the late morning air, now tinged with just a hint of rocket exhaust.

By now, of course, the deep thrum that had sent him running for the observation deck of the admin building had become a shrieking wail as the big rocketship slowed in the atmosphere, preparing for its final descent. Dexter shaded his eyes against the sun and looked for the telltale glint of metal and found it almost directly overhead. It grew rapidly as he realized with relief that he'd come out just in time. In seconds, the shiny glint had resolved itself into the definite contours of the latest model Mac-Donell-Douglas heavy lift Mars Shuttle. Dexter's heart pounded with pride and anticipation as he watched the huge vessel as it came down from the heavens aiming unerringly for its cradle along the old Rocket Row at the south end of the field. Soon, a plume of white hot flame burst from its main thrusters, and for a moment, it seemed as if the giant ship stood on a pillar of fire before once again moving gently downward. Then, just before it was about to touch down, vast clouds of steam burst from hidden chambers beneath the cradle as millions of gallons of seawater were used to cool the atmosphere around the landing pad.

Suddenly, the vibrations that had rumbled through the ground ceased and for a few seconds all was quiet with only the clouds of steam roiling about the landing pad. Then the all clear horn began to wail and Dexter could see the small fleet of hover vehicles as they left their pens begin to race out to the rocket cradle. A strong breeze came off of the sea just then, and like a curtain being pulled apart, the steam opened and revealed the Mars Shuttle, all silver and blue in the sunlight, resting as pretty as you please in its cradle. Dexter's heart skipped a beat when he saw it ranged against the descending line of ships standing at other cradles all down Rocket Row. In the distance, a small, two man rocket was just lifting off, the sound of its engines taking a few seconds to be heard. As a gantry slowly began to crawl toward the recently arrived Mars Shuttle, Dexter guessed it would be a few hours before the crew were debriefed and checked in. By then, if he worked it right, his duties would take him to the astronauts' reception area where family and friends could welcome their loved ones home.

Turning away from the launch area, Dexter once again found himself facing the admin building, a glassite structure of interconnected towers and tinted plexi-domes that allowed plenty of natural light into the offices and work areas inside. After watching the return of the Mars Shuttle, it took some bit of will power for Dexter to force himself to return indoors and to his custodial duties.

He still remembered the day he came to the Rocket Port and entered its confines officially for the first time. Not as a boy, face pressed against the chain link fence that surrounded the facility, eagerly watching the rockets come and go, but as an applicant for space duty! It was soon after he'd matriculated from secondary comp and, filled with anticipation, refused to waste any time in assuring officials of the Space Administration that he had something valuable to contribute to the exploration of space. He could see himself now, sitting nervously in the ante-room of the personnel office, looking at the walls covered in tri-D portraits of the early space pioneers all of whose names he knew by heart: there was Jerzy "Rocket" Bilboa, the first man to set foot on Mars; Philbin Nacroft, who found himself stranded on Deimos for six months before a rescue rocket could come back for him; Paul Martineau, who confirmed that the Martian canals were not natural formations; Scott Shaughnessy, the first living being to walk the streets of a Martian city in a million years; John and Phoebe Nelson, the first married couple to stand on a planet other than Earth (their first child was conceived on the tiny station on Uranus!); and Jack "Black" Stack, who'd walked the surfaces of more planets than any man in history! Then, suddenly, he'd heard his own name: "Dexter Snow?" He stood up, too quickly, he thought, and identified himself. "Will you please step into my office?"

Personnel Manager Jaunder was a friendly, understanding man, not like the typical bureaucrat Dexter had been led to expect by others who tried to warn him how unlikely it was that he would be hired for the Rocket Corps.

"So, Mr. Snow, you want to go into space I see," said Jaunder.

"Yes, sir," Dexter replied.

"I have reviewed your application papers and although I commend your enthusiasm, I must regretfully inform you that you do not possess any of the skills the Corps is currently seeking."

"I know my matriculation records show that I have not been more than an average achiever, but I am willing to learn and work hard and do whatever is required of me to qualify," Dexter said. "If only I am allowed to go into space!"

"I am sorry, Mr. Snow," said Jaunder with an amused smile on his lips. "But there is nothing an untrained person, with no particular scientific or technical specialty, could do in space. Room aboard a rocket ship is always at a premium and every person that goes into space must have some valuable skill needed by the crew or the colonists of the worlds the ships go to. In addition, our people often must be cross trained in two or more skills."

"But ever since I was a boy, I have dreamed of going into space, of going to Mars," said Dexter, aware that he was pleading, but not caring how he sounded, such was his yearning for the stars. "I have read all the holodiscs I could find about Mars, biographies and science books and every kind popular fiction too. I have kept up with all the latest discoveries..."

"Just loving Mars and knowing everything about its history and geography, its early explorers, is not enough, I am afraid," explained Jaunder, not unkindly.

Disheartened, Dexter rose from his seat and turned away, knowing that he could never master the technical skills needed to ride the rockets. Why had he come in the first place? Did he enjoy torturing himself at the sight of the rockets, leaving Earth without him? He should have listened to his family and friends who warned him that no ordinary person had a chance of going into space.

"Wait a moment, Mr. Snow," said Jaunder behind him. "If you are in need of employment and enjoy the sight of the rockets coming and going, perhaps you would consider duties other than space flight here at the Rocket Port?"

Dexter, suddenly forgetting how painful it was to see the rockets take off and being left behind, nodded eagerly, not caring what kind of work he was offered, so long as he could remain at the Rocket Port, close to the space ships.

And so, his application was transferred to the maintenance department and he began work with the custodial crew. It was true the money wasn't so good (although the benefits more than compensated for that) and due to automation and strict environment controls there really wasn't much for a janitor to do (he kept busy doing maintenance: changing the odd light bulb and replacing the occasional fuse...things that probably would never become automated), but the important thing was that the job kept him near the rockets. He was able to catch every take-off and landing, he watched them being serviced and every now and then, when he worked third shift, Maintenance Supervisor Howard would let him look around inside one of the rockets.

Dexter, turned on the magno-sweeper and as he began to pass it over the floor, his mind wandered, the way it always did when he was doing something particularly monotonous, to that day when Howard first let him aboard old *Daisy*.

Daisy, of course, wasn't the rocket's real name...according to Space Administration records, it was the XL76-T *Vindicator*...Capt. Mark Carpenter named it the *Daisy* after his daughter. It was tradition ever since the early days of regular space flight for the first captain of a new rocket to give his ship whatever name he wanted. And although the *Daisy* was an older vessel, to Dexter, it had fulfilled all the expectations of his youthful imagination. He still remembered the thrill he felt stepping through the ship's airlock...the first he had ever crossed...into the rocket's cool interior. There was the vague smell of plastic and metal in the air and the dull hum of the fusion generators created the impression that the ship was alive and ready to leap into the sky at a moment's notice. Power cables dangled from the crew compartments overhead or snaked up from the storage bays and engine rooms below and trailed out the airlock to test equipment on the gantry outside. By the airlock, a metal ladder extended the length of the ship, used while the rocket sat planetside and the demands of gravity forced the crew to climb hand over hand to get anywhere. But seeing the padded hand grips that lined the interior bulkhead of the ship allowed Dexter to imagine life aboard the rocket as it soared between worlds when gravity gave way to weightlessness and the crew passed from one end of the ship to the other moving hand over hand down its 1,700 foot length. With mounting excitement, he'd taken hold of the ladder and hauled himself up the dozen or so feet to the first of three levels that made up the crew compartment. He passed the sleeping quarters where each man had his own small, but comfortably private cubicle and a minute later, he was moving through the living quarters where the galley, disc library, and recreation equipment were located. Finally, he emerged onto the command deck, the heart and brain of the rocket where the heroic space captain would give his orders and take direct control of the landing procedure. From where he still clung to the ladder, Dexter could almost see the captain sitting in his upholstered command chair, hands firmly gripping the cyclic that controlled the rocket's stabilizing fins as he manually brought the giant, flaming rocket out of the vacuum of space and into the turbulent atmosphere of some far world. *How many worlds had the* Daisy *visited in her long career?* Dexter had wondered. The moons of Jupiter? Saturn? The asteroids? *Mars?* The mere thought that the ship he stood within might have sat shiny and tall amid the swirling pink dust of Mars set his pulse to racing! Slowly, almost reverently, he stepped from the ladder and approached the captain's chair. He ran his hand lightly over its old and cracked leather covering and saw in his mind's eye how the configuration of the ship would change once the rocket reached space and leveled off. Then, the crew's chairs would alter position and what was the deck while the rocket stood vertically on the Earth's surface, would become a bulkhead with the crew passing through it by the hatch that now stood closed in the center of the "deck." Overhead, it seemed strange to see the viewports and the controls for the pilots, the communications and navigations officers, fixed near the "ceiling" instead of the deck but it was all part of the glamour and the excitement associated with space travel that Dexter had always dreamed of. Since that time, Dexter had occasion to visit other rockets, but wonderful as they were, none seemed to capture the excitement he felt that day aboard the *Daisy*.

By the time Dexter had completed his recollections, he'd finished the floors of the admin wing and it was time to take the levitator down to the crew's reception area where he hoped to greet the men who'd just landed aboard the Mars Shuttle. Over the years since beginning his job at the Space Administration, Dexter had occasion to meet and talk to many of the tall men of the Space Corps and gloried in their willingness to accept him as one of the familiar faces welcoming them back from their often long and arduous jaunts among the planets. Their recognition of him as a friend was one of his proudest boasts and over the years, his appearance in the reception area to be among the first to greet them after the jaded and far less impressed technicians had completed their debriefs and post-mission check-ups, had become a small ritual Corpsmen had come to look forward to.

"Hello, Dexter!" waved Pilot Smith, the mission's captain.

"Hello, captain!" replied Dexter, placing the magno-sweeper on standby. "How was your flight?"

"Very smooth, very smooth," came the reply, as Smith thumped him on the back. "And how have things been Earthside? You still holding the Port together by your lonesome?"

"Without me, the place would fall apart," said Dexter, going along with the standing joke. "Who would replace the light bulbs if I were not around to do the job?"

"You are the only constant in a constantly changing world, Dexter," said Smith.

"But tell me, sir," said Dexter, "about Mars."

Smith paused, and for a moment, his features grew wistful and Dexter had no doubt that the man was a kindred spirit, in love with that wild, still mostly untamed planet, even as he was.

"Mars is still the same and still very beautiful," said Smith at last. "I remember the last night we were there. I was standing on the observation platform of Marineris Base 2, saying goodbye to the red sand and pink sky. All around me, a mild wind blew, kicking up the Martian dust but not as much as it used to in the days of Jack Stack, there is a heavier atmosphere these days, and the soil is able to hold more moisture. Soon, I thought, there would be vegetation growing in the valleys and orchards would stretch out from the Base instead of sand. Then, the rocky walls of the hillsides would become obscured in branches and leaves and the children will laugh as they pick the fruit. Things will be a great deal different then, but still beautiful."

"Maybe it will be the way Mars used to look in the days of the ancient race," added Science Officer Brown. "There is much evidence being found in the ruins of its cities to suggest that the Martians lived on a much more fertile world than we see today."

"Did you visit any of their cities, Science Officer Brown?" asked Dexter.

"Oh, yes," replied Brown. "I have colleagues on Mars who have been doing some interesting research on the Martians. As you know, the Martian alphabet has only recently been decyphered with the result that our knowledge of the Martians and the way they lived has increased greatly. They were a quiet, contemplative people; more taken by art and literature than science. They had very little in the way of electronics although they knew all about technology. They preferred to design their graceful buildings and write poetry than work with machines or computers."

"It was a great shame that they perished all those centuries ago," said Dexter, who mourned the Martians' passing just as if the great catastrophe had happened the day before.

"Indeed," agreed Brown. "And when I walked the streets of what was left of their great cities, I felt the loss greatly. Sadly, there is little that remains of them above the ground, but it is enough for those like you and I who feel keenly the Martians' absence, to give us a sense of the awe and mystery of Old Mars."

"Unfortunately, despite the scattered ruins, there is little of that Old Mars remaining," said Astrogator Jones. "The geologic upheavals that wracked the planet hundreds of thousands of years ago were very thorough in their work. Who knows how much of the Martian civilization was destroyed when the seas dried up and the continents fell away?"

"Did you see much evidence of those disastrous times, Astrogator Jones?" Dexter wanted to know, having only the holo images of Mars to go by, and who yearned to see for himself the monstrous formations that now dominated the Martian landscape.

"I have hiked the Martian backcountry many times on past visits," confirmed Jones. "I have taken flyers to Tharsis Ridge and followed the line of volcanoes as they wound along the waist of the planet, and hiked the Valles Marineris. And let me tell you, the early explorers were right when they said nothing on Earth compared with it! The sights of those towering volcanoes, many taller than any on Earth, and the canyons, remnants of a river system created when the seas of Mars were drained away after the continents sunk, make the Grand Canyon look like a mud flat. Never have I seen such wild, desolate, and beautiful country! And when a storm comes up and the dust flies through the pink air and the reddish sun is obscured...well! You fall in love with Mars and never want to leave."

"Astrogator Brown has already put in papers for permanent transfer to a Martian colony," said Smith.

"Is that true?" asked Dexter, almost breathless with envy.

"It is," confirmed Jones. "I have applied for work as a simple laborer in the archeological pits and in my spare time, intend to hike the backcountry and eventually, after suitable preparation, Olympus Mons itself."

Science Officer Brown laughed good naturedly. "If you reach the top, you will be the first human being to do it as that volcano is at least three times taller than Mt. Everest here on Earth. And unlike Everest, you will not only need the usual hiking gear, but an environment suit as well because the new atmosphere does not and will never reach all the way to the volcano's peak."

"True, and that will be the challenge," said Jones. "It will take years of study and preparation but when I have conquered the volcano, I will write a book of my adventure!"

The others laughed, all except Dexter, who only wished he could accompany Astrogator Jones on his journey.

"Well, Dexter," said Smith. "It has been a pleasure to see you again, but we must move on now; our families are waiting for us."

"Of course, Pilot Smith," said Dexter. "Good bye and welcome back!"

As the three men walked from the reception area, Dexter looked after them, wondering why Jones could be allowed to go to Mars simply to help dig in the archeological pits. How much skill could such labor demand? Why could he not be allowed to go to Mars and help dig for Martian artifacts? Such work did not require specialized skills! As he returned to his magno-sweeper, Dexter forced himself to suppress the resentment he felt at the double standard that permitted Jones to live on Mars but condemned ordinary folk such as himself to the humdrum existence of life on Earth.

And so, the days continued to pass much as they always had. Dexter continued to come to work at the Rocket Port four days a week to magno-sweep the halls of the Admin Building and supervise the robo-scrubbers as they washed the glassite buildings and change the occasional light bulb. Weekends he spent reading about Mars and the planets, but somehow, the energy he had once invested in the activity had drained away and the photo-comps of the Martian landscape no longer seemed to excite him as they always had. Even the occasional blast off or landing of a rocket was no longer enough to draw him outdoors to watch. Sitting one evening in his living unit high in the Canaveral Leisure Living Tower, it suddenly occurred to him that he was losing the one abiding interest that had made life at all endurable for him. Without his love of the rockets, his dream of going into space, of going to Mars some day, what did he have to look forward to day after day? Slowly, he felt a rising panic inside of him. If his dream was lost, what did anything matter?

A dull thrum came from outside and when he looked out his wall membrane, he could see a bright light coming down in the night sky. He didn't have to consult the schedule to know that it was the Uranus rocket just in from the outer planet run. Oh! How he wanted to be on it, on any rocket that was leaving Earth! The strength of his emotions surprised him because it proved that the love he had for space and Mars that he thought was dying, was still there, deep inside him, as strong as ever! He still wanted to go! He still wanted to go to Mars more than anything! Quickly, he grabbed his derma-jacket and exited his living unit. He descended the levitator to the Tower garage and maneuvered his flyer to the entrance and then to the hover way that led outside the city. He determined to make his case to Personnel Manager Jaunder. He would confront him with the Administration's hypocrisy and demand why Astrogator Jones could be allowed to go to Mars just to labor in the archeological digs when he was not. Surely, he was qualified do the same kind of thing?

Still fired with determination and resolved that if he was not permitted to go into space, he would quit his job, he arrived at the flyer port and settled his vehicle into the workers' lot. In his eagerness, he had forgotten that it was still early in the morning, still dark, in fact, and Personnel Manager Jaunder would not be in his office. Unwilling to return to the city, he was too keyed up for that, he decided to kill the time in the maintenance lounge watching the Uranus rocket being serviced. But no sooner had he settled in one of the thickly padded chairs than he fell asleep only to be awoken hours later when his name was being called over the speaker system.

"Will Dexter Snow please report to the personnel office? Dexter Snow to the personnel office. Thank you," said the female voice.

Dexter stood and straightened his tunic. All right then. Personnel Manager Jaunder probably wanted to discuss changes in his benefits package or his work schedule but the man would get a good deal more than he bargained for when he called for the page! Walking from the lounge, Dexter was determined to give Jaunder an ultimatum. Either he would allow him to apply for work on Mars, or he would quit his job immediately. So thinking, Dexter stepped into the personnel office where the pretty secretary motioned him to go right into Jaunder's office. "Mr. Snow is here, Mr. Jaunder," Dexter heard her say to the room in general.

"Good morning, Dexter," said Jaunder after Dexter had stepped into his office. "Please sit down."

"I would rather stand if you do not mind," said Dexter, nervous despite himself. "You see, Mr. Jaunder, I have made up my mind that if the Space Administration will not consider my application to go into space, then I no longer wish to be associated with the Rocket Port..."

"That is what I wanted to speak to you about, Mr. Snow," said Jaunder, unexpectedly.

Dexter blinked. "You do? I thought there was a change in my benefits..."

"There has been a change but not in your benefits package (which is a very good one by the way) but in the Administration's policy regarding space travel. Mr. Snow, I have not been unaware of your keen interest in going into space in general and to Mars in particular. Oh, yes; I recall our initial interview when I was forced, much to my discomfort, to deny your application for the Space Corps. My actions at the time, though unavoidable, were nevertheless painful to me. Thus, I never interfered when employees in the service department broke our rules to let you aboard idle rockets..." Jaunder held up a hand. "No need for protest. Nor have I ever complained about the times you ignored your duties to watch a rocket landing or taking off. Considering your great desire to go into space, I did not mind the occasional lapse. After all, we are all a little star struck here at the Space Administration...even Secretary Betty out there in the reception area." Dexter's eyes widened. "Oh, yes...but the rest of us manage to control our enthusiasms.

"Which brings me to the situation at hand," Jaunder continued, leaning forward and turning his desktop computer podium around so that Dexter could see the screen. "As you can see, I have here an official notice from Space Administration headquarters in Houston, an announcement of a change in policy. Recognizing the rapidly increasing population of our colonies on Mars and their swiftly moving reconfiguration from mostly quasi-governmental/scientific outposts to working towns complete with their own selectmen, private enterprises, churches, residences, etc., the administration has heeded the demand to match the number of specialists it continues to send with an equal number of general laborers. In short, what is needed most at the Mars bases now are cooks, secretaries, agricultural help, maintenance workers...and custodians." Dexter's eyes widened even more as his hands searched behind him for the chair he had spurned earlier in the interview. "So, Mr. Snow, are you still interested in applying for a position on Mars? It will not be with the Space Corps of course, as I understand it, the non-scientific positions are being offered by the Mars community itself and so, if hired, you would be an employee of say...Marsville, or Mars Base 2..."

"Yes! Oh, yes! I am still very much interested, Mr. Jaunder!" replied Dexter, with altogether too much enthusiasm, but he didn't care! To Mars! At last, he was going to Mars!

Signing the proper forms and applications was the work of a few minutes and a vigorous shake of the hand with Mr. Jaunder took even less time before Dexter dashed from the personnel office with a jaunty wave to Secretary Betty.

Biting his lip to hold back the tears of joy and relief, he quickly ascended the nearest levitator and made his way outside to an overlook where he could view the rockets lined up on the launch apron in all their silvery brightness. Soon, he would be boarding one of them, maybe the big blue liner or the old *Daisy* or better yet, the Mars Shuttle with Pilot Smith and his crew and some day, he and Astrogator Jones together would climb Olympus Mons!

And when he reached the top, and all Mars lay at his feet, Mars, with its volcanoes and empty canyons and haunted Martian cities and its pink dust and ruby red mountains and the new, strange life that would soon be growing in its reconstituted atmosphere, he'd open his arms wide and crush it all to him and shout like a prayer: "Mars, beautiful, mysterious, lovely Mars! I have dreamed of you and yearned for you and now I will have you forever!" And he would come down from the mountain and watch the rockets from Earth arrive, all silvery and bright, bringing more people, carpenters and homemakers and plumbers and farmers and clergy. No longer able to hold back his tears, Dexter allowed them to fall freely. And someday, the hills outside the Martian towns would be dotted with farmsteads and little villas and in old age, he would watch the children as they laughed and ran down to the rocket port to watch the rockets come and go and dream as he once did of going to the stars.

There Was a Rocket

13 years, 2 months, 6 days out from Sol

FRED JOSELY WAS HAVING trouble concentrating.

It had nothing to do with the stars clearly visible outside the *Endeavor*'s forward viewplate or the fact that he was trying to input data into the compu-board he held in his hand while fighting the effects of zero gravity, nor even the lingering disorientation that always bothered him in the first few hours after being awakened from hiber-sleep.

No, his lack of concentration had nothing to do with any of that. The problem was Pamela.

Even as Fred re-entered the same information into his compu-board for at least the third time, he knew he still had it wrong. Angry with himself, he punched the delete key with the intention of starting his calculations all over again but decided to give it up as a lost cause...at least for the next few minutes.

Casually, or as casually as he could muster in zero-gravity, he pushed himself away from the hiber-sleep monitoring console in the direction of the viewplate and just managed to let go of his compu-board in time to brace himself against the bulkhead from where he could stare outside.

Trying not to look too obvious, he turned his head just enough to catch a glimpse of Pamela out of the corner of his eye. Although her dark hair was caught up in a net to prevent it from becoming unmanageable in the zero G environment, Fred could make out her figure well enough in the tight fitting female cut of her coveralls and the slightly oval shape of her face as she watched readouts of communications from Earth that were days old at this distance from home.

Sighing, Fred looked away from Pamela and stared out of the viewplate. He was no astronomer so he could only guess as to which of the myriad stars outside was Sol, the home none of the 213 men and women aboard the *Endeavor* would ever see again.

Decades in the making, the *Endeavor* had been assembled in orbit above Mars while an intensive search was made to pick a crew who would then become settlers for Earth's first colony outside the solar system. But because it would take over 100 years to reach Magna III, the entire crew were to make the trip primarily in suspended animation. The plan was to have the ship's computer awaken crew members at intervals throughout the trip as their various specialties were needed to maintain operations and to monitor the complex web of positronic systems that actually conducted day to day activities aboard the *Endeavor*.

Chosen for their individual skills as well as their physical stamina, the crew ended up being a relatively young one and very close in age with the average being about 26.7 years. As such, planners on Earth theorized that even after having been awakened a number of times on the long voyage out, the crew would arrive on Magna III still youthful and thus best able to face the hard, early years of the colony's being established.

With staggered schedules, and infrequent awakenings by the ship's computer, it was determined that the development of personal relations among crew members would be unlikely and that such things would wait until planetfall had been completed.

But that was not the way it was working out for Fred who chanced another surreptitious glance in Pamela's direction. His heart skipped a beat as he saw that she had disappeared. Where had she gone? He twisted his body around more fully the better to take in the view of the entire control room but except for a few other crew members, there was no sign of her.

"Looking for me?"

Startled, Fred swung back in the opposite direction only to come face to face with Pamela.

Suddenly, his heart began to pound and his mind went blank.

"Um..." was all he could muster.

"Let me make it easy for you," said Pamela. "I've noticed you casting looks in my direction...they were pretty obvious...so why don't we go down to the cafeteria and I'll buy you a cup of synth-coffee?"

"Good idea," was all Fred could think of to say. He hoped he had put the right quality of carelessness into it but suspected he'd probably failed.

Attaching his compu-board to its place on the console, he drifted to the transit hatch with Pamela directly behind him. As the hatch matched up with that set in the rotating living section of the ship, he waved his arm indicating ladies first. Pamela didn't hesitate passing through, leaving plenty of time for Fred to follow before the two hatches had once again passed one another.

Inside the living section, they slowly settled to the deck as its revolving movement created a gravity 0.25 of Earth's; enough to allow the crew to walk normally albeit with a good spring in their step.

"It's always a relief to be able to walk on my own two feet," said Pamela as she led the way down a corridor, past a crew member or two, to a door that slid silently aside giving access to a small cafeteria.

"I was born on Earth but raised on Mars so this lighter gravity feels almost like home to me," Fred said, following Pamela to the food dispensers. "Do you take it black?"

"What?"

"Your coffee, do you like it black or...?"

"Oh! Synth-cream and glucose please."

Fred tried to keep the shake in his hands under control as he prepared the drinks. Congratulating himself on not spilling any, he nodded in the direction of a couple of unoccupied seats.

"So, you saw me looking at you, huh?" Fred said after a first sip of his coffee.

"I hope you didn't think a girl wouldn't notice?"

"Well...yeah, I did."

Pamela laughed and Fred thought the sound the most wonderful he'd ever heard. More, her smile completely changed the look of her face, lighting it up and making her seem even more attractive to him. Here was someone who could bring out feelings of tenderness in him with no effort at all.

"You know what I think?" said Fred. "I think you were looking at me as much as I was looking at you."

"So now you're a psychologist as well as a hiber-sleep technician?"

"Not at all, I just can't believe that I was as obvious as all that."

Pamela chose not to pursue the subject. Instead, she asked about his job.

"I began my career in the life sciences before focusing on hiber-sleep technology," explained Fred, feeling more comfortable talking about his work than answering questions intended to reveal more of his feelings than he wanted to let on. "Since the space program had the only interest in that kind of research, I applied for a job. Another lucky break was that because the field was so new, my department was a relatively small one and in no time, I found myself in charge. This project, the first deep space colonization effort, was also the first full scale application of everything I'd been working on for the past eight years. Not only did I want to be on hand to monitor and study the practical results of all my work, but I was really attracted by the sense of adventure the project offered."

"Well, speaking from the point of view of a hiber-sleep subject, it seems to be working fine," said Pamela. "We women need our beauty sleep you know."

"Not that I can tell," said Fred boldly.

"Never mind about that," returned Pamela. "We've been away from Earth for over 13 years now, has the process been working as you've expected?"

"Perfectly," said Fred. "If the ship's computer continues to function as it should, we ought to all arrive at Magna III at approximately the same age and no worse for wear."

"But once we get to Magna III, won't the usefulness of a hiber-sleep tech be ended?" said Pamela playfully.

"Well, I still have my background in life sciences to fall back on," said Fred. "We'll need someone who can keep track at how well we adapt to life on Magna III and how we can turn the planet's biology to our advantage.

"But what about you?" said Fred, turning the tables on Pamela. "What good is a positronic systems expert on a primitive new planet?"

"The short answer is: not much!" laughed Pamela. "But I expect to keep busy for a while with the ship's systems. You know from our mission briefing that we'll be expected to live aboard ship for years before most of us will be able to move permanently onto the planet. And even then, we'll have simply extended the ship's positronic systems to individual units planetside; they'll all still be connected to the main computer aboard *Endeavor*."

There was an awkward silence then until Pamela rose from her seat.

"Well, guess we'd better head back to work," she said. "We only have a few hours before returning to hiber-sleep."

"I guess so," said Fred, rising also.

"Why don't I detect any enthusiasm in your words, Fred? Don't tell me one of the developers of the hiber-sleep process doesn't care for it?"

"It's not that," said Fred as he tossed his cup into the recycling unit. "Actually, things are going to seem dull around here if I can't look forward to having coffee with you again."

Pamela stopped and stared at him expectantly.

"What do you say?" ventured Fred. "Want to share a cup with me during the next cycle?"

"Are you asking me for a date?"

"Sure, I guess you can put it that way. That is if you count it a date when the next time we meet might only be in ten years!"

"But in hiber-sleep it won't seem that long at all," replied Pamela. "Let me check my personal schedule..."

Reaching into a pocket in her coveralls, she pulled out a 'tronic note pad and asked the computer to match up her flight schedule with that of Fred Josely.

"Oh! We have a match!"

Fred secretly thrilled at the obvious delight in her voice as he leaned in to see the note pad's display window. Sure enough, there were nine days in which their schedules would over-lap during the next cycle.

"I tell you what, next time, let's do lunch," suggested Pamela.

"It's a date," said Fred happily. "See you in ten years!"

They both laughed at the absurdity of their situation, left the living section, and went back to work in the control section.

24 years, 8 months, 3 days out from Sol

Before Fred opened his eyes and just after consciousness began to return to him, there was a click and a faint sound of hissing air as the ship's computer, responding to a schedule arranged decades before when the *Endeavor* first went on line, gently woke him from hiber-sleep.

As he became more fully conscious, Fred raised his hands and pushed gently against the underside of the plasteel lid whose hermetic seal had been loosened and its latches undone. The lid lifted up and over as if it were weight-less and sitting up, he prepared himself for the passing nausea that was the usual aftereffect of prolonged hiber-sleep.

His stomach settled, Fred swung his legs from the hiber-pod and stood up. He waited for the expected wave of disorientation that always affected him when emerging from hiber-sleep and when it had passed, turned and lowered the lid of the pod. Around him, other pods, 213 of them, were ranged side by side in a number of rows that stretched upward with the deck that formed the inner bulkhead of the *Endeavor*'s drum shaped central section. This section was the only one of three that rotated on its own axis and that provided a measure of centrifugal force for the sleeping crew and the living spaces they needed when awake.

As he made his way up the corridor to the physician's office for a post-sleep checkup, Fred could hear the voices of other crew members as they went about their duties or returned to hiber-sleep. Work schedules aboard the *Endeavor* had been arranged by mission planners while the ship was still being assembled in Mars orbit and were intended to have specialists in many different operations awake and on duty at the same time. The total number of crew members was calculated so that duties could be shared while allowing each enough time in hiber-sleep that all could arrive at Magna III at an age that preserved their youthful vigor.

That was the theory anyway as Fred checked the ship's chronometer that indicated that they were into the 24th year of what was determined to be a 105 year journey to Magna III. He hardly felt as if any time had passed at all since the *Endeavor* left Mars orbit in 2164; in fact, it felt as if he had just left Pamela only a few minutes before. Suddenly, with the reminder, he felt a growing anticipation at the prospect of seeing her again and, unable to wait until she was scheduled to be awakened, headed in the direction of her hiber-pod.

It only took a few minutes to find her section and as he stood over her pod, he felt his heart swell in an affection that seemed inexplicable considering that he had only met with her once and that briefly. For some reason, she had removed the net that held her hair while working in zero gravity and her dark locks lay loose about her head. With her eyes closed and her hands folded demurely across her chest, her attitude served to remind him of what it was about her that first attracted him. It was something more than her physical features, something that he had only realized after sitting down and talking with her: when she gave him her attention, she gave him all of it. For those few minutes in the cafeteria, she made him feel as if she was actually interested in what he had to say; an attitude that gave him the confidence to speak his mind.

Placing his hand on the lid of the pod, he made a silent wish that their next meeting would go as well and that he did not say anything to ruin the budding relationship. Reluctantly, he left her form behind and headed to the scheduling office to find out what his work hours and duties were to be for the upcoming cycle.

Leaving the hiber-sleep area, he entered the living section where the administration, cafeteria, recreation rooms, and living quarters were located. There, he found the scheduling office and was told which shifts he would assume over the next month before returning to hiber-sleep. Not really interested in his personal assignments (they never really changed much), he made what he thought was an oblique inquiry as to Pamela's schedule. He knew he'd failed in keeping his particular interest from being suspected when he noticed that the scheduling officer seemed to give him a knowing look out of the corner of her eye.

"Pamela Letourneaux?" she asked.

"Yeah, she's a positronic systems tech," explained Fred. "I might need to interface with her some in checking over the hiber-sleep computer logs."

"Here she is," said the scheduling officer as her computer screen stopped scrolling. "She's scheduled to be woken next week. She'll be up for six weeks after that. Satisfied?"

"Um, sure..." mumbled Fred making a hasty exit under the lingering eye of the scheduling officer.

Fred next reported to the duty officer down the corridor and was told to get something in his stomach before heading over to the control section. After a light lunch, he transited into the weightless environment of the control section and using the hand grips that studded the bulkhead, swung himself over to the executive officer to report for duty.

"Good to see you, Fred," said duty officer Tom. "There seems to be a glitch in the hiber-sleep systems and we haven't had a regular hiber-sleep tech on duty for the last two cycles. Don't think it amounts to much, but you'd better look at that first."

"No problem, Tom," said Fred, getting down to business. "Has anyone been able to pinpoint the source? Is it the computer mainframe or simply a local systems failure?"

"Could be either so you better check both."

"Is there a positronic systems tech on duty?" asked Fred, for the first time hoping there wasn't.

"See John for that," replied Tom. "He's on duty until Pamela takes over next week."

For the next several hours, Fred busied himself trying to isolate the problem which involved an occasional "hiccup" in the fiber optic system cutting off power to a couple hiber-pods for as long as two milliseconds at a time. Not dangerous by any means, but still, something that needed to be addressed if only for his own peace of mind.

Although by the end of the first day he felt he was making progress, it was a problem that proved more difficult to track down than was initially thought. As a result, by the time Pamela was due to relieve John on the positronic systems, Fred was not much closer to solving the problem than he had been earlier in the week.

That was all right though as he looked forward to having an excuse for working closely with Pamela on the project.

When the day finally came, she took him as much by surprise as she did the last time.

"Hey, mister, didn't you hear me?"

Startled, Fred would have shot from his seat if he hadn't been strapped down. Looking over his shoulder, he found Pamela floating beside him.

"Pam! I mean, Pamela. I didn't see you there. I was so busy..."

"No need to explain," said Pamela holding up her free hand. "I can see you're hard at work. They told me you've been working on the same problem for the past week. Something about communications between the positronic systems and the local hiber-sleep computer?"

"I think that's what it is," replied Fred. "John was a good help but I'm glad you're here now."

"Why Fred, you'll turn my head!"

Suddenly, Fred felt his face begin to turn red.

"Is it warm in here?" he asked.

Pamela laughed before pulling herself down closer beside him.

"No, the air conditioning is working fine. Now tell me about the problem."

From that point on, not only did Fred lose all track of time, but it seemed to him that they made more progress than in the whole week before. By the time Pamela came over from her own positronic work station a few days later, he was sure that they had a lock on the cause of the problem.

"Hey, it's past quitting time, Fred," said Pamela. "We still have a date?"

Fred thought that he'd never get used to Pamela's abrupt nature, but he decided it was one of the things that he liked about her.

"Of course, what do you think I've been dreaming about for the past 11 years?"

"Oh, you *are* a sweetheart!" replied Pamela, clapping him playfully on the back. "I'm going back to my quarters to freshen up. I'll meet you in the cafeteria, okay?"

"You got it."

Fred wasn't sure what Pamela meant by freshening up, but when he laid eyes on her again in the cafeteria she somehow seemed more lively and attractive than she did all day. Could freeing her hair from the hairnet she wore on duty alone have that effect?

"Hey, Fred," said Pamela from where she sat at a table for two.

"Hey, Pam..." Fred began to say. "I mean Pamela..."

"Pam's okay," said Pamela. "We're friends now, aren't we?"

"I sure hope so!" said Fred hoping suddenly that there hadn't been too much of a note of desperation in his voice. "Shall we eat?"

"By all means, kind sir."

After they had made their selections and sat down again, there was a short, awkward silence before Fred brought up the subject of the technical problem they had been working on all day. Not exactly the topic he had hoped to talk about with Pamela over dinner, but at that moment, it was all he could think of. Gradually, however, they warmed to each other and conversation drifted into more personal areas. Fred talked about his life back on Mars, his family and friends, and Pamela did likewise. Fred found himself particularly fascinated with her girlhood on Earth.

"So you actually went for walks in the forest?" he was saying. "I mean, real woodland, not those parks where every tree and shrub is planned..."

"No, the real thing," said Pam. "Of course, there were some trails, but mostly it was completely wild and haphazard. And if the stars were right, sometimes I'd even see deer and beavers and such."

"Wow. We had nothing like that on Mars."

"But you had all those really interesting ruins to explore; and the old canals..."

Fred admitted that was true. By that point in the conversation, they had finished their meals and both had unconsciously leaned onto the table placing their faces no more than inches apart. There was silence again as they continued to stare into each other's eyes. Then, impulsively, Pamela moved in closer and gave Fred a peck on the lips, a kiss that lingered for a fraction of a second longer than it needed to but it was enough to send an electric shock through Fred all the way down to his toes.

"Hey, what was that for?" he asked, his eyes wide.

"Because I felt like it. You're not embarrassed are you?"

Fred looked around the room but no one there was looking at them. In fact, he noticed that there were plenty of other couples also engaged in quiet conversation.

"No, of course not. You just took me by surprise, that's all."

Pamela laughed and took his hands in hers.

"You know what would be fun?" he asked.

"Tell me," Pamela said, once again leaning close.

"If I could fix it, what would you say about a dinner date where we could be all by ourselves?" suggested Fred, emboldened by Pamela's positive attitude.

"By ourselves? How can you arrange that? There's no place aboard the *Endeavor* to..."

Fred lowered his voice.

"I'm chief hiber-sleep tech," reminded Fred. "It'd be easy for me to find a gap in the scheduling and arrange for us to be awakened at a time when everyone else is asleep."

"You can do that?"

"Sure. Completely unauthorized and against the rules but it wouldn't hurt anybody beyond adding a few hours to our lives."

"I don't know..."

"Fine, that's okay, it was a crazy idea anyway..."

"I didn't say no!" said Pamela hurriedly. "Don't you know that a girl's supposed to play hard to get? It sounds deliciously illicit! Let's do it!"

Fred found himself liking Pamela more and more.

"But *are* there gaps in the scheduling? I never heard of such a thing."

Fred nodded. "There are a few; mostly only of a couple hours duration when all the cycles find themselves in sync. Give me a couple of days to check and I'll get back to you with some options."

"Okay," Pamela giggled. "I think this is going to be fun!"

A few days later, Fred stepped into the cafeteria and immediately caught the move-ment of Pamela's arm as she waved him to their table.

"What did you find out?" asked Pamela without waiting for him to sit.

"We're all set," said Fred. "I found a two hour gap in the schedule four years from now and made the adjustments. It's a date!"

"You went ahead and did it?" asked Pamela incredulously. "Without checking back with me first?"

"Why? Are you going to be busy?" asked Fred, pleased with his joke.

Pamela smiled back. "You've got me there. Well that leaves us with just one problem."

"What's that?"

"What are we going to have for dinner?"

28 years, 9 months, 7 days out from Sol

Four years later, Fred was awakened by the familiar hiss of air as the seal of his hiber-pod gave way and the computer returned him to consciousness. There was no discernable break in his thoughts since he went back to sleep years before because his first was of Pamela and his desire to reach her side before she was awakened.

Disregarding the slight disorientation he felt, Fred swung himself from the pod, closed the lid, and sprinted quickly up the rows of sleeping figures to Pamela's enclosure. There, he saw that he was on time; the computer display showing the countdown to reawakening indicated she still had a few seconds before the seal was broken.

Fred looked down at the figure inside: she appeared the same as she did the last time he had visited her in the hiber-pod. Loosened hair, crossed arms, and was that the suggestion of a smile on her lips?

Suddenly, there was a hiss and the pod's lid parted from the couch and lifted wide. A few moments later, Pamela's eyes opened and seeing him standing over her, she smiled for real, sat up and reached out for his helping hand. She had no sooner gained her feet when on impulse, Fred gripped her lightly about the shoulders and kissed her. The fact that he could be so impulsive surprised him but not as much as when Pamela made no attempt to escape his grasp. Instead, her arms slipped around his waist and she leaned into the kiss herself.

They lingered there for what seemed hours but really was not more than a few seconds before separating. There were no words then; just each looking into the eyes of the other and reading there far more than either intended when they had laid their plans for a private dinner.

It was something that the developers of the hiber-sleep process never anticipated. It was always assumed, and that studies indicated, that while in hiber-sleep, individuals were not conscious in any way not even to dream and that the time between going to sleep and waking up was spent in a kind of mental shut-down enabling the individual to bridge the gap of years as if no time had passed at all. Thus there would be no continuing evolution of an interior life; an individual would simply pick up the threads of his or her life exactly where they left them when they abandoned consciousness early in the hiber-sleep process.

But now, it occurred to Fred with all the force of a revelation, that something else was happening. Far from the mind shutting down when the hiber-sleep process was in force, it seemed that on a sub-conscious level, at a point beyond the reach of instrumentation and measurement, the brain continued to correlate information, information that it then used to influence non-linear thinking such as basic emotions. How else to explain the deep longing he felt for Pamela despite having known her for no more than a handful of hours so far as the clock of their waking lives were concerned? When he set his eyes on her just now, it did not seem to him that they had just concluded their first date, but that in actuality, many years had gone by since he had seen her. It didn't matter that it seemed as though no time had passed since that dinner date four years ago, in the deepest portion of his mind, he was convinced that many years had passed since he had last seen Pamela with the result that he could not help but feel a deep longing for her, a longing that had compelled him to express his feelings with an impulsive embrace.

Looking into Pamela's eyes, he could tell that she understood what was happening as well.

"It's as if my feelings for you grew while I was in hiber-sleep," Pamela was saying. "As if in those four years, our relationship continued to grow and wasn't suspended at all."

"I was beginning to think it was all my imagination," replied Fred. "But it's a genuine phenomenon. All our research was wrong. Hiber-sleep may suspend all physical life functions, but not our emotions. Somehow, on the deepest psychological level, they continue to evolve based perhaps on the last experiences we had before entering the hiber-pods."

"It does seem as though hardly any time has passed since our dinner date," said Pamela. "But on the other hand, I feel as though I've known and...loved you, for all of those four years!"

"I didn't dare say it myself, Pam," said Fred looking into her eyes. "But that's the way I feel too. Somehow, over those unconscious four years, I've fallen in love with you."

Tenderly, they came together again and held each other close, not saying anything for a time.

At last, feeling more contented than they ever had in their lives, the couple parted and hand in hand, walked from the hiber-sleep area into the living quarters.

"If we're still going to have that quiet dinner together, we'd better get a move on," warned Pamela, smiling.

"Do we have to? I think I'd rather just hold you and look into your eyes."

"Okay, let's not get maudlin about the whole thing," Pamela said. "Let's go into the hold and see if we can find anything that I can make a real meal out of."

A few minutes later they had passed from the low gravity living section into the zero G environment of the aft section of the *Endeavor* which was made up mostly of a vast cargo hold containing all that a beginning colony would need to get on its feet. Beyond the storage area, at the extreme end of the ship was where the engine nacelles were located safely ensconced in their titanium sheaths.

After Pamela had accessed the hold's positronic work station, it was an easy task to find what they were looking for. In a short while, Fred had retrieved a portable self-powered oven unit and Pamela had filled a netted bag with various foodstuffs. With less than an hour and half to go until they needed to return to their pods, the two wasted no time getting back to the cafeteria and preparing their meal. Although Fred helped as much as he could, mostly it was Pamela's project and he ended spending some time in the control section double checking the hiber-sleep systems.

At last, he heard Pamela calling him over the comm link and he made his way back to the cafeteria. There, he paused in surprise as his nose picked up the scent of the first real cooking he had smelled since long before leaving Mars.

"Hey! That smells good," he said, wasting no time advancing to the table upon which Pamela had arranged the meal.

"It's not much but it's the best I could do on short notice and with a limited choice in victuals," said Pamela who nevertheless, beamed with some pride at her culinary skills.

"Shall we sit down?"

"Whenever you're ready, sir."

Fred surprised Pamela by moving behind her and holding her chair for her. Then he sat down himself. A few minutes later, he leaned back in his own chair and patted his belly playfully.

"I don't think I ever had such a delicious meal!"

"Oh, sure," replied Pamela, sipping at some orange juice concentrate. "Synth-steak, evaporated vegetables, and freeze-dried ice cream pellets?"

"But they were *cooked*, Pam!" Fred said. "Prepared in a real oven not dished out by a computer following a 30 year old program."

"I guess the human touch does make *some* difference."

"All the difference in the world," said Fred, rising. He felt a sudden surge of unaccountable tenderness toward this girl whom his mind kept reminding him he had only known for a few hours but that his heart insisted was years. He placed an arm around her shoulders and squeezed her to him, giving her a kiss on the cheek at the same time. "I love you," he whispered.

"We'd better clean up before our time runs out," said Pamela realistically and the two of them threw the remnants of the meal, utensils and all, into the recycling unit. Pamela waited for Fred in the hiber-pod area while he returned the oven to the hold. When he came back, she was waiting for him by the hatch and caught him as he transited through.

With their arms about each other's waists, they made their way back to Pamela's pod. There, they paused again and embraced.

"I love you too," Pamela said into his ear and kissed him. "See you in 19 years."

"Pam, when we see each other again, I want to get married," said Fred, realizing as he said it that the words were the most natural thing in the world to say.

"Oh, Fred," said Pamela. "There's nothing I'd want more but are we allowed? You know there hasn't been any provision in the flight schedule for marriage let alone romance!"

"Don't I know it," acknowledged Fred. "Whose research do you think it was that the scheduling was based on? With the scheduling we arranged, it was supposed that there wouldn't be any time for crew members to form romantic relationships. It was always intended that that would wait until planetfall."

"But I still don't want to wait!" insisted Pamela. "If the captain or one of the chaplains won't marry us, I say we find another gap in the scheduling cycle and do it ourselves."

Fred smiled at Pamela's determination, one that he agreed with completely.

"It'll tip our hand but I'm willing to approach the captain about it during our next common cycle," Fred said.

"Then it's settled," said Pamela, visibly relaxing. "Now kiss me good night and tuck me in."

47 years, 2 months, 16 days out from Sol

When Fred next awoke, his first thought was to worry that Pamela may have changed her mind about marriage. Hurriedly, he exited the hiber-pod and began to make his way toward her. He hadn't gone more than a few steps before Pamela herself appeared and ran into his arms.

"I thought I might have dreamt the whole thing, but as soon as I saw you, I knew it was all true," she said, her voice muffled against his shoulder.

"You still want to get married?" Fred asked wonderingly.

"Of course!"

He gently pushed her away from him and kissed her.

"I was afraid that you might have changed your mind..."

"Not hardly!" said Pamela, wiping a tear from the corner of her eye. "Do we approach the captain right away, or...?"

"Why not? If we're going to be court martialed for falling in love, then so be it."

Together, they made their way to the living area and then to the administrative offices. The captain's office had a holder on the door for removable labels. Just then, the label that had been slipped into the holder was for co-captain Henry Montez, one of twenty co-captains whose shifts were staggered so that no one would spend more than a combined total of five years awake during the *Endeavor*'s journey. Fred knocked on the door and a voice on the other side bade him enter.

Inside was a tiny cubicle with a man hardly older than himself sitting behind a desk that had been bolted to the deck. The rest of the room was sparse with all the information, records, and current ship's operations at the captain's fingertips by way of a computer console nestled in the surface of the desk.

"Fred Josely isn't it?" said Montez looking up. "Hiber-sleep expert?"

"Right. And this is Pamela Letourneaux, positronic systems technician."

"Of course."

Fred cleared his throat. "Captain, I don't know how to explain this except to say that I think there was a serious omission in the psychological research dealing with the hiber-sleep process."

"You think so?"

"Yes, because I have reason to believe that the subject's mental processes do not come to a complete halt during hiber-sleep."

"In what way do you mean?"

"Well, sir, that's the tricky part..."

"Then let me make it easy for you," said Montez. "You and Pamela are here to tell me that you've fallen in love and wish to get married."

Fred stood dumbfounded for a moment before turning to look at Pamela who seemed just as surprised as he was.

"How did you know that, sir?" asked Fred.

Montez sighed heavily and rubbed his forehead.

"Because you're about the tenth couple that I've seen come in here over my last two cycles," explained Montez. "Each asking for the same thing; permission to get married. I've checked the logs of the other co-captains and have found that there have been quite a few others that came forward in earlier cycles. In fact, those first couples have already been joined in wedlock by the captains on duty when they were awake."

Fred could only stare in continued surprise until Pamela broke the spell by slipping her hand into his.

"But sir, nothing like that was ever contemplated by the mission planners back home," Fred managed. "We thought, I mean Pam and I thought, well, that we were risking court martial by coming to you."

"Not hardly. Men and women being the way they are, none of this should have been unexpected. Such a blind spot could only have occurred to people cooped up in labs for too long. The truth is, many of the co-captains have discussed just this possibility many times before the *Endeavor* ever left Mars orbit."

"They did?"

Montez nodded. "And we decided that there was no way that we'd stand in the way of a couple who wanted to get married. The problem was how to rearrange the hiber-sleep schedule to accommodate them. You know, have each be up and about at the same time, etcetera? It's taken some doing and the changes haven't resulted in absolute coverage all the time..."

Startled, Fred now realized how it was that he had so easily discovered a gap in the scheduling that allowed he and Pam to awaken by themselves. It had most likely resulted from the changes in scheduling made by the captains to accommodate couples. How ironic!

"...so the captains have been marrying willing couples for a number of cycles now on the condition that they don't go around talking about it. The fewer marriages there are, the less problems we have in fixing the schedule."

"Would you do the honors for us, captain?" asked Pamela suddenly. "Until planetfall when the chaplains will be wakened?"

Montez sighed again. "You sure you want to do this? The life you have to look forward to over the next 70 years is going to be far from normal. In fact, I daresay they'll be pretty frustrating."

Fred and Pamela looked at one another for reassurance but there was never any doubt.

"We do," they both said at once and all three laughed.

"Well, then, by the power vested in me as ship's co-captain, I pronounce you man and wife," said Montez with little gravity. "You may kiss the bride, Fred."

Fred did so and then had his hand shaken by the captain.

With knowledge that they had not been the first couple to fall in love during the voyage, it seemed suddenly easy to spot those others that had preceded them in marital bliss. How could they not have noticed it before? Over the next few weeks before their next sleep period, Fred and Pamela each managed to speak to other men and women who had become couples, exchanging comments on the difficulties and peculiar pleasures of having to steal a few hours of each other's company over the decades. Inevitably, however, talk came around to the natural issue of wedded life and there everyone shared the same concerns: what to do about children?

It was a problem that for the time being Fred and Pamela could put aside as first Fred then Pamela reentered hiber-sleep to be awakened at the same time some 26 years hence.

73 years, 1 month, 22 days out from Sol

It had been the hardest thing for Fred to endure being awakened those times when Pamela's duty cycle did not match his. But now, at last, they would be together for the first time in decades and despite the feeling that no time had passed at all, it felt like an eternity since they had last been together.

What was different this time however, was that Pamela had been awake for almost a week before it was his turn to emerge from hiber-sleep and when he did, she was at his side ready to greet him. By now, the welcoming embrace was a familiar routine but instead of making their way immediately to the living quarters, Pamela held Fred back a moment.

"What's wrong?" asked Fred.

"There've been a lot of changes aboard ship since the last time we were together," observed Pamela.

"Oh? What sort of changes?"

"You remember all the couples we spoke to the last time, how many of them were already married and how there was a lot of talk about the problems of starting families out here?"

"Yes..." said Fred, wondering where the conversation was going.

"Well, problem solved!"

"What do you mean? How can...?"

"Wait. You'll see!" said Pamela pulling him insistently by the hand.

In another few minutes, they had stepped into the living quarters and immediately, Fred's ears were assaulted by the wail of a what could only have been an infant. He must have looked a question at Pamela because she answered it right away.

"Right. That's a baby! You remember Bill and Irma Johnstone? They were married a couple cycles ahead of us? It's theirs!"

"You're kidding!" exclaimed Fred. Despite the evidence of his ears, his mind refused to accept such an unheard of departure from the ship's routine, one that hundreds of technicians back on Earth had spent years devising and making foolproof. "How can that be?"

Pamela only looked at him with an expression that seemed to say "How else?"

"Well, you know...not that...I mean, how was it accommodated?"

"From what I've heard," replied Pamela lowering her voice. "It was a mutiny of sorts.

After a campaign by some of the couples to be allowed to have children that got no-where...they offered to stay out of hiber-sleep during the 9 months of pregnancy and then to have the children share a pod with their moth-ers...Sam and Janice decided to just go ahead and get pregnant...you remember how stub-born Janice has always been...she's a bio-nutritionist after all! Anyway, once her condi-tion was confirmed, there wasn't much the ad-ministration could do but go along with them. The co-captain on duty rearranged their duty schedules so that they could both stay awake for the full 9 months; that was almost 10 years ago now."

"That long? But what about the baby I'm hearing now? Was it put in hiber-sleep?"

"Weren't you listening? I said that baby be-longs to Bill and Irma not Sam and Janice..."

"You mean there are more?" asked Fred, taking a while to catch on.

For answer, Pamela led him to a door be-hind which Fred knew lay the ship's workout room but there had been changes, big changes. Inside, the exercise equipment had been pushed against one wall and the space created was taken up with makeshift bedding for a half dozen infants of varying ages and a table at which other, older children sat looking as if they were attending school.

"What's going on here?" Fred asked in-credulously.

"What's going on here is community," said a woman Fred recognized as Anne Bannister, a med tech who was supposed to have remained in hiber-sleep until planetfall.

"Community?" asked Fred.

"Something the planners back home never counted on happening, or at least not until arrival on Magna III," replied Anne. "They should have known that if you go putting a hundred or so young, healthy men and women together in a closed environment, things are going to happen. It's what human beings have been doing since the dawn of time: building families, social support structures, in short, communities. Absent an official roadmap, individuals aboard ship began to come together, get married, have children, and since people don't do that in a vacuum, they began to make their own rules. That's how the nursery ended up here."

"You mean none of this is sanctioned by the administration?"

"Well, not in the beginning, but what were they to do? Once Irma became pregnant and Dr. Jules ruled out as unsafe her going into hiber-sleep, that left only one option: the duty schedule had to change."

"So much for sacred writ!" laughed Fred. "But what about these other children, the older ones. What happens to them? There won't be enough hiber-pods for everyone."

"There are options," said Anne. "Parents have switched sleep time with single persons spending more time awake with their children; others have gone back to hiber-sleep sharing a pod with their children. That can be done safely so long as the children are young enough. Others have simply chosen not to wait preferring to stay awake permanently and raising their children aboard ship. By the time we arrive at Magna III, children will have grown to adulthood aboard ship and original crew members will have died of old age."

"That's too bad…"

"Not necessarily. According to some preliminary studies I've made, because of these changes, the ship's crew overall will arrive at Magna III healthier and more psychologically stable than the original models had suggested. With a more natural balance between young and old, the colony's odds for survival have increased almost infinitely! What machines and cold logic could not account for, human nature will accomplish."

"But the new scheduling needed to cover for all this activity must be a major headache for the administration," noted Fred.

"In the beginning it was, but it's getting easier."

"Speaking of scheduling, is there time available in room 20?" asked Pamela.

"Let me check," replied Anne taking a compu-board down from the bulkhead. "I can put you in for a sleep period in three standard days according to the ship's computer."

"Oh, good! Will you do that then?"

"No problem."

Heading back to the cafeteria, Fred wondered aloud. "There's one thing I still don't get, Pam."

"What's that?"

"Where in the world did all those couples find the time to...never mind that! Find the privacy to..."

"Remember what Anne said about how the crew began to make up its own rules in the absence of official regulations?" asked Pamela.

"You mean someone came up with new rules for...?"

"Well, it's not as radical as you make it sound!"

"So what, then?"

"Meet me in room 20 in three days and find out!"

97 years, 11 months, 12 days out from Sol

Fred and Pamela had managed to meet in room 20 a number of times over different cycles before Anne was able to tell them definitively that Pamela was pregnant. At the time, Fred didn't know whether to be overjoyed or deeply worried. With the pregnancy, their duty schedules would need to be completely rearranged with no returning to hiber-sleep for at least 9 months. Being awake for that length of time was a new experience for Fred and he wondered what he could do to keep busy since the ship mostly ran itself. One of the other factors he had to get used to was spending nights with his pregnant wife while sharing the same sleeping quarters with other couples. Of course, efforts had been taken under the new circumstances to create some measure of privacy for everyone and by mutual consent, room 20 continued to act as common ground for those trysts that could not be postponed.

But as Anne had said those many years before, the crew was busy building a new community and with only 213 adults and a small but growing contingent of children, it was easy to get to know and become comfortable with almost everyone aboard ship.

Finally, the day arrived when Pamela was ready to deliver and when she had finished, Fred was presented with a boy they called Victor. The birth however, presented them with a number of important decisions including when the family would reenter hiber-sleep and for how long a duration? It was determined over the years that a parent could safely share a hiber-pod until a child had reached the age of 6 or 7 years old; beyond that, the pod's systems could not maintain two people at once. Those facts gave them a window of a few years in which to proceed with another option if they chose.

For many months before the birth of Victor, Pamela had been intent on persuading Fred to accede to her desire to arrive on Magnus III with a complete and what many crewmembers had taken to calling a "well balanced" family unit. That is, Pamela wanted to delay returning to hiber-sleep pending the birth of their second child. When that was accomplished, they would then each take one child with them into their respective pods and wait out the years remaining to planetfall.

As it turned out, Fred wasn't completely opposed to the idea and after checking with administration about possible scheduling problems, agreed to the arrangement. Luckily, with only a few years remaining until planetfall, there would be no need to awaken neither he nor Pamela before the *Endeavor* arrived at its destination.

With his mind set at ease, Fred was able to concentrate on his marital obligations and after only a few turns in room 20, Pamela was able to declare success and give birth to a daughter that Fred insisted be named after its mother. By the time Dr. Jules had declared little Pam strong enough to bear the hiber-sleep process, the toddler was almost a year old. Then, after being out of hiber-sleep for almost 3 years, the family returned to their pods: little Pam with her mother and Victor with his father.

105 years, 3 months, 17 days out from Sol

Although Fred was still in hiber-sleep when it happened, he was assured that when the *Endeavor* arrived in orbit around Magna III all went according to what the planners back on Earth had intended. With all systems green, the co-captain on duty in the final cycle made sure that all those awake, including 27 children of all ages, were safely secured in improvised harnesses before initiating the descent sequence.

The rocket's outer hull grew warm as the big ship slowed in the upper atmosphere and passed through a thin cloud layer before coming into sight of the surface of Magna III. Then, allowing its positronic brain to guide it to the larger of the planet's two continents, one located in the northern, more temperate hemisphere, the captain took over on manual controls. Gradually, he used the rocket's jets to redirect the nose upward and with a final rumble and roar, the *Endeavor* settled gently to the ground on a plume of dust and steam.

There had been tests made of the planet's atmosphere but that was only a formality as unmanned satellites that had visited Magna III years before had already beamed the happy news that human life could survive on the surface in comfort. A stair descended from the base of the rocket to the ground and the duty captain was the first to emerge into the dull sunlight of a new world.

All around a forest of alien plant life, not jungle but not tundra either, spread invitingly to a distant mountain range whose peaks glistened under sheaths of glaciers. Then, with the all clear by the captain, the rest of the crew began to emerge from the rocket and among them, the Josely family with little Pam in her father's arms.

When the mission planners back on Earth finally received the visual feed from Magna III a strange and unanticipated sight would greet their wondering eyes. Emerging from the rocket was not the homogeneous group of young people that had been carefully chosen from among millions of candidates, but a ready made community of individuals young and old, those who had never been awakened during the entire journey and those born along the way.

There were those crewmembers grown elderly after choosing not to return to hiber-sleep and young people born and raised aboard ship who had never heard the hiss made by a hiber-pod as it broke its seal. There were children born on the crossing but with no memory of life aboard ship due to having returned with their parents to hiber-sleep while still infants and crew members not awakened until late in the voyage and married to young people who hadn't been born when they left Mars orbit.

Together they would help one another: the young would respect the wisdom of the old and the elderly would come to rely on the stamina and versatility of the young. There would be those who remembered Earth and Mars and those to whom Earth and Mars would be less than a dream but a dream that had bequeathed them the tools to survive and grow; tools necessary and useful no matter the alien environment; tools their ancestors learned and honed by ancient campfires and that enabled an infant humanity to overcome a hostile native world and break it to their will. They had family and community and as long as they stayed together and depended on one another, Magnus III would be their welcoming home for a long time to come.

"Not much to do here for a hiber-sleep technician," observed Fred as he looked out over their new world.

"I'm sure we'll find something to keep you busy!" said Pamela over her shoulder as she led Victor down from the rocket.

For Love of Old Earth

"HERE WE ARE, GRANDDAD. The place doesn't look much different than the last time we were here. A few more weeds maybe."

We sat in the late model land rover on a slight rise that overlooked the old rocket field. The last time I had seen the place, Virgil was only a boy and I had done the driving. Now, fifty years later, looking down at the rocket field with its vacant hangers and empty cradles, I couldn't help but think that the few changes that had taken place here over the intervening half century were in their way, like those that have happened to the world itself: deceptive.

"Oh, I don't know, Virgil," I replied. "I think a lot has changed."

Virgil engaged the frictionless drive and guided the rover along the crumbling roadway to the remains of the front gate. There, he was obliged to lower his speed in order to negotiate his way around the fallen fence but once on the field, he began to go faster. Trumbling along the grass tufted landing apron along the perimeter of the field, we passed in the shadow of rusted gantries and dilapidated hangars. Turning sharply toward the heart of the space center, Virgil drove along the length of a half assembled rocket lying on its side and looking like the partially devoured carcass of some antediluvian beast.

Pulling up in front of the administration complex, Virgil cut the power to the drive.

Wordlessly, we walked into the building, past the shattered glass doors, the weathered receptionist area, the ruined air lifts.

"Wait here, ganddad, while I check to make sure the stairs are still safe," said Virgil as he ducked past a fallen metal beam into the stairwell. "It's okay, c'mon."

Together, we walked up stairs I had first climbed with Jimmy James over 100 years ago, this time taking frequent time outs, until we reached the top and entered the control tower. There was not much left to it. What electronics that had not been stripped decades before had been turned by exposure to the weather into a useless mass of burnt out silicon. Everywhere, there was the dust of decades and through the empty windows, a strong spring breeze brought in the scent of heather and sweet new grass.

"Don't know why you wanted to come here again, granddad," Virgil was saying. "You and the other Founders took away everything that was useful a hundred years ago. That, and we'll be moving Newville south next year. You could've dropped by then."

"Just thought I'd like to see it again," I replied wistfully. "At 121, I don't think I'm going to be around long enough to make the trip to old Quebec."

"Hey, there's no need to talk like that!"

"Of course, you're right, Virgil," I smiled, clapping him on the back. "But still, it does seem so long ago when rockets were still lifting off from this field and we could feel their rumbles through the ground even as far north as Newville."

"You were supposed to be on one of the last of those rockets weren't you granddad?"

Of course, Virgil was completely familiar with the story having heard it many times while he was growing up; but I could tell that, sensing my mood, he wanted to hear me tell it again. Well, he had read me right. Looking at the featureless blue sky outside the tower window frames, I imagined that I could once again see the contrail of a rocket as it blasted off for some distant world in another solar system.

The sight had been a familiar one in my youth when my friends, Eric "Pip" Cyrano, Keith Gerald, and Jimmy James Lane and his little brother "big" Pete, and I used to ride our bikes tearing up the tundra outside Newville.

Our gang had become a regular feature of life in the town as we gathered in front of Keith's family domicile and planned the day's activities. At the top of the list was a mandatory ride down Rosy Lane to tease Harriet Linley and the other girls whose indignant replies were immediately lost in distance as we turned onto Main Street and headed for Croteau's Market. In a whirl of skids and fishtails, we would pull up in front of the store and march in, allowance credits in our pockets. Coming out of the store with packets of sugar free soda pop and crunchy health bars, we would remount and head out of town.

Beyond Newville's limits, the land stretched out in almost every direction in a featureless flatness broken only by the occasional low rise and covered with coarse, ground hugging plants common to terrain above the former Arctic Circle. There were no trees to speak of except the few that had been planted when Newville was first established on Devon Island late in the 22nd century.

The only natural formation for miles around, and the prime reason for Newville's being sited in such a desolate area, was a stone outcropping that rose from the surrounding tundra just outside of town.

One of hundreds of such facilities around the arctic and subarctic regions of the world, the refrigeration factory located atop the outcrop was vast, fully automated, and supplied a constant wave of cool air that rolled down the outcrop to dissipate in the plains below. While little of it reached Newville except on those days when the wind was right, most of the factory's output was thrust into the Earth's upper atmosphere through towering stacks that remained coated in ice all year round.

In winter months, with temperatures reaching as low as 60 degrees Fahrenheit, my friends and I liked to take our bikes to the top of the outcropping to look for chunks of fresh ice that had broken loose from the stacks and crashed to pieces on the ground surrounding the atmosphere facility. Finding some choice pieces, we would wrap them in thick folds of tissue paper and sit contendedly looking out over the vast tundra below and little Newville in the distance as we alternately sucked on the ice and sipped our soda packets.

It was on one of those days with the sound of the refrigerated air being forced from the stacks in a continuous roar that we were visited by the factory's lone caretaker, Phineas Walters.

Phineas was quite old, or at least he seemed so to me and my friends, and had been appointed to monitor operation of the factory in case anything went wrong...which so far as we knew, had never happened. As a result, it was our suspicion that old Phineas was frequently bored; why else would he have bothered with a bunch of kids like us?

"How's the ice fellas?" Phineas had asked one day, setting down the instrument package that he carried with him wherever he went.

"Cold!" we all said at once.

"Got some extra tissue paper?"

Big Pete pulled a roll out from his pack and handed it to Phineas who tore off a good sized piece. A moment later, he had retrieved a chunk of ice for himself and was sitting on a rock slightly above the rest of us.

We'd been sitting there quietly for some minutes, concentrating on our ice, when suddenly Jimmy James pointed excitedly to the south where the blue of the sky deepened almost to purple and there, sketching a great arc, was a white contrail indicating the departure of another rocket.

"Wow! There goes another one!" shouted Jimmy standing and shading his eyes with his hand. "Wonder where it's goin'?"

"Alpha Centauri, maybe?" guessed Pip.

"Nah, they must be overpopulated there by now," said Keith. "Must be headed for Rigel or even farther away!"

"I don't know why, but I get kinda sorry when I see 'em go like that," I said, revealing more of my feelings than I usually did to my friends.

"Why's that, Simon?"

"I don't know really," I found myself saying. "I like the idea of going off-planet someday and exploring other worlds, of being a pioneer like they say in the holo-posters, but I'll be sad to leave Newville too."

"Yeah, I know what you mean," agreed Pip. "I'll sure miss this place...and you guys...when it's our turn to go. I heard that even if we wound up on the same world, the colonies are small, no bigger than a family unit, and hundreds of miles apart."

"Why's that?" Keith wanted to know.

"Because there aren't enough resources in any single place to support more than a few people," replied Pip. "You need at least a hundred square miles of open land to support just one family."

"Why do we have to go at all?" sighed Keith. "I mean, if we don't want to go, why should we?"

"Because Mother Earth is gonna die, dummy," said Jimmy James. "Haven't you heard? It's global warming, Mother Earth is heating up all the time; been heating up for the past 200 years."

"Yeah, even I know that the ice pack at the north pole used to stretch a lot farther south then where it does now," said Big Pete. "It's because people years ago didn't care what happened to the environment...they just kept on burning oil and coal and sending chemicals and stuff into the air and started a greenhouse effect."

"That's why Newville was put so far north, where temperatures are still kinda temperate enough to make life comfortable," I said. "Where people used to live, in the old United States, it's either a jungle or a big desert now."

"And the seaboard cities are under water too," added Pip.

"Do you think it's true what they say, that there are only a few people remaining on Mother Earth and all the rest have left for other planets on those rocket ships?" Keith wanted to know.

"That's what my dad says," shrugged Big Pete. "He says any day now it'll be our turn to go."

"How come we have to be last?"

"Somethin' about making sure the factories keep running," I said. "They built 'em years ago to slow down the Earth's warming long enough to construct the rockets they needed to get everybody off-planet. By now, the human race must be scattered half way across the galaxy!"

"Gee, I sure hope we all get to go to the same colony at least," said Jimmy James.

Jimmy's concern was one we all had spoken about often and tried more than once to find out from our parents only to receive answers that were far from reassuring. As usual when conversation came around to leaving Earth, we all lapsed into our own private thoughts; thoughts I'm sure that we all shared: the fear that our camaraderie was doomed to end with the sound of a rocket's exhaust and a white contrail across the sky.

"'Greenhouse effect,' 'global warming,' phooey!" scoffed Phineas suddenly, breaking the gloomy spell. "There's nothing to them nor this 'Mother Earth' nonsense."

"Huh?" said Jimmy James perking up. "You don't love Mother Earth after all she's done for us?"

"What do you mean, Phineas?" I asked, shocked. I think it was the first time I had ever heard any adult mock the core beliefs that we had all grown up with.

"You heard right," said Phineas. "All that stuff about people being the reason for the Earth's temperature getting warmer just isn't true. And there's nothin' to this 'Mother Earth' business. Earth is just another planet circling its sun, the same as the rest."

We all went quiet for a few seconds after hearing what Phineas had said; calling into question the divinity of the Earth. It was something that most people at the time didn't really believe (except the Environmental Faithful) but would never dare express aloud, or even to themselves. In retrospect, I think that I at least, always doubted, even as a child and that attitude may have been the key factor in what happened later.

"You don't believe that the Earth is our Mother, who gave birth to humankind, nurtured us, and whose heart was broken after we took her for granted?" asked Keith, reciting the litany of the Environmental Faithful that we all learned in school.

"You believe that hogwash, kid?" asked Phineas dangerously. He risked losing his job and becoming a non-person if any of us reported his words to the environmental police.

"Well...yeah, I guess so..." replied Keith, suddenly unsure. "But if people aren't the reason for Mother Earth getting warmer, what's causing it? The ice is almost gone from the north and south poles and the glaciers have disappeared from the mountains."

"Oh, that's true enough," admitted Phineas. "But, it's not because of anything people did in the past. It's all part of the natural cycle of the Earth."

"What do you mean?" I had never heard of such a thing at school.

"The Earth has grown cooler then warmer over and over again throughout its long history," explained Phineas who had to have been a scientist of some sort to have been placed in charge of the factory. "Most likely, it's all tied in with activity on the sun which effects the composition of the Earth's atmosphere. Two hundred years ago there was a spike in such activity, everybody knew it, but there were parts of the world's society that had a lot invested in the idea it was the fault of people that the Earth was warming: too much manufacturing, too much fossil fuel being burned, just too many people...well, there ain't many people left nowadays."

We were all staring at each other, trying to understand what Phineas meant. Then, slowly, the implications of what he had said began to dawn on me.

"You mean, all those people, those billions of people who've been leaving in the rockets for the last two centuries...didn't need to go?"

Phineas chuckled.

"You got it exactly, Simon," he said. "They didn't need to go. But none of them listened. There were scientists who knew better; bioclimatologists, paleo-meteorologists, astrophysicists, but nobody listened to them. Instead, politicians eager for votes, gave the scare mongers money that was used in turn to conduct more propaganda. Eventually, anybody who disagreed with the accepted belief was shunned by the public and ostracized by their professional peers. People were afraid of speaking out for fear of losing their jobs, subjected to reeducation therapy, and later, placed in asylums. So people shut up and the factories closed, the oil wells capped, and civilization in general turned back almost a hundred years. Then, even that wasn't enough. As temperatures continued to climb, it was decided that the real problem was people themselves so the solution became how to get rid of them all? That was when some of the ban on manufacturing was lifted so that a rocket construction program could get started and no sooner than the first ship was built than they began sending people off-planet."

"And factories like this one?" asked Keith, pointing at the facility that towered over our heads.

"Built as part of the rocket program," said Phineas. "They thought that if they built enough of these refrigeration units, they could counteract the warming process long enough to get everyone off into space. And darn it, if they haven't done it!"

"Yeah, I hear there aren't but a hundred thousand people left in the whole world now," said Big Pete.

"All that's left are those folks in towns like Newville that were built for the folks needed to maintain the refrigerator factories," said Phineas. "Although truth to tell, they're designed so well, they've hardly needed any work at all. As a matter of fact, I'll let you in on a secret. These factories haven't been needed in a long time. The Earth stopped getting warmer a hundred years ago. If all the factories were shut down tomorrow, there'd be no change in the temperature."

"That's great!" exclaimed Jimmy James suddenly. "If Mother Earth isn't getting any warmer, that means we won't have to leave. We can live here and stay together until we grow old!"

"Hey, that's right!" said Pip. "Do you think our folks know?"

"I don't know, but I'm gonna tell 'em as soon as I get home!" said Big Pete.

"They ain't gonna believe you," warned Phineas. "It's like a religion to them now. No amount of facts or proof is going to shake their faith in global warming."

"We'll see about that!" said Pip getting to his feet.

"Hey, wait a minute," I said quickly. "If we go and tell our parents, I don't think we should say that we got the idea from Phineas."

Realizing that what we had all been thinking flirted with blasphemy, everyone calmed down for a moment. But our desire never to give up our homes and to preserve our camaraderie was too strong to suppress and we all determined to raise the subject with our families that night...even if we ended up on sewerage reclamation duty as a consequence.

Suddenly then, we were all getting our things together and headed to our bikes. A few minutes later, eager to tell our parents the good news, the gang was headed back down from the factory and toward the road that led into town.

———————

Later that evening, as the family was settling down for supper, I decided to raise the subject of staying on Earth with my dad. I waited as he and my mother worked their way through the main course of vegetables and starches and started on dessert before getting enough courage to speak up.

"Say, dad," I began.

"Yes, Simon?"

"I heard a funny thing today."

"Oh?"

"Yeah. About the Earth warming..."

"Well that's not exactly news, son," said dad laughing.

"I know that; but what I mean is, what if it's not warming any more. What if it's stopped?"

"Not likely."

"But what if it has? Would that mean we wouldn't have to leave Earth?"

"Is that what these questions are all about? Look, Simon, I understand how you feel. Newville is your home. Your friends are here. Of course you don't want to go. Nevertheless, it's out of our hands. Soon, Mother Earth won't be able to support human life anymore and by leaving, mankind is giving the planet a chance to recover from all the things that we did to it over the centuries."

"Listen to your father, Simon," said my mother. "He's Newville's environmental thought warden. He knows all about these things so he can make sure that people in town stay green and environmentally aware."

"We owe it to Mother Earth to leave, son," Dad said.

"But if the Earth isn't getting any worse, in fact that it might even be getting better, why do we have to go?"

"Simon, there's a very complicated boarding schedule in effect for the rocket program that's been in progress for almost a hundred years now," said Dad. "That schedule can't be upset. If we miss our boarding time, it would upset the schedule and cause all kinds of trouble."

"So you mean we have to go, whether we want to or not, because of decisions made for us by people who died a hundred years ago?"

"I don't think I like the tone in your voice, young man."

"Sorry, Dad."

I went to bed that night and for the first time in my young life, began to seriously question the assumptions embraced not only by my parents and every adult I had ever known, but that had been taught to me through seven years of school. I began to see my elders as being gripped by an ideology every bit as powerful as any faith and that they could no more question its dogma of Schedule and the pain suffered by "Mother Earth" than any sectarian.

Unable to sleep, I threw off my blankets and went to the open window. Outside, I could hear the occasional cricket in the thick grass and overhead, the stars winked and a crescent moon hung low in the sky. The universe was an inviting place and I had to admit to myself that I was curious to explore it, to walk on strange planets and visit alien suns but when my eyes drifted downward and met the vast tundra that stretched just beyond the last row of domiciles across the street, I felt an even stronger desire to explore my own world. Not "Mother Earth," but a planet called Sol III circling a sun on the edge of the Milky Way galaxy. As my imagination took hold of me, I saw the abandoned lands far to the south, the great belt of forest, the open plains of what my school books called Canada, the waste areas that stretched from the old United States to Brazil. All empty of people with their cities returning to dust and their highways disappearing beneath desert sands.

It all made for a forbidding vision and yet, I could also see myself, and Big Pete, Pip, Keith, and the others, on our bikes, our backpacks filled, pedaling free and unencumbered away from Newville, away from the rocket bases, away from our parents and into that world that was now become a new world for us; wide open for exploration, for wild jaunts, and endless, joyful companionship.

At last, some time later, I returned to my bed in the knowledge that I was an apostate but nevertheless able to sleep convinced that the scales had fallen from my eyes. The Earth belonged to mankind and there was no need to abandon it. But knowing now that it was useless to try and convince the elder generation that it was all right to stay, I made up my mind to remain behind when the final rocket took off, even if it meant being the last human being left on Earth.

———

But if the prospect of being alone in an empty world did give me second thoughts, I need not have worried. Meeting with my friends over the ensuing days reassured me that I would not have to remain behind by myself.

Over the course of several weeks, meeting in different places and exchanging views on our separate encounters with various parents and teachers, we all eventually arrived at the same conclusion: that it was useless to try and convince our elders to remain on Earth. Slowly, reluctantly, our opinions solidified, our plans firmed up, and our convictions grew stronger that we would never leave Earth and never abandon each other. At the same time, Newville being the small, close-knit community that it was, word of our discussions went around so that, one afternoon, the gang found itself crowded in the clubhouse in the empty spaces behind Big Pete's domicile. With us were a few other boys from the neighborhood and a contingent of girls that included Harriet Linley.

"So it's decided then?" I asked in the way of opening the discussion.

"You mean you're serious?" asked Leanne Remy standing by an opening in the clubhouse that served as a window.

"Of course we are," replied Pip without hesitation.

"If there's nothing wrong with the Earth, why should we leave for some other planet with a red sky or yellow oceans?" demanded Ricky Sterling who was in my class at school.

"Yuck! Yellow oceans?"

"Well, something like that," said Ricky. "I heard from one of my brothers in the Rocket Corps that there aren't any planets out there that are *exactly* like Earth..."

"So is there anyone here who wants to go to a planet with a yellow ocean when we've got oceans of the right color right here on Earth?" I asked.

There was no reply so I continued.

"Anyway, some of us here have already decided that when the last rocket takes off, we're not going; we're gonna stay here, together; ain't no one gonna break us up!"

"Gosh," said another one of the girls. "What about our moms and dads?"

"They've already said they're going to go," I said. "There was nothing any of us could say to convince them to stay. I don't know about the rest of you, but I don't want to leave all my friends, the best friends in the world, to go live on some other planet where you probably can't even ride a bicycle out in the open air. Not when we have the whole Earth right here all to ourselves!"

I didn't say it then, but deep down I felt closer to my friends than I did to my own parents whose conditioning had created a gap between us that became more unbridgeable every day.

"If Simon wants to stay, then I'm staying with him," declared Jimmy James.

"Me too," echoed Big Pete.

"Think how much fun it'll be to have the whole world to ourselves," said Keith. "We can ride and explore and go wherever we want."

"And never have to worry about being environmentally correct," said Johnny Askew who had spoken aloud what everyone in the room had been thinking.

"Anybody here that doesn't want to stay?" I asked.

I looked around the small room with rays of sunshine squeezing in between the cracks of the planks that made up its thin walls. The couple dozen kids who stared facing one another trying to read each other's thoughts, ranged in age from nine to fourteen but the important thing was that they were all friends...*we* were all friends...who had known each other our whole lives. More importantly, none of us would have been there that day if we had not already decided to go through with the plan of staying behind.

"Okay, then," I said when no one had spoken up. "We're all in."

After that historic meeting, we began to plan. Because Keith's dad was involved in work dealing with the Schedule, he was assigned the job of finding out exactly when the last rocket would be taking off and how preparation for takeoff would be made. From there, we could make our own preparations: caching food supplies; sneaking away equipment like self-powered flashlights, solar generators, and survival kits; writing farewell letters to our parents that were to be hidden away in their luggage.

When the day came when everyone in town were to board bus-vehicles for the long drive to the rocket port, two years had gone by. Counting on the rigidity with which planners clinged to the Schedule, we waited until the last minute before one by one, we slipped from our families and made our way to the hiding place where we hoped no one would think of looking for us. Oh, sure, it wasn't as easy as it sounds. We all loved our parents, younger siblings, and other residents of Newville, but we loved the Earth more and it was all we could do to keep the girls' courage up, comforting them with reminders of our future plans on an empty world all our own. But it was not any easier for us boys. I recall all too well the heartache that gripped me as I watched our elders scrambling at the last minute through the empty streets of Newville, heard their desperate voices calling our names. And then, it was all we could do to stay where we were as we saw the bus-vehicles slowly pull away from town and disappear down the long road headed south.

I can still remember as if it were yesterday, how we all drifted down from the hiding place in the refrigeration factory that old Phineas had once shown us and walked into a deserted Newville. We had wanted to stay partially to preserve the way of life we had always known but then, standing in the empty streets and looking into the darkened domiciles, we realized that we'd been wrong and that none of it would be quite the same as it was before.

That first night, I slept in my own room and in my own bed, but discovered that being alone in the domicile was too oppressive. It was something the others felt as well and over the next few days, we made new arrangements and eventually came to share a few homes clustered together in a single neighborhood. Then the work of bringing our supplies back into town, making inventory of whatever things were left behind, and otherwise sorting out our new lives kept our attention long enough to forget whatever regrets that might have crept upon us during that first lonely night.

Slowly, we began to explore the wide, empty world that had been left to us. At first, we rode our frictionless bikes aimlessly in every direction, following maps and visiting other towns and cities that had died or been abandoned in the years before Newville had been founded. Finally, overcoming the last vestiges of regret at our actions years before, we eventually arrived at the rocket port where the smell of exhaust fumes still clung to the tarmac. By that time, we had been on our own for a number of years and, tired of riding our bikes and needing to keep ourselves supplied, graduated to frictionless vehicles we found at the rocket port. The switch was not made without some sense that an important passage had been made from childhood to maturity. It was soon after that as I recall, that some of us boys began to grow closer to some of the girls. For myself, I found a surprising attraction to Harriet Linley and in the ensuing years, we moved back into my old domicile and began a family.

And in all that time, in all the years that we drifted into adulthood and beyond, the Earth's temperatures failed to rise but instead, fell steadily toward where they were 200 years before. Practical observation verified our findings with snowfall that lingered longer in the winter, glaciers that began to again creep down mountain valleys, and a seashore that receded every year as the polar ice caps expanded.

Now, as the Earth began to reawaken, I knew my personal golden age had finally come to an end. All my old friends, the Founders with whom I explored the empty world, rediscovered ancient cities, measured snowfall, struggled with self-education in electronics, mechanics, or computer technology, and raised children, one by one they reached the limits of age: Pip, Keith, Jimmy James, Big Pete, all fell away. And when it finally came time for Harriet too, I knew the adventure was over. A reborn Earth, with no mistakes in it, now belonged to our children's children. It would be their own golden age as they built new towns and reclaimed land that had been abandoned to sea and desert. Other children would ride their bikes in other towns as yet unnamed or even thought of and somewhere beyond the solar system, it could only be hoped that other children of men somehow had the chance to do the same.

"Ready to go now, granddad?" asked Virgil sensing that I had finished my tale.

"Sure," I said. "You must be sick of those old stories anyway. Let's head for home."

Virgil did not answer but smiled and clapped me on the shoulder instead. Together, we returned to the cracked tarmac and made for the land rover. Soon, the rocket port was a fading jumble on the horizon and ahead, I could already see the familiar streets of old Newville and imagine the gang dashing among them on their frictionless bikes beckoning me to join them. I would return to the old domicile where I was born and in a few weeks or months, as the snow began to fall, I would leave the good Earth on my own and not in a rocket.

The Return of Rocketman Ken Tobey

AFTER NEARLY TEN YEARS in the service, Rocketman Ken Tobey never thought that the press of a single Earth gravity could feel so good.

Smiling inside the confines of his plasteel helmet, he watched the indicators on his instrument panel spin crazily as the engines of the big solar rocket were cut off and the ship's lateral thrusters switched on. Slowly, the pressure on his body increased as the rocket slowed and began to right itself. Although the cabin where he rested in his padded stasis couch was completely soundproofed, still, he could imagine the screeching whine of the rocket as its stabilizing fins cut through the upper atmosphere and dipped below the first layer of cloud. Then, there was a final blast of the main engines and suddenly, as his couch was slowly leveled off by hidden gyros, Ken felt the comforting thud of the rocket as it came to rest in its prepared cradle.

Not waiting for the captain to give the formal order to get up, Ken joined the rest of the crew in eagerly divesting themselves of their flight suits, grabbing their duty bags and lining up at the exit hatch to await their first

"But of all the places you've been, which did you like the best?" asked Tommy.

Ken thought a moment, his mind wandering: sunsets on Mars, the ribbon of the Milky Way sparkling over the asteroid belt, the churning oceans of Venus that sent giant ripples slowly moving across the surface of its floating islands, the frozen beauty of distant Neptune, and the lonely removal of a distant sol as seen from the orbit of Pluto.

glimpse of home after years in space.

"What are you waiting for, Captain John?" someone at the head of the line said.

"We want to see the green hills of Earth!" said someone else.

"Or at least the landing apron of Campbell Field!" said still a third, as everyone laughed.

Ken thought they had a right to be in a jovial mood. After a tour of duty with the rocket service that included working the asteroid mines, terraforming on Mars, and siphoning gasses from Jupiter's atmosphere among other things, everyone was eager to feel warm sunshine on their unprotected bodies, to walk in normal gravity without a drag belt or helium suit, and to breathe fresh air instead of recycled atmospherics.

"Take it easy, men," said Captain John, his hand held tantalizingly over the big green knob that when pushed, would open the exit hatch and let in the outdoors. "In a few weeks, you'll be begging the service to take you up again to escape the boredom and fawning in-laws!"

The captain's jibe was met with laughter and vows that such a thing could never happen, not with this crew and then, suddenly, the door was open and over the heads of his crewmates, Ken could see a blue sky and a part of the glassite control buildings glistening in the sun.

One by one, the men exited the cabin and began descending a mobile staircase that had been pushed up against the flank of the rocket. They began at the top still shaky with their space legs but by the time they reached the bottom they were able to walk off in the confident, jaunty style that had become the mark of a former rocketman.

The captain's jibe was met with laughter and vows that such a thing could never happen, not with this crew and then, suddenly, the door was open and over the heads of his crewmates, Ken could see a blue sky and a part of the glassite control buildings glistening in the sun.

One by one, the men exited the cabin and began descending a mobile staircase that had been pushed up against the flank of the rocket. They began at the top still shaky with their space legs but by the time they reached the bottom they were able to walk off in the confident, jaunty style that had become the mark of a former rocketman.

Back at the head of the stairs however, Ken found himself unable to proceed. Struck by the quality of the late afternoon sunlight, he stood transfixed in the doorway caught between the heady scents of Earth and the stale, artificial smells from inside the rocket. Slowly, as he breathed in the outside air, he marveled at how easily he could differentiate among the outdoor elements: fresh soil, decaying leaves, various plant life, the musk of animals, wet tarmac, and even a stray wisp of a lady's perfume, all above the expected exhausts and fumes of a recently landed rocket.

How long he stood there at the top of the stairs, he did not know but it seemed an awful long time had passed before he became aware that someone was calling his name. Reluctantly, he looked down from a rapidly congealing sunset and saw for the first time that there were people waving to him from the edge of the landing apron. Was it...? Could it be...? Yes! It was mom and dad, little brother Tommy and...was that Betty Lou? His little sister all grown and become a young woman? It surely was and suddenly, even the delightful scents of Earth were momentarily forgotten as Ken rushed down the stairs and fairly flew into his mother's arms. And when she finally let him go, there was dad's firm hand gripping his shoulder.

"Dad..." said Ken, smiling.

"Ken...son...it's been a while," said dad, pulling the pipe from between his lips. Behind his glasses, his eyes were smiling seeing the boy who was the neighborhood astro ball champion rather then the man who explored other worlds.

"Hey, Ken, can you tell me all about what it was like up there?" said a breathless Tommy, all eagerness and curiosity as he stared in wide eyed adoration of the flight suited man before him. "It's all the kids in the neighborhood have been talking about for weeks!"

"Sure I will, Tommy; as soon as I get some of mom's apple pie in my belly," said Ken, giving his brother's scalp a quick Indian sunburn. Tommy twisted away and then reattached himself to Ken's leg like an iron filing drawn to a magnet.

"Betty Lou, aren't you going to say hello to your big brother?" asked mom, holding close to her husband's side.

"Hi, Ken," said Betty Lou, her hands clasped firmly behind her back.

"Is that any way to welcome home a famous rocketman who's been gone for ten years?" asked Ken.

Betty Lou smiled and took a hesitant step forward then, as if a light switch had been thrown, a big smile spread across her face and she flew into the circle of his arms.

"I'm going to squeeze you so tight you're eyes are going to pop!" whispered Ken in his sister's ear, just the way he used to when she was little.

Giggling, Betty Lou composed herself and said," I'm not a little girl anymore Ken!"

"Yeah, she's got a boyfriend now...or at least she thinks he's her boyfriend!"

"Oh, hush, Tommy!"

"It's Busby Kleiner!"

"Not Busy Busby?!"

"Tommy!"

Ken laughed then, the kind of free spirited, unselfconscious laugh that he suddenly realized he had not allowed himself for ten years. Come to think of it, he did not recall much laughter in space whether aboard ship or on station. Was it because things were that serious in space or only on Earth that he could breathe easily enough to let his inhibitions loose? Whatever the explanation, it felt good and he had no intention of spoiling things by examining the phenomenon too closely.

The drive through the abandoned country-side that lay between the rocket port and the outer ring of the city was like a dream for Ken as mom and dad talked about how nice it was going to be to have him back home again and Tommy and Betty Lou argued about whose friends they wanted him to meet first. Mostly though, Ken did not really listen, preferring instead to let his mind wander over the terrain of his youth, remembering how on warm summer days he and his friends would pack lunches and take off on their air cycles into the countryside. There, they would spend whole days exploring the ruins of the old commuter towns that were identifiable mostly in sub-divisions of weather beaten foundations and overgrown retail plazas.

Then dad pressed down on the air pedal and the car left the old ground road and slipped into one of the fly zones that eventually gave access into the city whose glassite towers glowed colorfully in the distance. Suddenly, they were swooping over the first dwellings of the outer ring and Ken could see people moving along the slidewalks that knit the different neighborhoods together. Now they were over a neighborhood center with its Post Office kiosk, retail domes, old style churches, and green common areas. Ken well remembered how his stomach had tied up in knots when, on a dare, he had taken his air cycle into the city and flew it to the highest point atop the pink hued astral tower and there, tethered to the 3-D needle that crowned its topmost floors, he had an epiphany. Looking down, there was nothing to see except misty clouds that hid the rest of the city from view but when he shifted his gaze upward, the world opened up to him. Over his head, the blue sky was piled high in fleecy white clouds but beyond them, he knew there was nothing that separated him from the solar system beyond. Enraptured, he stayed there for hours, waiting for day to end and when the stars became visible at last, he felt close enough to reach out and touch them. But surprisingly, he felt neither awe nor wonderment at the sight instead, what he felt was a sense of familiarity, like space was simply a place he had been to before. Perhaps the feeling came from reading stories of the early space explorers, books he had devoured with a hungry voraciousness in those days. In any case, it was right then, sitting on the swaying flimsiness of his air cycle high above the city that he first determined to be a rocketman...

"...for dinner, Ken?"

Suddenly, the remembered vision of that night vanished and Ken found himself back in the air car and mom was asking him something.

"I'm sorry, mom," said Ken. "What were you saying?"

"I was wondering what you wanted for dinner tonight?"

"Anything, mom," replied Ken. "Anything would taste swell after ten years of insta-food."

"Those insta-food menus are pretty good," said Tommy. "We tried some at school once."

"They are the first few months you have them, but after that, they're not so hot," Ken said. "There's not much variety in them you know."

"What about ribs and grits with plenty of greens on the side?" asked mom.

"Sounds great!" said Ken with real enthusiasm.

"And I've got you're choice of apple or blueberry pie."

"Mom baked them from scratch," said a wondering Betty Lou. "Flour and milk and eggs. I peeled the apples."

"Stop it girl, you're torturing me!"

Everyone was still laughing when dad finally slowed the air car and veered from the fly zone onto a glide path that took them directly into neighborhood #1133. Suddenly, everywhere Ken looked there seemed to be a familiar landmark: there was Russ Mann's dwelling where the 1133 gang had built an elaborate tree house (no girls allowed!); and next door was Mr. Monahan's dwelling where he saw his first scientifiction book (and thereafter devoured every one in Mr. Monahan's collection); and just down the slidewalk at #1130 was Mary Jill Lochek's double domed dwelling where he received his first kiss... And then they were pulling onto the airpad before his own home which was a retro-design based on mid-twentieth century suburban architecture, all sloping roof lines, imitation clapboard, and small paned louvered windows. Outside there was plenty of shrubbery, some big shade trees, and even a white picket fence out front that he remembered mom having insisted on putting in. How long ago was that? He thought Betty

Lou may not even have been born yet. As the airfoils died down, dad settled the car neatly on the airpad and everyone piled out.

As the public air car lifted off for the return flight to the depot, Ken saw that nothing much seemed to have changed inside either. The dwelling was furnished much as it always had been with dad's vibra-recliner still in its usual place before the family's entertainment center while the pipe rack that Ken had made for him on his 45th birthday sat on a table in the living room. Family holographs of cousins and aunts and uncles still stared from control frames on the walls. Even his old room, as spare and unlived in as it had been, was much as he had left it. Throwing his duty bag onto the bed, he walked over to the open natural-tint window and looked out over the backyard, inhaling the scents coming from mom's flower bed. And as night fell on the neighborhood and #1133 basked in the multi-colored glow of the city's glassite towers, only the brightest of stars could be seen in the darkening sky.

———

The next day, Ken was relaxing out back listening to a newspad and catching up on current events when Tommy poked his head over the fence that separated the yard from the dwelling next door.

"What's up, kid?" asked Ken, when it seemed Tommy would never speak up.

"Are you busy, Ken?"

"Not for my favorite little brother."

"How about your favorite little brother's friends, Jiff and Jimmy the Kid?"

Suddenly, Ken saw two more heads begin to poke up over the top of the fence.

"No problem, bring them over." Ken well remembered what it was like to be a boy and watch the big rockets taking off from over the hills and wondering where they were headed to. He did not blame his brother and his friends for wanting to hear the stories he had to tell.

The next moment there was a scrabbling of feet and the three boys had climbed over the fence and thumped down in the yard. Ken put down the newspad as they approached.

"So what is it you guys want," asked Ken, already knowing the answer.

"Can you tell the fellas what it was like to be a rocketman?" asked Tommy.

"What was it like in the asteroid farms?" asked one of the boys.

"That's Jiff," said Tommy. "And this is Jimmy the Kid."

"Did you see any aliens?" said Jimmy the Kid breathlessly.

"To tell you the truth, life on the spaceways was mostly dull routine with lots of waiting," began Ken. "But if you're the kind that sees beauty in a night sky and can find excitement in any change of situation, then being in space can be the most thrilling experience in your life. For instance, you wouldn't think that polishing those giant mirrors attached to the solar collectors in orbit around the sun could be much fun..."

"No, no, no," said all three boys in wide eyed chorus. "That sounds great!" "Exciting!" "Awesome!"

"...but seeing the sun that close up, even through the polarized lens of an environmental suit, was nothing short of spectacular. Now, some guys I worked with, they didn't think it was anything special. They just wanted to collect their duty pay and get back to Mercury Station to watch the latest vids from Earth."

"Wow," said all three boys in unison.

"Tell us about the time you went to Venus..." prompted Tommy, settling down in the grass.

"Oh, the floating islands," said Ken. "Venus being a liquid world has no fixed land, no continents like there are on Earth. Instead, it has floating islands made up of sedimentary filaments that have grown and intertwined to form single units drifting freely in the ocean currents. Over thousands of years, they grow to the size of continents with their surfaces littered with encrustations that have reacted with the atmosphere to create different kinds of minerals that can be harvested for use in food or other products."

"Gee," said the boys, other worldly visions obvious in their wondering eyes.

"I was assigned to continent G-12 in the southern hemisphere where I spent a year helping to gather stony bulbs from encrustations that are ground up for use as solar spice that your mothers sprinkle in their tea..."

"I love spice candy bars!" said Jiff.

"So do I," said Ken. "Then there was the time I worked on one of the atmosphere factories on Jupiter."

"Is that one of those things that work like giant vacuum cleaners, sucking up the atmosphere?" asked Jimmy the Kid.

Ken laughed. "Kind of. An atmosphere factory floats in the upper atmosphere of the planet and harvests methane gas in a huge balloon. When the balloon is filled, it's released and bobs to the upper levels of the atmosphere where it can be snagged by rocket service ships and taken on the long haul back to Earth. Back home, the gas is converted into fuel, mostly for use on the moon colonies."

"Have you been to the moon, Ken?" Tommy wanted to know.

"Only briefly," admitted Ken. "When I was on layover from Earth and waiting transport to the asteroid belt. That was my first assignment after I'd completed off world training at Canaveral. They call it 'asteroid farming,' but really, what goes on out there is raising biological cultures that can only be grown in a zero G environment. The larger asteroids are perfect for that because they offer plenty of room and can bc isolated in case of accident...and they're zero G off course!"

"But of all the places you've been, which did you like the best?" asked Tommy.

Ken thought a moment, his mind wandering: sunsets on Mars, the ribbon of the Milky Way sparkling over the asteroid belt, the churning oceans of Venus that sent giant ripples slowly moving across the surface of its floating islands, the frozen beauty of distant Neptune, and the lonely removal of a distant sol as seen from the orbit of Pluto. But none seemed to match the wonder of his own back-yard right here in #1133. What, in the whole solar system, could match a lawn of closely knit grass or a maple tree swaying in a warm summer breeze? What was it about the shape of the roofline on the Anderson's house and the way it was outlined against a starry night sky? And could any of the barren landscapes of the moon or Mars equal the mystery of what might lay behind the line of trees marking the end of his neighborhood and the beginning of the out-lying countryside?

"I don't expect you to believe me, guys," said Ken finally. "But nothing in space beats what I can see from right here, sitting in this lawn chair." He pointed to an empty lot next door that had become a tangled wilderness of towering ancient trees, underbrush, rampant vines, and hanging mosses. "Look at that. Isn't that the strangest landscape you've ever seen? There's nothing in there, whether trees, ani-mals, or insects, that's less alien than anything you'd find on Mars or Venus. You want to ex-plore? Then you don't have to go any farther than next door..."

Not the answer they were expecting, the boys looked at one another doubtfully, not cer-tain if the veteran rocketman was joking.

"Aw, c'mon, stop fooling with us, Ken, what did you really like best?" persisted Jiff.

But Ken did not reply. Lost in thought, his gaze locked on the wooded lot, he seemed to forget that the boys were there. And when at last, he came to himself, he found that he was alone and that it was nearer to noon than early morning.

———————

It was a few days after his return home that Ken saw Mr. Monahan trimming the hedges that separated his property from the Tobeys.' At the time, Mr. Monahan was displaying some of the eccentricity with which he was famous in the neighborhood: instead of a laser trimmer, he was using an old fashioned pair of giant scissors. Smiling at the recollection of all the times he had visited Mr. Monahan looking for a book to read, Ken decided to go over and say hello.

Pausing in his work, Mr. Monahan looked up and smiled at the boy he once knew now become a man.

"Well, hello there young fella," Mr. Monahan said. "And what brings you back to old Terra?"

It was Ken's turn to smile then, remembering Mr. Monahan's fondness for twentieth century scientifiction. He never could reconcile himself to the fact that the world had failed to adopt many of the terms that had been popular in the scientifiction stories of the 1940s and 50s.

"I missed the trees," replied Ken, taking Mr. Monahan's hand in a welcoming grip. "I see nothing's changed here. Still have an affection for things twentieth century?"

"These?" Mr. Monahan held up the trimmers. "Had them for 40 years and they still work fine. I notice that your dad has gone through quite a few laser trimmers in that time..."

"You're right, nothing's built to last these days," laughed Ken.

"Well, except for the rockets," said Mr. Monahan who, as an astro-tech for the rocket service, was the first to take Ken down to Campbell Field to see them up close. "Have to admit lots of great engineering skill went into those, especially the latest models."

"I can tell you first hand that the new Bradbury Needles are absolutely reliable," said Ken. "All of us rocketmen swear by them!"

"So I hear," said Mr. Monahan. "And you, Ken. Still keeping up with your reading? Or have you become one of those guys seduced by the vids?"

"Oh, I'm not against watching a good vid now and then, but yes, I still read...not actual books mind you...they're just not convenient while on duty. While in space I did most of my 'reading' by listening to a newspad."

"Understandable, but do they keep any of the classics stored in among the new junk?"

Ken did not need to be told what Mr. Monahan meant by "classics;" the great scientification novels and stories that had been popular in the last century.

"You'd be surprised," said Ken. "But certainly nowhere near the breadth of material you have in your collection. You do still have it don't you?"

"Now that's a silly question!" said Mr. Monahan with mock surprise.

"In that case, is there any chance I can borrow something to read while I'm home?"

Mr. Monahan's face lit up as Ken knew it would.

"Need you ask?" said Mr. Monahan, putting the trimmers down in an old wheel barrel that had been resting out of sight on the other side of the hedges. "C'mon over and you can pick out what you want."

Moments later, Ken was standing in a spare bedroom at the rear of Mr. Monahan's dwelling that had been converted into a library. Everywhere, the walls were lined with bookcases containing thousands of colorful "paperbacks" and "magazines" that were probably worth a fortune to antique collectors but which had not prevented Mr. Monahan from letting the boys of #1133 take whichever they wanted home to read. To be sure, he must have lost some along the way but as he always said, it was all intended to be read not preserved "under glass."

Scanning the shelves while Mr. Monahan prepared lemonade in the kitchen, Ken found his memory thrown back to lazy summer days spent reading Isaac Asimov, Edmund Hamilton, Henry Kuttner, C.M.Kornbluth and a score of other authors whose visions of the future inspired him to be a rocketman.

Carefully, Ken removed one of the books from the shelf and slipped it out of its plaz sleeve. It was a copy of Frank Herbert's *Dune*, a paperback edition published in 1969. Opening the book, Ken caught the scent of old time pulp paper and immediately felt a rush of nostalgia as he was transported back to Donny Metzler's back yard where he and his friend would lay on the cool grass each reading books they had borrowed from Mr. Monahan. How long ago was that? It seemed like it must have happened to someone else in another lifetime.

"Here you go," said Mr. Monahan, breaking into his thoughts and handing Ken a glass of lemonade. "I put a pinch of solar spice in it. My concession to what the future used to be."

Ken took the glass and took a long drink, amused to hear again Mr. Monahan's favorite phrase.

"So what'll it be? Heinlein? Pohl? Weinbaum? Or maybe a couple of magazines?"

"I hadn't really anything specific in mind," said Ken. "Except maybe something more down to Earth...no pun intended."

Mr. Monahan laughed. "No problem, Ken. I can see how you might have had your fill of wonder...if such a thing is possible."

Moving over to a smaller section of Mr. Monahan's library, Ken stooped and looked over a group of books that he'd disdained when he was a teenager. Picking out a volume, Ken stood and said, "I'll take this one."

"*Walden?*" asked Mr. Monahan looking at the title. "Not something I'd have expected you to choose. Any particular reason?"

"I'm not sure," admitted Ken. "But maybe I'll find out after I read it."

"Ken, is there anything wrong?" asked mom one day about a month after Ken had returned home.

"Why do you ask?" replied Ken, putting down the book he had borrowed from Mr. Monahan.

"Well, it's just that you seem so distracted lately," mom said stepping into his room. "More than once we've noticed how you don't finish a sentence and right in the middle of a conversation, you seem to tune people out and just stare at nothing. And the other day, you came in from the rain soaked to the skin and when I asked you why you didn't come home sooner, you acted as if you hadn't even realized it was raining."

Ken remembered that night, but for the life of him, could not recall where he had been for the hours between dinner when he had left for a walk and when he returned after midnight. That was something however, that he had no intention of worrying his mom with at the moment.

"And you frightened Tommy before when all you did was stare at an anthill for a whole morning last week," mom continued. "Tommy said that he tried to talk to you but it was like you never even heard him."

"I'm sorry, mom," said Ken. "I guess maybe I have been a little distracted, but only because it feels so good to be home again. Life here is so different from the way it is in space where there isn't any. Even now, after a full month, I still have to keep reminding myself that I don't need to go through a life support check before going outside. And sometimes, it's only when I get to the table and actually see the meal there that it occurs to me that I don't have to eat instafood any more."

Mom reached out and placed her hand against his cheek the way she used to do when he was a boy.

"I just want you to know that there's nothing to be concerned about," mom said. "All those worries you must have had while in space are over now. You don't have to be constantly on guard to make sure of your life support. You're home now, where it's safe."

"I know that mom, and thanks," said Ken, rising to his feet. "Just give me a little time."

Deciding he needed some fresh air, Ken left the dwelling and on a lark, hopped on Tommy's air cycle and headed down the glide path to the edge of #1133. It was a beautiful day, just like the ones he remembered when he was a boy. Under a warm sun, he crossed the outer ring of neighborhoods and reached the countryside where nature had overrun the old commuter towns. Drifting slowly along the line of trees that marked the edge of the third growth forest, Ken kept an eye out for the familiar break in the underbrush that he and his friends used to use to access the woods. He had to make a couple of passes before he spotted the almost invisible opening and turning around, carefully maneuvered the cycle into the cool shade of the forest.

Trying to avoid getting tangled in overhanging branches, Ken bobbed and weaved until he broke into a clearing dotted with the weather worn foundations of former dwellings. Slowly, he drifted up the road where fossil fuel powered vehicles had once driven but that now was barely discernable beneath creeping grasses and weeds. At last, he arrived at a confluence of old roads that suggested a town center and settled the cycle on a hilltop dotted with stones worn down to nubs. The commuter towns had been abandoned when the old fossil fuels became prohibitively expensive. After that, people began moving back to the city. Later, after the forests had reclaimed the commuter towns, the outer ring of new neighborhoods were built on a limited basis with those interested placing their names on a list for occupancy of one of the new dwellings when it became available. Understandably, not many people wanted to leave the convenience of the city so the wait for a dwelling was never too long. But with limited public services and no private transportation, the number of neighborhoods were kept to a minimum and so the old commuter towns remained undisturbed.

Picking a long blade of grass, Ken stuck it between his teeth and looked over the forgotten cemetery, wondering about the people who were buried there and the lives they had led, lives bereft even of the knowledge of space flight and rocket travel. When he was a boy, he used to pity them for their earthbound lives, bound forever by gravity and undeveloped technology. Those poor people, with no hope of ever seeing the rings of Saturn up close, feel the heat of a solar flare as it licked at a rocket, or the view from atop Olympus Mons on Mars! But now, after experiencing those things for himself, he was not sure if those old Terrans did not in the end have it good. What had they missed after all? They were still able to sense the warmth of the sun on their faces, feel the soft purr of a housecat, endure the cold of a sparkling winter, and heat of a summer day. Ken looked at the tall trees around him, the way vines crept up their boles and hung in festoons from their branches. He listened as a cicada chirped in the heat of the day. Watched as white clouds scudded across the blue sky. What was there in the whole universe to match such sights? What did the pink atmosphere of Mars have over the blue skies of Earth? Were the dead methane seas of Uranus more awesome than the green waters of Earth that teemed with all kinds of marine life? The more he thought about it, the more he came to realize that the people buried beneath him did not have it so bad after all.

With a considerably lightened spirit, Ken returned to the air cycle and made his way back through the forest to the outer ring and neighborhood #1133. He was still in thought as he drifted up the glide path not far from his dwelling when he heard someone calling his name.

"Ken!" said the voice. "Ken Tobey!"

Ken slowed the cycle to a hover and looked around. Though not his own, the neighborhood looked familiar...was it #1130?

"Over here, Ken!"

Someone was waving to him from the front step of a double domed dwelling. Instantly, Ken recognized it as the home of Mary Jill Lochek, who had once dominated his youthful thoughts when he first laid eyes on her at the regional learning center. At the time, they had both been in fifth form but the day Ken would never forget was the one in eighth form when they sneaked a kiss up in her brother's tree house...the first he had ever experienced.

With mixed feelings after so long a time, Ken spun the air cycle around and scooted off the glide path to the slideway before the Lochek's dwelling.

"Mary Jill?" he asked unnecessarily.

"You know very well who I am," Mary Jill said with a laugh; the same laugh that so enchanted...and frightened...him in fourth form.

"I guess I do," admitted Ken.

"Isn't that cycle a little tame for a rocketman?" said Mary Jill in the same teasing tone that used to drive him crazy when they were children.

"It gets me around," said Ken. "Besides, my rocket would probably wake up the neighbors."

"As if that would ever have bothered you before," said Mary Jill. "Why don't you put that thing in hover mode and come on the veranda. I'll go inside and get you something cool to drink."

Ken hesitated for only a moment before dismounting and drawing the air cycle into the enclosure of shrubbery that bordered the front yard.

Stepping onto the veranda, Ken found a swing fastened to the ceiling and sat down, remembering the view from another time when darkness had fallen and he had brought Mary Jill home from a junior spacer's dance at the rocket field. At the time he had been nervous and jumpy all evening and the walk back from the air bus stop to Mary Jill's dwelling seemed to take an eternity. When Mary Jill had asked him to stay for a while for a juice drink, Ken was so nervous he almost ran away while she was inside. But he had conquered his fear and remained and later that evening was rewarded with a kiss...

"Here you go," said Mary Jill, breaking into his thoughts and holding out a compact power drink whose container was wet with condensation.

"Oh, thanks," Ken said, taking the container in his hand. "I see you're still doing some gardening."

"Oh, yes," said Mary Jill taking a place beside him on the swing. "I have a unit in the city these days but I like to come home on weekends for the fresh air and to tend my flowers. But roses and daffodils must be pretty dull for you after Venus and Mars."

"Not really," said Ken absently, staring at a row of potted plants that rested on a table at the edge of the veranda. "Did you know that the floating continents of Venus don't have any plant life? Nor even dandelions? I used to hate those things...my father had me weeding almost every day it seemed to rid our lawn of the pesky things."

"I know how that feels," replied Mary Jill, not noticing the dreaminess in Ken's voice. "The crabgrass in our yard is something terrible."

"Don't knock crabgrass," said Ken, suddenly standing. "Imagine a world without it. Without a single living green thing. Did you know that on Venus, we could never even touch the mineral knobs we were sent there to harvest? Even those mean looking sediments that resembled scrub moss? You had to wear a heavy environmental suit at all times...if you touched anything it was only between multiple layers of insulation and flexsteel. And on Mars, the one place in the solar system besides Earth where you could step outside without a suit, the only thing you could actually touch were rocks and sand. Dead things without a trace of life."

Trancelike, Ken had forgotten his drink and had dug his fingers into the soil of a potted cactus plant. Gently, carefully, he scooped the moist dirt from the pot and held it in the palm of his cupped hand.

Wonderingly, he moved his hand and watched as the granules of soil sifted between his fingers and fell back into the pot. Such a simple thing, he thought, and yet so complicated, so impossible to reproduce anywhere else in the solar system.

Ken shifted his gaze to the cactus and reaching out for it, pricked his hand on its spiny quills. So unappreciated by people. A plant with apparently no useful purpose. Like crabgrass or dandelions, something to be dismissed, to be associated with the dead and lonely spaces of the Earth. But such places were nothing but illusion. In reality, deserts were teeming with life that often went unnoticed. People ought to see Mars or Mercury to find out what lifelessness was really like!

"...listening, Ken?" Mary Jill was saying.

Slowly, Ken became aware of his surroundings and realized that he had once again drifted off in thought.

"What was that, Mary Jill?"

"I said are you even listening to me? I don't think you've heard a word I've said."

"I'm sorry," Ken said. "You're right. My mind was wandering. It seems to be doing that pretty often these days. What was it you were saying?"

"Never mind," said Mary Jill, obviously exasperated. "It seems you haven't changed that much after all."

Not changed? It was the first time since returning home that Ken had considered the question. What was that old saying? If a person questions his sanity, then he is not likely insane? But what to make of his frequent lapses in attention? Why did his mind insist on wandering? Or was it wandering? Was it, instead, trying to lead his thoughts in a specific direction? What was it his subconscious was trying to tell him?

"I guess I'll see you around, Mary Jill," he said finally, more abruptly than he wished.

"It was good seeing you again, Ken," said Mary Jill, not certain at Ken's sudden change in demeanor.

Guiding his air cycle through the front gate, Ken hopped on and took off down the slideway forgetting to wave goodbye to Mary Jill.

Late that evening, after the rest of the family had gone to bed, Ken left his dwelling and went for a walk. It was a warm summer night with the soft wind in the trees the only sound to break the stillness. Even the glide path was quiet with no traffic to activate its hidden machinery. Feeling more content than he had been for a long time, Ken realized suddenly that it had taken ten years in space to teach him the value of his own world, his city...even his own neighborhood. Looking around, he took in the familiar rooflines, the way the trees blocked out the sky, the clouds drifting across the starry sky glowing white in the moonlight, the smell of Mrs. Ronda's flower garden two slideways off. The soft rustle of leaves caught his attention as he neared the edge of the neighborhoods and the row of trees that marked the start of the abandoned commuter towns.

Beyond that rank of trees, there was only darkness and for a moment, he heard the solitary call of some night bird in the forest. Making his way to the top of a nearby rise, he found a half buried boulder at the summit and, surrounded by tall grass that had gone to seed, he propped himself against the stone and lay down. Gazing at the sky, he soon found himself tracing the great constellations, just the way he used to do when he was boy and only dreaming of going into space. When he was younger, those stars seemed to beckon him like old friends. Unlike some other rocketmen, he was never fearful or nervous about going into space, and once there felt at home. But somehow, over time, the comfort and ease he found among the planets must have changed. If familiarity breeds contempt, then it must have been something like that because now, lying here with the Earth beneath him, he felt no inclination to return to space. Those distant lights no longer held any fascination for him. Oh, he would always feel a wistful appreciation for what they had once meant to him, but like old friends he had outgrown, he no longer needed to be with them. Ironically however, another old friend that he had somehow forgotten had suddenly, unexpectedly superceded them.

Plucking a blade of grass, Ken placed the stem between his teeth and tasted its bitter juices on his tongue. Vaguely, he removed the blade from his mouth and held it before his eyes, a black line against the starry heavens. How simple in design it was! For so long, he had taken such a thing for granted. The presence of grass had been such a normal thing that he had never bothered to question it but after being in space so long, it now fascinated him endlessly. Staring at grass, Ken's mind dove deep wondering about its life processes going from seed to mature plant and sowing seeds of its own and then covering the earth with its kind. He wondered about the soil it sprang from, the insects and worms that made their way through it, and how they all fit together in the grand tapestry of life. In space, where life was completely absent, contemplation veered inward instead of outward. There, the self became the chief subject of consideration, an intellectual and spiritual dead end. On Earth, as he had discovered, the incredible diversity of life that covered every aspect of the planet from the macro to the circumscribed surroundings of neighborhood #1133 allowed for a flowering of rediscovery. It was ironic then, that the simple life of neighborhood #1133 allowed for a fuller appreciation of the universe than all the rest of the sterile worlds of the solar system.

Suddenly, Ken heard the distant howl of some canine from deep in the forests of the old commuter towns. Getting to his feet and turning in the direction of the silent trees, he listened and heard it again, farther away. It was then that the full realization struck him that there had been no need to go into space to discover new worlds or strange life forms, all of that was right here on Earth the whole time. Staring at the dark rows of trees, he felt the old growth woodland with its silent vestiges of a past way of life calling to him, insisting that he immerse himself in all the wonders of nature. Inspired, Ken turned back toward home and ran to his dwelling as fast as his legs could carry him.

It had been almost a year since Ken had resigned his commission in the rocket service surprising his family as well as his colleagues when he had applied for early retirement benefits. He used almost all of the earned credits and took advantage of the high respect many had for rocketmen to buy a lot in the old commuter towns from the government for construction of his own dwelling. As was to be expected, the request caused consternation. After all, who would want to build a home so far from any public services or utilities? At the time, Ken had simply smiled patiently and accepted the deed.

In the following months, after he had recruited Tommy and his friends to help, they constructed a dwelling using mostly material they found in the ruins of old buildings and from nature itself. When they had finished, the boys, as boys would, admired the rough log cabin. While not exactly as primitive as it looked (generators provided power for air circulation, lighting, and various appliances) water was still supplied by a well and for personal relief, an outhouse was located a hundred yards from the dwelling.

Excited in the beginning, the novelty of Ken's dwelling eventually wore off and the boys' visits dwindled. Which was all right with the former rocketman whose continuing fascination with life on Earth kept him constantly enthralled with his bucolic surroundings. He figured to enjoy it while he could because he strongly suspected that as soon as his fellow rocketmen heard what he had done, they would come visiting, many to stay and do the same. As for the boys, let them scratch their heads and wonder how a rocketman could trade the glamor of space for the dull familiarity of a forest trail. The only way they could ever understand was to go into space and discover the reasons for themselves.

Happy and content, Ken put down *Walden* and stepped out of his dwelling, anxious to explore his new world...

How Jeremy Bonner Saved the Future

"...HAWAII BECAME THE ALOHA State yesterday following action by Congress and the President in formally admitting the former territory into the Union. The action follows that of Alaska which was admitted as the 49th state in January..."

Jeremy Bonner snapped off the radio and stepped out the kitchen door of his modest Maple Street home. Making his way along the row of hedges that separated his property from that of his neighbor's, he reached the front yard and pushed past the gate in the white picket fence.

"Hello, Mrs. Frenwick," he called to the woman waiting at the bus stop with a group of children. "Beautiful day isn't it?"

Not waiting for a reply, Jeremy hopped into the shiny new Chevy Impala convertible parked at the curb and paused a moment to look around. Taking a deep breath of cool morning air, he admired the orderly quaintness of the surrounding neighborhood: the single family homes adequately spaced, the quiet tree lined streets, the leafy sidewalks just filling with children walking to school. Overhead, beyond the surrounding oak and poplar trees, a blue

Dispirited after only a few minutes of study, Jeremy little wondered at how supinely the people of this dark future seemed to accept a destiny that pointed inevitably to the grave. Under such circumstances, civilization was doomed and he had no desire at all to be there when it ended.

sky beckoned with nary a cloud to ruin its deep, intoxicating color.

He had to admit, after the upheaval of the war that had ended over ten years before, it was a world the victors felt justified in having fought for.

Breathing a contented sigh, Jeremy leaned forward and turned the key in the car's ignition and listened, satisfied, as the big engine purred to life. Yes, indeed, life in these here United States was good and with a future that promised so much more! Turning on the radio, he pulled the automatic transmission lever into drive and edged away from the curb.

"...put down an uprising in Tibet forcing its spiritual leader, the Dalai Lama into exile. The action comes only months following strongman Fidel Castro's seizure of power in Cuba earlier in the year and marks continued expansion and consolidation in the Communist world..."

Well, of course, nothing was perfect, not even the world of 1959 but in his small corner of it, Jeremy was convinced that civilization had reached its apex. Or, at least, come pretty close to it. With the opening up of space exploration, the use of nuclear energy for peaceful purposes, and a free market economy that had made the lives of everyone better, easier, and safer, the future presented only an unending vista of improvement.

As proof, Jeremy considered his own life as a microcosm of the United States as a whole. When he had returned home from the Pacific Theater in 1946, he took advantage of the GI Bill and graduated from MIT with a degree in physics and electronics. By then, the future of electronics lay with the integrated circuit and the development of calculating machines so it was natural for him to wind up with FutureTech, a start up company concentrating on the new technology. These days though, the trendy word was "computer" and already, dinosaurs like univac were beginning to seem old fashioned.

"...confirmed the flight earlier in the year of a new X-15 rocket plane which obtained a record breaking speed of Mach 6. The new type aircraft made its first flight after being released from the belly of a B-52 bomber and flew to the edge of space before being brought back to earth..."

It was the possibilities promised by modern science, particularly information technology, that excited Jeremy the most. What the development of high powered computers could mean for pure scientific research was anybody's guess but it was that suggestion of unlimited horizons that had first caught his imagination back in college and convinced him that the post-war era would prove to be the most exciting in the history of mankind. That was why, as an employee of FutureTech, he felt he was a part of that inevitable progress toward a shining future that he had first glimpsed as a child at the old New York World's Fair.

It was that future of glistening towers, trackless public transportation, and spotlessly efficient household instrumentation that fired not only his own imagination as a boy, but the expectations of everyone who saw those exciting displays.

"...what has become popularly known as the 'kitchen debate' when Vice President Richard Nixon debated Soviet Premier Nikita Krushchev in a model of a typical American kitchen on display at the American National Exposition in Moscow. Kruschev had expressed doubt that the model depicted the average American kitchen..."

Jeremy's confidence in the future was shared by FutureTech president and founder Bill Trender, a veteran of White Sands whose loose management style encouraged employees to pursue their own projects when time permitted. Nothing was off the table and if any showed promise, Trender was willing to put the company's resources behind its development.

Such had been the case with a pet theory Jeremy had come up with a few years before during the first Eisenhower administration, before he really knew just how difficult a job it was that he had undertaken. Remaining after hours when time was available on the company's up to date computers, he had been working on a new number theory requiring strings of mathematical formulae held together by the slimmest of equations. Often, it seemed more like a mental juggling act than mathematics.

But it was worth it. Along with the long hours and the overtime, were the rewards of a good paycheck which had enabled him to purchase the little house on Maple Street as well as wining and dining Marya Demarais, a pretty brunette he met one day in the company cafeteria. Jeremy had already decided to propose to the lucky girl and was only waiting for a decent amount of time to pass before popping the question. But that was for the future, right now, he was supposed to be on his way to work and today of all days, he didn't want to be late.

After driving for some minutes along tree lined boulevards, school yards filling up with happy children, and downtown shops where storefront awnings were just being let down for the day, Jeremy pulled into a new industrial park located on the opposite side of town. There, he joined other commuters as they made their way to work following an orderly internal traffic pattern. Low lying industrial parks located in the suburbs were another post-war innovation that not only relieved cities of unsightly, polluting, red brick factories, but shunted auto traffic on newly constructed roadways designed specifically to handle the increased number of automobiles that had proliferated over the last decade. Everything about the new industrial park movement spoke to Jeremy of modernism and forward thinking futurism.

In moments, he entered the parking lot for the FutureTech building which sat amid generous landscaping and boasted an architectural design that was all glass and shiny marble. Grabbing his briefcase, Jeremy strode across the tarmac, waving greetings to fellow employees and making no effort to differentiate between researchers, administrators, or maintenance workers. As Bill Trender often said, they were a team with each member performing a vital task in keeping the company moving toward the future. Jeremy liked that!

Once through the heavy glass doors, Jeremy stepped into the air conditioned lobby, once again struck by the building's controlled internal environment. He still recalled stifling hot days before the war when the use of fans was the only way to keep cool indoors. Air conditioning had been a revolutionary improvement for the work environment helping to maintain worker efficiency and extend working hours even during the hottest parts of the summer.

Before going any further, Jeremy paused to attach his identity card to his coat pocket and as he headed to the cafeteria, the security guard barely gave it a glance before waving him past his station.

"Good morning, Mr. Bonner," he welcomed.

"Good morning, Fred," replied Jeremy. "How're the Red Sox doing?"

"Not bad. Maybe this is the year we win the pennant."

"Could be," Bonner said as he followed other arrivals streaming to the cafeteria's coffee machines.

As had become his habit, the first thing he did upon stepping into the cafeteria was to look out for Marya. She was easy to spot; she was only the best looking woman working for FutureTech.

"Looking for me?" said a voice almost at his elbow.

"How did you guess?" said Jeremy, smiling. Seeing Marya every morning was like a tonic to him.

"Not so hard," Marya said. She was holding a cup of coffee in each hand and extended one to Jeremy. "Cream and half a dozen sugars?"

"You read my mind!"

"Not likely. We've only been meeting like this for the last six months and your order never changes."

"But it's that dependability that you love!"

"I do!" agreed Marya laughing.

Jeremy glanced around and spotted an empty table. Cocking his head in its direction, he led the way over and presented Marya with a chair.

"Thank you, kind sir."

"You're welcome milady."

"So are you going to be working late again tonight?" asked Marya after she had sat down and taken her first tentative sip of java.

"We don't have anything planned for tonight, do we?" asked Jeremy worriedly.

"Don't fret, pet," said Marya, patting his hand. "It's not Friday yet. I was just wondering, seeing as how you've been putting in a lot of after hours in the lab lately...on to something big?"

"Hopefully," replied Jeremy. "I'm closing in on a new mathematical paradigm that could make the basic logic used by computers simpler than ever. If I'm successful, FutureTech could leap ahead of everyone else in making computers easier to program and accessible to more users."

"It sounds exciting but how many more users could there be?" asked Marya reasonably. "Everyone who needs a computer probably already has one."

"Right now maybe," replied Jeremy, warming to his subject. "But computers won't always remain at the size they are now. Miniaturization is constantly improving and we're hearing predictions that some day computers could even get small enough to fit on a desk top without any loss of capacity."

"Now I know you're kidding me!" said Marya who passed by the room sized univac model every day in the course of her duties.

"I'm not; you'll see." Jeremy glanced at the wall clock and noted the time. "You better get going or you'll be late for work. You know how Jonesy gets if his people aren't at their desks on time."

Marya rolled her eyes. "Tell me about it!"

Jeremy took his cup of coffee with him to the laboratory and promptly forgot all about it the minute he emptied his briefcase and began to glance over the figures he had worked out the evening before. It was stone cold by the time his co-workers began to drift past his door on their way back to the parking lot and home. The day had passed as it always did for Jeremy; very quickly once he became immersed in his calculations. But the sudden increase in activity around him loosened his concentration enough to begin winding up his work for the company. By the time the corridors were quiet again, he was ready for a return trip to the cafeteria for a second cup of coffee and a quick bite to eat.

On the way back to his office, he stopped to check the inter-office mail and found what he was looking for rolled up in his box. Pulling the papers out, he opened them tentatively and saw that they held the calculations he had requested of univac earlier in the day.

Pulling the shades in his office against the late afternoon sun, Jeremy settled down at his desk to go over the numbers provided by the computer. If his predictions were correct, the computer's calculations ought to confirm his own and verify the first three principles of his theory.

Sipping his coffee, the complicated string of numbers and equations began tumbling through his brain, falling neatly into place, faster and faster; his excitement mounted as he began to sense that his object was in sight. The language he needed to create in order to more easily program computers was within his grasp...almost there...

Suddenly, Jeremy felt himself fall from his chair and when he recovered, noticed that it was pitch dark in the room. Had night fallen already? Reaching up to his desk for support in getting to his feet, his hand felt nothing. Moving his arms in wider arcs, he still failed to find the desk or even his chair. Puzzled, he regained his footing without any help and carefully made his way to the light switch by the door. But after feeling around on the wall for a minute, gave that search up as well. Going to the windows with the intention of drawing the blinds, all he found was a blank wall.

"What the heck?"

Groping his way back to the doorway, he stepped through and immediately sensed that he had entered a large room, a very large room that had the effect of dampening a low humming sound that reminded Jeremy of immense but harnessed power. Feeling the urge to panic, he controlled himself until finally spotting a light in the far distance. Making his way there, he discovered that although there was no particular source for the light itself, it seemed focused on a glass booth of some sort. Tapping the glass, Jeremy was convinced that the material was not glass after all but some kind of clear plastic. He was startled by a hiss of air as an opening in the booth appeared without any visible movement of a doorway. Cautiously, he stepped inside and another hiss told him that he was now enclosed. Wondering what came next, Jeremy thought the booth reminded him of some kind of elevator...

Whoosh!!

Stumbling against a wall, Jeremy would have panicked except that he didn't have the time. In moments, the sense of motion he had felt halted and his eyes were struck by the glare of the sun. When they had adjusted themselves to the abrupt change in light, Jeremy was able to see through the clear enclosure of the "elevator" and take in the incredible sight of a city where a city had no right to be. Before he woke up in the darkened room below, he'd been sitting at his desk in the corporate headquarters of FutureTech, located in the leafy suburbs. There weren't any buildings taller than a couple floors anywhere around for miles. How then, was it possible that he now looked over a cityscape of towering buildings that had more in common with the hanging gardens of Babylon than Chicago? Slowly, as his senses took in the incredible scene, he began to notice movement among the buildings and gradually he made out cars or trams that sailed smoothly in and around the buildings on a monorail system that allowed passengers to disembark at different heights. Farther down at what he supposed was street level, other vehicles moved smoothly along roadways they barely seemed to touch.

He'd begun to move closer to the edge of the roof in order to look directly downward when a voice startled him and almost made him lose his balance.

"Hello, Jeremy," said the voice from behind him. "I can't tell you how delighted I am to see you here!"

When he'd recovered his balance, Jeremy turned to see a pleasant faced young man with short cropped hair standing a few feet away. He was dressed in a colorful ensemble of tight yet comfortable fitting top and slacks of an indeterminate material while at his back rested a sleek vehicle of some kind. Jeremy's amazement only grew the greater when he noticed that the vehicle not only had no wheels, but hovered a few inches from the surface of the roof.

"You seem to have the advantage over me," was all Jeremy could muster in the face of such strangeness.

"Sorry," said the young man. "My name's Wilbur; Wilbur Fentis. No one special...at least to you. I mean, I'm not anyone that you'd know."

"Then what are you doing here and...is that car hovering?"

Fentis looked back at the strange vehicle before returning his attention to Jeremy.

"Yes," he said. "They're the primary source of personal transportation these days. As to what I'm doing here, I'm here to welcome you to the year 2023."

Jeremy was struck speechless a moment before replying. Did he just say the year 2023?

"I see by the look on your face that you're confused," continued Fentis nonchalantly. "Don't worry. You're not crazy and neither am I. You see, the calculations you were working on in your office back in 1959 had an unexpected consequence. I'm not sure exactly how your calculations ran...I'm only going by what you reported to William Trender, your employer at the time..."

"Stop!" said Jeremy suddenly, holding up his hands. "Just a minute! I have no idea what you're talking about. How do you know about what I was working on and what did I report to Bill? I don't recall ever having spoken to him on the issue aside from getting his permission for time with univac..."

"Sorry," replied Fentis. "I should have started from the beginning. I know you must be a bit disoriented right now. You see, you're now 66 years in the future...well, the present now actually...but for you it's the future. By momentarily substituting a particular function in the sixteenth equation group coupled with a limited field in the last subset, you altered the intended solution of your problem. With the date also included in the equational chain, you severed your connection with 1959 and connected with 2023."

"But that's impossible...isn't it?"

Fentis shrugged. "You're here aren't you? But obviously, and this was the conclusion you reached in consultation with your employer at FutureTech, somewhere in univac's calculations which you had been reviewing at the time, the computer had stumbled upon a quantum variant that changed the nature of the whole problem."

"And I spoke about this to Bill Trender?"

"Well, not yet...at least from your perspective, you haven't spoken to him about it yet, but from anyone living in this era, you have," said Fentis. "Time travel does tend to make things more complicated than they ought to be."

"So I'll speak about this with Bill?"

"The records show that you went back to 1959, consulted with your employer, and upon his advice, you dropped further work on the project that resulted in your traveling into the future."

"Why would Bill ask that I discontinue my research if I'd had such spectacular results?"

"According to a report you wrote that was filed away in FutureTech's records, your employer thought that time travel posed too many dangers including the creation of alternate timelines and the introduction of knowledge into the 'present' that society might not have been prepared for."

"I guess that makes sense...sort of," admitted Jeremy, rubbing his chin. "But then, if the report was kept secret, how is it you're here to meet me?"

Shuffling his feet, Fentis looked embarrassed.

"Naturally, over the years, no information, no matter how confidential, ever remains secret permanently," Fentis said. "FutureTech was sold to another company which in turn was taken over by another. Eventually, records were lost or donated to university libraries. Such was the fate of your report to William Trender. Historians doing research on the origins of the modern era of course, used records of your time to determine the facts and it was one of them who found the report of your discovery. The report, of course, failed to include the equation with which you were able to travel in time and because of that, your assertion of having visited the future wasn't believed."

"But you did believe it?"

Fentis nodded. "I wasn't sure, mind you. You have to admit, on the face of it, it was a pretty preposterous notion. But the possibility of it kept nagging at me and I must confess to feelings of embarrassment when I finally decided to meet you here when you appeared...if you appeared."

"Well, I'm glad you did," said a grateful Jeremy. "And I suppose that I mentioned exactly where I was to appear in my report?"

"Yes; time and place, so it was a simple matter for me to fly over at the proper time and satisfy my curiosity as to the report's claim."

"Did my report mention meeting anyone here?"

"No. My guess is that you had your reasons."

"Well, at least I know I won't be stuck here," said Jeremy. "Not that I don't like it; on the contrary, the future is almost exactly the way I always imagined it would be. In fact, it looks a lot like the predictions made at the New York World's Fair that I visited when I was a boy."

"You mentioned that observation in your report," said Fentis, pleased. "I'm not sure if it happened during your visit to our era, but if you'd like, I'd be happy to show you the sights via my air car."

"Would I?" said Jeremy eagerly. "Let's go. I'll worry about figuring out how to get back to 1959 later!"

Fentis led the way across the rooftop to where his vehicle hovered and directed Jeremy to take the seat next to him as he climbed into the driver's position. Placing his fingers into grips obviously fashioned to the shape of the human hand, Fentis manipulated them in such a fashion so as to seal the vehicle in a clear bubble of plexiglass. Thus protected against buffeting by strong winds that blasted from between the city's towering buildings, Jeremy felt himself lifted into the air and directed toward the edge of the roof.

"The air car is powered by a nuclear particle that provides a limitless source of energy for the turbo-fans that keep it in motion," Fentis explained. "By directing a series of cantilevers beneath the 'car, I can move it in any way I choose."

So saying, Fentis pushed the air car over the edge of the roof where thick hanging vines hung over the sides and down the face of its upper floors. On different terraces down the face of the building, other plantings grew giving it the Babylonian look that Jeremy had noticed throughout the city when he had first set eyes upon it. For a moment, he felt dizzy staring down to where the building was anchored to the ground but as the flight continued, the feeling passed and he began to enjoy himself.

So far, there were few other vehicles moving at the height from which Fentis had left the roof. Below however, Jeremy noticed how traffic increased closer to the ground.

"Hardly anyone travels at this height," said Fentis sensing his questions. "By law, most traffic is confined to the first three flight levels and public transportation such as the monorail system is used to reach the upper areas of the city. If there weren't such restrictions, air travel would be much more dangerous. In fact, I needed to apply for a special permit to take my 'car to the rooftop where I met you. For now though, we'll need to go below. For that, I'll use a grav-way that will take us quickly and safely through the different traffic levels to the one we want."

So saying, Fentis eased the 'car into an area of sky empty save for a blinking light that seemed to float freely in the air. Suddenly, Jeremy had the sensation of freefalling as his stomach went up his throat and his hands gripped his seat in panic. In no time, the feeling passed and the 'car emerged from the grav-way and slid easily into a traffic lane whose invisible boundaries were obviously known to all the drivers.

"For now, I can give over control of the 'car to the automatic pilot that's programmed with all of the city's traffic patterns," said Fentis. "It knows exactly in what lanes we're allowed to travel and which to stay out of."

"This is all so fantastic!" was all Jeremy could muster as his gaze sought to take in everything at once. What impressed him the most was the cleanliness of the city and how it was designed in such a way that no matter the number and height of its buildings, sufficient sunlight was able to find its way into every corner relieving it of the gloom that sometimes settled over cities of his own era. And with more sunlight there was a healthier climate overall for both people and plants which flourished in every nook and cranny of the city. Obviously its residents loved the outdoors and nature in particular as they filled their streets with arboreal largess and the faces of their buildings overflowed with hanging vines, flowering shrubs, and overhanging miniature trees. The effect was one of an ancient city that had been hidden in the jungle for hundreds of years but with its plant life arranged with far more order and thought.

At "street level," where 'cars seemed prohibited, thousands of pedestrians walked along elaborate gardens on one hand, and store fronts filled with the latest products of an advanced society on the other. For those in more of a hurry, moving sidewalks conducted pedestrians swiftly and safely in long avenues hidden behind a thick screening of plants. Jeremy quickly found himself entranced by this wondrous and orderly society.

"Shall we land?" asked Fentis, seeing his interest.

"By all means!" replied Jeremy as Fentis took manual control of the air car and veered out of the traffic level and into another gravway that dropped them to the lowest level only a few hundred feet above the ground. From there, he steered the vehicle into a public parking area housed inside one of the plant hung buildings. Exiting the 'car, they joined a few other riders heading to a grav-pulse elevator that lowered them all gently to the ground floor. There, they passed through the building's lobby whose periphery was lined with banks of other grav-pulse elevators. In a great, open concourse in the center of the lobby, a multitude of snack bars and lunch counters offered a dizzying variety of foods while patrons sat amid a jungle of plants that included even some full grown trees. As he watched them sipping exotic drinks or quietly reading hand held devices that caught them up on the day's news, Jeremy found himself tempted to mingle with the meal time crowds.

Unfortunately, there was still too much else to see as he allowed himself to be escorted outside where Fentis led the way along the grand sidewalks overhung with towering shade trees. Amid the thronging crowds, many of the pedestrians appeared to be families on holiday with fathers holding older childrens' hands while mothers conducted strollers that seemed to operate on the same principal as the air cars.

"Are those cameras?" asked Jeremy of the impossibly small devices some people were aiming at different points of interest.

"Yes," replied Fentis.

"But they're so small," marveled Jeremy. "Where do they keep the film?"

"They don't need film. Everything is digital today."

Instead of trying to find out what Fentis meant by 'digital,' Jeremy decided to let the subject drop. It was only one of dozens of questions he had that he knew either would be answered in time or not at all before he had to return to 1959.

In the meantime, he was busy marveling at window displays featuring a dizzying variety of electronic devices all meant to make life in the 21st century a comfortable one freeing the average person to spend more time with family members or pursuing personal interests.

Jeremy was still trying to figure out what half the consumer devices actually were when he and Fentis arrived at a vast open space set in the heart of the city. Featuring a rolling landscape of low hills dotted here and there by rocky outcrops and crowded with trees and shrubs that in places might be described as forest land, the area was a garden criss-crossed with pathways, some paved and some moving, that attracted those seeking some solitude from the hurly burly of city life. Taking a path leading to a high point atop a jumble of boulders, Jeremy noticed that the open space seemed to be a favorite of young people who walked hand in hand amid the greenery or simply sat close together on benches or on blankets spread in the grass. Elsewhere, youth's played games of sport in areas set off for teams or on courts where opponents faced off one on one. Everywhere, there was peace and harmony, cleanliness and orderliness, and Jeremy noticed that people were unfailingly polite and considerate of one another. There was also one other thing that he noticed.

"Wilbur," Jeremy said. "I haven't noticed any policemen going about their rounds."

"That's because there aren't any," replied Fentis. "Not that there's no need for them. From time to time, there is an altercation that might require the attention of law enforcement, but such incidents are rare. For that matter, the world itself has been an unusually peaceful place ever since the end of the Cold War and the ascendancy of Western ideals of democracy."

"Then the threat posed by communism has ended?"

"Yes, thanks to the vigilance of the United States," said Fentis. "With the old Soviet Union gone, its satellites soon followed opening the world up to commerce and the blessings of a prosperity that has since encompassed most of the globe. The discovery of alternative sources of energy especially nuclear power, freed the world from its dependency on oil and enabled a vast expansion of the economy."

As evidence of the expansion that had liberated vast sums of money from the wastage of war, Jeremy saw that at some point in the past, the United States had broken the bonds of Earth and began an era of space exploration. With mounting excitement, he watched a news report from the screen of a full color television set of the events surrounding the expansion of a Mars colony. With a picture whose resolution suggested three dimensional imagery, he witnessed a brief summation of the history of space exploration from the first landings on the moon to the establishment of lunar cities with a total population of well over 3,000 people.

Meanwhile, beneath the ocean, permanent underwater labs enabled men to explore the sea bed and even work there tapping its untold wealth of mineral deposits. Jeremy was puzzled, but nevertheless impressed, with early efforts at cleaning up the environment to the point where industry proceeded unchecked but with less and less pollution. Finally, it was strange but somehow satisfying to see people of different races mixing freely with one another, each contributing equally to the improvement of daily life.

"Fentis, from what I can see, the future, your present, will be the fulfillment of every dream we of the mid-20th century had always imagined it would be," concluded Jeremy. "The American way of life, triumphing over the final tyranny of communism will finally lead the world into the paradise we always believed we could make of it. Now, I can go back to my own time content in the knowledge that we will have this wonderful legacy with which to leave our children."

"Then you've decided not to stay?"

For a moment, Jeremy was nonplussed. He hadn't actually considered it. Why bother going back to his own time when he could have the wonders of the 21st century not in 75 years, but right now? It was a good idea but one he entertained for barely a moment.

"I'd like to, but I can't," he finally replied. "You see, there's someone in my own time that I care about and well, I guess I love her and life, even a life as wonderful as it would be in this time, would ultimately be meaningless without her."

"I understand completely," said Fentis. "To tell you the truth, when all the records I could find indicated that you had not decided to stay, I guessed it would have had to be for exactly such a reason."

"Well, then, I guess I should be thinking about getting back."

"What's the hurry? Can't you spend a few more days here? After all, with time travel, you can always go back to the moment you left and lose no time at all."

"You're right!" said Jeremy with enthusiasm. "I'll do it! So now that that's settled, what can you show me next?"

"Are you hungry?" And with that, the two were off for lunch at one of the city's tower top restaurants with a grand view of the mountains many miles in the distance. Jeremy spent the next few days following an agenda filled with sights and surprises that delighted and filled him with anticipation for the years he planned to spend with Marya as they watched events unfold and that would eventually lead to the sparkling future that he had previewed with his unintended visit.

At last, however, the time came when he had seen all that he desired and to see more would mean to have seen too much. And so Fentis conducted him back to the building that had grown over the spot where, 75 years in the past, the FutureTech plant had stood. With some solemnity, Jeremy thanked his host for all that he had done for him before entering the grav-pulse elevator that with a thought, plunged him to the building's foundations where he had first awakened in the year 2023.

Deliberately this time, Jeremy again took up the papers he had been holding when he thought himself into the future. Scanning the information prepared by univac, he reviewed the equations, consciously substituting the crucial data that would complete the equational string and send him back into the past....

The date on his calendar was the same as when he had come in to work that morning and outdoors, the light indicated that it was late afternoon. The clock on the wall showed 6:35 p.m. and the outside corridor was quiet. Faced with such normalcy, Jeremy was inclined to believe that he'd merely fallen asleep and dreamed his adventure in the future...except for the simple viz-pad in his pocket. Given to him by Wilbur expressly to prove to himself that he hadn't dreamed the whole thing, the viz-pad was a simple storage device for visual imagery and contained a short series of images taken of that future world. Scrolling through them, Jeremy grinned.

Conscious that he was now simply playing a part in a pre-destined future, Jeremy left his office and made his way to that of Bill Trender's. As he expected, the FutureTech ramrod was at his own desk working late but at Jeremy's quiet knock, looked up and invited him in.

Jeremy never told Marya about the future world he had visited. There really was no need to. And as Wilbur had predicted, Bill Trender had warned of the danger of his discovery and recommended he forget about it. Although he agreed with him, there was enough of the scientist in Jeremy to want to write up his discovery and so for his own satisfaction, he drew up a report that did not include the crucial details and had Trender file it away with the company's most sensitive records.

He and Marya eventually married and the two of them had ten very happy years together as Jeremy secretly watched the various events he recalled from the future as they unfolded around them. Sadly, however, Marya passed away in 1967 leaving the marriage a childless one. A less cheerful Jeremy went on with his life as he continued working in the burgeoning computer industry. By that time, FutureTech had long since seized to exist and he had moved on to IBM becoming a senior research technician there. But through all the years, Jeremy never forgot that fantastic trip to the future, which seemed more and more like a dream to him, until finally, weary of life without Marya, he decided the time had come to try again and this time, he intended to remain in the 21st century.

And so, late one night in 1969, he pulled out the yellowed papers that he had saved against Bill Trender's advice, and began to pore over them. Having anticipated this day for some time, he had arranged his affairs in such a way as to make sure he had a nest egg waiting for him in the future; one that ought to tide him over until he could find gainful employment...perhaps a position in a university teaching 20th century history or as a guest lecturer. Briefly he worried about where he would find himself fifty years in the future if he traveled there from his Maple Street home but if he recalled rightly from his previous visit, there had been little development this far out in the suburbs. He would take his chances.

Carefully he went over his old notes, step by step filling in an integer there and substituting a term there. Finally, he filled in the size of the field, the desired date and...there was muted lighting in the room he suddenly found himself in and looking around, he realized that it was the same room that he had just left. Or had he left at all? Looking around at the familiar layout, he realized that he was still in his own home. His heart sinking, he rose to his feet and went over to the windows to look outside. There, he saw the familiar neighborhood that he had lived in for the past ten years. For a minute, he thought that he might have made an error with the formula but then he began to notice differences. The neighborhood was the same but many of the houses had changed. Some had new additions; or rather, they had been new once, now, like the rest of the homes they had been built onto, they simply looked run down in their old coats of peeling paint or worn out siding. Almost all of the trees that used to shade the street were gone with some of the old stumps rotting in denuded front yards. Grass was dead or patchy, trash was unsecured, and everywhere, automobiles that still rode on tires crowded the street and filled many yards. One passed by the house obviously still burning gas for fuel as it chugged along trailing a cloud of unsightly exhaust. And of the residents he saw moving about, most seemed to be foreigners. Where were the monorails? The gleaming towers? The air cars? If this was indeed the future, nothing much it seemed, had changed; at least technologically. It was all more of the same but dingier.

Disappointed and wondering what had gone wrong, Jeremy backed away from the windows, bumping into a desk that occupied one end of the front room. Nervously, he spun about, wondering if anyone was home.

"Hello?" he called tentatively. "Hello?"

No answer. He made a careful inspection of the house but found no one. A few pictures held on the refrigerator by magnetic ornaments revealed the smiling faces of strangers that Jeremy assumed now lived in the home that used to be his.

Back in the front room, Jeremy was beginning to wonder what to do next when he noticed a curious instrument on the desk that he had bumped into earlier. Consisting of monitoring screen and a keyboard attached via wiring, it seemed to hum as if alive. Recognizing the arrangement as a computer, but one far less bulky than those mostly in service with the Defense Department in his own time, he wondered what such a thing was doing in a private home. Idly, he pecked at one of the keys and immediately, the screen on the monitor sprung to life displaying a message prompting the user to engage it further. Curious, Jeremy followed the instructions of the promptings and soon found himself on something he gathered was called the "internet," a marvelous form of communication that apparently allowed any citizen access to a limitless store of information.

Forgetting where he was, Jeremy began to experiment and in very little time found himself able to "surf" the various options available on the internet and soon he was accessing various news sites in an attempt to discover what had happened in the years since 1969. But the more he read, the greater his alarm. What had happened to the post-war world his generation had bequeathed to the future? What happened to the boundless optimism which had fueled the country's space program and computer industry; the determination to overcome the communist threat; the courage of Americans' belief in themselves and their way of life? As he viewed aspects of the world of 2023, Jeremy saw little that he could recognize as the virtues of his fellow countrymen. Why, even after a series of successful moon landings, the space program was cut back and eventually abandoned.

It was now a world firmly divided by an unbending ideology whose first tenet was that Western civilization had been at the root of all the world's problems, that had caused all of its deadly conflicts, its rank injustices, its oppressions, and unfairnesses. As a result, measures had to be taken to redress the wrongs and place things in proper balance. After fifty years of such programs, in all areas of society women and non-Europeans had replaced fully 63 percent of leadership roles, educational positions, and the workforce. No matter that overall efficiency and progress had suffered or even halted as a result. Correcting historic injustices was the more important goal whatever the cost to society. Such sweeping societal changes had not only sapped industry of its creative energies, but robbed people of any desire to take risks or even to lead. With emergent societies with more cohesive ideologies and citizens more certain in their beliefs, the west had suffered a catastrophic decline littered with policies of appeasement, apology, and self-indulgence. Stripped of the elements that had once provided them with reasons to be virtuous, courageous, and honorable people, westerners were now philosophically and intellectually defenseless against the outside forces that sought to overthrow them. Reeling at a society so corrupt and narcissistic, Jeremy was still unprepared for the casual acceptance of perverted behavior, the denial of parental rights, the wholesale destruction of unborn children, the collapse of national borders and the resultant economic disruption that bankrupted whole countries and subverted their political systems. As public services eroded, the quality of education declined, and opportunity based mostly on gender or race prevailed, there was no longer any motivation to defend such a corrupt system; a system that defied logic and turned common sense on its head.

Dispirited after only a few minutes of study, Jeremy little wondered at how supinely the people of this dark future seemed to accept a destiny that pointed inevitably to the grave. Under such circumstances, civilization was doomed and he had no desire at all to be there when it ended.

Obviously, this was a different future than the one he had visited in 1959, one that had come into existence as a result of events that had occurred between that year and 1969. But what? Certainly, the 1960s had been a tumultuous decade and though society may have seemed to be in turmoil on nightly television, Jeremy knew that was only an illusion created by the immediacy of television and modern communications. Most ordinary Americans remained true to the values and principals that had seen the country through more trying circumstances. So what could have happened? Whatever it was, it had led to this dystopian future that should never have been. Determined to leave it and perhaps save the future at the same time, Jeremy began to form a plan.

Retrieving his notes, he used the calculator function programmed into the computer to help with the changes he needed to make in the time travel formula. Much faster and able to hold far more information than univac, the computer enabled him to make the necessary calculations in good time and, leaving behind a self-deleting command with the computer, Jeremy left the future and returned to 1959.

His home was just as he remembered it from the days before he was married. Looking out the window, he once again saw the old neighborhood as it once was and couldn't help comparing it to what it would become down that other corridor of history. Shuddering, he determined to save the future for all those generations to come by insuring with his presence there, traveling from 1959 instead of 1969, that whatever evil events that had transpired between those years would never happen.

So thinking, he returned to the neighborhood of FutureTech, once again went over his notes, and soon found himself in the basement of the building in which he had first arrived in the future of 2023. Familiar with his surroundings, he walked over to the grav-pulse elevator and...whoosh...in no time, found himself on the roof. There, he was relieved to find the future just as he had left it, all clean, and orderly, and satisfying...the fulfillment of every dream the people of 1959 had expected. Looking out over that city of beauty and sanity, he shuddered involuntarily at thought of that other Orwellian future where up was down and wrong was right.

Aware that he now served as the anchor that would hold back the past from drifting into that other, terrible future, he made certain the timeline would remain pointed in the proper direction by taking a single match from his pocket and using it to set fire to his yellowing notes. Making sure the fire caught, he released the remnants into the air and watched as they were reduced to a puff of ash on the evening breeze.

Satisfied, he turned back to the grav-pulse elevator with the intention of catching the monorail on the sixteenth floor. As he whooshed downward, he wondered what Fentis was doing for dinner that night and how surprised he'd be not only to see him back again, but also how he'd saved the future!

The Robot that Adapted

"HOW ARE YOU THIS morning?" Joozy heard Mr. Heinkel say.

Most times, Joozy would not have thought such a greeting a strange one to make on a pink Martian morning, but what he did find odd was that Mr. Heinkel had been addressing his floater when he made it.

The thing was, Joozy should not have been so surprised as Mr. Heinkel had a reputation in the neighborhood for eccentricity. Still, it was rather disconcerting to see a grown man talking to his floater as if it were an old friend. Admittedly, being only nine years old, Joozy had little experience upon which to form a proper judgment on the behavior of adults, but on that bright morning when the sun's glare shown through the thin Martian atmosphere and brought everything into crystal sharpness, he felt he had the right to wonder about the peculiarity of Mr. Heinkel's actions.

Of course, here and there, he had picked up stories about Mr. Heinkel: how he kept to himself within the grounds of the oldest dwelling in the neighborhood; how he seldom said hello to anyone and seemed to resent other people; how he talked to himself through his machines and household appliances.

But as interesting as those facts might have been to Joozy, whose entire life experience consisted of Redrock Enclave where he and everyone he ever knew was born, most intriguing was speculation on the possibility that Mr. Heinkel was the oldest settler in town. If true, it suggested to Joozy visions of the early days of colonization when fleets of big stratoliners soared from Earth to Mars and filled Nova Planum with a forest of upright rockets from which the first settlers emerged.

Those were the days, thought Joozy, whose hazy notion of the first wave of colonists included opened cargo doors in the sides of tall rockets spewing forth terrain moving tractors, heavy duty floaters loaded with building materials, and personal floaters piled high with the belongings of the early settlers.

The decades that followed were conflated in Joozy's mind so it seemed that in no time at all, a road network was established and towns and cities sprung up along their course including Redrock Enclave whose domed dwellings appeared like mushrooms up the sides of a steep hill overlooking an important spur in the ancient canal system that crisscrossed the planet.

From what he heard outside of school, it was Joozy's understanding that before the rockfoam composing the domes of the town's other dwellings had been poured, that of Mr. Heinkel's had already been situated near the top of the hill.

Standing on the side of the road where he had heard Mr. Heinkel offer greetings to his floater, Joozy could see the old man's dwelling perched as it was high over the other domes dotting the face of the slope leading down to the canal below. Unlike the other dwellings, including his own home, that of Mr. Heinkel was swathed in the stunted trees and prickly shrubbery specially bred for life on a planet much dryer than that of Earth. Nearly hidden among the purples and violets and bursts of white, the dome showed its age in the many nicks, pock marks, and even cracks that could be seen only at close range. Around the base of the dome were the traditional banks of windows made of thick clearsteel through which Joozy could see for himself the old fashioned furnishings that littered the interior. If nothing else, those objects offered circumstantial evidence that the dwelling's owner had been around for a while.

It was Joozy's own curiosity that had lured him up the hill, past the oldest dwellings in the neighborhood, to the gate barring the entrance to Mr. Heinkel's property. There, he stood beside his personal floater and watched the grounds for some time before determining on a closer look. Surreptitiously, he hid his floater behind some rocks farther back along the road and returned on foot. At the gate again, he checked to make sure no one was about and climbed over the stone fence that walled off the compound from the road. Slipping among the thick ranks of plants that crowded the front yard and careful not to catch his clothing on their prickly stems, Joozy approached the heavy dome. It was there that he heard someone emerge from the front entrance way and saw Mr. Heinkel step outside. He had been on his way to the front gate to retrieve the early pad of the Martian Digital-News when Joozy heard him ask his floater how it was doing.

"No reply, hey?" Mr. Heinkel was saying. "That's okay. As you can recall, I can be a patient fellow. Take your time to adjust. I'll be here when you do."

Joozy crouched in his hiding place, eyes wide at this evidence of everything he had heard others say about Mr. Heinkel's eccentricities. Certainly, no one he had ever known spoke to their floaters in such familiar terms. His interest more than ever piqued, Joozy determined to remain at his post and learn all he could about the definitely strange Mr. Heinkel.

All the rest of that day, he remained on the premises, shifting his position from time to time hoping to catch further instances of Mr. Heinkel's communications with his machines. However, his subject returned indoors after retrieving the Digital-News and all Joozy could observe for the rest of the day was Mr. Heinkel moving his lips as if he were speaking to himself. Disappointed, but still eager to learn more, Joozy returned home that night, avoided his parents' questions regarding his activities during the day, and went to bed wondering about what Mr. Heinkel had to say when he spoke to himself.

The next few days were occupied with more of the same. Joozy soon learned that each morning, Mr. Heinkel greeted his floater in the same way and each day he retreated back into his dwelling to putter around and speak to himself. It was not until the third day that Joozy caught a break. On that day, he had wormed his way around to the rear of the big dome and discovered that the old fashioned arrangement of fastenings, gratings, and leads connecting the dwelling to its individualized atmosphere reconditioning system allowed for the transmission of sound from indoors. Finally, Joozy learned that Mr. Heinkel had not been speaking to himself those times he had observed him, but to the various appliances and machines that occupied his home.

"Not feeling well today?" asked Mr. Heinkel of his electro-entertainment module.

"The pulse from the planetary oxygen generator down in Bradbury City is especially noticeable today; hope that doesn't bother you?" Mr. Heinkel said, addressing the dwelling's food heating unit.

"That's a great view you've chosen today!" Mr. Heinkel declared of the Earth vista being displayed by the wall projector in the living room.

"Couldn't feel better," said Mr. Heinkel to the automated treadmill holo-scene inducer. "Think I'll take a walk outside today instead of using the treadmill."

Throughout, Mr. Heinkel would connect questions and observations with a stream of conversation just as if he were addressing other people in the dwelling with him. By the end of a week, Joozy's observations had become so routine that he no longer found the old man's strange habit so strange anymore. In fact...

"Aren't you getting tired of sneaking around in these prickly shrubs, young man?" asked a voice from behind him.

Immediately, Joozy shot to his feet, his head and shoulders plunging into a network of branches thick with bristles that tangled in his hair and pricked his face.

"Ouch!" he could not help ejaculating.

Mr. Heinkel's face screwed up in sympathy with Joozy's situation.

"I know how that must feel!" said the old man reaching over and helping to ease Joozy's head out of the branches and away from the prickly etensil tree that screened the dome's window banks from the rest of the neighborhood.

"Thanks," said Joozy, painfully picking bristles from his hair.

"Why don't we go inside and I'll see about getting the rest out where we can see them more easily," suggested Mr. Heinkel, guiding the boy around the dome to the front entrance.

Inside, Joozy was directed to a comfortable chair near the east window bank while Mr. Heinkel proceeded to pluck the remaining bristles from his hair. When he had finished, he offered Joozy a cool drink.

"Thank you," said the boy, relieved that the old man had not chosen to be angry at his prowling.

"Now then," said Mr. Heinkel. "Maybe you can tell me your name?"

"Joozy," said Joozy gulping down a mouthful of his drink. "Joolial Moofta actually. I live down the hill at 62 Rockslide Lane."

"The pink colored dome?"

"That's the one."

"Your mother has good taste; I see her landscaping all the time. She has much better sense than most about the proper balance between stones and plants."

"How do you know that?" asked Joozy wonderingly. "You never leave your yard?"

Mr. Heinkel chuckled. "You'd be surprised. But really, I can see your dome perfectly well from my back yard. In fact, I can see pretty much everything from here. That's why I picked this spot for my dome when I first moved here nearly fifty years ago...fifty years Earth time that is."

"Then you are old!" blurted Joozy before realizing that he may have hurt the old man's feelings. "Oh, sorry! I didn't mean..."

"Don't worry, to a young person, even someone only a couple years older often seems ancient, so what are they to make of someone like me?" questioned Mr. Heinkel. "But you are right. I am getting on in years."

"How old are you?" ventured Joozy.

"Well..." began Mr. Heinkel with a laugh in his voice. "I'm older than Redrock Enclave. Older than this cracked dome. Older even than the road down there leading from Marsville. Not older than that canal though...that was here before all of us."

"Did you come to Mars on the old startoliners? Did you see the old Martians before they all went away?"

Mr. Heinkel laughed and walked over to the window bank that looked down on the dusty canal at the foot of the hill. "I'm not that old, son. Never saw a Martian, neither. But my parents came from Earth. Homesteaded along the Great Central Canal...only that's not what they called it in those days. My father was one of the first to grow Martian wheat, genetically altered plants that could grow on Mars. In those days, the atmosphere was still pretty thin...planetary oxygen generators hadn't been in operation for more than sixty years so dad had to do most of the field work with a portable breather on his back. Now that was hard work, let me tell you."

"Is that where you grew up? On a farm?"

"That's right. Didn't stay there long though. Work was too hard. Left that to my two brothers. Instead, I got into Martian archeology and made some good sales of artifacts to Earth collectors. That was enough for me to stake a claim for the land at the top of this hill and build a dome of my own. Been here off and on ever since."

More in awe of the old man than ever, Joozy simply sat in his chair, speechless for a moment.

"It must get lonely up here all by yourself," observed Joozy at last.

"I'm never lonely," replied Mr. Heinkel. "Why do you say that?"

"Well, because you talk to yourself all day?"

"I'm not talking to myself, boy," said Mr. Heinkel grinning. "I'm talking to an old friend of mine."

"A friend?" Joozy said, looking around. "I don't see anybody here. And I haven't seen anybody around the whole time I've been..."

"Spying on me?"

Joozy gulped.

"Why have you been poking around up here, boy? Come on, now it's your turn to come clean."

"Well, I...I've heard so much about you and I wanted to find out for myself if any of it was true."

"And what did you find out?"

"That you never leave your property, that you were older than anyone in Redrock Enclave, and..." Joozy hesitated but decided to plunge ahead and be completely truthful. "...that you talked to your machines."

"And you find that odd do you?" asked Mr. Heinkel, latching immediately on to the final eccentricity.

"Well, I don't know of anyone who talks to their floater or food heating unit," replied Joozy. "Except maybe to curse at them when they don't work."

"There you go then, I'm not the only one who talks to machines!"

"But you don't just curse them when they don't work, you have whole conversations with them!" insisted Joozy.

Mr. Heinkel rubbed his chin then, obviously arrested by the force of Joozy's logic.

"That's true, I suppose. But I have good reason."

"You do?"

"Certainly. You don't think I'm one of those old timers who's lost his senses do you?"

"No, sir."

"Didn't it ever occur to you that I might have a good reason to talk to my machines?"

"No, sir...that is, I never gave that possibility much thought."

"Didn't think so. Well, anyway, I do have a good reason." Silence met the old man's statement. "Well, it's a long story and I'll have to start at the beginning."

Joozy wriggled down farther in his chair and settled down to listen.

"I've told you how I was raised on a farm," began Mr. Heinkel. "Well, I couldn't have been much older than you are that day when I was turning over the soil on the south forty where our land ran along the edge of the Great Central Canal. The ground there turned out to be pretty easy to turn over with the help of a graviton-force plow so that by lunch time I was finished. Usually, I'd eat my lunch and head back to our dome but that day I decided to do some exploring. I knew that a couple miles further down along the canal were the ruins of an old Martian city. My dad had taken me and my brothers exploring there once before but we didn't get to stay long. He didn't know it, but my dad turned out to be the one that got me interested in archeology and eventually to leave the farm. Anyway, that day I decided to take a closer look around the ruins.

"I must have poked around for hours finding nothing much before ending up at the launch along the canal. The launch, at least that's how I thought of it; don't know to this day what the old Martians used those things for. Anyway, it stuck out over the canal a good ways. Maybe it was part of an old bridge or a place where the natives used to shove human sacrifices into the water that once rushed by on its way south, I don't know. But when I came near to it, I found the head of a crumbly staircase that went down the side of the canal to the bottom. It was even more of a mystery to me why the old Martians had built stairs going to a place that had probably been hundreds of feet below water at one time, but at that moment I didn't really care. I was too excited! Maybe I'd found something new that nobody else had seen before. Call it the stupidity of youth, but almost as soon as I found it, I headed down those stairs. Remember I said that they were crumbly? Well, they sure were and a couple of times I almost turned back. But after I spotted a funny shaped rock at the bottom, I determined to keep going.

"Of course, the bottom of that canal was heaped in desert sand that had collected there for who knows how many thousands of years and here and there, parts of the canal walls had collapsed too, including a portion near the old city with the debris piled up near the foot of the stairs. From the top, it looked like nothing special, just a jumble of rocks and masonry; but as I moved closer, one of those rocks stood out from the rest due to its regular shape. It was a giant cube. Sure, it could have just been a piece of masonry; but it was a goal to aim for and I used it as the excuse I needed to continue down those stairs to the bottom of the canal.

"There, it seemed as though I was at the bottom of a huge canyon with the walls towering over my head. It wasn't without a little nervousness that I began to move away from the stairs and toward that jumble of rubble. But as I drew closer and realized that the cube wasn't a piece of masonry after all, I forgot about my fears and concentrated more on the object in front of me.

"It was big, but not gigantic, and had what looked like metal bands reinforcing the corners and edges. All over, the surface was worn and pitted like something that had sat under water for hundreds of years and then exposed to the desert winds for a thousand more. But none of that mattered because after I'd come within a few feet of it, I heard something click and it began to open!

"You can just bet that I flew back in sudden fright! I stumbled over a piece of fallen masonry but before I could get up again, the block was unfolding, opening up like a flower and inside, was a solid piece of metal in the shape of shiny cube. I sat there on the ground, holding my breath, too frightened and fascinated to move when the cube began to change shape. At first it seemed to soften and melt and then it began to fold in on itself. It flattened out, then expanded to ten times its original size, then shrunk again into the shape of a sphere. It stayed that shape for a few seconds and then it seemed to harden and at a speed too fast for me to follow, began to unfold and eventually took the shape of some kind of mobile exploratory vehicle. It had tracks and an array of antennae and other appendages I couldn't recognize and began to come down one of the sloping sides of the unfolded block and onto the sandy bottom of the canal.

"As it came closer to me, I snapped out of my fright and scrambled to my feet. The thing must have sensed my movements because it stopped suddenly and aimed some of its electronic gear in my direction. I froze, wide eyed; holding my breath for the heat ray I felt sure was going to be turned on me. But nothing happened. The thing seemed to be waiting for something. Not knowing what to do and too afraid to turn my back on it, I said: 'Please, don't hurt me. I won't come here any more, I promise.'

"Not exactly the most intelligent thing to say in a situation like that, right? Maybe so, but it did get a reaction from the machine. I heard some sounds from deep inside it, like it was thinking over what I'd said.

"'More, please,' it said in a voice that sounded like my own and let me tell you, I almost fell down a second time when I'd heard it!

"'More what?' I asked.

"'More, please.'

"'More *what*?' I repeated more frustrated then, than fearful. 'What do you want?'

"'I want more.'

"'Well, if you want more, you're going to have to talk to me,' I said, pretty boldly under the circumstances, I have to say.

"'I want you to talk more to me.'

"Then it occurred to me that what it was trying to do was to communicate with me and wanted to learn more of the English language. Already, it had taken the few words I'd spoken, intuited their meaning, and rearranged them to ask me questions. The darn thing learned fast; much faster than any 9-year-old boy could! So I started to talk to it about anything that came into my head and pretty soon, the robot thing could speak English as well as I could...and in my own voice to boot! Of course, by then, I'd completely lost any fear I had of it and decided to ask if it wanted to come home with me. Wouldn't my parents and brothers be surprised?

"'So, what are your plans...say, what's your name anyway?'

"'I don't have a name,' said the robot thing with a hint of regret in its voice. 'Only a designation.'

"'A designation? What's that? Like a number or something?'

"'Correct.'

"'That's too bad. But it wouldn't feel right to go around calling you RUR231 or something...especially now that we're friends.'

It didn't say anything.

"'Would you like to have a name?'

"'Yes, I think so.'

"'Hmmm, okay. Let's see now. How about Vinzee? Or Skallio? Nah...there must be better names than that. I know! Tarkas! That's a good Martian name.'

"'Good, I shall be known as Tarkas.'

"'And you better do something about that voice too,' I said. 'People are going to get confused if we both sound exactly alike.'

"'How's this?' said Tarkas, lowering the timbre of his voice an octave.

"'Perfect!' I said. 'Now you're ready to come home with me.'

"'Home? Will your parents approve?'

"'I'm sure they will! You're a genuine Martian...or at least the closest thing to a Martian that anyone's ever found so far as I know. You're going to be big news in these parts!'

"'Then I'll go with you, Skivas,' said Tarkas. It was the first time he'd said my name and it sent a little shiver of pleasure down my spine. 'You're my friend.'

"'It's settled then,' I said, happy and excited to have a friend like Tarkas. 'But we'd better get going now, it's a long way to the top of those stairs. Do you think you can make it?'

"Tarkas was still in his tractor form and it looked to me like it might even have been impossible for him to negotiate the steps leading out of the canal.

" There were more sounds from inside his body and the sensor array on his surface began to agitate and suddenly, there was that rapid unfolding motion again and in seconds Tarkas had changed his shape and become a spiderish thing with many legs. A clear canopy rested at the center of the legs and even as I watched, it sprung open and inside, there was a compartment big enough for a person to fit in.

"'Please take a seat,' said Tarkas.

"Without hesitation, I climbed aboard and as soon as the canopy snapped closed, Tarkas began to climb the sheer wall of the canal using the fine tips of his spider legs to find holds and lift us to the top. What had taken me almost an hour to come down by the stairs, my new friend accomplished in a few minutes. In no time, we were on the surface again and he was asking me which way to go from there. Delighted, I pointed in the direction of home but then had second thoughts.

"'What's wrong?' asked Tarkas noting my hesitation.

"'It's the way you look,' I replied. 'I don't know how my mom and dad will react if they see me riding home in the belly of a giant metal spider.'

"Tarkas considered what I'd said with those funny sounds coming from somewhere inside of him. Then he began to transform again and in a few seconds an exact replica of myself stood before me. Except for being metallic, Tarkas had fashioned himself in my likeness right down to the clothes I wore.

"'That's great!' I said, delighted. 'But do you think you can do something about your face? So it doesn't look exactly like me?'

"There was a flicker of movement over Tarkas' face and when it stopped, he looked different.

"'Perfect! When we get home, I'll lend you some of my clothes and except for your head, you'll pass for any normal boy on Mars!'

"With that, we set out for home although truth to tell, I don't remember much about it as

I was just too darned excited at a turn of events that promised us all kinds of new adventures. I had visions of Tarkas telling me all about Mars; the people who used to live there, how they built the canals, and what happened to them. Then I'd leave the farm and we'd set out to explore the planet together and make discoveries that would astonish everyone who read of them. Tarkas and I would be in all the vid-casts and kids back on Earth would have to learn about us in school!

"It was late by the time we reached home and the sun was only a red smear on the horizon. But the lights around our dome were bright and welcoming and as I approached the front entrance, I began to have second thoughts about bringing in Tarkas unannounced. It occurred to me that my parents might have the same reaction I did when I first laid eyes on him so I asked Tarkas to wait outside while I went in to smooth things over.

"Inside, my parents weren't too surprised to see me come in after sundown. On a farm, you keep late hours and working in distant fields usually meant coming home late.

"'Come in Skivas,' said my mother hovering over the kitchen table. 'Supper is ready.'

"I moved into the circle of light around the table where my two brothers and father were already sitting. They noticed my hesitation.

"'What's wrong, son?' asked my father.

"'Well, I kinda brought home a friend,' I said.

"'A friend?' said my brother, Jondis. 'Where did you find a friend out here?'

"'Hush, Jondis,' said my mother. 'Where is this friend? Why didn't you invite him in?'

"'I wanted to tell you about him before I brought him inside,' I said. 'He's not what you'd expect.' I saw my father put down his eating utensil and turn in his chair to face me more directly. 'I mean, he's different.'

"'How different?' Jondis wanted to know.

"'Look, son. Why don't you just tell him to come in,' said my father.

"Gulping, I went back to the foyer and signaled for Tarkas to come in. There were more than a couple gasps in the room when my friend stepped fully into the light and everyone noticed his metallic skin.

"'What is this?' demanded my father rising.

"'He looks like he's wearing a mask or something,' said my younger brother Hildon.

"'Who are you?' my father asked Tarkas seriously.

"'My name is Tarkas.'

"'Tarkas?'

"'I called him that, dad,' I said hurriedly. 'He didn't have a name when I found him.'

"'Found him?'

"'Yeah.' I gulped again as I was forced to admit that I'd left work to do some exploring. 'I found him in a big box at the bottom of the canal.'

"Naturally, that revelation brought an exclamation from my mother expressing concern about my doing such a dangerous thing and didn't I think about what might have happened to me?

"'That's enough Elida,' said my father. 'What's done is done. We'll have a talk to Skivas about that later. 'Tarkas. Are you a product of Martian technology?'

"The way my father had asked the question surprised me somewhat. I never heard him speak with quite that tone of authority in his voice. For the first time in my young life, I realized that there was far more to him than I ever suspected. As indeed there was. Farming on Mars was something he took up only after a successful career in Earth's air forces and interplanetary program so he was well trained in many technical fields.

"'My proper designation is untranslatable into English,' replied Tarkas. 'I am a multipurpose mechanoid programmed to serve in any number of capacities.'

"'Do you understand what I'm talking about when I use the term "Martian?"'

"'Skivas has informed me that is the term used to identify the former inhabitants of this planet, now all deceased.'

"'Does the removal of your creators pose any problems with your programming?'

"'None.'

"'Well, son,' said my father after some thought. 'You certainly have made an important discovery here. So far as I know, this is the first solid evidence that has ever been found of the existence of Martian technology.'

"Let me tell you, that left a big smile on my face, one that vanished as quickly after my father's next words.

"'And as such, we have an obligation to re-port the finding to authorities on Earth.'

"'But dad,' I pleaded. 'If they find out, they might take Tarkas away!'

"'I won't deny that; but you must under-stand that a discovery this big can't be kept to ourselves. Besides, sooner of later, word about...Tarkas...would get out and the situa-tion would be out of our control. By taking the initiative ourselves, we'll have some say in how the situation is handled.'

"I didn't like it because I was already thinking of Tarkas as a friend and not a ma-chine but deep inside, I knew my father was right.

"'But dear, what are we going to do with it in the meantime?' asked my mother.

"My father shrugged. 'Give it some chores?'

"And so my life with Tarkas began. As things turned out, it would be years before rep-resentatives on Mars and then the authorities on Earth finally decided what was to be done with Tarkas. At the time I didn't understand the details but to be sure it involved turf battles and time consuming debate over which de-partment had primacy, whose interests were more important, and what ultimately, was to be done in order to exploit the new technology presented by Tarkas.

"In the meantime, the fear of losing Tarkas had receded in my mind and each day was filled with wonder and delight at his continuing development into a more rounded individual. During the days, we'd work side by side on the farm, and in the evenings he would learn with me as I did my school work and sat with the family in the front yard as we looked at the stars, played word games, or teased Jondis about a girl he'd met at a farmers' dance. Nights, Tarkas would lie in the extra bunk in my bedroom and talk softly with me of the old Martians until I fell asleep.

"Thus, we grew up together with Tarkas becoming more and more human-like as the days passed. To be sure, he continued to hold his metallic features, but he wore our clothing with increasing assuredness and took to sporting hats so that little of even his face could be seen. He helped my mother around the kitchen even to preparing meals for the family those times she was out and talked with my father for hours about technical subjects far removed from farming. Even my brothers came to like him and like me, they seemed to forget he was a machine and treated him no different than we all treated each other, that is, like a brother.

"And then the time that I had dreaded arrived. A stranger came to our dome to speak to my father and by the markings on his floater I knew he had been sent by Mars Control. All that day I worked in the fields with Tarkas dreading supper time when I knew my father would give us the bad news. My silence, however, didn't go unnoticed by Tarkas.

"'You're worried about what the man from Mars Control is going to say, aren't you Skivas?'

"I didn't answer.

"'Hey, we're friends aren't we, Skivas?' Tarkas asked.

"'Of course we are,' I replied, getting up from where I'd been watching the gauges on the water inducer.

"'Then why don't you want to talk to me?'

"'Because all we'll end up talking about is your leaving.'

"'We knew that would happen one of these days,' Tarkas said not unreasonably.

"'So you think that will make it any easier to see you go?'

"'I guess not,' said Tarkas. 'I'll miss you terribly, Skivas. And the rest of the family.'

"'I don't want you to go!' I blurted finally, feeling the tears well up in my eyes and a lump the size of a goose egg swelling in my throat. 'Let's run away! Let's get out of here before anyone knows we're gone. We can hide out in one of the old Martian cities that only you know about.'

"But Tarkas only shook his head. 'That's not realistic, Skivas, and you know it. I owe it to your parents not to let you do any such thing.'

"'But they'll probably take you apart, break you down for analysis!'

"'I was built to serve,' Tarkas reminded me. 'Only now, I'll serve your people instead of the old Martians. But I'll tell you this: whatever happens, if any part of myself is used in the creation of a hybrid Earth-Mars technology, I will be there.'

"'What do you mean?' I said, wiping the tears from my eyes.

"'I mean that the technology with which the old Martians had created me is not strictly

mechanical or even electronic, but organo-
siliconic,' explained Tarkas. 'I was built up from
the molecular level so that each atom of my
being contains my complete consciousness.
Should any of those atoms find their way into
any other mechanism, their programming
would override that of the host machine and
some part of my original consciousness would
eventually become dominant.'

"'You mean if I could find a machine in
which some part of you had been used to create, we can be together again?'

"'Not as satisfyingly as we have been, but
yes, we could.'

"You have no idea with how much relief I
heard those words! My friend wouldn't be taken
away from me. Some day, there was every possibility that we would meet again and with the
mutable nature of Martian technology, maybe it
was even possible that he could reform himself
back into the Tarkas I knew! That part, however was only a hope I had, as Tarkas himself
rejected the notion.

"So it was that even though I still dreaded
Tarkas being taken away from me, it was with
a considerably lightened heart that I returned
to the dome that evening. When we arrived
there, my father met us at the door and led us
into his small office.

"'You know someone from Mars Control
came by this morning so I'll give it to you
straight,' he began. 'It's been decided that the
research labs here on Mars are better equipped
and staffed with more people knowledgeable
about the old Martians than those back on

Earth are. So in a way, Tarkas will at least be staying close to home. Yes, he'll have to leave us as we all knew he someday would have to. We all know how Skivas feels about you, Tarkas, but I don't think it will come as a surprise to you that the rest of the family, including myself, feel any differently. In the few years you've lived with us you've become an important part of our lives and we will all miss you terribly.'

"'I appreciate the sentiments, Mr. Heinkel,' said Tarkas gravely. 'And understand that my feelings are no less conflicted. I will miss you all.'

"My father rose from his chair then and took Tarkas by the hand. 'The people from Mars Control will be by in the morning to pick you up. Goodbye, Tarkas and good luck.'

"'Thank you, Mr. Heinkel.'

"That last night with Tarkas was the longest of my life. We lay in our bunks and talked through the night, long after my brothers had fallen asleep. We talked about how we first met, the night I brought him to meet my family, the days working in the fields and hothouses, the exploring we did and all the things he'd told me about the old Martians. By the time I fell asleep, it was almost dawn with the sky beginning to grow pink on the horizon.

"The next morning, they came for him and while the rest of the family lingered by the dome, I walked with Tarkas the rest of the way to the Mars Control floater that hovered at the end of the walk. In the end, seeing him off wasn't as difficult as I'd imagined. We had a good long talk the night before and his calm acceptance of a situation we both knew was bound to come helped me to maintain my composure.

"'Goodbye, Tarkas,' I said. 'I'll sure miss you.'

"'I'll miss you too, Skivas,' he replied, holding out his hand.

"But I couldn't hold back the emotional tide that had been welling up in me since the day before. Ignoring his hand, I threw my arms around him and embraced him in a manly hug of farewell. He returned the gesture and for a moment, his face flickered in a manner I hadn't seen since the first time I found him: he changed his features, if only fleetingly, to those that reflected my own. He smiled, released me, and stepped into the floater.

"I stood there looking after him long after the vehicle had disappeared over the rise that sloped downward toward the more settled regions of the county. After that, life on the farm was never the same for me. I'd always felt the urge to go off exploring and now that feeling took over completely. My last years there were an interminable period of waiting before I could attend classes at the science college in Bradbury City. I graduated with a degree in Martian archeology and using what I'd learned from Tarkas, became the most successful archeologist on the planet. I wrote a number of books and had the satisfaction of seeing my words studied by students on two worlds. Eventually though, even poking about the ruins left by the old Martians lost its interest for me as more and more I yearned to see my friend again.

"Over the years I'd learned a bit about what happened to him. Mars Control conducted a number of exhaustive tests on him before finally getting around to studying his composition on a molecular level. Although they thought they understood the Martian technology that allowed Tarkas to reform, rebuild, and repair himself, I never heard or read anything about his retaining some part of his identity on the molecular level. No one ever asked me about it and I never volunteered any information. It was to be a secret between Tarkas and I."

"And you never saw Tarkas again?" Joozy asked, wide eyed.

"Never," replied Mr. Heinkel solemnly. "Anyway, to finish my story, researchers were able to replicate the molecular makeup with which Tarkas was composed and to apply it to other machines. That's where my friend made his greatest contribution. Scientists were able to replicate Martian technology in our own manufactures so that today, every machine from floaters to household appliances, can maintain themselves so none of them ever break down. Sometimes the Martian based machines can even improve themselves so that toasters never burn toast and floaters never break down. But early on, elements of Tarkas himself were used in some new machines and those are the ones that hold the potential for his programming to reassert itself."

"Gosh!" gasped Joozy. "So is that why you talk to your floater? Because part of it might be Tarkas?"

"Right," said Mr. Heinkel. "When we talked that last day we were together, Tarkas said that every atom of his being contained not just a piece of his consciousness, but his complete consciousness. He said that over time, the programming of any host machine that contained a part of him no matter how small would at some point be overridden and his own programming would become dominant. If that's the case, why shouldn't Tarkas find some way to communicate with his old friend? The only question is, which machines were built with original elements taken from Tarkas himself?"

Hearing that, Joozy began looking around him, suddenly aware of all the different machines involved in his daily life and how any one of them could suddenly begin thinking on its own.

"Do you think Tarkas could be my friend too?" Joozy finally asked. "I mean, if I talked to machines the way you do?"

"I don't see why not," replied Mr. Heinkel. "Tarkas always was a big hearted kind of fellow. Yes, I'm sure he wouldn't mind at all having another friend."

"But what about the secret?" asked Joozy suddenly. "Won't Tarkas be angry if he finds out you told me about him?"

Mr. Heinkel chuckled. "At this late date, who would believe it? People in town think I'm odd for talking to my machines don't they?"

"That's true," agreed Joozy. "Not that I agree with them!"

"Certainly not!" said Mr. Heinkel. "It'll be a secret just the two of us will share...and Tarkas of course!"

"Right!"

"Now I think, it's time you should be running along," said Mr. Heinkel. "Your parents will be wondering where you are. And the next time you visit, come by the front entrance. No need for sneaking around!"

"I will," called Joozy, waving goodbye.

It was not many years later that Mr. Heinkel died. Joozy had visited him often in his dome atop the hill and together they had many spirited conversations with the machines around his dwelling. And though he never saw the old man in anything less than a happy, upbeat mood, Joozy suspected that it was with great disappointment that his old friend Tarkas was never able to communicate with him. Indeed, there was a time when Joozy himself grew to doubt Mr. Heinkel's story and stopped talking to machines lest he was caught and people began to wonder about his own sanity. Later, after Joozy had moved from Redrock Enclave to attend university in Bradbury City, he understandably saw a good deal less of Mr. Heinkel and wondered often how he was getting along. The report of his death when it finally came to him, was sad but not unexpected. What Joozy could never have predicted however, was the news that ownership of Mr. Heinkel's dome had been left to him. It had been such a long time since those days when he visited often with Mr. Heinkel that he was sure that whatever sentimentality in which he was held by the old man had long been forgotten.

So it was that Joozy deliberately chose not to visit his new property until after Mr. Heinkel had been laid to rest in the little cemetery outside Redrock Enclave He remembered that day as being very bright and pink and cool and the walk up the main road as it wound about the hill to Mr. Heinkel's dome passed quickly. At last however, he arrived at the front gate and pausing only long enough to recall the day he first met Mr. Heinkel, he passed through and headed to the front entrance of the old dome.

In the drive sat the same early model floater that he had first seen Mr. Heinkel talking to those long years ago. Smiling to himself, hands in his pockets, a sprig of hair falling over his forehead, Joozy chuckled.

"And how are you today?" he asked the floater. "Don't worry old fellow, I don't intend on sending you away from home."

Entering the dome, Joozy moved into the main sitting room and looked around. There on one wall were the odd findings from the various digs Mr. Heinkel had worked in his days as an archeologist. On another, were the bookshelves holding his research literaries and the handful of books he had written and that had made his name in scientific circles. And there was the chair he had sat in when Mr. Heinkel first told him about his friend Tarkas.

Joozy stepped down into the sunken floor of the sitting room and looked out at the garden beyond the broad window bank then turned to face the interior again.

"Hope you're all feeling good today," he said to no one and nothing in particular but understanding within himself that he was speaking to all of the machines within earshot. "I know Mr. Heinkel was your friend and that you will miss him very much. So will I. In fact he saw fit to leave me this dome and it is my fond wish to live here now that he is gone. I hope that you will come to regard me as your friend as you did him."

Joozy didn't know why he said those things. In fact, he felt a bit foolish after having done so but at the same time somehow relieved. It had meant so much to Mr. Heinkel to believe in his story of the Martian robot and it seemed fitting to put an end to it in a fashion that he would have approved.

Suddenly, his thoughts were interrupted by a sound from the kitchen area. Was that the food heater? He walked to the kitchen and upon entering was immediately struck by the smells of a fresh cooked meal. Had the estate left instructions that lunch be prepared for the new owner? As he considered that possibility, he noticed that his favorite piece of classical Earth music was playing softly throughout the dome and that the indoor climate had been altered to suit his taste. And now, for the first time, he noticed a subtle sound coming from somewhere deep in the interior of the dome's machine network.

"Hello, Joozy," said a voice. "Skivas has told me a lot about you."

There Are No Regrets in Sky-view Tower

STONEY VANDER SIGHED HEAVILY as he gazed outside over the municiplex. It was an unusually clear day and for that reason, he was able to look down and see the foundations upon which Skyview Tower had been built and in the distance, between neighboring towers, the hint of green wild beyond the point where civilization ended and unsupervised nature began.

What was out there? Wondered Stoney Vander.

According to the Board of Supervisors, there was nothing but unregulated nature, a wilderness of tangled vines and creepers, thick forests of trees whose branches swept the ground and whipped their leaves in the wind, swamps of disease ridden water, and matted grasslands woven with ground crawling thorns and infested with biting, stinging insects of every kind.

Just the thought of it all sent shivers down Stoney Vander's spine...shivers of anticipation, that is. The truth was, he often found himself like this; instead of working or studying, his attention was drawn to the tower's expansive window banks and the green wild when it was visible on clear days. The view never failed to send his mind wandering down paths other citizens of the town of Sunshine would surely consider perverse. But why was it perversion to think of life outside Skyview Tower? What was wrong with feeling the wind on your bare flesh instead of the tower's climate controlled atmosphere or to breath air unfiltered by its ventilation systems?

Against all tradition and common sense, Stoney Vander yearned to feel the spring of real grass beneath his feet instead of the artificial turf preferred by his fellow citizens. And it was with guilty pleasure that he sometimes stood in the garage stall at home when the exit panel lifted and the outside air rushed in. He remembered one time years before, when his mother caught him doing just that and horrified, restricted him to his room for a week.

Looking back, he had always known that he was different. Unlike other children, he took no pleasure in their games intended to reinforce order in preparation for their lives as adult citizens of Sunshine. In games of mathematical logic he deliberately set out to confuse his fellow players by reciting numbers at random and preventing the others from concentrating on the proper equations needed to win. In other games, he always made his moves out of order to see what the unexpected results might be while at the same time upsetting his playmates when events did not go as everyone knew they had to.

As a young man, he upset his parents when female companions who had been carefully chosen by the administration for their compatibility factors were sent home in tears when he refused to practice the accepted courtship rituals. In school, he was a constant challenge to his instructors with his questions that usually landed him in tutorial where he was required to memorize the 367 dictums required of orderly life in the town of Sunshine.

Behind his peers in entering the workforce, he was assigned maintenance closet #224 in design wing, employment Level IV where he was expected to spend his career making sure the work environment for the designers was kept clean and pleasant. Some day, if he were diligent in his duties and if a position unwanted by any reparations card holder opened up, he might move up to junior designer and himself help to create schematics for newly upgraded food preparation units, the chief manufactured export of Sunshine.

And so, here he stood at the window banks he had gazed longingly out of since his arrival on employment Level IV trying to catch a glimpse of the green wild that more and more, represented the one thing not provided in Sunshine or Skyview Tower for that matter: release. Disappointed, he saw that a mist was drifting across the large lake on whose shores the municiplex was located. Once again, it would obscure the base of the towers and the green wild would vanish from sight. The view outdoors would shrink until all that remained were the upper levels of the towers that dotted the municiplex.

"Daydreaming again Stoney Vander?" asked a voice from over his shoulder.

Stoney Vander turned quickly, dropping onto the floor the vaporizer with which he had been cleaning the cracked window banks.

"The time of prayer to the Prophet is over," pointed out design wing supervisor Mehmed Trumbel.

"I am sorry design wing supervisor Mehmed Trumbel," replied Stoney Vander. "I had not noticed."

"You must learn to take notice of such things Stoney Vander," admonished design wing supervisor Mehmed Trumbel not unkindly. "You know that as a citizen of European descent, you bear much of the guilt for past evils perpetrated on non-European peoples. It is incumbent upon you to be especially sensitive to the feelings of Sunshine's citizens of color."

"I understand that, design wing supervisor Mehmed Trumbel," said Stoney Vander with appropriate humility.

In order to redress past injustices, the municiplex had long ago instituted a reparations card system based on the gender or gradation of a citizen's skin pigmentation. The darker a citizen's skin color or if the citizen were a woman, the more credit points that person was entitled to. Thus, at the extreme end, reparations cards could be issued to some citizens that freed them of labor and entitled them to a free education, free housing, first choice on the selection of spouses, and many other benefits. Lighter skinned citizens receiving less credit might only need to work part time or pay only a portion of his rent. Credit could also be used to pro-rate test scores in school, improve employment evaluations on the job, or entitle the bearer to promotion regardless of skill level or competence. Of course, as a citizen of European descent, Stoney Vander did not possess any credit at all but was required to turn over 83 percent of his income in taxes to subsidize the reparations card system.

"The city depends on all of its citizens to perform their assigned duties to the best of their abilities," said design wing supervisor Mehmed Trumbel who was himself a citizen of color. "Today we're working on the latest improvements to Sunshine's food preparation units, one of our specialties and important to the economy of the town. Your work, though seemingly insignificant, is actually integral to creating the proper atmosphere for our designers to do their work. You do realize the importance of completing the drawings for the transverse microwave frequency modulators, one of the most crucial elements of the Mark IX automated food processing unit?"

"Of course, design wing supervisor Mehmed Trumbel," replied Stoney Vander, who had been trained as a designer himself and graduated in the same form as the design wing supervisor.

"The city of Cloudscape in Thunder Tower has already pre-ordered 3,000 units and expects delivery and installation by the end of the quarter," design wing supervisor Mehmed Trumbel continued. "Do I need to say any more?"

"No, design wing supervisor Mehmed Trumbel," replied a chastised Stoney Vander despite his knowledge that the level of quality of the product designed by Sunshine employees would never be that good due largely to a lack of incentive on the part of its workers; a fact that citizens were strictly forbidden to discuss or even consider. "I realize the importance of my role in the production schedule and will perform my duties with the proper diligence."

"That is good, Stoney Vander," said design wing supervisor Mehmed Trumbel not unkindly. "You may continue working."

As design wing supervisor Mehmed Trumbel walked away, hands clasped behind his back, Stoney Vander picked up his dropped vaporizer and looked over the vast room that housed design wing, employment Level IV. In all directions, rows of desks radiated away from his position by the window banks, most occupied by employees of color and all now busy at their tasks: some hunched over drafting boards, some milling about on errands delivering completed work or picking up new assignments, and still others conferring with one another no doubt seeking advice on some technical problem or other. Over all was the same glow of even light radiated from ceiling panels and in the distance, rows of design wing supervisors' offices lined the wall that faced inward toward the central hub of the town of Sunshine.

The central hub extended through the heart of Sunshine to other towns both above and below Skyview Tower. According to what

Stoney Vander had learned in history class when he was in school, Skyview and the other towers of the municiplex had once been the headquarters of global corporations that had governed the world many years before. While no one was really certain how it happened, the corporations evolved into a new form of civic organization that stratified their different functions into separate departments in their tower headquarters. Over time, functions such as management, manufacturing, sales, design, product development, transportation, and customer support, grew increasingly independent until they separated from one another and incorporated themselves into towns and cities depending on how many levels they occupied.

Sunshine had been the corporation's design department occupying only a dozen levels near the top of the tower when it became an independent town with a permanent population of 15,679. With limited room and resources, the towns evolved a strict social regimen over the years until every facet of municipal life had been addressed. Such were the benefits bestowed on their citizens that there was less and less need for venturing beyond municipal limits. Except for the occasional flight by air car to neighboring towers for business, a citizen could spend his entire life in a town like Sunshine and never leave.

Which did not prevent Stoney Vander from daydreaming about doing that very thing. Once when very young, he used to suggest to his friends that they play imaginary games where they would leave Skyview Tower and have adventures outside the municiplex but as he grew older, he became aware of how uncomfortable his ideas were to others. By the time he became a teenager, he had learned to keep such fantasies to himself. Nevertheless, he continued to entertain them, wondering what life was like in towns lower down in Skyview Tower or in other towers of the municiplex for that matter. Later, it occurred to him that although life in the other towers was probably much the same as in his own, how radically different it must be in the green wild where no one had ventured for almost two centuries. Just the same, he kept such musings to himself, half convinced that there was something wrong with him for continuing to wonder long after his peers had moved on to thoughts of taking their places in the ordered society of Sunshine.

Stoney Vander was jolted from his reverie by the blare of the shift klaxon sounding the end of the employment day. Relieved, he carefully replaced his work satchel in maintenance closet #224 and began his rounds activating the dust shields over the designers' drawing boards. Finished, he extinguished the lights and joined his co-workers as they continued to crowd the central hub.

Stoney Vander, aware of the great weight that always seemed to lift from him following an interminable day spent at the dull routine of work, emerged onto the promenade of design wing, employment Level IV and mingled with the thousands of other workers from other wings including planning, administration, and maintenance. Passing the myriad shops, compu-newsstands, and cafeterias, he ignored the slow moving escalators that served pedestrian traffic between levels and headed directly to the bank of high speed lifts that afforded transportation directly to the residential levels above.

Joining a group of other citizens, Stoney Vander entered the lift designated for Level VII and was immediately whisked upward past the levels dedicated to public recreation and administration to the residential level. A few seconds later, he stepped out into the central hub for Level VII where the atmosphere was much more subdued than it had been on employment Level IV. With fewer citizens moving about and walls covered in sound deadening materials, an air of peace and tranquility more suitable to rest and retreat from the busy working day was created. As a maintenance worker, Stoney Vander never failed to notice the lack of attention paid to areas of the city other than the design wing upon which Sunshine's livelihood depended. Annoyed without quite understanding why, he looked with disapproval at the shabby nature of Level VII where there was little to attract a citizen's attention. Certainly not the drab and run down nature of the central hub where many of the automated devices intended for banking and food dispensing had broken down for lack of repair, floors were dull and dirty for lack of regular cleaning, and plants had withered and died for lack of watering. It was all unfortunate but understandable. If so much of a citizen's income was taken in taxes, why should he exert more effort than was required to do his job? With little in the central hub to draw his attention, Stoney Vander made his way to residential unit #491 where a swipe of his palm over a hidden sensor caused the door panel to move aside giving him entry.

"Good afternoon, son," called his father Aris Vander from another part of the residence.

"Good afternoon, father," replied Stoney Vander stepping into the foyer and shrugging out of his vestsmock. "Is mother home yet?"

"No, but she communicated a little while ago by earphone to say that she would be in time for dinner," said Aris Vander appearing from the general direction of the kitchen. "How does old style baked potatoes sound for dinner? The food processors at Cirrus Tower have perfected them such that I can't see how anyone can improve on the taste."

"Wonderful!" said Stoney Vander; old style baked potatoes were his favorite. "What is the occasion?"

"Your sister has some good news for us," said Aris Vander. "She plans to tell us all about it over dinner."

With a vague sense of depression, Stoney Vander suspected what the news would be and was not at all sure why he should not be as happy to hear it as he ought to have been.

Throwing himself into an old plush chair in the living room, Stoney Vander sighed heavily before undoing the shirt stud at his throat. He snapped his fingers to activate the wall viewer and settled back to receive the news of the day but when his father finally called him to the table, he realized he had not heard a word of the report.

"Good afternoon, dear," said his mother Vivy Vander-Hool in a voice filled with laughter. Stoney Vander figured that she also must have guessed what the news would be from his sister. "How is work treating you?"

"No change," said Stoney Vander as he took his accustomed place at the dinner table. "Design wing is working on a new component of the Mark IX food preparation unit, the latest model being marketed by Sunshine. I am told that it will completely supercede all previous models."

"What is wrong with the current model?" Aris Vander wanted to know. "It has 508 different settings, holds food preparation data in its memory for 10,000 items, and misfunctions hardly at all."

"Nevertheless, I am told that the maintenance department will begin replacing the old units in the residence levels in a few months," said Stoney Vander. "It would not do to market a new model while the town itself does not use it in its own residences."

"Well I just hope my new living unit in Clearsky will have all the latest conveniences," declared Immomia Vander.

Stoney Vander looked at his sister as did his parents and asked, "What is this about Clearsky? Have you been assigned a living unit already?"

Immomia Vander smiled broadly, delighted in her not so secret news.

"Mother, father," Immomia Vander began. "I have the pleasure of informing you that I will soon enter union with a Clearsky male and have already been assigned living unit #112...on the east side!"

Immediately, Vivy Vander-Hool burst into tears and threw her arms around her daughter, who was a few years older than Stoney Vander. Aris Vander merely beamed in pride and the anticipation of the expected grandchildren.

"Will your partner be a citizen of color?" asked Stoney Vander.

"Unfortunately, no," said Immomia Vander momentarily crestfallen.

Clearsky was the next town below Sunshine and was the home of many of Stoney Vander's first cousins. Administration made sure that second cousins united with citizens from the next town downwards or upwards and so on until the family lost touch with succeeding generations who continued to unite with partners farther up or down along the tower's height. It was only unfortunate that Immomia Vander was a brunette, if she had been a blonde, for sure she would have been requested by a person of color which would have immediately lifted her to an improved living status. As it was, as a couple of European descent, the living unit she and her husband had been assigned would not command the best view from the tower and would probably be located near a noisy central service duct or high speed lift.

"Congratulations, sister," mustered Stoney Vander. "Do you know who the lucky male is yet?"

"No, but I am told he is my own age and praised by his supervisors as one of the town's most savvy marketers," replied Immomia Vander. "As a result, he has earned early promotion. In fact, I think one or two of his ideas have contributed greatly to the upcoming advertising campaign for the Mark IX."

"Is that so?" said Stoney Vander not without a twinge of jealousy. "And have you previewed living unit #112?"

"Oh, yes!" said Immomia Vander. "As soon as administration informed me that my civil partner had been chosen, I asked if a living unit had been arranged...you know that sometimes there is a delay between the announcement of unions and the assignment of a living unit? But I was lucky. One was immediately available and even more fortunate, it was located on the east side so that not only will we be away from the lifts, but we will also have as many as two bedrooms."

"You are so lucky, Immomia," said Vivy Vander-Hool. "Aris and I had to wait almost 23 years before we were able to move into this living unit with its three bedrooms and view outside."

"Has a date been fixed for the union?" Aris Vander wanted to know as he tucked a napkin in front of his shirt.

"Next month, and administration has arranged for it to take place in the rooftop chapel gardens," said Immomia Vander.

"How thrilling!" said Vivy Vander-Hool already making plans in her head.

"Well, it seems that Immomia Vander's news will definitely eclipse my own," said Aris Vander with a twinkle in his eye.

"What do you mean, Aris Vander?" asked Vivy Vander-Hool suddenly quiet.

"I have been promoted from first design team to junior planner," announced Aris Vander.

"Oh, that's wonderful!" beamed Vivy Vander-Hool. "That is a position you have been aiming for since before we were united. I still remember the day I arrived in Sunshine from Moonglow up above and moved into our first living unit to get it ready for our union day."

"I remember that," admitted Aris Vander. "I was only a maintenance worker then, like Stoney Vander here. But I worked hard, impressed my supervisors, and suggested improvements in some of the designs the men were working on as often as I could. My efforts paid off when my supervisors were promoted on the basis of my suggestions and to keep me around, managed to have me named to the design team. The increases in salary were what enabled us to move from the north side to the unit we currently occupy. With this promotion, I will have to do less design work and more actual planning. I will be out of the design wing more often, moving among the different towns of Skyview Tower interfacing with our representatives in manufacturing and sales. Of course, it will also mean that I will have less time for my chores here in the living unit."

"It all sounds so exciting doesn't it, son?" asked Vivy Vander-Hool, not at all concerned that her husband would likely not be home to welcome her after a hard day working on office Level III.

"Very," agreed Stoney Vander, trying to sound encouraging.

The truth was, the very thought of spending endless years giving his ideas away to designers and supervisors unqualified for their positions in hopes that their resulting success would carry him along did not appeal to him in the slightest.

"You sound underwhelmed, son," noted Aris Vander.

"No, I'm happy for you father," said Stoney Vander.

"But there is something else."

"Well...well it seems to me this success should have happened far sooner."

"How so?"

"Since many of the ideas that helped your supervisors advance were your own, wouldn't it make more sense for you to be the one to have benefited?" blurted Stoney Vander to gasps from Vivy and Immomia Vander. "Why should less qualified employees be promoted ahead of you simply because of the color of their skin?"

There was silence for quite a few minutes following Stoney Vander's intemperate question. Such things were not mentioned in polite company.

"Son, I don't have to remind you of the past evils visited upon our citizens of color by those of us of European descent..." began Aris Vander.

"But no one alive today, or for the last 250 years for that matter, has ever suffered or even witnessed such evils," pointed out Stoney Vander. "Why should they continue to benefit from the misfortunes of their long dead ancestors?"

Even Aris Vander was taken somewhat aback by such a statement so baldly put. Unconsciously, he looked about as if checking to make sure no one outside the family was listening, leaned forward, and whispered "Son, the sentiments you've expressed can be very dangerous if overheard and could cost our family its position in the community, not to mention my impending promotion. Now, you have always been a bit out of step with your friends and all, but you should be mature enough now to understand the ways of the town..."

"All I understand is the seeming injustice of it all," insisted Stoney Vander.

"It's injustice that the laws of the municiplex have been created to redress," said Immomia Vander dutifully. "Certainly, our family is not of the upper echelons, and I regret not being assigned a citizen of color with which to unite, but some day our fortunes will change and we can begin the process of full integration."

"Of course, son," soothed Vivy Vander-Hool, resting her hand gently on Stoney Vander's. "Soon, it will be your turn to be assigned a female with which to unite and there is every possibility that she will be a citizen of color..."

"That is not my point," insisted Stoney Vander, taking his hand away. "I simply demand that promotion on the employment levels be based on merit and not on some antiquated system of pigmentation!"

"I think that is quite enough of that, son," said Aris Vander, his voice assuming its accustomed air of command. "The city provides us with all our wants and a means of moving up and bettering ourselves..."

"At the expense of losing our identities?" asked Stoney Vander. "At the expense of pandering to unqualified superiors? If that's the case, then I'm not interested in what the city can provide me!"

"What more do you want then?"

The question brought Stoney Vander up short. What *did* he want?

"I don't know...but something is missing. I'm tired of living on the sunless side of Skyview Tower; I'm tired of cleaning the window banks and human waste depositories. I know my contributions to the life of Sunshine can be more substantial if only I had the opportunity."

"But you will have the opportunity, son. You simply must be more patient, work with your supervisors, and in ten or twenty years, you should be promoted to junior designer..."

"Ten or twenty years!" spat Stoney Vander. "Pfah! Why should anyone with genuine ability wait so long while others with far less qualifications are given the top positions?"

"But it is their right as citizens of color..." began Immomia Vander.

"I don't want to hear that!" shouted Stoney Vander getting up from the table. "In fact, I don't want to continue this conversation at all."

With that, he stormed from the room and into the private lift that whisked him up to the stall where the family kept its air car. There, Stoney Vander walked purposely to the control panel, waved a hand over the instruments and watched as the plasti-steel exit door rose into the wall above. Instantly, he felt the pressure of the outside air press against him as it whipped his hair about his head. Moving around the air car, he approached the edge of the stall where it fell away the half mile or so to the ground hidden somewhere below by drifting clouds.

Often when he was younger and feeling the same kind of frustrations he was feeling now, he would come here alone, raise the door, stand as close to the edge of the stall as he dared, and stand in the wind that whooshed inward from the outside. On it, he thought he smelled the exotic scents of the distant green wild: trees and flowers and soft, moist earth. Occasionally, an insect would be carried into the stall with the breeze and he would entertain himself by capturing it and studying its strange ways. Today however, he felt none of that. Instead, he seemed to be held in the grip of emotions that compelled him closer to the edge of the stall than he had ever dared before. Looking down and seeing the cloud layer slowly moving past the towers of the municiplex, it seemed to him that he stood on the deck of a moving ship as it cut its way across some vast and trackless ocean; an ocean that called to him, that urged him to step out and lose himself in its comforting quiet...

Suddenly, an insect carried by the wind struck Stoney Vander in the face, startling him out of the reverie that had seemed to possess him. Stepping back from the brink, he made a decision. Turning inward, he approached the family air car and waved the door open. With a hiss, it rose upward and he slid into the conductor's seat. Unbidden, the door fell shut and the turbine powered fans automatically began to turn in standby mode. Unlike most other families in Skyview Tower, the Vanders took pride in maintaining their air car and though seldom used, it was in such condition that Stoney Vander had no qualms about taking it out on a moment's notice.

With all systems showing green, Stoney Vander released the fans from standby and the air car immediately rose on a cushion of air only a few inches off the floor. With directional compressors engaged, he began moving the air car out of the stall and outside the building. Minding the high winds that wound about Skyview Tower, he was careful to keep the car under tight control, moving slowly. As he brought the car around, the glassy smoothness of Skyview Tower loomed on his left and he was momentarily surprised at the number of cracked and broken window banks there were in the cylindrical structure whose height he could only guess at but which continued to extend upward for many more thousands of feet above the levels assigned to Sunshine. The town was well named as its position in the tower placed it well above the clouds and in near perpetual sunlight. Craning his neck, Stoney Vander noticed for the first time that a new town being constructed at the top of the tower seemed to have gone unfinished for some time judging by the great blotches of rust on the exposed iron work and the lengths of empty window banks.

Turning back to his flying, Stoney Vander veered the air car away from Skyview Tower and toward an inviting open area amid the man-made forest of towers that made up the municiplex. Slowly, he began to descend straight down into the cloud layer and in seconds found himself surrounded by a gray haze that if not for the 'car's sensor instruments, would have been cause for concern. But gradually, the clouds began to break up until he had clearly fallen below them into the drab, rainy world of the lower levels where the manufacturing and transportation towns were located. As he continued to descend, the old, largely disused roadways connecting the towers became visible and he was made aware somewhat of the ancient beginnings of the municiplex. Now able to see a good distance ahead, Stoney Vander allowed himself more speed and weaving among the towers, soon found himself outside the limits of the municiplex where concrete and crumbling tarmac gave way to ground cover of a more vegetative nature.

Once seen only at a distance, the green wild rose up in the distance with much finer detail than Stoney Vander had ever noticed before. At once, his pulse began to quicken in anticipation of discovery...or was it something else? Stoney Vander was not so foolish as not to realize that what he was doing was escaping from the oppressive confines of Skyview Tower in a desperate search for what he would have called "freedom" if such a term had occurred to him. Nevertheless, at the moment, the band of green that stretched darkly along the growing horizon lured him on and in some part of his mind where dreams were left unexpressed, he imagined that beyond it he would find whatever it was that he was looking for.

As he swooped closer to the ground, the closest he had ever been in his life, he noticed that there were few roadways and the ones there were, were crumbling and buckled with trees and other plants. They snaked into the dark interior of the green wild where they were swallowed up as if they had never been. *Where had they once led?* Stoney Vander wondered. To other towers? Other prisons that suppressed creativity and rewarded failure and called it justice? Watching his power gauge, Stoney Vander continued on toward a line of low hills even as the terrain beneath him merged into a single, trackless expanse of forest. Suddenly, however, he spied a patch of open grassland amid the tangle and on impulse, decided to set the air car down.

Angling the directional compressors forward, he slowed the turbine fans and brought the air car hovering within a few feet of the ground. Gently, he lowered the vehicle the rest of the way and cut the power to the turbines. As the whir of the fans died away, Stoney Vander engaged the door lift and in another second, he was breathing the pollen laden air of the green wild. Not without some trepidation, he stepped from the conductor's seat and for the first time, felt the ground beneath his feet. All around him, tall grasses lay flattened from the force of his landing and beyond the few feet surrounding the air car, the plants stood as high as his waist. In the distance, he could see in the late afternoon sunlight where the forest began with a few tall trees acting as outriders.

But now that he was down, Stoney Vander was faced with the question of what to do next. Although he was in no mood yet to return home, he really had not thought out his actions when he exited Skyview Tower. Should he stay put or venture out on foot? Presently, the sound of insects chirping from the tall grass and of birds swooping over the distant trees decided the issue for him and he chose to explore a short distance within the tree line. Passing through the tall grass was simpler than he expected and so it was with an emboldened spirit that he found the vague remnants of a road and passed beneath the thick canopy of trees that formed the green wild.

He had been walking for some distance, marveling at the myriad sounds of nature, when he noticed how dark it had become in the forest. Looking up, he was surprised to find that the setting sun had become almost completely hidden from view behind not only a thick tangle of branches but also a kind of netting that hung upon the upper terraces of the forest. Looking more closely, Stoney Vander decided that the netting was not natural and that over the years it had become worn with great rents in its fabric that here and there permitted a stray shaft of sunlight to penetrate to the forest floor. Who had placed the netting like that and why? Just then, his thoughts were interrupted by a sound that stood out from those made by insects or the wind by its unnatural regularity. Wary, Stoney Vander left the old road to hide behind the thick bole of an ancient conifer and watched as the sounds very definitely indicated that they were being made by some mechanical device.

At last, a small, two person ground car hovered into view. Not unrelieved at the sight, Stoney Vander stepped out from hiding and into the old road waving a friendly hand at the silver haired driver who slowed the vehicle to a halt.

"Good day to you citizen," said Stoney Vander when the whir of the vehicle's fans had subsided.

"Hello yourself, stranger," replied the man.

"My name is Stoney Vander, a resident of the town of Sunshine in Skyview Tower."

"Thought you might be from the 'plex," said the man. "Your clothes tell the whole story. But I didn't think by this time there was anyone of European descent left in the 'plex."

"Oh, there are quite a few," said Stoney Vander unselfconsciously. "But fewer all the time. Within another fifty years or so it's projected that every citizen of Skyview Tower will be a person of color in one grade or another."

"So they're still judging one another by their skin color are they?"

"I wouldn't go so far as to say that," insisted Stoney Vander, surprised at finding himself defending the very practices that had driven him from Skyview Tower earlier in the day. "There is a great deal of past wrongs perpetrated on our citizens of color that need to be corrected."

"Hmm. I'm not in the mood to go into that old argument right now," said the man. "I'm Stu Daidin by the way. I work a farm outside Vigilanceville."

"A farm?"

"Yeah. I guess you couldn't know much about raising crops being a citizen of the 'plex and all," mused Stu Daidin. "I suppose they still got those automated food dispensers working up there? Hard to believe after this long. Anyway, out here, we grow our food naturally from the soil; the way our ancestors always did. One of the reasons for the war."

"The war?" Stoney Vander was becoming confused. Apparently there were gaps in the education he had received in Sunshine.

"Don't they teach you anything up there in those fancy towers?" asked Stu Daidin. "The people who lived in the big cities wanted farmers to stop raising animals and the big corporations tried to take over all the farms so they could grow their engineered crops. No way was any of that going to happen. But it was only one reason for the war. There were plenty of others. Anyway, it's been years since the fighting ended but that don't mean we've stopped keeping a lookout for the enemy. That's why I'm afraid I'm going to have to ask you to come with me. It'll be up to the town council in Vigilanceville to decide what to do with you; either let you go or hand you over to the feds."

"So, I'm to regard myself as your prisoner?" asked Stoney Vander with some trepidation.

"Prisoner sounds like too strong a word," said Stu Daidin. "What say we call you a guest? You can stay at my place until the council makes its decision."

Stoney Vander hesitated. By that time, the sun had touched the horizon and was sinking fast. It would be dark soon and his absence would be noticed at home. What would his parents say? Thought of his home and family impressed upon him for the first time the strangeness of his situation. Why did he leave Skyview Tower? The green wild was like an alien world to him; uninviting and apart. Suddenly, he felt a great urge to return to the familiar surroundings of Sunshine, even to the comfortable sameness of his job in design wing, employment Level IV.

"I don't think I want to go with you," ventured Stoney Vander at last.

"Sorry son, but you don't have a choice," replied Stu Daidin touching what appeared to be a firearm strapped to his hip. Stoney Vander, alarmed, had not noticed it before. "It's likely not going to be for long anyway. Just a few days. And life on my farm isn't so bad, I promise."

"Well, since it appears I don't really have a choice..."

Stoney Vander climbed into the ground car and sat in the seat alongside Stu Daidin who revved up the turbines and spun the vehicle around to face the direction from which he had come.

Presently, as the forest grew darker with the setting of the sun, Stoney Vander forgot about his earlier objections and began once again to enjoy his little adventure. As the ground car moved farther into the green wild, the roadway over which it hovered improved and he settled back to watch the changing landscape.

"Stu Daidin," he said at last. "What did you mean by a war? Was it actually fought between citizens of the municiplex and those outside the tower communities?"

"Like I said, you city folks, or your ancestors at least, wanted everyone to live the way they wanted them to," explained Stu Daidin. "They didn't just want to tell farmers how to raise their crops, they wanted to tell everyone what to eat and how to live. It began when they got ahold of the medical insurance system. Once they got the government to take it over, individual choice began to disappear. First it was which doctor to visit, then it was telling people what to eat and not to eat to stay healthy, then when people went to see their own doctors outside the government system, they began to arrest both doctors and patients. Anyone who operated outside the approved system were considered out of their minds so they were declared insane and forced into camps, only they didn't call them camps, they called them re-education centers, to change the way they thought. Next, it was decided that having more than a couple babies was unhealthy for the mothers, abortion became mandatory after a second child and finally, they began to take children away from their parents because practically everything a parent did was considered unhealthy for their children."

Stoney Vander said nothing; reflecting on similar laws enforced in the municiplex.

"Of course, that was only one small part of the problem," continued Stu Daidin. "Then there was the whole reparations movement that bankrupted the country and the wholesale re-assignment of jobs, placement in schools, and first claim on rationed goods to women and persons of color."

"And there were some who objected to the new order?"

"Damn right there were!" said Stu Daidin somewhat emphatically. "Mostly they were religious folk, but there were plenty of others who agreed that the government was in violation of the Old Constitution. By that time though, there weren't many of the religious folk left. They had no power, no influence. The government and the city folk had long since outlawed most of their practices, declared them the cause of most of the bad things that had happened in the history of the world and forced them to keep their faith to themselves. Some religions they allowed, which didn't make any sense, but then, not much they favored did. They favored some because it was felt that they were more genuine not being part of European culture and all. They finally got around to closing all the churches when pastors questioned the laws legalizing certain kinds of behavior...that came after the arrests of doctors and scientists who questioned the same things or who dared to speak out against what they called in those days 'global warming.'

"Anyway, there was a lot more but the main thing is people, ordinary people, finally got sick and tired of it all; the hypocrisy, the nonsense, the policies that flew in the face of common sense," said Stu Daidin. "They began to organize and took out the guns that the government and the city folk were never able to take away from them. Battle lines were drawn that ended up dividing the cities from the countryside and later, just the big cities. Both sides purged themselves of elements that disagreed with the majority. It was an ugly time and a lot of what happened no one could take pride in on either side, but they were things that had to be done to secure each society. Luckily for us, the military, what was left of it, turned out to be on our side. That left the government helpless to force its will on us. But instead of going in for total war, we decided to fight a war of attrition. We isolated those cities that refused give up and they became what you call the municiplex, self-sufficient communities run under the old laws that prevent personal enterprise and favor one group of people over another. That's why over the last 100 years or so, they've been slowly dying. The way they do things flies in the face of common sense."

That was news to Stoney Vander...who now considered for the first time the run down condition of Sunshine, the faulty manufactures of Skyview Tower, the lack of initiative on the part of its citizenry.

"We get a few people every now and then trying to escape the 'plex, but not many," observed Stu Daidin. "Guess they still keep a pretty tight lid on things over there, huh?"

"The idea never occurred to me, but maybe they do," replied Stoney Vander, who had never given the matter much thought. If there were rules against leaving the municiplex, then surely someone would have attempted to stop him from taking the air car from the family stall? He recalled the reeducation sessions he had been forced to attend when he was a boy.

There was silence between the two men for some minutes before the ground car topped a rise and the landscape beyond was spread out like a multi-hued carpet for miles in every direction. Stoney Vander marveled at sight of the green wild which seemed much less wild at the moment due to a network of roadways that crisscrossed the valley connecting small clusters of buildings that huddled amid carefully kept fields and pastures. In the distance, at the head of the valley, was what looked like a miniature municiplex with modest towers reaching above the tree tops.

"That's Vigilanceville over there," said Stu Daidin pointing at the distant municiplex. "That's where the council meets. About 45 miles beyond is the state capitol where the feds have offices."

"The state capitol?"

"Of Wisconsin. Well, new capitol anyway. Madison was isolated during the war and I hear there are still some holdouts up there. Anyway, over there's my farm."

Stoney Vander looked where Stu Daidin was pointing and saw one of the small clusters of buildings he had noticed. Looking closer, he could see fenced off areas with what might have been domesticated animals moving about them. Further away from the buildings, there were squared pastures of varying hues of green and brown.

Without further word, Stu Daidin drove the ground car further along the road until it dipped into the valley headed in the direction of his farm. Soon, they were below the ridgeline of the hills and amid the trees of the forest again but now Stoney Vander could see open fields between their branches and many of them were covered with plants arranged in long rows that seemed to stretch on forever.

"Do those plants grow that way naturally?"

Stu Daidin laughed shortly. "Of course not; they have to be planted. We grow corn on the south side of the farm mostly for feed, but in these pastures I like to diversify growing squash, beets, and potatoes."

"Potatoes!" exclaimed Stoney Vander, recalling his last meal that had consisted of old style baked potatoes...that now seemed a long time ago.

"You've had potatoes before, haven't you?" asked Stu Daidin, not sure what people ate in the 'plex.

"Of course, but they're served through a kitchen food dispenser," said Stoney Vander, at once feeling stupid. Of course he had learned in school how food was grown and processed. But the reality of it still came as a surprise.

"A dispenser, you say?" mused Stu Daidin. "But where did they come from before they got into the dispenser?"

"Hydroponic production methods," said Stoney Vander. "Although I'm not sure how the process actually works, growing edibles not being one of the activities of Skyview Tower."

"Then you might be in for a number of surprises before long," warned Stu Daidin as he pulled the ground car through a gate and drove up before a neat looking cottage close by a barn and other buildings that obviously housed the various animals Stoney Vander had seen from the hill top.

Trained as a designer, Stoney Vander was struck at the simple lines of the two story home. A wide porch encircled the front and one side with flowering plants hanging from hooks along the roof edge. The windows betrayed a feminine touch with curtains enclosing them indoors and shutters flanking them on the outside. With the sun now well behind the trees, it was growing dark quickly and a light over the front door had already been turned on.

"You'll stay here for a few days until I can get in to Vigilanceville and speak to the council," Stu Daidin was saying. "We've got a spare room..."

But Stu Daidin never finished his sentence as the next moment, the front door flew open and out stepped a young woman whose attractive features immediately caught Stoney Vander's attention.

"Dad! So you're finally home! I thought you weren't going to make it for supper..." The young woman stopped speaking suddenly when she noticed that Stu Daidin was not alone. "Oh, I'm sorry. I didn't know you brought company home."

"Merrybelle, this here's Stoney Vander; found him in the woods over in the hills toward the 'plex," reported Stu Daidin. "Stoney Vander, this is my daughter, Merrybelle Daidin."

"How do you do?" Stoney Vander managed, not sure if he should extend his hand in greeting. He decided such a gesture might be too familiar and simply nodded his head instead.

"Fine, thank you," replied Merrybelle Daidin. "I don't recognize you. You're not from around here are you?"

"I've come from the municiplex," replied Stoney Vander. "Specifically, I'm a citizen of Skyview Tower. I was taking a ride in my air car and landed on the other side of those hills there when your father..."

"You can get all the details inside while we have supper, Merrybelle," said Stu Daidin, mounting the steps and heading for the door. "Just let me show our guest which room he can use."

"Will he be staying until we get word from the council?"

"Yeah, so I was thinking he might be able to use some of your brothers' clothes for a couple days if he needs them."

"I'll get some sets of shirts and trousers from the cupboard," said Merrybelle Daidin.

"That's very kind of you, Stu Daidin," said Stoney Vander stepping into a large sitting room just inside the door.

"No problem. My boys are away engaged in upper learning these days so they won't be needing them."

After he had been shown his room on the second floor and the clothes placed in a neat pile at the foot of the bed, Stoney Vander followed his hosts downstairs to the kitchen where pleasant smells met his nostrils. Despite his having eaten supper with his own family some hours before, he found he was hungry again and eager to eat whatever was offered. That, however, was before he discovered what was on the menu.

"Meat!" he declared, dropping his eating utensils with a clatter.

Unfortunately, the discovery was made only after he had cut and eaten a number of morsels from the steaming portion that Merrybelle Daidin had laid in his plate. Assuming it was some kind of vegetable with which he was unfamiliar, he had cut pieces from it and eaten them, not without some pleasure at the taste. Merrybelle Daidin, it seemed, was a very good cook.

"Hmmm, this is quite good," he had commented. "What is it?"

"Pork," said Merrybelle Daidin as she daintily placed a small bit of her own portion into her mouth.

"And you say you prepared it yourself...over an open flame?"

"Well, I wouldn't call it an 'open flame!'" laughed Merrybelle Daidin. "I sautéed it in a pan on the stove top. Most people use microwave ranges these days, but my mother preferred cooking over a real fire, she claimed it gave her better control over the cooking process, so our stove is an older model gas range."

"And you don't mind taking the time to cook yourself even after coming home from work?"

"What do you mean by work? I work here on the farm so I arrange my own schedule. It's not like having a regular job. Is it different in the 'plex?"

"In Skyview Tower, all women are entitled to employment outside the residences," replied Stoney Vander. "They would consider it an insult to be confined to domestic chores. Often, for those men still waiting for employment slots in positions of greater responsibility, it falls to caring for the home and preparing meals...but meals are much easier to prepare as the process is completely automated."

"So women don't help with the domestic chores?"

"They have no time," said Stoney Vander. "They hold many of the upper employment slots due to their having been exploited in the times before the establishment of the municiplex. Men, on the other hand, who have given up the preferred employment slots to more deserving women and citizens of color, suffer from much less stress as a result and are expected to maintain the family's living unit and create a comfortable home life for their harder working spouses and daughters."

"Do you mean to tell me that men are employed only in menial labor?"

"Mostly, but they have every opportunity for promotion if no woman or citizen of color desires a particular position," said Stoney Vander. "My father, for instance, has recently been promoted to junior planner after only 23 years."

Stoney Vander did not understand the meaning of his words until he saw the look of consternation on the face of Merrybelle Daidin. It was then that he suddenly realized that it might seem to her that he was defending Sunshine's way of life. The irony of the situation was that it was one that he had opposed most vociferously only a few hours before at his parents' dinner table.

"I didn't mean to sound as if I approved of the way things are done in the municiplex," confessed Stoney Vander. "In fact, it is something that I have often struggled with."

"Is that what you were doing outside the 'plex when my father found you?"

"As a matter of fact, it was," said Stoney Vander truthfully. "It seemed the injustices I perceived in Sunshine grew too great for me to contain without making some outburst that would have brought trouble upon me. In truth, I may have upset my parents with some of the things I said and if that were ever discovered outside the family, I could be required to attend a round of sensitivity training."

"Sensitivity training?" asked Merrybelle Daidin.

"A program intended to point out to offenders the error in their way of thinking and to redirect their thoughts into correct channels."

"Brainwashing?" said Merrybelle Daidin not without some horror.

"Hardly!" said Stoney Vander. "There are ways that citizens in an ordered society are expected to behave. Surely you don't condone anti-social behavior for instance? Or damaging another's self esteem? Or hurting someone's feelings?"

"Not necessarily, but when a person is forced to alter their thoughts to conform to non-criminal behavior, I call that brainwashing."

"Oh, I hardly think so," said Stoney Vander, still wondering why he found himself defending things that he had so recently criticized. Seeking to change the subject, he asked about the food he was eating. "You called this pork? I don't think I've ever had any before. What kind of vegetable is it?"

"It's not a vegetable, silly, it's meat."

"Meat!" cried Stoney Vander, half choking on his food. "You're joking, right?"

"Of course not," said Merrybelle Daidin. "Why should I joke about it?"

"Eating the meat of animals is disrespectful of other living creatures with whom humans share the Earth," explained Stoney Vander, disgusted at the thought that a fellow being had been callously slaughtered simply for food. Unbidden, he felt his gorge begin to rise. "One might as well eat other human beings as animals."

"You don't mean that, do you?" said Merrybelle Daidin, surprised.

"I'm afraid he does, Merrybelle," said Stu Daidin, his patience finally worn out by all the nonsense having been spouted by their guest.

"But an animal...is only an animal," said Merrybelle Daidin trying to understand. "Are you saying that there is no difference in status between an animal and a human being?"

"Certainly!" retorted Stoney Vander pushing his plate away. "Animals have as much right to live out their lives in happiness and security as we humans do. To hunt them and eat them is barbaric!"

In the silence that followed, Stoney Vander was suddenly aware that his outburst may have caused insult to his hosts and worse, hurt their self-esteem. Quickly, he moved to reassure them that he did not hold them responsible for their beliefs.

"I apologize if my intemperate words offended you," Stoney Vander said. "I did not mean for them to do so. It was just the shock of finding out that I had been eating meat..."

"We understand," said Stu Daidin. "You've lived your entire life in a single isolated community with its own set of peculiar beliefs. The same beliefs that the rest of us outside the 'plex rejected years ago. We can't expect you to drop them in only the few hours you've been with us."

Stoney Vander said nothing, but inwardly he began to seriously question his rebellious nature and wondered if he might have been wrong after all. It was one thing to question the fairness of Sunshine's system of employment, quite another to be asked to accept such outrageous practices as institutionalized anti-social behavior and cannibalism!

Luckily for him, his hosts were just as reluctant to reopen conversation as he was and presently, he was able to excuse himself and retire to his room for the night. There, he disrobed and lay atop the coverings, the back of his head cupped in his hands as he gazed at the stars outside the window. The same stars he used to see outside the window banks of his parents' living unit in Sunshine. Were they even now looking outside, wondering what had become of him? Placing himself in their position had the effect of bringing home to Stoney Vander the utter strangeness of the world outside the walls of Skyview Tower and the ordered society of the municiplex. If he were not allowed to return home, could he ever adjust to life in the green wild? As much as he disliked how some things were done in Sunshine, was it any worse than the topsy turvy beliefs of Stu and Merrybelle Daidin? Such thoughts turned over and over in his mind until he finally fell asleep to the unaccustomed sounds of nocturnal insects.

By the next morning, the sound of insects was replaced with the pleasant music of birds chirping happily in a nearby orchard and Stoney Vander arose in a better mood than he had felt the evening before. Dressing in the clothes Merrybelle Daidin had laid out for him, he descended to the building's first floor only to discover that Stu Daidin had already risen. He wanted an early start on the day's work before going in to Vigilanceville to report to the council.

"Good morning," Merrybelle Daidin said in a manner that left Stoney Vander feeling unaccountably thrilled.

"Good morning," he replied moving to a place at the table already set with an empty plate and clean utensils.

"I have breakfast all ready," said Merrybelle Daidin scooping something from a pan that rested over an open flame on the stove. "And don't worry, it's not meat."

Stoney Vander shivered involuntarily. "Thank you for your consideration."

Sooner than he had expected, Stoney Vander had completely devoured the meal Merrybelle Daidin had placed in front of him and leaned back in his chair, satisfied.

"That was fast!" exclaimed Merrybelle Daidin who was only part way through her own flapjacks.

"They were very good, especially with that peculiar tasting syrup over them," said Stoney Vander around a gulp of coffee.

"It's made from maple gathered from our own trees," said Merrybelle Daidin not without some pride. "Almost everything we eat on the farm we raise or grow ourselves."

"That's a most interesting observation," said Stoney Vander.

"After breakfast, you can come with me while I do my chores and I'll show you the farm," suggested Merrybelle Daidin.

"I would enjoy that very much."

Not long afterward, the two young people stepped out the back door of the house onto a porch where Merrybelle Daidin pointed out a small garden through which a path led to a barn and a pair of long, low buildings from which the strangest squawking sounds emanated.

"This is my kitchen garden," Merrybelle Daidin was saying. "I tend these plants myself. Most of the farm is dedicated to cereals like corn and wheat with some potatoes and squashes but the rest of the vegetables we need, I grow here."

Moving among the various plants, Merrybelle Daidin lifted leaves to give her guest a better view of the fruit growing beneath and other times picked those vegetables that were ripe and deposited them in a basket she allowed Stoney Vander to hold. Soon, the basket was full and after leaving it on the porch, the two followed the well worn path in the direction of the barn.

There, Stoney Vander's senses were assaulted in a number of ways one of which came from a foul odor that he soon learned belonged to the cows that stood in specially constructed stalls which allowed workers in the employ of Stu Daidin to retrieve the "milk" from a score of bovines at the same time. The process itself came as a shock to Stoney Vander who had to control his stomach when he learned that the white substance being removed from the cows was intended for human consumption and that in fact, he himself had drunk some of it at the meals he had shared with his hosts.

It was with relief that they moved from the barn to one of the longer, low lying buildings behind it. There, Stoney Vander was no less surprised to find them filled with hundreds of chickens all clucking and screaming at the same time so that he could hardly understand it when Merrybelle Daidin explained to him that the birds were kept for their eggs which were boxed and sold to markets in cities and towns across the state.

"You actually eat these creatures' unborn offspring?" asked Stoney Vander surprised at his continued capacity to be shocked.

"Of course," replied Merrybelle Daidin, who had come to expect her guest's objections to anything that had to do with the consumption of anything other than plant based foodstuffs. "You do realize that for a healthy diet, a human being must eat balanced meals?"

"Naturally, but we in the municiplex have long had available insta-foods manufactured from hydroponically grown sorghum and soy products that can be fashioned into any number of nutritious variations. There are a number of cities in other towers than Skyview that specialize in their production."

"So you eat no real meat or dairy products such as milk, eggs, or cheese?"

Stoney Vander made a face. "Certainly not! Of course, there are artificial substitutes that can serve just as well."

"That may be, but I'm sure they don't provide you with all the proper vitamins a human being needs to remain healthy," replied Merrybelle Daidin eyeing her guest's anemic looking physiognomy. "Perhaps that explains your pale complexion and underweight appearance...maybe even your height; you do seem shorter than most of the men I've seen."

Unsure if he should have been insulted or not, Stoney Vander unconsciously straightened. "My appearance is not any different than most citizens of Sunshine. We rarely suffer from malnutrition or any kind of disease."

"I'm sure," said Merrybelle Daidin, smiling. "Anyway, I have a project that will keep you busy for a few hours while I return to the house and get some of the farm's accounting done."

"What do you want me to do?" asked Stoney Vander, happy to be of assistance.

Handing him a piece of paper with a number code written on it, Merrybelle Daidin pointed to a ground car outfitted as a work vehicle and instructed him to take it to the barn and tell the workers there that he was to load it with meal for the chickens. After he had the car loaded, he was to go to the chicken coops and fill all the feeders there with the meal.

"That should keep you busy until lunch time," said Merrybelle Daidin with amusement. "Think you can handle it?"

"No problem," said Stoney Vander. He watched as the girl turned and walked back up the path to the house and for the first time noticed how more fully formed she appeared in comparison to the women of Sunshine. She was well rounded in all the right places while her body moved in such a manner that he found himself becoming more and more enchanted with her. Shaking off the feeling with some difficulty, he managed to put Merrybelle Daidin out of his mind long enough to make his way to the ground car, punch the access code into the ignition panel, and conduct it to the barn. The balance of the morning was taken up with his assigned duties which he completed with less disgust than he had anticipated. In fact, the repetitive nature of the work freed his mind and allowed his training as a designer to come up with a number of improvements that could be made to the building and the manner in which the chickens were fed that he intended to suggest to Stu Daidin when he saw him next.

When he saw Merrybelle Daidin again at lunch time, it was not without the realization that he had missed her presence after she had left him that morning. Having been attracted to other young women in Sunshine, he recognized the symptoms and realized that he had become attracted to the lovely outsider.

"Well you must have built up an appetite after all that work," Merrybelle Daidin was saying.

"I did," replied Stoney Vander seating himself at the table, noticing that the meal Merrybelle Daidin had prepared did not include any meat or poultry products; a fact not unappreciated by her guest.

"After lunch I thought we'd take a ride into town," said Merrybelle Daidin taking her place at the table. "I have some errands to run."

"I'd be happy to go."

With their meal over and the dishes safely in the automated dishwasher, the two young people stepped outside and into a waiting ground car that Stoney Vander judged to be Merrybelle Daidin's personal vehicle due to a number of feminine touches made to its interior. In another few minutes the vehicle had cleared the main gate and reached a road running through the surrounding woodland.

Such was the ground car's speed, that soon, Merrybelle Daidin was obliged to slow as she approached the main highway that led directly to Vigilanceville. Turning onto the highway, the girl picked up speed and soon, Stoney Vander was treated to a passing view of the neighboring countryside which was dotted with farmsteads similar to that of his hosts and surrounded by a patchwork of fields covered in various kinds of crops. Despite his discomfort with many of their odd practices, the panorama that unfolded before his eyes was admired by Stoney Vander for the initiative it represented on the part of the local citizens. An initiative that he found lacking in his own people back in Sunshine.

With the speed of the ground car, it was not long before they pulled within the city limits of Vigilanceville. Stoney Vander was struck by how the homes in what Merrybelle Daidin called the suburbs were spread out with much wasted open land between them.

"Is something wrong, Stoney Vander?" asked Merrybelle Daidin.

"I'm simply struck by the amount of space that is wasted in your city," Stoney Vander said. "What is the use of all that open ground covered in nothing but grass?"

"Some people want their privacy," explained the girl. "They don't want to live cheek by jowl with their neighbors. Also, good sized yard space enables some to retain a connection to the land. See? Many have smaller versions of my kitchen garden in the back."

"It's just disconcerting to see citizens living horizontally instead of vertically," said Stoney Vander. "Such isolation one from the other would make me lonely."

"It's something you'll have to get used to if the council decides you can't go back," said Merrybelle Daidin, not without some concern in her voice. "Really, it's not so bad living outside the 'plex. If you end up staying, you'll see what I mean."

Stoney Vander kept his thoughts to himself, doubting that he could ever get used to such a confusing lifestyle. He appreciated the girl's thoughts however and wondered if they could mean anything more when his musings were interrupted by the sight of an unusual looking structure.

"What kind of building is that?" Stoney Vander asked, pointing.

"Where? Oh, that's a church."

"Really? Are there many worshippers of the Prophet on the outside?"

"Prophet? What are you talking about? A church is where Christians meet."

"Christians! You mean to tell me that there are enough Christians to fill such a building?"

"Of course, and many more. There are many churches in Vigilanceville used by different sects of the religion." Merrybelle Daidin chanced a look away from her driving to Stoney Vander. "Don't tell me there are no Christians in the 'plex?"

"Oh, I'm sure there are," replied Stoney Vander. "It's just that I've never met any. I'm told there are a few who practice their faith but if so, they don't advertise the fact."

"Why not?"

"Like citizens of European descent, the Christian religion was responsible for much suffering in the world and for that reason has long since been removed from society and those who continue to cling to it have been marginalized," said Stoney Vander matter of factly. "I suppose it still has its believers but today, worship of the Prophet is the sanctioned religion."

"So as far as you're aware, there are no Christians in the 'plex?" asked Merrybelle Daidin, clearly disturbed.

"No. That's why I'm surprised to hear you say there are enough on the outside to demand the use of so many church buildings. You mean to tell me that the Christian religion is still practiced here?"

"Of course! The Christian religion is a beautiful faith directed by a desire for peace and love for all. Why should anyone want to remove such a thing from society?"

"On the face of it, I'll admit your definition sounds attractive, but religion has been responsible for more bloodshed throughout history than any other factor," said Stoney Vander.

"So your society has chosen to embrace the evil men have done in the name of religion instead of the peaceful intent of the religion itself?" commented Merrybelle Daidin. "And certainly, the twentieth century regimes of Germany, Russia, and China alone far surpassed in bloodshed anything that could be laid at the doorstep of religion? The slaughter engendered by those political entities was not done for religious reasons but for those of the state...the same kind of state that currently rules in the 'plex. How many citizens have lost their lives or who have never been permitted to be born because of the laws of the towers limiting population growth? How many millions over the centuries since the war?"

For once Stoney Vander had no reply. It had never occurred to him to look at the situation in quite that way. Due to the finite nature of its resources, the administration of Sunshine did indeed control the number of births in town, euthonize its elderly and, more in the early years of the municiplex than currently, put to death thousands of people in order to bring population levels down to numbers that could be managed in the closed environment of the towers. For the first time, Stoney Vander sensed if only dimly, the vast crime perpetuated by the administration of the towers on its citizens.

Recoiling from such notions as he would from the edge of a deep pit, Stoney Vander quickly chose to change the subject.

"Do you belong to any of these churches?" he asked.

"I do," replied Merrybelle Daidin without elaboration. There was silence then and he knew that he had upset her with the conversation regarding Christianity. And though try as he might to get her to speak again, she refused and it was not until the ground car had come to rest in a lot containing many other similar vehicles that she deigned to speak to him again. "We'll leave the car here while we do our errands. First the bank."

The balance of the afternoon was spent checking on the Daidin account at the bank, shopping in the local food store for items not available on the farm, and simply walking about with Merrybelle Daidin showing Stoney Vander the sights.

In viewing the city, Stoney Vander was struck by the ease with which those of European descent and other citizens of color moved among each other. Just as surprising was the fact that there seemed to be many more of European descent than citizens of color and that both groups held positions of employment at all levels regardless of the pigmentation of their skin.

"How are citizens assigned employment in Vigilanceville?" Stoney Vander asked.

"No one is assigned employment," replied Merrybelle Daidin. "Employers own their own businesses and hire whom they please. If they wish to succeed, they make sure to hire the best person suited to the job."

"And does this system apply as well to civil unions?"

"What do you mean?"

"Do men and women choose their own partners as they choose their own employees?"

"Of course, silly!" replied Merrybelle Daidin.

"That would explain why so many couples are made up of people of the same skin color," said Stoney Vander, thinking aloud. "Are citizens then forbidden from choosing mates of different skin color?"

"No," said Merrybelle Daidin. "Like I said, people are free to choose whomever they want to be with. Look, there's a mixed couple there."

The contradictions of the society he found himself in continued to pile up, giving Stoney Vander a headache. Would he ever figure out how such a chaotic community could possibly remain healthy and viable?

But the question was one he soon abandoned as he began to feel more comfortable in the presence of Merrybelle Daidin who, by the end of the afternoon, had slipped her arm into his and held him close. Stoney Vander found the contact more thrilling than any he had ever experienced. Certainly there had been young women in Sunshine that he had known but contact with them was usually within the strict rules governing the activities of unmated individuals. Rarely...no, never, had he felt the kind of pleasurable sensations he was feeling now with Merrybelle Daidin, who proved to be a free spirited young woman.

Thus it was that by the time they had returned to the farm, Stoney Vander was quite taken by the vivacious Merrybelle Daidin, a fact he had some time to ponder over as she turned him out of doors while she prepared the evening meal.

Outside, he wandered through the kitchen garden and out to the edge of the corn fields where he walked quietly along the rows of stalks toward the sunset. Unbidden, memories of the life he had left in Sunshine paraded through his mind and he was seized by a sudden longing to return home and the familiar routine of work and home life. He thought of his parents and sister and how they must be worried about him and he was struck by the strangeness of life outdoors. Suddenly the open sky overhead made him nervous and the feel of the wind on his skin carried with it a sense of vulnerability. Sounds from the chicken coops and barn underscored the air of unnaturalness and from somewhere deep inside of him, the feeling grew of wanting to run, to get away from these odd people, back to his air car, and to go home where all was normal and sane.

But the panic that had been welling within him dissipated with the sound of Merrybelle Daidin's voice calling him from the house. The evening meal was ready; Stu Daidin would be there with news of the council and for the first time, Stoney Vander was not sure what he wanted that to be.

Inside, he was relieved to find that once again, Merrybelle Daidin had prepared a meal for him that did not include meat or dairy products. The food before him was pleasing in its variety of greens and yellows and a big bowl of fresh fruit sat at the center of the table.

"Is this what you call a meal for a hungry man?" demanded Stu Daidin half-jokingly.

"In deference to our guest, I prepared supper without any meat," replied Merrybelle Daidin sweetly, looking at Stoney Vander out of the corners of her eyes.

The smile he saw on her face chased all of his doubts of the last hour away and Stoney Vander knew only the desire to remain in her company as long as possible.

"I appreciate the effort," he said, smiling himself.

"Hmmm," was all Stu Daidin could muster, looking at a bunch of lettuce leaves where he had them stuck on the end of his utensil.

After a few minutes of silence while they ate, Stoney Vander ventured the question that all of them knew was coming.

"So, did the council decide what is to be done with me?"

"No," replied Stu Daidin picking an apple from the fruit bowl. "They spent all morning and part of the afternoon arguing about the situation until finally deciding to pass the problem on to the feds at the capital. It seems that it's been longer than I thought since the last time someone from the 'plex wandered outside. No one really knows if any of the old rules about what to do with such people still apply. It seemed pretty harsh to simply shoot you like they did in the days immediately after the war."

"I'm happy to hear that!"

"Me too!" said Merrybelle Daidin with such emphasis that it caused Stoney Vander's heart to leap.

Stoney Vander finished his second night on the outside watching some televised programming on the family's entertainment center and listening as Merrybelle Daidin played an old fashioned upright piano in the living room. She was very good, at least judged by Stoney Vander's limited experience but he decided that simply being with Merrybelle Daidin was pleasant enough.

After he had retired for the evening and was alone with his thoughts, Stoney Vander had to admit that he was conflicted. He recalled the electric thrill he had had whenever Merrybelle Daidin held his arm or came into contact with him for any reason and the empty feeling he felt whenever he was away from her. Admitting a growing affection for the girl, one that he believed strongly was reciprocated, he found the situation unsettling. Being raised outside the municiplex, placed Merrybelle Daidin at odds with his own beliefs which, despite her arguments, failed to weaken. It was for that reason he felt that whatever relationship he might consider entering with the girl was doomed to failure. In fact, whenever he felt the possibility of things becoming serious between them, he grew conflicted, fearful, and wary of giving up his beliefs and way of life for hers, which he still considered alien and unreal.

Twisted up inside over his growing desire for the company of Merrybelle Daidin and his yearning to return to the comforting familiarity of Sunshine, it was a long time before he finally was able to fall asleep.

And so the nights passed, sleepless mostly for Stoney Vander as he wrestled with the possibility, growing more real with each passing day, that he would have to make a choice between staying on the outside with Merrybelle Daidin or returning to Sunshine where increasingly, he felt he belonged. Each night he fell asleep wanting nothing more than to forget the girl and go home and each morning he would descend to breakfast, lay eyes on her, and immediately forget all of his arguments of the evening before desiring nothing more than to be with her.

As they awaited word from the feds about what to do about Stoney Vander, he and Merrybelle Daidin filled their days with chores on the farm, jaunts into Vigilanceville, long walks beneath the green bowers of the forest, and warm evenings talking on the front porch or laughing at the actors in the latest televised dramas. All the while, Stoney Vander was certain, Merrybelle Daidin was as cognizant as he was that depending on the kind of news that finally came from the feds, a decision would have to be made, a very serious decision that would effect them for the rest of their lives. At night, alone in his room, Stoney Vander sometimes trembled at the thought of making that decision; the position in which he found himself, doing nothing to discourage the belief by

Merrybelle Daidin that he wanted nothing more than to stay with her, made it more difficult all the time to refute her affections and return to Sunshine. So much did he dread that moment, that he grew more and more nervous to the point where his heart pounded and his hands shook. Finally, the waiting became too much. Admitting to himself that he was a coward, and hating himself for it, Stoney Daidin decided to escape the outside and return to Sunshine before the others discovered his absence.

And so, late one night, some weeks after his arrival, Stoney Vander, dressed in the clothes with which he had first left home, slipped quietly from his second floor room and left the house. Behind him, on the dresser, he had placed the portable message screen given him by the Daidins and preserved on it a note explaining the reasons for his leaving, all of them lies. Ashamed and relieved at the same time, he engaged the near silent turbines of Merrybelle Daidin's ground car and as it rose on a cushion of air, pushed it from the front yard to the gate at the entrance of the farm. Looking back, he wondered if he was making a mistake; brushing the thought aside, he entered the ground car. Punching Merrybelle Daidin's personal code into the ignition pad, something he had seen her do many times, he brought the fans up to full power and with a dull whine impossible for anyone to hear from the house, he directed the vehicle up the road to the crest of the hill over which Stu Daidin had first brought him to the farm.

Dawn was brightening the eastern sky when he passed beneath the ragged remnants of the camouflage netting and entered upon the portion of the old road that had been abandoned to the encroaching forest. Leaving instructions in the ground car's nav-system, he jumped out and watched as it spun on its axis, picked up speed, and headed back to the farm. Turning, he continued walking along the pitted and cracked roadway until it emerged onto the grassy dell where he had landed his air car weeks before.

Catching sight of the air car among the tall grasses, its familiar lines brought back to him all the comfortable feelings of home and suddenly, he was more eager than ever to leave the green wild and return to the family and friends whom he had abandoned so precipitously. How they must have worried when he did not return! Anxiously, he waved the door of the 'car open and as the vehicle rose on a cushion of air, he took the conductor's seat and coded the ignition pad. Instantly, all systems showed green and as the fans increased their rotation to full flight mode, he cast a last look at the distant tree line, engaged the directional compressors, and moved quickly to gain altitude.

Immediately, he saw the green wild spread out beneath him to the line of hills over which he knew lay the world of Merrybelle Daidin. For a moment, he felt a pang of regret at not having had the courage to remain, but he ignored it and determined to make the most of life in Skyview Tower. A few minutes later, the hills had disappeared beneath the horizon and the misty towers of the municiplex began to make themselves apparent in the distance. Gradually, they resolved themselves into gleaming cylinders that pierced the thin clouds of vapor that presaged the coming of a storm front over the great lake on whose shores the municiplex had been located.

Soon, Stoney Vander found himself reducing the air car's speed as it made its way among the towers of the municiplex. Presently, Skyview Tower came into view and an automated beacon from the air car signaled the exit door to the family's stall to open. The next moment, within the stall, he felt the air car settle onto its accustomed markings as its power wound down. Gradually, quiet returned to the stall as first the outer door closed shut and then the turbines stopped in the air car. Alerted that the stall door had been activated, Aris Vander appeared at the lift entrance, relief expressed on his face as he saw his son exiting from the vehicle. Behind him, he was joined by Vivy Vander-Hool who could not contain her happiness at seeing her missing son return.

No less happy to see them again, Stoney Vander embraced his mother and shook his father's hand. Together, they all returned to the living unit where Vivy Vander-Hool prepared a quick meal which, to Stoney Vander's relief, did not include the flesh of animals. After he had eaten and the family had settled in the living room, Stoney Vander told them of his adventures.

"I have been to the outside and discovered many things different from what we learn in our history books," Stoney Vander began. When he had finished, his parents had many questions, most of them tinged with horror at the lives of those desperate remnants of a war fought hundreds of years before.

"My heart goes out to those poor creatures," said Vivy Vander-Hool, her hand held delicately over her breast. "To be ruled by the superstitions of religion, to feast on the flesh of fellow beings, to submit themselves to the uncertainty of random pairings...brrrr"

"It does all seem quite incredible," agreed Aris Vander from where he sat at the end of the sofa. "And you say this Stu Daidin grew his own foodstuffs from the ground beneath an open sky and not hydroponically?"

"I found it hard to believe myself until I saw it with my own eyes," replied Stoney Vander who had played down his relationship with Merrybelle Daidin.

That night, alone in his own room at last, Stoney Vander had time to think and what he found was that he missed the exciting presence of Merrybelle Daidin. He missed the softness of her touch, the sound of her carefree laughter, even the times when she ignored him through some slight he hardly knew he had caused. At the same time, he feared what remaining with her would have done to him. Would his own personality have been subsumed in a new relationship with her? Would he come to forget his life in Sunshine or would he live to regret every day his decision to remain with her? Angry at not knowing, he worried that the regret at a possible opportunity lost would hound him the rest of his life.

And so the weeks and months passed until some years following his impetuous excursion to the outside, he found himself promoted to entry level designer and assigned a new civil partner. In this he was luckier than his sister Immomia Vander-Skit in that he had been paired with a citizen of color enabling he and his partner to occupy a choice living unit with a view out the west side of Skyview Tower. Less fortunate for Stoney Vander's conscience however, was that on exceedingly clear days the view was unobstructed such that he could see the dark line of trees that marked the edge of the green wild. On those days, he could not keep his thoughts from drifting to Merrybelle Daidin and the life that could have been his but for his lack of courage. Ashamed and frustrated, he would turn from the window banks and watch his partner take up her prayer mat and prepare to leave for her office in Sunshine's administrative level. By the door he would see the hated vestsmock he wore as an entry level designer and be reminded how it was often his ideas that allowed unqualified superiors to advance. It was in those times that he would suddenly be overcome by the now familiar urge to flee; to find an air car still in operating condition and escape from the municiplex as he had done before and return to Merrybelle Daidin to beg her forgiveness. Then, a moment later, the initial panic would subside, and only a vague emptiness would remain. Instinctively, he would don his vestsmock, leave the living unit, and join the line of his fellow citizens as they headed for the employment levels. And as he squeezed in to the lift that would take him down to design wing, employment Level IV, he knew that despite the 367 dictums needed for an orderly life in the town of Sunshine, he was not simply headed for another day of work, but descending into a personal hell of lost opportunity and regret.

Down the Long Long Years

AT FIRST, JIP NORFLINGER wasn't sure what had woken him.

It was still the middle of the night and from where he sat bolt upright in the upper bunk, he could plainly see the Milky Way framed in the open window of the clubhouse as its band of glistening stars stretched across the summer sky. Outside, all was quiet, but something had nevertheless awakened him from a sound sleep.

Or had it been so sound? Concentrating a moment, Jip tried to remember what it was he'd been dreaming about just before waking up. But try as he might, he couldn't recall anything, only impressions of frustration and disappointment that left him vaguely depressed.

"Did you hear that?" whispered Tyler Murfree from where he lay in the lower bunk. His words broke Jip's concentration and he forgot all about whatever it was that he might have been dreaming.

"It sounded like a sonic boom, but a kind I never heard before," replied Danny Ouelette from the folds of his sleeping bag on the other side of the small room. Danny occupied a third,

...outside the gate, unauthorized personnel were permitted to gather and see what they could through the chain links in the gray metal fence that surrounded the test center. There, the boys joined a number of other curiosity seekers who had been driven from their homes by the late night booms.

single bunk that rested beneath another window in the clubhouse.

"I know what it was," said Jip finally. "It was a multiple sonic boom!"

"More than one? From a single flight?" asked Tyler.

"Yeah, that was it," said Danny. "The booms came close together so they sounded more like thunder."

"It must mean there's a plane out tonight!"

"It's a beautiful night for it," said Tyler, going to the window and looking up at the sky. "Not a cloud in sight and it's so bright outside, the lakes must be shining almost like they would in daylight."

Throwing the fold of his sleeping bag off, Jip crawled closer to his window and looked outside. Around the clubhouse there were a few scraps of desert scrub and the odd cactus and close by he could see the silhouettes of base housing against the horizon. In the distance, between the low lying homes, he caught the shimmer of the salt pans that made up the dry lake beds giving Edwards Air Force Base its reputation as the perfect place for testing America's advanced aircraft.

Together, the three boys continued to scan the night skies, straining their eyes to spot the single moving light among the stars that would reveal it not as a natural object, but one that was man made.

"There it is!" cried Danny, pointing suddenly. The others looked in the direction he indicated and a moment later they spotted the small dot of red that moved against the stars.

"What do you think it is?" wondered Tyler.

"Some new jet obviously," said Danny.

"I know that," replied Tyler testily. "I meant what model?"

"Can't tell from here," said Tyler.

Suddenly the very atmosphere seemed to cave in upon their senses and Jip could have sworn he felt a sudden drop in air pressure just before their ears were assaulted by a triple boom that must have woken everyone in the base compound.

"Wow!" was all Tyler could say, holding his ears.

"That was a double for sure!" exclaimed Danny in open mouthed awe.

"No, a triple!" insisted Jip. "It's the X-2! I'm sure of it!"

"Tonight?" asked Danny. "It wasn't due to fly for another two weeks. My dad told me so."

Normally, Jip wouldn't be inclined to argue with Danny if that was what his father had told him. Armand Ouelette was a top engineer at the flight research center on base so his information was no doubt good, but Jip was positive he'd heard a triple boom.

"Only one way to make sure..." said Tyler, expressing the thought they all were thinking.

"Let's go!" said Danny, springing to his feet and getting into his clothes.

Seconds later, the three boys had tumbled from the clubhouse and were making for the bicycles they had left lying on the ground a few feet away. In homes all around them, lights were coming on.

As Jip picked up speed and followed his friends into the road in front for the Murfree house, his eyes continued to look skyward for evidence of the Bell X-2 he knew had to be up there somewhere. He could imagine what it must be like for the pilot, protected in a pressure suit and breathing with the aid of a helmet and oxygen mask, flying over 100,000 feet above the Earth while at the same time fighting against the pressure of traveling three times faster than the speed of sound.

Ever since he could remember, he dreamed of doing the same: of soaring high above the Earth to the edge of space as his father himself sometimes did when it was his turn in the rotation cycle to take one of the experimental X-planes up into the wild blue yonder.

Jake Norflinger had been an ace fighter pilot in World War II before being reassigned to Edwards in 1949 just when the Air force base was beginning to acquire its reputation as the place to be for pilots seeking to push the outside of the envelope. At that time, fellow pilot Chuck Yeager ruled the roost after becoming the first man to break the sound barrier in 1947 but as things turned out, with the cold war heating up, there was plenty of work to go around.

As the boys left the base housing area and rode down the unpaved road in the direction of the testing range, Jip wondered if his father was flying the plane that had caused the curious series of booms...but no, he recalled his mother saying, not without a note of relief in her voice, that he had ground duties tonight. Jip, however, thought little of the danger flying the experimental X-planes posed for his father; instead, it was the glamour of flight, of pushing the edge of the unknown, of barriers of sound and spinning gauges and screaming metal, and the sudden unexpected cold of space as stars began to twinkle through cloud cover in what was supposed to be the middle of the day. More than anything, he wanted to be up there, on the new frontier, being the first...

Jip's thoughts were interrupted as he and his friends were forced to skid to a halt at the gate that barred entrance to the Flight Test Center. Forbidden to all but authorized personnel, a guard booth outside the gate lent emphasis to the seriousness with which base command took the restrictions. And if anyone failed to get the message from signs posted with the words "Authorized Personnel Only Beyond This Point," then surely, they'd understand the ugly butts of loaded revolvers on the hips of the white helmeted sentries.

But outside the gate, unauthorized personnel were permitted to gather and see what they could through the chain links in the gray metal fence that surrounded the test center. There, the boys joined a number of other curiosity seekers who had been driven from their homes by the late night booms.

Squeezing their way to the front of the crowd, the boys twined their fingers into the chain link fence and pressed close against it.

"See anything?" asked Danny.

"Nothin' yet," replied Tyler.

Saying nothing, Jip dug the toes of his Keds into the chain links and hauled himself up near the top of the fence for an unobstructed view of the airfield that stretched beyond the vague bulk of the lab buildings. Soon he was joined by his friends and together, they speculated about what plane could have caused the booms. The question of which model had been used was an important one as a successful flight, one that broke speed records, would indicate research that was yielding the best results.

"Wait!" hissed Jip, straining his eyes into the dark of the field. "I see lights. Something's being moved along the runway."

"Can you see what it is?" said Danny, unconsciously leaning forward for a better look.

"Not yet...It's the X-2!"

Lying on a trailer being pulled by a jeep, was the white form of a sleek little one man plane. Red lights winked on the ends of its wings upon which the legend "USAF" was emblazoned in proud letters. As the plane moved into view, Jip found it hard to believe that such an average looking aircraft could have traveled at mach 1 let along mach 3 as the series of booms had indicated. Then the plane had been hauled out of sight and into a hanger beyond the cluster of lab buildings.

"Guess that's all the excitement we're going to get tonight," sighed Tyler, lowering himself to the ground.

"I'll find out form my dad tomorrow if the X-2 really did break mach 3," said Danny.

"Well, it sure sounded like it did to me," said Jip, picking up his bike and throwing himself across the seat. "Maybe my dad will have some news about it too."

"If they're allowed to talk about it at all," added a pessimistic Tyler.

Of course, that was possible seeing as much that happened at Edwards was classified top secret; on the other hand, news involving record breaking flights often seemed to circulate pretty freely even making the newspapers within a few days of the event. Jip's father guessed that such news was good publicity for the Air Force and was reported to the press in order to hold the public's interest.

Back at the clubhouse behind the Murfree home, the boys stripped to their skivvies and crawled back into heir sleeping bags. They lay awake for some time speculating on the night's events until one by one they fell asleep. The last thing Jip remembered was looking at the stars outside the window, his fingers knitted behind his head, and wondering if one of the stars he was watching was the planet Mars...

———

Jip didn't wake suddenly, but instead his consciousness seemed to rise slowly to the surface of full alertness as one by one his senses began to pick up evidences of the world that existed beyond the walls of sleep.

First to signal his mind that it was time to get up was his sense of hearing that detected the muted thrum of the internal generators as they worked to supply the minimum power needed to keep the ship's life support systems functioning. It was his sense of touch that brought him to the next level of awareness as his entire body felt the faint vibrations caused by the generators as they traveled along the ship's titanium and aluminum hull and interior bulkheads. Finally, he could tell through his closed eyelids that the cabin lights had come on and by the film that lined his mouth, knew he needed to brush his teeth.

Reluctantly, he unbuckled the restraining straps that held him to the bunk and battled weightlessness while slipping into his coveralls as fast as he could. Sitting up, he swung his feet to the cold deck and finding his metallic footwear, slipped his feet into them. Feeling his boots cling to the ship's magnetized flooring, he tried to rub the sleep from his eyes but it did no good. When his vision cleared, he found that he was still in the same tiny room that had been assigned to the mission commander. He sighed heavily and not for the first time wondered when it had occurred to him that hitting the sack meant more to him than the mission.

The mission! What did it ever mean for him except more responsibility, more study, more training, more hassle? It was hard for him to remember now that there had been a time when he enjoyed his job; when he couldn't wait to hop into the pilot's seat and start the engines of whatever bird he happened to be assigned to. Whether it was an A-10 Thunderbolt, F-16 Fighting Falcon, or an F-18 Hornet, they were all great aircraft and all a hoot to fly.

Heck, he still remembered the thrill he felt when he first went aboard an old Air Force T-37 Cessna trainer back at Edwards. How many years ago was that? He couldn't have been more than 14 or 15. It hadn't been the first time he'd left the ground in a plane though; his father had been an Air Force pilot since before they called it the Air Force and had taken him up a few times before. But that first lesson in the old Cessna was the first time he'd been airborne for purposes of his own; to learn to fly and finally take wing all by his lonesome. That happened about a year after he'd begun taking lessons when he soloed, passed, and received his pilot's license. That was a proud day not only for himself but for his father too. He remembered that the thrill of flying stayed with him for a long time. Through the Air Force Academy and all the years serving stateside and then over the SAM infested skies of North Vietnam. Then came a tour in Europe before he received word that he'd been accepted by NASA for astronaut training.

Was it then that the fun began to drain out of flying? As a pilot on one of the last moon shots, there was little for him to do what with most control of the spacecraft being handled by ground based technicians back on Earth. The spacecraft was so well designed that there was little chance of anything going wrong. As a result, most of the time, he'd felt like a passenger instead of a pilot. He hadn't liked the feeling then, and didn't like it any better now as the tin can he and four other men were riding hurtled through space toward Mars.

They'd been in space for over nineteen weeks not counting the time they'd spent in Earth orbit prepping for the mission which was to be an historic one: the first manned landing on the surface of Mars. It was an event that every astronaut in the corps had vied for with Jip and four crewmen, navigator and co-pilot Mart Binger, physician Jersey Slater, bio-geologist Will Montegue, and communications and electronics expert Kent Carpenter winning out in the end. But curiously, the news, when it came, had seemed less thrilling than he had expected. His heart should have been filled with pride and happiness and his mind eager for the challenge; it should have been the cul-mination of a career that had been filled with one triumph after another. Instead, all he'd felt was the anticipated drudgery of the inevitable paperwork, the reports to be written and filed, the intensive regimen of study, the cross train-ing in multiple disciplines, and above all, the personal responsibility that would be his as commander of the mission.

All of that had come to pass, in spades; until now, well past the half way point on the way to Mars, he felt the accumulated weight of it all pressing down on him, dampening his spirits and turning the mission into something to be endured rather than anticipated. Despis-ing himself for those feelings, he couldn't help but think they were a betrayal of everything he'd ever dreamed about, everything he ever yearned for when looking after the contrails of those experimental aircraft his father used to fly at Edwards and wondering what lay beyond the thin envelope of atmosphere that protected the Earth from the vacuum of outer space.

Determined to shake off his feelings of despondency, Jip pulled aside the thin doorway that separated his quarters from the short corridor outside and stepped onto the command deck. There, the main cabin lights were off with most of the illumination emanating from the scores of dials and gauges that studded the various instrument panels that filled every available space above and below a set of small view ports that looked out over the nose of the Eagle-1 as it hurtled thousands of miles an hour toward its destination. Just then, soft classical music was being piped through the cabin's sound systems which meant that Mart Binger had to be on duty.

Sure enough, when Jip's metal boots clanged into the cabin, it was Mart who turned to face him from his position in the navigator's chair.

"Hey, skipper," said Mart with too much good humor in his voice. "Am I relieved already?"

"You got it," replied Jip throwing himself in the chair beside the navigator. "Are we still on course?"

"Yep. We'll be there in about four months," Mart said as he shut down the instruments at his station. "Am I free to go?"

"Take off," said Jip, already running his hands over his own instrument panel that lit screens and booted up his computer. "Make sure Kent gets up on time before you turn in, okay? He's missed the start of his watch twice in a row now and I get grumpy when I'm hungry."

"Will do but I can't figure out how that prefab food we've been eating for the last few months does anything to improve your disposition," observed Mart.

"Get going!"

Alone on the command deck, Jip turned to the ship's log and began reading over the entries made by the crew since his last watch. Determined to concentrate on his work for the next five hours so as to make the time pass more quickly, he read through the log making notes of points that he intended to follow up on either by questioning the crew, having the ship's computer run back the information, or checking into it himself. But going through the log was the pleasant part of his job. Far worse was scrolling through the data stream that arrived from Earth in a constant flow of information that was received by the ship's computer and automatically acted upon. If anything was received from Earth's human operators, it was flagged for the commander's personal attention and although little of it demanded any kind of response, in practice, all of it had to be looked over anyway. Meanwhile, the Eagle-1 was also sending its own data stream the millions of miles back to Earth; mostly binary impulses detailing the tens of thousands of individual operations needed to make the ship run, but occasionally carrying official responses by the commander or personal messages from the crew to the families they had left behind.

"How's it goin' skipper?" said a voice behind him, rousing Jip from his work.

Looking over his shoulder, he saw that the voice belonged to Kent. Was his five hours up already?

"What time is it?" asked Jip, letting his electro-pad float freely for a moment.

"Time for me to change this music," said Kent as he reached overhead and played with some switches. A moment later, the latest swing-rock fusion music then popular back home replaced the Bach fugue that had been filling the cabin with is sonorous notes. "Better, huh?"

Jip shrugged. "I'm just glad to get out of here. Let me finish these notes so you can get them off to Earth."

As Kent took a seat at the communications console, Jip put the finishing touches on the day's progress report and handed the electro-pad to Kent. "Take care of that for me will you?"

"No prob," replied Kent, booting up the instruments.

Getting up from his seat, Jip ducked out of the command deck and moved into the narrow corridor that divided the Eagle-1 in exactly half. To his left were the three living units, one his own, and the others shared by a pair of crewmen each. On his right was a small galley and what the crew grandly called the "rec room" that contained a few pieces of exercise and health monitoring equipment and instrumentation for conducting various kinds of scientific research. At the moment, Jip caught sight of

Mart as the crewman worked the bike while fitted out with restraining straps and stirrups designed to keep the operator from floating away while he applied enough pressure on the pedals to get a decent workout in the otherwise zero g environment. On the other side of the rec room, Jersey was monitoring Mart's heart rate.

Continuing to the end of the corridor, Jip slipped into a small room that separated the forward part of the ship with its aft section and quickly closed the hatch behind him. The nerve center of the ship's computer system, the temperature here was a good 10 degrees cooler than in the crew's quarters the slightest variation of which would stet off alarms that would require Jip to fill out two days worth of paperwork and write up a complete report of whatever incident had caused the problem for transmission to Earth.

Strapping himself into a chair at one of two consoles, Jip punched in a password that allowed him access to a computer program that displayed a lengthy checklist of items representing every aspect of the ship's functions. Sighing, he began to scroll down stopping whenever he encountered a highlighted item and opening the file, did whatever he was required to solve the problem presented. The flagged items included either concerns raised by NASA staff back on Earth or those of his own found after studying the ship's log since the last time he'd been on duty.

When he finally emerged from the computer room, it was well into the third watch and he was ready for something to eat, a little exercise, and some sleep. It was the sleep he looked forward to the most though. Somehow, unobtrusively, it had become his salvation on the long voyage; the vaguely satisfying dreams he'd been having since leaving Earth orbit the only thing that seemed to bolster his spirits and fortify him for the next watch. In the soothing darkness of his quarters, he could forget the straps that held him to his bunk and the deadening routine aboard ship that threatened to rob him of the joy that had been his guiding star since he was a boy...

Jip leaned back against the main stem of the Joshua tree in which he was sitting and stared up at the blue sky stretching cloudless over the desert that made up California's Antelope Valley. Overhead, the heavens were crisscrossed with white contrails, most in varying degrees of dissipation. At the moment, one streak was in the process of being created as some plane, too high to be visible, thundered toward the north.

"Wonder what plane that is?" asked Danny from where he sat on the other side of the tree.

"Dunno," said Jip, still staring. He'd been feeling out of sorts all that morning, ever since waking up from a dream he'd had the night before, one that left him with a strong feeling of claustrophobia. There had been a sense of being trapped but he wasn't sure if it was due to limits on his physical movements or great frustrations that preyed on his mind. Try as he might, he couldn't recall exactly what his dream had been about but he was sure that if it had gone on any longer, he would eventually have been overcome with panic of some kind. The only way he'd found to successfully shake the gloomy feelings was to get outdoors, under the sky, and do his dreaming with his eyes open.

In his mind's eye, it wasn't the high flying plane that he saw streaking across the sky overhead, it was himself as he sat in the cockpit of an advanced model X-plane not yet built but perhaps in the planning stages or simply in the mind of some nameless engineer. Suited up in pressure gear, an airtight helmet sealed to a metal ring around his neck, Jip imagined himself easing up on a joy stick as his plane leveled off somewhere in the stratosphere. Beneath him, the Earth was draped in clouds that obscured the ground and overhead, the dark of space was punctured by a million stars...

"Scuttlebutt says there's a new plane they're working on; one that'll go right into space..." offered Tyler. "I head it's supposed to be fastened onto the belly of a B-52 and only dropped loose when both are miles above the ground."

"The X-15?"

"Shhh! Not so loud! It's supposed to be top secret!"

"Then how come everyone on the base knows about it?"

"The name is only its model number, those don't mean a thing."

"Still, I hope full development can wait until I get my wings," said Danny.

"Flying's all right, but I want to be in with the design team," said Tyler. "If my grades are good in high school, my dad said he'd see about getting me admitted to MIT."

"You've got no imagination, you know that Ty?" kidded Danny. "Hey! You guys want to go over to the Point and see if there's anything doing over a Rogers Lake?"

Rogers Lake was the smaller of two dry lake beds that also included the Rosamond. Together, they totaled 44.5 square miles of salt pan, the best in the world for testing high speed aircraft. Which was the reason why the Army Air Corps first began to use them as part of an airbase in the 1940s. Interestingly, though the lake beds were dry, there was some precipitation in the area but high winds kept the water from collecting and instead, picked it up and used it to scour the lake beds almost to a mirror like smoothness. In fact, the lakes were so hard and flat, that lines could be painted directly on their playa surfaces for use in designating runways for top performing aircraft.

When the Army first came to the area, they called the new base Muroc Army Air Field but following the death of pilot Glen Edwards in 1949 testing the Northrop YB-49, the base was renamed Edwards AFB and became the nation's number one test flight center where all the latest aircraft types from fixed wing and vertol to upright pogo planes and flying platforms were given their trial runs. Also tested at

Edwards were early rockets that at first were based on the German V-2 and then later prototypes for the Atlas and Titan missiles. As part of that testing regimen, tracks were laid for deceleration tests and, pioneered by Dr. John Stapp, the most powerful mechanical braking systems ever built were developed for use in high speed vehicles. Although begun with the idea of testing new aircraft designs, by the 1950s, Edwards had clearly evolved into something more: the cradle from which Americans would some day conquer even outer space.

"You think they might be using the rocket sled?" asked Tyler, perking up at mention of Rogers Lake.

"I thought I heard some engine noises up there when I got up this morning," said Danny promisingly.

Since Stapp's first sled, nicknamed the Gee Whiz, Air Force brass, impressed by the results, had gone ahead and built a longer, 10,000 foot model where the SM-62 Snark Cruise Missile became the first test subject.

Tyler stood up on the big rock that he'd been sitting on. "Then what are we waiting for? Why didn't you speak up sooner?"

Danny shrugged. "Forgot to mention it."

"Well, let's go," insisted Tyler. ""I've got the binoculars with my bike."

Giving in to the will of the majority, Jip shook off the lethargy he'd been feeling and jumped down from his perch. Making his way to where his bicycle stood by the edge of the unpaved road, he hit the kickstand with the heel of his foot and hopped into the saddle. A moment later, he and his friends had taken the road past the base housing and out into the desert heading the few miles to Lookout Point from where it would be easy to watch the doings around the rocket sled through Tyler's powerful binoculars.

By the time they reached the Point and had dropped their bikes onto the ground, the sun was high in the sky and the desert landscape around them shimmered in the heat. Sweating, Jip threw himself onto his belly at the crest of the small rise and waited his turn for the binoculars.

"See anything?" Danny asked Tyler.

"Just a sec," replied Tyler as he adjusted the lenses. "Yeah. There's definitely something going on down there. I see somebody sitting on the sled."

"Let me see," said Danny taking the binoculars. "You're right but I can't tell who it is."

"Do you really think that Stapp was the fastest man on Earth?" asked Tyler suddenly.

"I thought the Flash was the fastest man on Earth?" said Jip, smiling at his little joke.

"I mean the real thing, dummy!"

"Sure, why not? Anybody else ever go as fast as he did...before they broke the sound barrier that is?"

"My turn," said Jip, holding his hand out for the glasses. Danny handed them over.

Jip had hardly finished adjusting the lenses when a sudden roar came over the flat expanse of the dry lake bed and he saw something speed along the 10,000 feet of track faster than the eye could follow. Split seconds later, it was over and all he could see were men running to the figure strapped in the deceleration chair attached to the rocket sled. The figure reached up to remove its helmet and Jip saw him shaking his head as if to clear it.

"What happened? Is it over?" demanded Tyler grabbing the binoculars from in front of Jip's face.

"Wow!" exclaimed Jip, still stricken by how fast it had all happened. "That chair must have been going a thousand miles an hour!"

"And I missed it!" groaned Tyler, still trying to adjust the glasses.

"If a man is ever going to ride a missile into space, they must figure he has to be able to stand the same kind of acceleration that the rocket will," mused Jip. "That's why they're putting test pilots on the same sled that they tested the rockets on."

"Gosh!" breathed Danny. "Don't know if I want to go through that! My breakfast would've come up inside my helmet."

"Yech!"

"Well, there's not much shaking out there now," said Jip. "How about going for a swim at the base club?"

"Last one there's a rotten egg!"

That night, Jip finished the last chapter in Isaac Asimov's *Second Foundation* and put the book down on the night stand by his bed. Lying atop the sheets, he stared at the darkened desert outside the window and thought of the unknown pilot who had been flying the plane he had seen earlier in the day and the other man who had ridden the rocket sled. Each would very likely be rocketing into space some day soon and he couldn't help feeling a twinge of envy. Some day he would do the same; he only hoped that there would be some world left to explore or record to break by the time he did.

———————

Jip had woken up that morning wanting to look forward to his job; he really did.

He wasn't sure what had changed...maybe a good night's sleep. He'd dreamed about something he was sure, but exactly what, he couldn't say at least until he'd entered the command deck and glanced at the bank of display screens. There, he saw one crisscrossed with lines representing the tracks of various objects detected outside by the ship's sensors. For some reason, the pattern of the white lines seemed familiar. Then he made the connection: they looked like the contrails left by planes across an open sky, an effect that he was sure he'd dreamt about the night before. Seeing them, he felt his spirits boosted the way they used to be when he'd flown test planes into the sky early in his career.

Thinking about it now, he realized that he hadn't felt that kind of emotion for more years than he cared to count. How many times had he been pressed back into his pressure chair as the rocket he rode lifted off from its launch pad with tens of thousands of pounds of thrust pushing against the Earth? How many times was it that he felt the pressure of take off ease and the weightlessness of zero g take over?

More to the point, how many take offs had he endured before the thrill of being launched into space had vanished?

Suddenly, he found himself not wanting to think about it. Instead, he preferred to recall those early flights when it seemed all the study, all the responsibility, all the preparation was more than worth it. The eagerness he felt in loosing himself from the pull of the Earth and embracing the endless universe beyond was worth it all. How well he remembered those few precious days spent in orbit, at first strapped the whole time in his pressure chair, but on later missions able to move about a larger cabin. And that first space walk! First tethered to the spacecraft and later, in literal freefall when all he wore was a thruster pack to bridge the gulf between his ship and another. The months spent aboard the early space stations and then on the moon...it hardly seemed like months at all but only weeks...days!

Jip's thoughts of the happy times playing moon golf with the other veterans of the early space program ended abruptly when one of the crewmembers poked his head into the command deck.

"Hey, skipper, Mart says he needs to see you aft," said Jersey, jerking a thumb toward the rear of the spacecraft.

"Thanks, Jersey," said Jip without turning his head. Sighing, he turned off the computer he was using to review the ship's log, unbuckled himself from his chair, and pushed himself erect.

Passing from the command deck into the connecting corridor, Jip wondered what had evoked those memories of growing up at the old Edwards AFB before the base was closed? He smiled. It *had* been a while since he'd thought about those long gone days. *Whatever happened to Tyler Murfree?* he wondered. The two of them went through the Air Force Academy together and after earning their wings, were both assigned to Southeast Asia. Tyler was the first to run out of luck when he was shot down over North Vietnam but got it back again after he managed to walk out of the jungle near Khe Sanh three weeks later. After that, they both joined the space program and for a while they were paired for some early missions. Then Ty struck paydirt with a publisher who accepted a science fiction novel he'd written and the next thing he knew, his friend had switched careers. His books were pretty good too: all about the "high frontier" and whatnot. Hard SF it was called with nary a bug eyed monster in sight.

And Danny Ouelette? He and Ty lost touch with Danny early on. That's the way things were for military families. Always on the go. Always new schools to get used to and new friends to make. He supposed old Danny ended up in engineering the same as his dad.

But while they were all at Edwards, they were the best of friends. Nothing could separate them. During the days, they tore around the base on their bikes trying to find ways around security for a glimpse of an X-plane or some other crazy gadget the engineers were always dreaming up. At night, it seemed they never slept in their own beds but were always in the clubhouse at Tyler's house. He remembered building that clubhouse; how they scrounged all over the base for castoff material from corrugated iron sheets to wood scraps...they even stole a couple windows frames from a construction site at the north base! How many nights did he lay in that top bunk gazing out one of the stolen windows, looking at the stars, and wondering if he'd ever get to visit them?

Now here he was. Stopping for a moment, Jip turned to look back into the command deck where the bank of view ports gave a restricted view of the exterior. Because of the cabin lights, it was impossible to see outside, let alone the stars, but he knew they were there. For a moment a familiar feeling stole over him but almost as quickly was gone.

Needing to get back to business, Jip shook the thoughts from his mind and continued aft. Arriving at the hatch leading to the computer room, he passed through, secured it shut behind him and went to a second, circular hatch set in the opposite wall. Punching a green knob with his fist, the round hatch popped open and stooping, Jip peered inside.

"You there, Mart?" he called.

"Yeah, you want to come in here a minute, skipper?"

Jip took hold of a handle bar located above the hatch and lifted his legs through the opening. Inside, he found himself aboard the Eagle-2, the landing module that would separate itself from the Eagle-1 command craft and do the actual landing on Mars. At the moment, legs

folded, it was held in the ship's hold and protected from open space by a pair of long cargo
doors that enclosed the entire storage area.
Large enough for a crew of four, mission parameters actually called for only two members
to descend to the planet's surface: himself and
Will Montegue.

"Anything wrong?" asked Jip, knowing that
there must be otherwise Mart would not have
asked to see him. At the moment, his co-pilot
was looking at a computer screen showing the
module's planned descent path, one designed
years before by NASA engineers to take it to a
soft landing amid the ridged plains of the Valles
Marineris.

Jip settled down in the pressure chair
alongside Mart. "What's the problem?"

"I was running a routine test on the module's systems. Everything was fine until I got to
the descent parameters. Look."

Mart ran his fingers over the keypad and
hit enter but the screen didn't change. Still
displayed was the same descent pattern it had
shown since Jip sat down.

"Don't tell me the screen's frozen!"

Mart shrugged. "Okay, I won't."

"Did you try to reboot the system?"

"Yeah, but no dice."

"What about back up systems?"

"No good."

"Damn!" exclaimed Jip. "This would happen with only days before we go into orbit."

The program that ran the descent pattern
was vital in taking the module from Eagle-1
safely to the surface of Mars. Without it, there

were only two options left: either the landing portion of the mission would have to be aborted, or Jip would have to take the module down on manual; something the mission planners back home had hoped would never need to be considered.

Jip sighed with the knowledge that if the problem weren't fixed, he faced a tedious time delayed dialogue with mission control that would no doubt mean extending the time Eagle-1 would have to remain in orbit around Mars. He had no problem with taking the module down himself, but it was a worst case scenario that mission planners had hoped would never come to pass preferring to trust in their computers rather than human beings. For that reason, relatively little effort had been expended in training to prepare either commander or co-pilot for a possible manual descent.

Sighing, Jip banged his fist on the edge of the console.

"Look, Mart," he said. "Keep trying to get around the glitch, dig into the hyper text if you have to..."

"You sure about that? I mean, I'm not exactly trained for that..."

"We've got no choice," said Jip. "You can't screw it up any worse than it is now. I've got to have a good case when I lay it all before mission control; and I have to have the report ready to transmit in a couple days at the latest."

"Are you going to suggest completing the mission manually?"

"What else can I do? Sure as hell we haven't come all the way out here for nothing."

A few hours later, the situation had not improved and Jip became resigned to a lengthy exchange with mission planners via data stream. After sending his initial notice and his tentative plan to take the module in himself, he retired to his cabin for some rest before the expected replies began to come in.

He was busy strapping himself into his bunk when it occurred to him that he wasn't as upset about the potential change in plan as he ought to have been. In the past, even the slightest deviation from routine or expectation was enough to tie his stomach in knots of frustration and repressed anger but now, for some reason, there was none of that. Instead, he felt the corners of his mouth tending upward in a smile and there was a lightheartedness to his spirits that was completely unaccounted for given the unexpected glitch in the module's programming. Was he actually looking forward to flying the cumbersome thing down himself?

Unbidden, he once again thought of his old pals, Danny and Tyler and their days at Edwards when the thought of some day flying was still new and a notion filled with wonder and excitement. Curious, Jip reached overhead and pulled down his personal console from the ceiling panel. He tapped some keys accessing the ship's library. What was the name of Ty's first book? Something about stars or space or something... He tried searching for the key words and immediately a long column of book titles appeared, scrolling down to Murfree...there couldn't be many authors by that name...he found it: *To Pierce the Edge of Space.*

He hadn't intended to actually read the book, but it took only the first graph to draw him in and when he finally fell asleep hours later, it was with a clear understanding that it had been the lure of the unknown, the urge to be free, cut off from the bonds of Earth, that had first drawn he and his friends to flight, to go for the stars that twinkled just out of their reach as well as their imaginations. And though he had gone farther than either Danny or Tyler, he had still been held back by the limitations of his machines. Tyler was the first to go beyond the limits, to be the first into outer space if only in his imagination. But now, Jip had the opportunity to confirm what his friend believed even without first hand evidence. Suddenly, he seemed filled with purpose again and for the first time in years, he was looking forward to the unknown, regardless of the uncertainty, because that, after all, was why he had come.

Jip and his friends were killing time in the PX, enjoying the air conditioning and being out of the mid-afternoon heat. He and Danny sat on piles of newspapers that lined the bottom shelf of the store's magazine section while Tyler spun a wire rack holding a colorful array of comic books. Although the supply sergeant in charge of the store didn't care for kids hanging around and reading the comics without paying for them, he usually said nothing if he was able to make some token sales off them. In that respect, the three boys had already ante'd up their nickels for some giant sized freeze pops and between slurps, were able to flip through the latest issues of *Mystery in Space, Rawhide Kid*, and *Archie.*

"I don't know why you bother with those Archie comics," Jip was telling Danny. "They're dull."

"Says you," replied Danny without raising his head from the comic he was reading.

"I'll bet it's the girls he likes, Betty and Veronica!" teased Tyler from the spinner rack.

"It is not!" insisted Danny, his face flushing. "They're just funny."

"Sure!" said Tyler.

"Well, take this *Mystery in Space*," said Jip holding up the comic he was reading. It sported a garish cover with big red rockets, green BEMs, and a spaceman firing a ray gun. "Lots of adventure and hardly a girl in sight."

"Ah, even those comics are too stupid for anybody over 8 years old," said Tyler, dismissing the title. "Now for good science fiction stories, there's nothing like an old EC comic."

"Those old comics you got at home?" asked Jip.

"Right. Those are real stories with lots to read and good twist endings. The rockets in them look like they could really fly and the stories about jet fights in the Korean War are pretty authentic at least that's what my dad said."

"How come we never see any of those comics for sale?" Danny wanted to know. "I liked the *Aces High* comics you have."

"Don't know. The company went out of business I guess."

Moving over to the book section, Tyler found some new science fiction titles that drew his attention.

"Hey! Check this out! Some new Asimov and Arthur C. Clarke books!"

Immediately the other two were on their feet and looking over his shoulder at the paperbacks with their shiny new covers.

"I loved Asimov's *Foundaton* series," said Tyler thumbing through the contents page of a new anthology.

"Me too, " said Jip, looking over at the book section as the cover of a Lewis Padgett collection jumped out at him. "Lewis Padgett! I loved 'Mimsy Were the Borogoves' and The Twonky!' I'm getting this one."

"A paperback? That's going to set you back!"

"It'll be worth it!"

Together, the boys made their purchases and left the cool of the PX for the warmth of the desert sun.

"Let's get a Coke at my house then go over to the clubhouse to read some," suggested Jip.

"Sounds good," agreed Danny as he tucked his comics inside his shirt and hopped onto his Schwinn flyer. The others did the same and a little later they were in the clubhouse in varying states of relaxation and all absorbed in their latest purchases. As the afternoon wore on and temperatures began to cool, Danny's mother came out with tall glasses of lemonade slick with condensation and as the boys took long sips around floating ice cubes, conversation drifted as they often did, to subjects far from the mundane reality of Earth.

"Sure wish there were spaceships around today," said Tyler, who had been reading "The Calistan Menace," an early tale by Asimov. "We could take off for a quick spin around the Earth or maybe get marooned on some unexplored world. Wouldn't that be fun?"

"Sure, but how likely is that?" said a more logical Danny.

"My dad says that the space program is already planning to build a fleet of space shuttles; reusable space ships that'll be able to go into space and then land back on Earth. No disposable stages like in regular rockets," said Jip.

"Yeah, in the year 2000 maybe," replied a morose Tyler.

"Things'll be great then," said Danny with more enthusiasm. "There'll be monorails, and cities built up to the clouds, and everyone will have their own personal flyer!"

Jip took the paperback of Clarke stories he'd been reading and placed it on a shelf beside other SF books including those by Edmund Hamilton, Doc Smith, Jack Williamson, and Fred Pohl. One book however, suddenly caught his eye...*The Martian Chronicles* by Ray Bradbury...and suddenly something came to him. It teased at the edges of his consciousness until he realized it had been something he dreamed about the night before. What was it? Something he'd been dreaming about often lately...

"Something wrong, Jip?" asked Danny, noticing that his friend had frozen in place, the Clarke book still held in his hand, half way to the shelf.

"I was just trying to remember something I dreamed last night," said Jip, pushing the book into place and returning to where he'd been sitting on one of the bunks. "I think it was something to do with Mars."

"Mars, huh?"

"Yeah, give me a second," Jip said, getting up again and looking at the binding of the Bradbury book again. It was curled and worn, evidence of having passed through a number of hands and when he read the word "Mars" on its spine, it all began to come back to him. "Now I remember. I was on a spaceship headed to Mars. I was the commander."

"Was I there too?" Tyler wanted to know.

Jip shook his head. "No, I don't think so. It seemed as if I was alone aboard the ship even though I know there were others. There was something bothering me that kept me from enjoying the trip, from looking forward to being the first man on Mars."

"Boy, when you dream, you don't kid around!" said Danny, impressed. "Tell us more."

"I don't remember much else," said Jip. "Just that I should have been filled with anticipation and eagerness for being the first man on Mars, to step foot on another planet, but I wasn't. Then something happened to cheer me up and I began to feel better again."

"Wow," said Danny. "You think there's anything to dreams being hints about the future?"

"Nah," said Tyler. "That's just superstition. How could dreams tell the future? It's all psychology. Jip reads a lot of science fiction and comic books, see? Then he goes to sleep and dreams about what he read. Where's the mystery in that? Just don't tell my mom and dad I said so though...they'll use it against me the next time they need an argument to take away my comics when my grades start to slip!"

Danny laughed not noticing that Jip hadn't joined him. Soon after that, it was time for supper and the friends broke up each heading to their respective homes.

That night, Jip only picked at his food, a situation that didn't go unnoticed by his parents. His mother thought that he might be coming down with something, but his father, who had been a boy once himself, decided that it wasn't that.

"Leave the boy be, Eunice," advised his father. "I'll talk to him later."

After supper, unable to read or even concentrate on the television, Jip wandered outside. Sitting atop the rail fence that cut off the backyard from the open desert, he sat quietly watching the stars. A meteor shot across the heavens briefly and vanished in silence and he wondered about living and working in space. Not for the first time, it seemed to him that the stars were familiar friends of long acquaintance. Why was that?

"What's on your mind, Jip?" said his father suddenly.

Jip didn't turn around but simply replied: "Don't know, dad. Something about the stars tonight..."

"Friendly are they?"

Now Jip turned. "How do you figure that?"

His father leaned against the top rail of the fence, knitting his fingers together. "Known them all my life. Used to count on 'em to find my way back home when I was a Boy Scout in Nebraska. Later, when my old P-38 went down in the Solomons, they saved my life by helping me to find the fleet."

"What about when you fly, dad? When you take an X-plane way up to the edge of space. Do the stars still seem friendly up close?"

His father paused and considered before replying.

"I'll tell you something I've never told anyone else, son," said his father. "When I get up there close to the edge of space where the stars are all cold and real and twinkling, they call out to me. Like they really were old friends who'd been waiting out there patiently for me. When I feel their welcoming, it sometimes takes everything I have not to keep going but then I remember you and your mother and it becomes easy to say goodbye and take that long roll back to Earth. Maybe those stars are your friends too, Jip. And maybe some day, you'll do what I couldn't and go out there to meet them at last. If you do, don't forget to say 'hey' for me, will you?"

For the first time since recalling his dream earlier that afternoon, Jip smiled and knew everything would turn out all right. He would learn to fly, join the Air Force, become a rocketman; and if he had the chance, he'd go to Mars too.

Turning to go back to the house, feeling his father's arm around his shoulders, Jip looked back at the desert sky and noticed the red glint of Mars as it began to rise above the horizon.

"Be seeing you," he whispered under his breath.

——— —— ——

Jip woke up that day, the 251st of the over 56,000,000 kilometer journey from Earth to the red planet, with the realization that it had always been his intention to be the first to set foot on Mars.

Seemingly for the first time during the long voyage he felt calm in being where he was and a satisfaction in the simple anticipation of entering upon a new world, a feeling that he hadn't felt since he was a boy. Unbidden, he recalled the stars over the California desert that he had studied so often and noticed for the first time that they didn't look much different than those that stared in at him from outside the Eagle.

Standing at the entrance of the command deck, he watched his crew work the computer consoles, double checking their orbit around the planet that now dominated the scene outside the cabin's view ports. Had it only been a few days before that the Eagle made its final approach to Mars, completing the Hohman transfer orbit that had taken advantage of the planet's closest approach to Earth and brought it neatly into orbit at the conclusion of the nine month journey? Everyone, including himself, had held their breath when it came time to let the computers take over, what with the continuing problem with the landing program, no one was sure whether anything would go wrong with the orbital insertion program as well. Luckily nothing did and they soon found themselves chasing down the supply drone that had been launched from Earth two years ahead of their own departure in anticipation of this historic day.

"There it is," declared Mart from his place in the pilot's chair. Although previously detected and tracked by the ship's computers, the supply drone had only then become visible to the naked eye and the co-pilot was the first to spot it.

"I see it," said Will, leaning over from his console for a better look outside.

Jip found himself drawn further into the cabin as he too tried to lay eyes on the drone. Slowly, the greater velocity of the Eagle began to close the gap between the two vessels and in another hour, with the bulk of the drone filling the scene out the forward view ports, everyone felt the gentle nudge that indicated the ships had come into contact.

"Secure docking latches," ordered Jip.

"Latches secured," replied Mart running his hands over his computer console.

"Open inner seals and release the oxygen," said Jip.

"Done," said Mart, as the faint sound of hissing air was heard from beyond a hatch set beneath the forward consoles. "Indicators show green."

"I'm going forward," said Jip, ducking into the well and releasing the latches holding the hatch shut.

A moment later, the portal had opened and Jip slipped through into the narrow space separating the nose of the Eagle and a second hatch giving access to the interior of the drone. When that had also opened, he passed into the other ship. His entry caused the lights to come on and a quick inspection verified that the supplies were safe.

"Everything's set," said Jip after he had returned to the Eagle and dogged the hatch shut again. "We can start our pre-flight schedule right after lunch."

"Yay bo!" shouted Mart, coming out of his chair so fast that he almost hit the ceiling of the cabin.

A message was boosted back to Earth notifying mission control of the successful docking and while waiting for the expected reply, the crew enjoyed their last meal together, at least for the next several months. Afterwards, while Jip and Will ran through the pre-flight schedule on Eagle-2, Kent, Mart, and Jersey transferred a portion of the supplies from the drone. When they were finished, Jip joined them on the command deck and watched as the drone was detached from the Eagle and with its retro rockets firing, directed into an eccentric orbit that would take it on a one way trip to the surface of Mars ahead of the landing module.

With that done, the crew retired to their bunks for a few hours sleep and when they returned to duty refreshed, Jersey gave Jip and Will a last minute checkup before allowing them to suit up and enter the landing module. Mart, with Jersey standing by, then made sure the hatch was secure and gave the "okay" sign to the two inside by way of a tiny porthole.

A few minutes later, the radiophone crackled inside his helmet and Jip heard Mart's voice saying "One, two, three, testing."

"Testing," replied Jip, adjusting the frequency and eliminating the crackle. "Got you coming in loud and clear."

"Roger that, skipper," said Mart. "I'm piping in a transmission from control."

A moment later, Jip heard the familiar voice from Earth. Winston Joy, chief mission control officer at NASA who had shepherded the crew every inch of the way from orientation to take-off.

"This is mission control," said Joy, his transmission boosted to near real time. "Am I clear with the Eagle-2?"

"You're clear," replied Jip. "Go ahead, Win."

"Jip, we read all systems go at this end; how do you read?"

"Green, green, green," said Jip. "The supply module has been successfully deposited on ground zero, the Valles Marineris, as planned. Will and I have just completed the pre-flight protocol and everything is go for a manual launch."

"You sure you still want to go through with this, Jip?" asked Win. "You know you can cancel any time with no blame from this end."

"I know, Win. But I've discussed the situation with Will and the rest of the crew and they have expressed every confidence in my ability. We're all prepared to see the mission through."

"I realize that saying anything at this point would be superfluous because you already know how important the successful conclusion of this mission is to the agency and the nation," said Win, saying what everyone already knew. "Closer to home, there are thousands of people who have put millions of man hours into this project and I'm sure I don't have to remind you how much they have invested personally in this project. But be that as it may, the crew's safety has always been uppermost in their minds and if you felt it was unwise to continue with the mission, no one would blame you for turning back."

Jip smiled at the sentiments. "The crew is well aware of the feelings of everyone involved with the project and have vowed not to let either them or the country down."

"Then Godspeed Eagle!"

"Roger that, control."

"We're all set here," said Mart over Jip's headset. "Ready when you are."

"Then let's go!"

A dull thrum began to vibrate through the module as bright sunlight suddenly lanced into the aft storage compartment where Eagle-2 lay like a moth in its cocoon. Then, as the cargo doors reached their fullest extension, the launch rail upon which the module rested began to rise and as it did, the lander's spindly legs started to unfold like the limbs of a butterfly. Inside, Jip had begun the launch sequence that saw small retro rockets outside the lander flame to life and Eagle-2 to pull against its restraints as if eager to be free.

"Releasing restraints," said Jip, feeling the pressure of acceleration almost immediately as the module shot from its launch rail and away from Eagle-1.

Controlling his excitement, Jip ran his hands expertly over the lander's control console even as he called for readings on the status of the module's systems. Not hearing but absorbing on a subconscious level the information Will was reading off to him, Jip inserted the lander into the proper orbit and began its powered descent. As the vehicle approached closer and closer to a planetary surface unobscured by any atmosphere to speak of, geographical details resolved themselves easily and his pilot's eye for landscape began to make out such features as mountains and valleys and canyons and desert wastes. Lower still, and he saw great rubble strewn plains veined with what looked like dry river beds that early astronomers had once thought were "canals."

And with the lander's ever increasing speed, the closer it approached to the surface, the more exhilarated Jip felt. At last, all the alienation and dissatisfaction he had experienced on the long voyage from Earth dissipated completely, like the morning dew that Mars had never seen. He was once again the boy who soloed when he had earned his pilot's license, the young man who had earned his wings in the Air Force, the soldier who had fought for his life in the skies over Vietnam, the veteran who had succeeded his father in testing X-planes over the American desert, the astronaut who had walked in space and set foot on the moon. How could he ever have forgotten those thrilling moments of triumph and joy? As a boy he had yearned to break the bonds of Earth's gravity and reach for the stars; old friends whom he had already visited in dreams borne of science fiction and hours spent stargazing in his backyard.

Suddenly, even as the module righted itself in anticipation of landing and its main rocket flamed on to slow its descent, Jip's mind leaped back 20 years to the desert at Edwards AFB, a night filled with stars, and a reassuring hand on his shoulder.

The red landscape outside the lander's tiny view ports was rushing by now almost too fast to see and all that was visible was a reddish landscape relieved only by an occasional shadow. But Jip didn't need to see anything more as he expertly guided the module to a successful landing.

On the surface at last, the roar of the engines silent, neither Jip nor Will said anything, both absorbed in the historic moment.

Hours later, after the two men had emerged from the lander and done their duty for the cameras and the people back home, Jip found a moment to walk by himself for a few minutes and to stare out over the flat, red landscape that rose abruptly to meet a pinkish sky in the distance. It was the Mars so many had dreamed of: his father's, Danny and Ty's, even writers like Ray Bradbury and Edgar Rice Burroughs. And now, at last, it was his too and with his heart bursting in the fulfillment of a lifelong passion he had lost for a time but only now was beginning to understand, he greeted the ancient world like an old friend and delivered a message given to him many years before.

"Told you I'd be seeing you," said Jip. "And Jake Norflinger said to say hey!"

The Day the Computers Failed

JON KINESPEE REMEMBERED HOW it was before baseball, before cooking, and even before
the existence of Time.

In those days, when he was much younger,
machines had done it all and people did nothing for themselves...except for Mr. Lenoir who
alone knew what to do in the days immediately
following the arrival of the Pulse.

The funny thing was that before the Pulse,
no one realized that anything was missing from
their lives. Not Jon's dad, not his mom, not his
little sister Sal, not even his dog Spot, or the
two goldfish the family kept in a compu-tank in
the living room.

Life had always been complete from the
automated homes people lived in to the smart
highways that they drove along to the intel-
games they played. Nothing was left out; nothing left to chance; nothing missing.

Every morning began the same way when
the house computer would awaken family
members to begin a new day. First, dad and
mom would be woken with the soothing tones
of a wordless ditty and when they had reached
the required level of post-sleep consciousness,
the computer's strategically hidden speakers
would resonate with carefully chosen words

whose modulation were designed to bring its listeners to full alertness with the least chance of discomfort.

When fully awake, dad would get up and head for a shower that was already running with water at a temperature intended to complement the wakening process. Emerging from the shower, dad would take his place in the auto-chair where machines would shave his face, comb his hair, brush his teeth, and massage his body with scientific exactitude. Getting to his feet once more, dad would step into his clothes for the day which were also chosen by the house computer on the basis of information provided by the business computer that ran dad's place of employment.

Meanwhile, a similar procedure had been performed on mom in her own computerized bathroom and when she emerged to head for the kitchen, the bed was already made and any loose articles left around the night before picked up and put away or whisked into hidden laundry chutes. In the kitchen, mom arrived just in time to make sure breakfast was ready before saying good morning to Jon and Sal.

Although timed by the house computer to all arrive in the kitchen at the same time for breakfast, the children had undergone a slightly different early morning procedure than their parents.

Both Jon and Sal were awakened in the same soothing manner as the adults and gently urged into their separate bathrooms for their morning ablutions. Among other things, Jon's hair was applied with an oily compound then popular with 11-year-olds that allowed it to be molded into any shape desired while Sal's dress was adorned in the latest ankle length style with a trim of tiny bells attached around the hem.

Eventually, the entire family was gathered in the kitchen and as they took their places around the table, an assortment of mechanical instruments emerged from beneath the surface to serve breakfast.

"Will you be home at the regular time this evening, dear?" asked mother of her husband.

"6:15 as always," replied father dabbing lightly at the corners of his mouth with a disposable napkin. "You know my schedule has been arranged all in advance by the company's central computer. I'm sure the house computer will be informed if there's any change."

"I'm sure," said mother. "It's just that I won't be home for dinner this evening as I have choir practice tonight."

"The church computer on the blink again?"

"No, but I have to make sure the new arrangement downloads have been installed properly by the music company computer."

"Don't trust the machines?" It was a rhetorical question, an old joke really, that had lost all meaning over the decades since the last major computer malfunction in 2057.

"I don't understand why we can't just go to school at home," complained Sal only for the thousandth time it seemed. "We can plug in to the virtual classroom just as easily here as across town."

"You know the answer to that question as well as I do," said mother. "Computer studies have shown that children need regular interaction with young people their own age. Walking to school with the other children is valuable for proper social development."

"Humph," said Sal, holding her mouth open to allow the computer assisted spoon to place cereal in it for her.

Jon watched as his own spoon vanished into the table top along with his cereal bowl and sighed as he lifted a glass of orange juice on his own and downed its contents in a few gulps.

"Jon!" said his mother. "Where are your manners? Let the computer feed you."

"Aw, ma! I'm too old for that now."

Following breakfast, father headed for the garage stall while the children kissed their mother goodbye and left the house by the front door.

In the garage, the door to the family car opened by itself and father slipped into the driver's seat. Disregarding the steering wheel (a relic from 2057), he hit the start button and the vehicle's automated systems came to life. Light's glowed and a familiar hum emanated from the computer regulated engine that operated on a microscopic fragment of atomic material. Slowly, the garage door began to rise and in another few seconds the car rolled outside and down the driveway to the road in front of the house.

Sitting back and catching the news on the vid monitor mounted in the dashboard, father let the on board computer do the driving as it opened communications with the city's master computer that recognized the family's particular vehicle and integrated its intended course with hundreds of thousands of others that made up the morning traffic stream. The trip to work however, was far from the frustrating experience that had once plagued commuters as the master computer, in cooperation of the thousands of other workplace computers, arranged work schedules in such a way that hindrances in traffic were reduced to nothing. Accidents involving motor vehicles were unheard of.

Meanwhile, after leaving their home, Jon and Sal stepped onto the sidewalk conveyor that took them and other neighborhood children to a branch conveyor down the street and with increasing numbers of young people, they were conducted to PS 12 where they were met by their teachers who separated them by grade and led them to their respective classrooms. There, each child immediately took their places at personal consoles, placed learning hoods over their heads, and entered a virtual classroom for their first lesson of the day.

Back at home, mother went to the house computer console to begin setting the program for the rest of the day. During the morning, she would observe the house electronic aparati as they made the beds, dusted the furniture, tended the yard, and a hundred other tasks, making sure that all was done according to her wishes. In the afternoon, she might take the sidewalk conveyor to do some errands, work on her column for the daily newspaper, and finally join other women in the neighborhood for refreshments and conversation while they waited for the children to come home from school.

Yes, to Jon, life in those days seemed complete with nothing left to chance...except for old Mr. Lenoir.

Mr. Lenoir lived by himself in the big house at the top of the street. Dominating the neighborhood, the house looked down over the rest of the community as if it were a creature out of time, which in a sense it was, because unlike other buildings of its kind, it was the only one Jon knew that did not have a house computer. And strange as it seemed, Mr. Lenoir didn't mind the personal hardship of being cut off from the electronic network that made life as easy as it was. In fact, Jon recalled more than once seeing him puttering about his well manicured yard trimming the hedges, mowing the lawn, or pruning the apple trees while humming a jaunty tune or two; exactly as if he were enjoying himself.

Indoors, or so Jon had heard from adults who shook their heads in pity for the old man, Mr. Lenoir was similarly bereft of computerized help doing his own housework, preparing his own meals, and even driving his own car! Jon could hardly imagine what that kind of life could be like with its tedium and drudgery but it was one they would all learn much more about the day after the Pulse hit the Earth.

Afterwards, Jon had heard on the television that the Pulse had begun somewhere far out in space, maybe following the collapse of a dead star, or an unexpected shift in the radio waves caused by the collision of negative and positive galaxies, or the sudden surge of dark matter emanating from a black hole. Whatever its origins, the Pulse had probably been traveling through space for thousands or millions of years before striking the Earth and shorting out every computer on the planet.

In an instant, without any warning, the memory banks of every electronic brain from vast and complex central cores that coordinated the activities of whole continents to Jon's personal all purpose GPS monitor were wiped clean and all activity linked to any kind of computer at all seized, throwing the whole world into chaos and confusion.

Luckily, however, there were no real panics and government agencies stepped into the breach to reassure the public that the disaster was not life threatening. Quicker than most people realized (at least so it seemed to Jon at the time), the major functions of civilization were taken over by human operators, albeit with chores being accomplished at a much slower rate. Traffic for instance, became a confusing mess for a while and for a few months food distribution became spotty. But all that was on a scale beyond Jon's direct experience. For he and Sal and their friends, the new world created by the Pulse was a frightening one filled with an uncertainty that even their parents were hard pressed to comfort them over.

Then reassurance came from an unexpected quarter.

One by one, people in the neighborhood began to make the trek up the hill to the home of Mr. Lenoir. At first, forced by the inexorable plant growth around their homes, they asked to borrow his hand tools: hedge clippers and grass cutters, then water cans and yard rakes. Following their husbands' example, the women of the neighborhood began to appear at Mr. Lenoir's back door at first seeking advice on how to prepare food themselves and later for items that were suddenly indispensable in preparing those meals: sugar and flour and eggs.

Suddenly thrown onto their own resources, Jon and his friends were at a loss how to entertain themselves. Temporarily suspended from school as lesson programs were reorganized, the children discovered that they had plenty of free time to do what they wanted but with no idea how to use it. Their virtual vid helmets were useless and the games and music available on their all purpose GPS monitors had been erased. In addition, their individualized home entertainment systems that allowed them to visit and play anywhere they wanted to from ancient China to the ice fields of Pluto were down for the count.

As a result, children were seen wandering about the neighborhood in aimless circles or sitting on the curb beside the useless sidewalk conveyors or simply sprawled on their beds listlessly waiting for the computers to come back on. At last, frustrated with the situation, Jon tore his useless virtual vid helmet from his head and dashed it to the floor with such violence that the pieces flew in every direction.

With a growl in his throat, he stomped to the bedroom window and looked out over the dead streets of the empty neighborhood.

It was a hot summer day and the green leaves of the trees fluttered here and there in stray gusts of warm wind. Along the streets, he could see some of the neighbors as they attacked lawns and shrubbery that had grown noticeably longer and shaggier in the days since the computers failed. Forced to do the work themselves, many of those adults who had gone to Mr. Lenoir for advice had returned with borrowed tools which they had to operate by hand. Not familiar yet with how to use them, the results of their yard work was spotty at best and not at all as uniformly efficient as when it had been performed by domestic machines. But seeing the work being done gave Jon an idea. If the adults could get useful information on how to cope with the new situation, why couldn't he?

Energized by the revolutionary thought, Jon left his room and took himself outdoors. There, in the bright sunshine, he walked up the street along the stilled sidewalk conveyors in the direction of Mr. Lenoir's house.

As he approached, the first thing he noticed was that there were no security cams around the property nor were there any garden robots anywhere in sight. Although both would have been out of order due to the Pulse, their metallic carcasses should have still been in place or stored somewhere around the property. But what surprised him was how neat the landscaping around the old house was in spite of Mr. Lenoir never having used robots to keep things trim. Somehow, Jon had never considered that it could be possible for a single person to keep up with the trimming, cutting, pruning, painting, sweeping, and all the other work incumbent upon home ownership. At the very least, he had expected a ragged look to everything with a yard that resembled more a jungle than a well manicured garden.

So it was with rising curiosity that he approached the big front door and waited to be scanned and announced but after a few minutes he suddenly realized that even if Mr. Lenoir had employed a house computer, it would not have been operational. Feeling somewhat foolish, Jon knocked on the door the way he had seen others do it in virtual vids depicting the times before computers. His knocking was rewarded with the sound of approaching footsteps from inside the house and a moment later the door swung wide and Mr. Lenoir stood in the opening.

"Well, young man, what can I do for you?" he said.

Suddenly, Jon was at a loss for words. He had indeed been bored but what exactly was he looking for to relieve the tedium? What could Mr. Lenoir, who had never relied on computers, offer him in the way of divertissement?

"Cat got your tongue, lad?"

Jon stared at Mr. Lenoir's kindly features. He had thought him elderly but now on closer examination, he seemed younger than that. In fact, he did not seem that much older than his father. His hair was gray to be sure, but it still had many dark threads woven among the white and only the corners of his eyes displayed wrinkles that appeared when he squinted. His posture was erect and when he extended his hand in greeting, Jon could not help but notice how firm it was.

"I know you," said Mr. Lenoir then. "You're the Kinespee boy aren't you?"

"Yes, sir," said Jon, finding his voice at last.

"Come here because your mother has a question about what to fix for supper? Your father want to know how to change a spark plug in the lawn mower?"

"Uh, not exactly," said Jon. "I came to ask you something for myself."

"I see! Well, then, why don't you step inside so we can discuss the matter?"

Jon did so and as Mr. Lenoir closed the door behind him, he noticed immediately a strange smell that permeated the inside of the house.

"Something bothering you, lad?" asked Mr. Lenoir, noticing how Jon's nose had wrinkled up at the smell.

"Just something in the air I guess...what are those?" asked Jon suddenly, pointing at the rows of shelves that lined the walls of the house.

"Haven't you ever seen books before?" asked Mr. Lenoir not without some irritation.

"Is that what they are? I've never seen real books before. Just in the virtual vids."

Mr. Lenoir shook his head in pity.

"Never seen a real book before? Never held one in your hands? Never felt the spine of a new book crinkle when it was opened for the first time? Never smelled that aroma of ink and pulp paper?"

"Is that what I'm smelling?"

In reply, Mr. Lenoir took down one of the books from the shelf, opened it and held it up to Jon's nose.

"Breath deep," said Mr. Lenoir. "Because if you were *20,000 Leagues Under the Sea* with Captain Nemo, it's a sure bet you wouldn't be able to."

Jon did so and the peculiar aroma tickled to the back of his throat and he almost sneezed.

"Here try this one," said Mr. Lenoir, replacing the first book and taking down another. "Can you smell the water of the mighty Mississippi in *Huckleberry Finn?*"

"No," said Jon with some disappointment. "It sort of smells just like the other book."

"Pshaw!" declared Mr. Lenoir in disgust. "You're nose is just out of practice. You don't read enough."

"Read? The computer teacher does that for me. And besides, reading is too slow, too dull!"

As soon as the words were out of his mouth, Jon knew he had said the wrong thing.

"Reading...dull?! Impossible! Listen, lad; have you ever actually read a book before?"

Jon had to admit that he had not.

"Then how do you know what you're talking about? Don't you know that every book has its own scent? *The Maltese Falcon* smells of gunpowder and *The Call of the Wild* like wet animal fur. You can almost smell the rotting jungle in *Tarzan of the Apes* and the dank scent of soggy moors in *Jane Eyre*; but best of all is the rocket fumes in books like *The Martian Chronicles* and *The Gray Lensman*! But never mind about those, you can start with Doc Savage" he said, handing a very old book to Jon with the cover long since missing. "There's the smell of the ocean in that one and sweat and laboratory experiments gone wrong, and even a dash of talcum powder...but never mind all that for now. First, read it and savor it and enjoy it. You'll be back for more in no time, I'll guarantee it!"

Jon said nothing, preferring not to upset Mr. Lenoir more than he had already done. Carefully, he slipped the battered paperback into the front pocket of his shirt.

"Now here," Mr. Lenoir was saying, "I keep my magazines filled with adventures in time and space and every exotic land in between..."

"Uh, Mr. Lenoir..." said Jon, clearing his throat.

"Yes, lad?"

"What I really came for was to ask if you had any ideas for what I could do with my friends now that all of our virtual vids aren't working..."

"Bored, eh?" said Mr. Lenoir immediately.

Jon nodded. "I thought that maybe you could give us some advice the way you've been doing with the adults."

Mr. Lenoir paused and rubbed his chin.

"Ever hear of baseball?" he asked suddenly.

"Wasn't it a show they used to have a long time ago on something called a television?"

"Pshaw!" said Mr. Lenoir again. "No one ever intended baseball to simply be watched but played and played by real live people...running, jumping, catching, hitting!"

"Hitting?" said Jon, slightly alarmed.

"A ball, lad. Why do you think the game is called base-*ball*?"

"Oh," was all a relieved Jon could muster.

"I take it you haven't got a base or a ball...or even a bat?"

"What are they?"

Mr. Lenoir heaved with the heaviest sigh Jon had ever seen.

"Looks like I'll have to start from the beginning. Come with me, lad."

Jon followed Mr. Lenoir through the house to a door that led down a flight of wooden stairs to a musty basement filled with tools and another smell that he later learned to associate with the cutting of wood.

Mr. Lenoir reached up and pulled a cord that lit a fluorescent light situated over a work table cluttered with tools and metal receptacles filled with nails. Fascinated, Jon picked up a hammer and wondered at how it felt in his hand.

"Like that feel?" asked Mr. Lenoir, recognizing instantly the instinctual connection of a boy to a tool. "Here's what I'm looking for."

Mr. Lenoir had taken a broom with a long wooden handle and laying it lengthwise in a vise clamped to the work table, he spun a handle until the sweeping implement was held in a fast grip. Next, he took a hand saw down from the wall, measured a length of the broom handle with his eye, and began to cut.

Jon watched Mr. Lenoir work with fascination, never having seen anyone do such a thing.

In a remarkably short time, Mr. Lenoir had cut through the broom handle and was giving the loose piece a few tentative swings in the air. Satisfied, he put it down and began rummaging among some old boxes on the floor. Presently, he returned with something in his hand. He tossed it to Jon.

"Think quick!" Mr. Lenoir said with a chuckle.

Startled, Jon reached out and tried to catch what proved to be a soft sponge rubber ball but missed.

"You'll have to do better than that if you want to win at baseball," said Mr. Lenoir watching him as he scrambled to retrieve the loose ball. "Now toss it back to me."

Finally in control of the ball, Jon did as he was told and was surprised to see how easily the old man caught the ball even while holding the broom handle in one of his hands.

"Don't look so astonished," he said. "It's simple once you get the hang of it and you will, faster than you think."

At that point, Mr. Lenoir led the way back upstairs and at the kitchen table with glasses of lemonade at their elbows, he drew a diagram of a diamond shaped object that Jon soon learned was a representation of the field upon which baseball was played. At first, as the old man explained the concept of "bases" and "outs" and "home runs," it all seemed terribly confusing to Jon, but gradually as the rules began to sink in, the picture in his mind jelled and soon he was imagining himself swinging the broom handle at the ball and running around the bases with the wind running through his hair.

At last, Mr. Lenoir folded up the paper with the diagram and tucked it in Jon's shirt pocket along with the copy of the Doc Savage book and conferred on him the broom handle and sponge ball with all the gravity of a king of old giving a knight his sword.

"There you are, lad," said Mr. Lenoir stepping back. "Go forth and play baseball!"

Not sure how the other children in the neighborhood would take to the new game, Jon determined to at least give it a try. After all, the old man had insisted that it was more fun than a virtual vid, which even Jon found hard to believe.

After a lunch of ham sandwiches, a wedge of angel food cake, and chocolate milk (which his mother took pride in having prepared herself), Jon left the house to round up as many of his friends as he could find. When he did, and they were all standing together in a rough group in an empty lot a few streets away from his house, it was a strange sensation because he could not remember a time when he had associated at the same time with more than one or two other boys in his life. More often, they gathered on the virtual plane to play Dungeons and Swords or World Wrecker or to go mountain climbing in Tibet. As a result, there was quite a bit of foot shuffling with no one really sure how to associate with the others on a personal level. At last, by reason of his having interfaced with Mr. Lenoir, Jon took control of the situation.

"All right, gather round," he said as he crouched down and unfolded the paper with the diagram that Mr. Lenoir had given him. "I'll explain to you how we're going to play this game."

"What did you say it was called?" asked Swifty.

"'Baseball,'" said Jon as he flattened the paper on the grass.

"Never heard of it," said Tom. "Is it like virtual bashback?"

"No, nothing like that," replied Jon. "You play this for real."

"For real?" said Swifty. "Like in we have to run and stuff?"

"Yeah, what's so bad about that?"

Swifty shrugged. "Just don't feel like knockin' myself out chasin' a ball all over the place."

"Oh, get over it," said Jon, exasperated by an attitude he himself had shared not a few hours before. Since then, the idea of playing a game for real had grown on him and he was anxious to give it a try. "Now here's how it's played."

The next half hour was taken up with explanations and answers to his friend's questions. In the meantime, other children who had observed them from nearby homes began to drift over, drawn by the possibility of being relieved of their boredom. In no time, there were enough children to form the "teams" Mr. Lenoir had spoken about.

Finding bits of metal and disposal waste containers around the lot, Jon instructed the others how to place them to represent the "bases" and standing in a circle, they began to toss the ball to each other, getting used to its feel and how to move in order to catch it before it struck the ground.

Soon however, with a young boy's patience being what it is, there was a general consensus that the game should begin. Choosing "teams" in the manner Mr. Lenoir had showed him how to do Jon, acting as one of the "captains" asked for another for the opposing team and when Tom stepped forward, they began to choose sides. That done, the broom handle was thrown to Jon who caught it in a single hand (a skill that delighted and surprised more than one of the boys). Tom then placed his hand above Jon's followed by Jon's free hand and in such manner, Tom's team was selected to "bat" first.

After that, Jon lost all track of time as did everyone else as cautious and clumsy play slowly evolved into something resembling self-confidence. By late afternoon, at least two games had already been concluded with everyone exhausted but paradoxically exhilarated from running back and forth in the "outfield" and dashing madly from base to base. It took no time at all for them to discover the pleasure of sliding into home base under a wild throw from the "infield" or diving full length for "fly balls" in the outfield so that by supper time there was not a boy whose clothes was not streaked in dirt and who didn't take pride in knees covered in grass stains. They were having so much fun that supper time had come and gone and the glow of the streetlights had been illuminated for quite a while before anyone noticed how late it was.

"Gee, my mother's going to be wondering where I am!" muttered Tom.

"I didn't even notice that it got dark!" exclaimed a breathless Swifty.

"Should we quit and go home?" asked another boy.

There was silence. Although the streetlight gave some illumination, it was near impossible in the dark to see a ball plunging into the outfield. Nevertheless, it was proving difficult for anyone to tear themselves away from the "diamond" that by then had been etched in the grass. Suddenly, however, the problem was solved when Jon's father appeared from the darkness.

"Jon, is that you?"

"It's me dad," replied Jon, stepping into the glow cast by the streetlight.

"Wow! Are you a sight!" exclaimed his father who found it difficult to recognize his son beneath the grime that covered his face and arms and the dirty clothes that boasted a number of tears that had not been in them when Jon left home that morning.

"Sorry," said Jon, looking down at himself. "We were playing baseball."

"Baseball, huh?"

"You know it?" asked Jon, catching a strange tone in his father's voice.

"I remember the word," said his father, rubbing his chin. "I think your grandfather mentioned it to me once...something people used to play before virtual vids."

"That's it. It's a game like we play on the virtual plane except you play it for real."

His father wrinkled his nose at the notion. "Running and jumping and skipping? Ugh. Anyway, time to head for home. It's late and you missed your supper."

"See you guys tomorrow?" asked Jon in a last look over his shoulder.

"You bet!" said the other boys all at once clapping each other on the shoulder and shaking hands as they broke up and headed to their various homes.

Jon saw the family car parked alongside the road directly beneath the streetlight and when he had slid into the passenger seat, noticed that a number of components were missing from the dashboard.

"What happened to the vid monitor?" asked Jon.

"Didn't need it any more," replied his father as he actually turned a key in the ignition to start the engine. "I had a technician take it out but had to make an appointment to go back and have the space filled with a computer free music console. It'll have a receiver so that I can hear the traffic reports on the way to work. No more computers to automatically avoid slow downs you know."

Jon marveled as he watched his father take hold of the steering column and guide the car away from the curb and into the middle of the road. All the way home, he fought against holding his breath while the car moved strictly under the guidance of a human hand. The whole experience was positively eerie.

Later that evening, all scrubbed clean and feeling more contented than he had ever felt in his life, a smiling Jon lay back in his bed, his hands folded behind the back of his head and dreaming of all the homeruns he would make the next day. What fun baseball was! How exhilarating to use his body and expend his youthful energy for tumbling in the grass, racing from base to base, swinging the bat with all his might and watching the ball as it climbed into the blue heavens and then arc down almost out of sight!

Looking around his room, Jon's eyes spotted the vid helmet lying useless on the floor. He had no desire at all to put it on, even if he hadn't smashed it earlier in the day. The vistas of Tibet and Mars and the bottom of the Atlantic Ocean now seemed unreal and unsatisfying. How could he ever have thought living in that world was fun, even fulfilling? With a new perspective, he realized how empty and shallow those worlds were with their too sharp images and perfect settings that didn't even allow him to suffer so much as a scratch even after wrestling with Bengal tigers or Venusian swamp snakes. Touching one of the half dozen scratches that adorned his body, the sting reminded him of the day's exertions, and proved that he had actually gone and done the things he remembered doing. Could he ever have said the same thing about the worlds he had visited in virtual vids?

Jon swung his legs off the bed and going over to the remains of his helmet, picked it up and took it to the window. Lifting the sash, he flung the helmet out into the darkness and listening, heard a satisfying crash as it struck the pavement of the street out front. Back inside again, he began to pull the room's house computer unit and individualized home entertainment system outlets from their housings; wires snapped and fastenings groaned their resistance to being ripped from the wall, but at last they were all free and collected in a pile in the center of the floor. Tomorrow, he would throw them all out.

Suddenly there was a noise behind him and whirling, he saw Sal at the door. She was staring at the pile of wires and switch panels on the floor.

"You think father and mother will be angry?" asked Jon.

"Maybe, except that I think I saw mother herself throwing out components," said Sal. "She said she needed more room in the kitchen for groceries. C'mon."

Jon followed his sister into her own room and there found a pile of junk on the floor that looked very much like the one he had made.

"You too?"

"I've got better things to do than play house with Neptunian ice princesses and designing clothes for the miss alien species pageant," said Sal.

"Oh, yeah? Like what?"

As if waiting for the opportunity, Sal rushed up to Jon, her hands clasped at her breast, and said, "I went to see old Mr. Lenoir today and..."

"Mr. Lenoir!" said Jon, startled. "Why did you go see him?"

"I was bored with nothing to do so I thought if Mr. Lenoir can show mom and dad how to get along without the computers, then he could do the same for me," said Sal. "And I was right. He told me about this wonderful game I could play with my friends and we've been playing it all day! In fact, according to Mr. Lenoir, the game can be even more exciting after dark!"

Jon, recalling how well Mr. Lenoir's advice had served him, found himself eager to discover what other game he may have come up with for Sal and her friends. If it was anything as fun as baseball...and could be played after dark when baseball became difficult...

"What's this game called?"

"Kick the can," reported Sal. "You see, we get a can (Mr. Lenoir gave us one of his but told us soon they'd be a lot more plentiful when the new supermarkets open) and someone is chosen to count to 100 while everybody else runs to hide. After that..."

Virgil listened with increasing interest and found himself wondering what other games Mr.

Lenoir could teach them. At last however, with exhaustion overtaking him, he yawned and said goodnight to his sister.

In his room again, Jon sat back in bed. He was just reaching over to switch off the light when he noticed the old book that Mr. Lenoir had lent him peeking from the pocket of his shirt. Curious, he reached over and plucked it out.

The Submarine Mystery read the title.

Flipping through the yellowing pages, Jon speculated that if Mr. Lenoir had been right about baseball being fun, could he have also been right about reading?

In the proper frame of mind to experiment further, Jon turned to the first page of the book and as he struggled through the first chapter, the chore of reading began to fade and was replaced with delight and wonder as he plunged not only into the world of Doc Savage, but also on a voyage of discovery of his own little dreaming of the amazing vistas that lay beyond the pages of a book or the boundaries of a baseball diamond...

Pioneer Stock

OSCAR THAD, PRIVATE INVESTIGATOR, needed a few minutes to get his bearings.

Thirty-five minutes was hardly enough time for him to adapt to the vast change in surroundings moving from his two room living unit located in the older, original part of the colony to the newer made up of gleaming office towers and spacious residences that dominated the upper class section of Bradbury City.

Just now he was sitting in the penthouse office suite of industrialist Magnus Pendleton that gave an impressive view of the bright lights and broad boulevards of the first city of Mars.

Thad was not impressed which accounted for the lack of expression on his face and the careless manner in which he occupied the chair he had been offered...one of those newer models that conformed to the body of whoever sat in it.

"I'm glad you could make it, Mr. Thad," Pendleton was saying.

"You caught me at a good time, Mr. Pendleton," replied Thad. "I wasn't doing anything."

Pendleton harrumphed and came to the point.

"Back then, life was far from easy and women had to be every bit as tough and strong as their men. My great-grandmother was one of those women. She came to Mars with her husband in the hold of one of those old tin cans they had the nerve to call a stellar liner.

"I checked around and found that you were a good man for locating missing persons."

"I've found my share of runaway husbands and lost dogs," admitted Thad.

"Well how are you at finding missing persons?" asked Pendleton, who apparently did not consider husbands as human beings.

"If you've done your homework as you said, you already know the answer to that," said Thad, leaning forward and resting his elbows on his knees. "Who do you want me to find?"

"My daughter, Althea," replied Pendleton. "She's been missing for almost a week."

"Is that unusual?"

"It is. She's never been gone so long without leaving me some word of her whereabouts."

"So she has taken off before?"

"Well, yes, but only for a few days at a time."

"She didn't leave any note or messages anywhere?

"I've checked all her electronic devices and there was nothing. She took her personal flyer out for what she said was a day trip to Deimos but never returned."

"What did she plan on doing on Deimos?"

"Visit with a friend," said Pendleton, clearly concerned.

"Did the friend have a name?"

"Joval Stevens," said Pendleton. "She used to see him when he attended the Mars College of Interplanetary Geology. After he graduated, he was hired by Martian Mining on my recommendation."

"Have you spoken to him?"

"No, I haven't been able to reach him."

Pendleton began to pace across the office; there was plenty of room for it.

"I've been out of my mind with worry, Mr. Thad," said the industrialist unnecessarily. "What could have happened to my daughter? Was she kidnapped by business rivals? Things like that had been known to happen in the early days of the colony...not much these days to be sure, but...or was her flyer hijacked by space pirates? Could she even now be languishing on some foul planetoid, ravished by one of those brutish aliens we keep hearing about?"

"Take it easy, Mr. Pendleton," said Thad, getting to his feet. "No alien has ever imposed itself on an Earth woman so far as I've heard...those are old wives' tales. And pirates would have to be out of their minds to operate between Mars and its moons. That leaves your 'business rivals' or simple accident...but it's even more likely that your little girl is living it up somewhere and has just forgotten to call home. Now, do you have a holo of your daughter?"

"Yes, right here," said Pendleton. "You can have this one."

Thad took the holo and held it up to the lights of the city coming through the office's big glassite window. Just as he thought. Althea was a knockout all right and obviously not the type to hang around at home where daddy could keep an eye on her. Yeah, he knew the type: a spoiled rich kid who probably liked to spend all her time by the swimming pool, in toning parlors and saunas, and under the care of massage-bots while sipping iced drinks with her friends. He'd had lots of cases like her be- fore and expected to have to take care of a few more. Sure it was cynical, but who wouldn't become jaded in a business that involved itself mostly with the seedier aspects of human civili- zation?

Anyway, so far as he was able to tell, women these days were pretty much the same no matter if they were rich or poor, Terran or Martian: they wanted their creature comforts, the ones they were bombarded with by an om- nipresent media that seemed to exist solely to hold up the debauched lives of useless celebri- ties as examples to be followed. Take away the artificial veneer of civilization and they wouldn't be able to survive a day in the real world. Where were all the hardy women who accom- panied their men to the frontier in the early days of settlement? Thad wasn't an expert but he was pretty sure the pioneer women of Mars didn't spend their days worrying about chip- ping their fingernails or keeping up with the latest impractical fashions; they had been too busy working side by side with their men trying to scratch a living out of the planet's water parched soil.

"What do you say, Thad?" Pendleton was asking. "Can you find her?"

"No guarantees, Mr. Pendleton," said Thad, pocketing the holo. "But I've had better luck than most in this business if that's any conso- lation."

"I assure you, if your efforts meet with success, I can be very generous."

"That's swell, Mr. Pendleton but for right now, I'll be satisfied if you just credit my regular fee to the account number I gave you."

———

After double checking to make sure that Althea really had taken out her own flyer, Thad confirmed with off world traffic control that a flyer answering to her call numbers was tracked leaving Mars over a week before. Sorry, no destination was filed.

That piece of business settled, Thad rolled out his own vehicle, not a late model, but reliable, and cleared take-off with control. The transit to Deimos wasn't bad and he landed at the moon's single colony with little trouble.

Thad hadn't been to Deimos for years, but the place hadn't changed much. In fact, it was hardly the place that a jet setting girl would find attractive. Mostly a mining settlement, the Deimos colony didn't even have a name and its population of 73,000 was made up mostly of hard working folk who frowned on too much gaiety. Anybody over the age of 21 with an ounce of brains in them usually abandoned the colony as fast as they could find a flyer that would take them to Mars and points beyond; which was the main reason why Thad placed little hope of finding any trace of Althea there. With luck however, she might have touched down briefly to preserve a cover story for her father before taking off to parts unknown.

Thad took the conveyor tube into the Deimos colony and wasted little time visiting with the sleepy traffic control office to see if there was any record of Althea's flyer having come down any time over the past week. No luck. Next, a call placed with Martian Mining revealed that one Joval Stevens hadn't worked for the company since the previous year and in fact, had quit suddenly and returned to Earth. A sick aunt no doubt.

Things seemed to be getting complicated but not more so than Thad had encountered in other cases. Now, if he were a spoiled rich kid who wanted to do something that he didn't want his parents to find out about, where would he go? It was a no-brainer: the vacation spots of Arcturus naturally, with their gambling parlors, swanky salons, zero G bars, and public saunas. The action never stopped in places like that.

The flight to Arcturus was an uneventful one and when he checked flight records there covering the previous few weeks, he hit paydirt. Althea had been there all right. Unfortunately, she didn't stay long. Just the time it took to refuel her flyer and move on. This was definitely not fitting the pattern Thad had had in mind and furthermore, it was getting expensive. Where could the girl have gone? With the amount of fuel she took on, she could have gone anywhere from Procyon II to the Horsehead Nebula. Losing his patience, Thad decided to take a long shot and check out the little used spacelanes out by Rigel Prime. The traditional hangout of space pirates and other desperados, it was a worst case scenario that he hoped to eliminate from contention as soon as possible. Arriving in the area some days after leaving Arcturus, Thad went for his ace in the hole: a dimensional wave receiver he'd invested in a few years before designed to pick up the signal of the black beacon that was installed as a safety device by manufacturers in every space going vehicle. Installation of the black beacon was mandated by law, one that was little known by the public, a fact that was of great service to law enforcement and especially for private investigators needing to defend reputations for finding missing persons.

"Eureka!" shouted Thad, his voice filling the small cabin of his flyer.

No sooner had he turned on the receiver than it picked up the signal from Althea's late model Boeing Stratolane flyer. With a range of only a few light years, he felt lucky in being able to pick up the girl's beacon on the first try.

Locking in on the signal, Thad allowed his own flyer to ride the beacon to what his instruments indicated was an Earth-normal planet located well off the beaten spacelanes. Once in orbit, he double checked the receiver's data stream and confirmed that Althea's signal was indeed coming up from the planet beneath him. Instruments also indicated that the planet was not only devoid of any sign of civilization, but was almost without fauna of any kind.

"What in the world is she doing here?" wondered Thad aloud.

Shrugging, he strapped himself into a seat, punched landing instructions into the on-board computer, and prepared for planetfall. The entire process took about four hours as the flyer followed a shallow descent calculated to bring the flyer into the area where Althea's beacon was flashing. Outside the little vehicle's plasteel windows, clouds began to stream past until suddenly there was a break in air speed and the flyer began to settle to the ground. Now the tops of tropical style vegetation rose up before the windows and in no time, the entire view was blocked by a thick canopy of jungle. There was a soft thump as the flyer hit the ground followed by the whine of the engines as the computer returned the ship's systems to active normal. Thad released the crash harness and switched the computer from landing to internal life support mode before checking the external cameras. He didn't have to look long before spotting Althea's flyer only a few dozen yards from his own. Not bad.

Zipping himself into an all purpose jumpsuit, Thad stepped into a tiny airlock at the rear of his flyer and then watched as the outer hatch unsealed itself and slid aside. Immediately, he was hit by a wave of shuddering heat and a moment later, his nostrils were filled with the pungent odor of decaying plants and moist soil. Taking hold of a hand grip beside the hatch, he hopped down onto the ground where his booted feet sank about two inches in the spongy surface. He made sure his utility harness was fastened securely around his body and then began to make his way through the underbrush to the other flyer. Bird sounds echoed distantly in the forest and vines as thick as his wrists looped from the trees that towered over his head. Luckily there didn't seem to be any insects on this world.

A few minutes later, he reached the abandoned flyer. After an inspection revealed no evidence of external damage, Thad used a police signal key to activate the electronic lock. It worked, and a hatch opened in the side of the ship. With the aid of a built-in step, he hoisted himself up and peeked into the airlock.

"Althea?" he called. "Anyone in here?"

There was no reply.

Inside the flyer, the aft power console revealed that the ship's engine was still operative and that there was plenty of fuel remaining. Up forward, the rest of the flyer showed no signs of a struggle.

Now it was Thad's turn to imagine the worst: had the girl been abducted? Captured by piratical slavers? Was she injured and wandering the jungle lost? Worried, he left the flyer for a closer look outside.

There, he found traces of recent passage: a broken branch here and a crushed fern there, indicating that someone had left the vicinity of the ship and entered into the jungle. Looking more closely, he noted some footprints in the soft soil whose size and number suggested that they were made by a single person, a woman. Obviously Althea's, but what was the kid up to? She leaves home without leaving any kind of message, lands on an uncharted planet, and then just wanders off into the jungle by herself? It didn't make sense and if she lost herself out there it would only serve her right. Spoiled rich kid without an ounce of brains in her pretty little head...

Eager to get the job over with and collect his fee, Thad went back to his own flyer and filled a pack with food, water, and gear to cover an extended hike, shouldered it, and plunged into the surrounding rain forest.

Following the trail was no problem in daylight, but as the sun began to set behind the trees, darkness fell with unnerving suddenness. In no time it seemed, Thad could barely see where he was going. Time to find a spot to hole up for the night. Up in a tree maybe? He stopped to survey the terrain, not wishing to move too far off the trail, and peered into the jungle around him. Suddenly, his attention was drawn to a flickering light off in the distance. Concentrating on it, he took it for what it was: a campfire. So it seemed Miss Pendleton wasn't as helpless as he thought. Immediately, her estimation in his eyes went up several notches. He was impressed. Still, he imagined she was pretty desperate by this time; no doubt huddling frightened and bewildered by the fire and wondering what ever came over her to come out here by herself.

Adjusting the pack around his shoulders, Thad moved in the direction of the campfire. Of course, as unlikely as it might be, it was possible that the fire did not belong to Althea so he decided to approach cautiously, not calling out until he was sure whose fire it was.

He made his way through the underbrush as best he could until he was close enough to see into the circle of light cast by the fire.

There, he was satisfied to see the familiar figure of Althea warming herself in its glow. Good to see also was the fact that her hands were free and that there didn't seem to be anyone else around.

"Come on out," said the girl suddenly getting to her feet and facing him where he stood in the darkness just beyond the circle of light. "I know you're there."

Thad wasn't much surprised that she had detected him; he must have made plenty of noise thrashing though the jungle in the dark.

"Althea Pendleton, I presume?" said Thad as he stepped from the underbrush into the light.

"The same," said Althea. "I suppose that my father sent you to find me?"

"He did," replied Thad truthfully. "Mind if I get closer to the fire?"

"Be my guest."

Thad tossed his pack to the ground and stood close to the fire, enjoying its warmth. Around them, the jungle was dark and preternaturally quiet. Overhead, unfamiliar stars twinkled between overhanging branches.

"My name's Oscar," said Thad in the way of introduction. "I'm a private investigator. Your father hired me to find you and I don't mind saying, you've given me a good chase."

"Really?" said Althea, smiling. "I wasn't trying to."

"What were you trying to do? This isn't exactly the usual destination for a young lady like you."

"What do you mean 'like me?'" asked Al-thea, putting her hands on her hips.

"Rich, with plenty of leisure time to kill." Thad shrugged. "That usually spells pursuit of pleasure, not roughing it on uncharted plan-ets."

"Doesn't it?"

Thad looked at the girl and their eyes met. Althea's were steady and unblinking. There was stubbornness there, but also determination and pride. Looking around, he noticed how tidy the campsite was: a pack was hanging on a tree branch out of reach of any wild creatures; an enviro-tent had been pitched a safe distance from the fire; the fire itself was a good one with plenty of heavy pieces of wood glowing red with heat; the remains of a meal sat neatly on a portable stove just beyond the fire; and the butt of a sturdy pulse pistol poked out from one of the girl's trouser pockets. Althea herself was dressed sensibly for the wilderness, there was nothing there to indicate that she had in-tended on spending any time on a pleasure planet.

Despite his expectations, Thad was im-pressed.

"You came here deliberately," he said at last.

"You figured that out all by yourself, did you?"

"Just answer the question," said Thad.

The girl shrugged. "What do you know about my family, the Pendletons?"

"Not much," admitted Thad. "Well, nothing at all actually."

"So you didn't know that the Pendletons were one of the first families who came to Mars to stay permanently?"

"One of the first of the old pioneers? No."

"Well we were," said the girl. "Back then, life was far from easy and women had to be every bit as tough and strong as their men. My great-grandmother was one of those women. She came to Mars with her husband in the hold of one of those old tin cans they had the nerve to call a stellar liner. Most of the three month trip out from Earth they spent frozen in barely heated quarters and once on the planet had precious little support from home. But my great-grandfather staked a claim near the arctic and after they both nearly died of thirst, managed to drill a well that reached water 3,000 feet below the planet's surface. At first they lived in a pre-fab dwelling that was mostly kept up with an air pump, but after a few hard years the aquifer they found made large scale operations on Mars possible. In no time, my great-grandfather was being pursued by big corporations looking to establish factories on Mars and after signing a couple short term contracts, he went into business for himself and...well you can figure out the rest of the story."

"I can."

"Anyway, I admit to having lived the kind of life you imagined I'd be pursuing when you set out to find me," continued Althea. "But believe it or not, you get tired of the personal pampering; at least I did, and pretty fast. I wanted to prove to myself that I could leave the life I was living any time I wanted. I wanted to prove to myself that I could have done what my great-grandmother did; what all those early pioneering women did. But how? Not on Mars, that's for sure. So I asked around; I visited the stevedores at Burroughsport and the miners on Deimos and learned about this place..." she looked around at the darkened jungle... "off the usual spacelanes and without too many dangerous species roaming about. It hasn't turned out to be a paradise but then, that's what I was looking for; something to give me a challenge in adapting to its wild conditions."

"Still, this is pretty extreme," observed Thad, looking around. "How have you found it so far?"

"More difficult than I anticipated but I've been managing," said Althea, lifting her chin in the direction of the fire and indicating the remains of a small creature roasting on a spit.

"Smells pretty good too," said Thad, turning the spit to prevent the meat from burning.

"I decided to get away from my ship and found this spot to make camp," continued Althea. "Once I was well oriented here, I though I'd take some day hikes into a nearby valley to explore. I think I saw some interesting geological formations down there."

Despite himself, and the fee paid him by Althea's father to find her, he was surprised to discover a growing admiration for the determined Althea. She'd been out here for a few weeks and didn't seem any the worse for wear. Maybe, he thought, there was hope yet for kids like her.

Thad grew quiet then and realized that his inclination was to let the girl alone; leave her here to prove herself as she wished. But that left him with a problem: how to tell Pendleton that after finding his daughter, he chose to leave her behind?

"Are you thinking about taking me back?" The question was put to him quietly, but he could tell she was worried. She really didn't want to back...not yet at least. Thad decided that he liked the girl's pluck.

"It's what I was paid to do," said Thad aloud but inwardly the answer to his own dilemma came more easily than he expected. "On the other hand, I suppose I could use the sub-space radio to assure your father that you were safe but that there might be a delay in getting home."

"You could, but what would stop you from going back and telling him yourself?" asked Althea. "Not frightened of him are you?"

"He can be an intimidating man," replied Thad facetiously. "On the other hand, you're the kind of girl I wouldn't mind keeping company with."

"What do you have in mind?" asked Althea, crossing her arms defiantly across her chest.

"Is there room on the expedition for another member?"

No Choice at All

10:23:08 GMT

THE CHANGES WERE LITTLE noticed at first. A stronger wind here, a snow flurry there. But then the weather turned for the worse. Against all expectations, seven inches of snow fell in New England, an impenetrable fog left London at a standstill for two days, rain seized to fall in North Africa, the monsoons returned to the China Sea. Everywhere, the seasons became elastic, beginning and ending in such a way that they were impossible to predict. By the end of the year, farmers were reporting either surges in production or steep drop offs and re- sorts off the coast of France, the mountains in the American west, the African veldt, and the Pacific islands experienced wild fluctuations in tourism. The changes quickly affected local economies that soon sent tremors across the old national borders and finally caught the at- tention of members of the Supreme Bureau of World Affairs. After consultation with econo- mists, geologists, social scientists, and meteor- ologists, it was decided to send for the Chief of the Office of Chrono Scheduling.

The Chief of Chrono Scheduling arrived in Helsinki close to midnight and was whisked immediately into conference with members of the Supreme Bureau. There, behind closed doors, matters of the highest importance to global security were discussed with the result that the worst fear of public officials was confirmed: changes in the weather had skewed the Master Schedule and thrown the world into imminent chaos and panic.

"Something must be done!" demanded the President of the Supreme Bureau.

"Matters must not be allowed to continue in this way," added the Vice-President of the Supreme Bureau.

"The Master Schedule must be adhered to at all cost!" insisted the Secretary of the Supreme Bureau.

"Should weather patterns not conform to those demanded in the Master Schedule, they will cause a ripple effect that could reach every aspect of society," observed the Treasurer of the Supreme Bureau. "Society could not withstand such a shock. Above all, expectations must be met, nothing must be left to chance, the Master Schedule must be maintained."

Clearly, noted the Chief of the Office of Chrono Scheduling, panic was setting in and if it were not to spread beyond the stead walls of the Supreme Bureau of World Affairs, confidence must be restored to the world's leaders.

"Obviously the source of the problem does not lie in the Master Schedule," soothed the Chief of Chrono Scheduling. "The Master Schedule is infallible. So long as all factors that have contributed to its formulation continue to function as predicted, nothing can threaten the beauty of its symmetry. However, should there be any kind of variance in the performance of even one of those factors, it would pose a grave danger to the delicate checks and balances upon which the Master Schedule depends. The slightest alteration, even if imperceptible at first, would grow until the whole mighty machine would grind to a halt."

Pausing a moment, the Chief of Chrono Scheduling saw that he had erred. Instead of calming the fears of the government officials, he had only exacerbated them.

"The good news," hurried on the Chief of Chrono Scheduling, "is that we seem to have identified the problem that is posing the first threat to the Master Schedule in over 172 years. I'm sure the meteorologists among your staff of consultants will agree with me that the problems we are currently suffering can be traced back to unplanned fluctuations in the world's weather. Thus, the solution is a simple one: someone must go into space and investigate conditions aboard Weather One."

"Of course!" expostulated the President.

"Naturally!" agreed the Vice-President.

"Why didn't we think of it sooner?" wondered the Secretary.

"Has anyone heard from the weather officer aboard Weather One?" the Treasurer wanted to know.

Immediately, all eyes turned to the Director of the Department of Outer Space Activity for an answer.

"Ahem," said the Director of the Department of Outer Space Activity, clearing his throat. "The weather officer aboard Weather One has been in regular contact with ground control."

"How regular?" asked the Chief of Chrono Scheduling innocently.

"Ahem," said the Director. "He has replied to messages from control whenever he has received them..."

"And?"

"But has been less than punctual..." a collected gasp from everyone in the room..."in making his own reports."

"And did you not connect this shocking lapse in his personal Schedule with the unplanned weather patterns the world has been experiencing?"

"We did find it unsettling..."

"Mr. Director," scolded the President. "I find this failure to recognize the problem a serious one the result of which has not only threatened the Master Schedule, but shaken the confidence of every man, woman, and child in the world in the superiority of the Planned State. The consequences of which I'm sure you are aware."

"Of course, I..."

"Should the general populace lose faith in the Master Schedule, chaos could be the result and a return to wholesale individualism," continued the President. "Where would the world be if 40 billion people were to take it upon themselves to make their own decisions?"

"There would be no guarantee of anything," answered the Vice-President without waiting for a reply. "The world would return to uneven wealth, unreliable food distribution, unpredictable energy consumption, unfair distribution of wealth. Why, it could even mean the return of war and violence as groups competed with each other to obtain scarce commodities..."

There was a visible shiver among officials in the room at the possibility of the return of free will.

"Now, now," said the Secretary. "We must remain calm."

"But already, we have been thrown off the Master Schedule," said the Treasurer. "Surely, such a contingency could not have been planned for?"

"No," admitted the Chief of Chrono Scheduling to more gasps. "For the first time in 172 years, we are left to fend for ourselves. We must make a decision on our own without the help of the Master Schedule. For that reason, it is imperative that we correct the situation as quickly as possible because if we do not, every passing hour will force us to make more and more original decisions not included in the Master Schedule. And with each one of those decisions, it becomes less likely that we will ever be able to reset circumstances back to those taken into account by thc Master Schedule."

There was a sober silence then around the room until the President spoke.

"Mr. Director, you will send a personal representative up to Weather One to find out why meteorological conditions on Earth have been so erratic of late," ordered the President. "Should your representative find anything amiss, he is to replace the weather officer and return him to control for questioning and discipline."

"Yes, sir," replied the Director, rising from his place and hurrying from the room, thankful that no more questions would be aimed his way.

"Gentlemen," concluded the Chief of Chrono Scheduling. "With confidence that the problem does not lie in the Master Schedule, I am certain that with order restored to Weather One, things on Earth will soon return to normal and from that point, events will take care of themselves until the Master Schedule has been restored."

There was an audible sigh of relief from everyone gathered in the room.

22:16:50 GMT

Astronaut Mandrake Willins glanced at the digital chrono display window set amid the thousand and one gauges, screens, buttons, levers, panels, and various other instrumentation surrounding the pilot's chair assuring himself that the rocket shuttle was on schedule for docking with Weather One at 23:52:12.

Double checking his controls, he was satisfied to see that all systems registered green and that the rocket's attitude was in the correct position to fit the port side air lock with that of the space station when the two spacecraft finally rendezvoused. Free to take his eyes off of his instruments, Astronaut Willins allowed himself a few seconds to look out the small forward window and catch sight of the weather station as it rose like a planetary body over the Earth's horizon.

All angles and antennas, the station bulged with a number of protuberances including a pair to which outer atmosphere only craft could be docked. From the outside at least, nothing seemed amiss.

"See anything wrong?" asked the man sitting in the co-pilot's chair.

"Nothing that I can tell," replied Astronaut Willins.

"Appearances, as they say, can be deceiving," commented Weather Officer Hugh Pannin.

"True," acknowledged Astronaut Willins. "And if control is correct about Weather One being the reason why the world has been thrown off the Master Schedule, it will be our duty to make sure the situation within the station conforms to that prevalent everywhere else."

"Weather One is the source of the problem," said Weather Officer Pannin definitely. "The Master Schedule accounts for all circumstances on Earth, including the weather. Control of the weather is crucial to a number of other factors that, if interrupted, can affect matters such that it would take years maybe even decades to resynchronize. If that happens, there is a good chance that we will never be able to restore the Master Schedule to its original timeline."

Astronaut Willins shuddered.

"Thus, straying from the Master Schedule would create an exponential affect causing so many secondary variances that some believe would make it impossible for even the Office of Chrono Scheduling to keep up with," finished Weather Officer Pannin grimly as he glanced at his personal Chrono-piece.

22:23:12 GMT

Desperate to keep the situation under control, the Office of Chrono Scheduling had worked its giant air cooled computers non-stop to devise new personal Schedules for both Astronaut Willins and Weather Officer Pannin in order to cover their emergency flight to Weather One. Calculations were planned down to the millisecond and were intended to fit exactly within the time frame between the beginning of the weather disturbances and the point at which they were expected to be brought back under control. The assumption was that Astronaut Willins and Weather Officer Pannin would correct the situation within that time frame and calculations allowed no room for further deviance.

"Something must be done to bring the weather back under control and operating according to the Master Schedule," said Weather Officer Pannin more to himself than to his companion. "If rain fails to fall when it is expected, if there is not enough sunlight where it is needed, if there are unplanned changes in temperature, the Earth could once again fall prey to swarming insects, unrestricted breeding patterns, devastating hurricanes, monsoons, or even earthquakes. In fact, chrono theoreticians are still unsure how the weather might affect human sexual activity!"

"Are you suggesting that it could mean un-Scheduled births?" asked Astronaut Willins, shocked.

"If hurricanes for instance prevent farmers from working their fields or snow keeps office workers homebound for extended periods..."

"...people would need to find things to do to keep themselves busy until the weather improved," finished Astronaut Willins.

"And as pre-Schedule history tells us, when other divertissements such as electronic entertainment is exhausted, humans often revert to more instinctive, unregulated activity such as..."

"But that would mean..."

"Exactly."

For the first time, the deadly seriousness of the situation imposed itself on Astronaut Willins whose imagination suddenly began to conjure a world where couples had more than a single child and the State, overburdened by the unexpected increase in human fertility, would quickly find its carefully planned post-natal system of child rearing unequal to the task. Concerned with caring for multiple children, women might be forced to abandon their duties in support of the economy. Disruptions would surely follow and Astronaut Willins wondered if even the Office of Chrono Scheduling could adjust the Master Schedule to compensate. Although Astronaut Willins knew he could never indulge in un-Scheduled sexual activity with his wife, he could not be sure about anyone else. Surely, the drive to procreate was one of the most powerful expressions of individualism available to human beings and one of the last to be brought under control by the Office of Chrono Scheduling. Once that particular genii was out of the bottle, could it ever be replaced?

It was with a new sense of urgency that Astronaut Willins again checked the chrono display window to make sure there had been no deviation from the mission's Schedule.

22:36:11 GMT

Only a few minutes more before docking was to take place. According to the mission Schedule, it was time for contact with weather officer Leteen aboard Weather One to begin docking procedures.

"Astronaut Willins calling Weather Officer Marvin Leteen," called Astronaut Willins toggling his communicator. "Astronaut Willins calling Weather Officer Marvin Leteen."

Even with the knowledge that there had been a serious breach in the Master Schedule over the past weeks, the fact that there was no immediate reply from Weather Officer Leteen still shook Astronaut Willins. The newly devised mission Schedule was as perfect as the Office of Chrono Scheduling could make it, that is, planned down to the milli-second. There was no excuse for Weather Officer Leteen not to have been standing by awaiting contact from the rocket shuttle.

Anxiously, Astronaut Willins called again. "Astronaut Willins to Weather Officer Leteen..."

"This is Weather Officer Leteen," a voice crackled loudly over the ship's speaker system.

Astronaut Willins looked over at Weather Officer Pannin who sat stiffly erect in his chair. Obviously he too was not happy with the deviation from the mission Schedule.

"This is Astronaut Willins in the relief shuttle," said Astronaut Willins. "As per the revised mission Schedule, I have arrived in company with your relief, Weather Officer Pannin. You will begin docking procedures in exactly...2 minutes, 36 seconds..."

"Sorry, Astronaut Willins," came the astonishing reply. "But there will be a slight delay. You see, I'm not at the docking controls but on deck three overseeing some rather delicate adjustments to the orientation of Weather Fourteen. Can't leave here for another few minutes. I'm sure you understand. Please stand by."

Dumbfounded, Astronaut Willins did not even think of acknowledging the request. He simply stared out the observation port at the bulk of Weather One as the shuttle's auto-systems oriented it for docking.

"The situation is worse than we thought," said Weather Officer Pannin, breaking the silence.

"He deliberately ignored the mission Schedule!" said Astronaut Willins still a bit in shock. He was not used to such blatant disregard for timeliness. Quickly, he consulted the mission itinerary and after only checking the first few items on the agenda gave up as lost any attempt to keep to the carefully arranged revised Schedule. "This is disastrous!"

"It seems, Astronaut Willins, that we have been thrown onto our own resources in the matter of how to proceed," said Weather Officer Pannin with unusual self control.

"What do we do now?" asked Astronaut Willins at a loss. "Anything we do could throw the mission Schedule even more askew. We'll never be able to get back on Schedule!"

"I'm as aware of the problem as you are," said Weather Officer Pannin. "I think we should contact control and make them aware of the situation. Maybe they will be able to suggest how we can proceed."

"What if they order us to abandon the mission and return to Earth until a new mission Schedule can be drawn up?"

"Then that's what we'll have to do," said Weather Officer Pannin. "Of course, they could order us to proceed with the mission."

"But to do that, we'd have to..." Astronaut Willins lowered his voice to a whisper. "...improvise."

Weather Officer Pannin gulped loudly. "Let's hope not! Hurry, contact control and find out what they want us to do. It's a good thing an emergency call to control was included in the mission Schedule!"

Astronaut Willins passed the sleeve of his jumpsuit across his forehead and exhaled a shuddery breath at how close they had come to being stranded in space without the wherewithal to take a next step. It was truly fortunate that the computers of the Office of Chrono Scheduling had included a fail safe option in the mission Schedule!

Facing an abyss of uncertainty, Astronaut Willins once again engaged the communicator and messaged to control.

"Astronaut Willins to ground control," called Astronaut Willins. "Astronaut Willins to ground control..."

"This is ground control," came the immediate reply, loud and clear. "What is the problem, Astronaut Willins? This is an un-Scheduled call..."

"We have an emergency situation up here, control," said Astronaut Willins. "It appears that Weather Officer Leteen aboard Weather One, in direct violation of the revised mission Schedule, is calling for a delay of several minutes in docking procedures."

Astronaut Willins left his message at that...no need to throw control into complete chaos!

There was several minutes of silence during which Astronaut Willins became almost certain that the mission would be abandoned and he and Weather Officer Pannin doomed to orbit the Earth for the rest of their lives. He did not realize he'd been holding his breath until the communicator crackled and the voice of control came over the speaker system.

"Astronaut Willins," said control. "We have consulted with representatives of the Supreme Bureau of World Affairs and the Office of Chrono Scheduling and considering the seriousness of the situation, we have been instructed to tell you to proceed with the mission. You are to disregard the entire itinerary save for the time in which the shuttle is to disengage from Weather One and return to Earth. Until the time of your Scheduled return to Earth, you are free to do whatever you must to correct what you deem necessary on Weather One to restore Scheduled weather patterns. Do you understand?"

Stunned at the unheard of freedom of action, Astronaut Willins took some seconds in which to reply.

"Am I to understand that Weather Officer Pannin and I have been freed from all Scheduling and will be required to make decisions on our own?"

"That is correct, Astronaut Willins."

Astronaut Willins looked uncertainly at Weather Officer Pannin who nodded his understanding.

"Understood, control," said Astronaut Willins, signing out.

Feeling as if he were groping in the dark along a narrow chasm into which he could fall at any moment, Astronaut Willins returned his hands to the attitude controls of the shuttle. Suddenly, he was faced with an uncertain future, a void that could only be filled by the results of decisions he made. For the first time in his life, he was forced to wonder what lay ahead without a personal Schedule mapping out his activities and the thought scared him almost to death. His immediate instinct was to freeze, to shut his mind down and not think of anything. If he ignored the problem, he wouldn't have to make any decisions. But that was a decision in itself wasn't it? Had he just made his first decision? Was he in the future now, one he was mapping out for himself? He wasn't sure because he didn't know where he was heading. Wait! He was supposed to be headed for Weather One wasn't he? Yes...and that decision had already been made for him hadn't it?

"Weather Officer Leteen to Astronaut Willins," said a voice over the speaker system. "Weather Officer Leteen to Astronaut Willins. I'm ready to guide you in now."

Still struggling to overcome his mental paralysis, Astronaut Willins automatically looked over to the chrono display window and was surprised to see the time.

24:13:22 GMT

Where had the time gone? Astronaut Willins asked himself. Is this what he was supposed to expect after deviating from the mission Schedule? A wholesale loss of time? What happened to those lost minutes? How would they be accounted for?

Worriedly, Astronaut Willins looked at Weather Officer Pannin out of the corner of his eyes but it didn't seem that he had noticed the same phenomenon.

"Astronaut Willins?" queried Weather Officer Leteen over the speaker system.

"I'm here," replied Astronaut Willins in a voice much calmer than he expected. "We have been instructed by control to proceed with the mission. Are docking protocols engaged?"

There was a pause, then: "Yes. You're cleared to approach the station."

Astronaut Willins enabled the automatic piloting system and with his hands on the controls in case of emergency, watched his instruments as the shuttle's computer guided the vehicle to the docking collar that protruded from the weather satellite. Slowly, the cavity inside the collar grew larger and larger until it vanished out of view beneath the nose of the shuttle. Presently, Astronaut Willins felt the slight jar that indicated contact between the two vehicles and an audio signal indicated that the latches of the docking collar had clamped into place around the nose of the shuttle. A row of green lights on his instrument panel showed it was safe to shut down the main computer and place the ship in standby mode.

"That's it," said Astronaut Willins to Weather Officer Pannin. "We can leave our seats now."

"I'll grab our ditty bags and pass them forward," offered Weather Officer Pannin as he floated free of his seat and maneuvered himself to the rear of the cabin.

Meanwhile, Astronaut Willins stepped downward and pulled open the hatch that covered the short passage leading from the shuttle's cabin into the weather station. Together, the two men entered the passage and alerted Weather Officer Leteen on the other side that it was safe to open the hatch leading into Weather One. There was a hiss of air and the hatch cracked open. In a moment, the newcomers had straightened and stood in a small ready room as Weather Officer Leteen slammed the hatch shut and spun the locking mechanism.

"Welcome aboard," said Weather Officer Leteen after he had turned from the hatch to the others. "Sorry for the delay, but as I said, I was busy with Weather Fourteen."

"Why was that work not done when it was indicated in the station's mission Schedule?" asked Weather Officer Pannin without preamble.

Weather Officer Leteen chose not to reply and instead indicated the way to the station's living quarters.

"It'll be a little crowded with three of us on board, but we'll manage," he said.

As Weather Officer Leteen led them slowly along the narrow, instrument lined corridors and up a ladder to the overhead decks, they exchanged small talk and while Weather Officer Pannin engaged him in more technical comments regarding the weather satellite, Astronaut Willins could not help but notice a certain demeanor about their host. He seemed to lack the gravity normal with the rest of humanity. He never glanced at his personal chrono-piece or any of the digital clocks located at numerous places throughout the station. In fact, he seemed almost criminally negligent of the passage of time. But there was something else about him, something less definable and Astronaut Willins struggled to find the proper words with which to label it.

Slowly, older phrases that had once been used before the creation of the Master Schedule came back to him. He recalled learning about them in the psychology courses he had taken during astronaut training. Then, his instructors had warned students against indulging in feelings of "euphoria" or "happiness." Emotions that were dangerous to anyone wishing to keep to the Master Schedule. Were those the kind of emotions that he was observing in Weather Officer Leteen? If so, they made Astronaut Willins uncomfortable in what they suggested.

At last, the small party reached deck one where the living quarters were located and Weather Officer Leteen indicated a narrow stateroom that had been prepared for his two guests.

Astronaut Willins looked around the small room and was immediately struck by a strange phenomenon: the digital clock on the wall appeared to be keeping the wrong time. Not sure whether to believe his senses or not, he stared at it for some time and then compared it to his own personal chrono-piece. There could be no doubt; the wall clock was off by several hours. Disturbed and unable to take his eyes from the display, he nudged Weather Officer Pannin with his elbow and inclined his chin in the direction of the clock. Beside him, he sensed the weather officer stiffen in surprise.

"Weather Officer Leteen," ventured Astronaut Willins. "Am I mistaken or is the time on this clock wrong?"

"The time on that clock is wrong," replied Weather Officer Leteen nonchalantly. "In fact, all the clocks aboard the station are off...by several days as a matter of fact."

Shaken, Astronaut Willins was dumb-founded. It was Weather Officer Pannin who broke the strained silence.

"How could all the clocks be wrong?"

Weather Officer Leteen shrugged. "It happened a few months ago when there was an unusual amount of solar activity. As near as I can figure it, there was one particularly powerful emission and it was soon after that that much of the power on the station was interrupted including that needed to keep the clocks running."

"Didn't that upset you?"

"Certainly it did," admitted Weather Officer Leteen. "As you can imagine, I was frantic and quickly tried to get things back on line. It took some time but after a few days, I was able to restore the power and attempt contact with ground control for further advice."

"But control claims it hasn't heard from you since your last official report well before the time when you said the clocks all failed..."

"Correct. It was only after I tried to contact control that I discovered that the restoration of power had not effected the station's communications equipment. They were still down. "

"I can imagine the panic you must have felt when the clocks failed," sympathized Weather Officer Pannin.

"I can assure you, it was awful," said his colleague.

"But there's one thing I don't understand," continued Weather Officer Pannin. "You said you managed to restore power in the station?"

"Yes."

"And at that point, everything except the communications equipment came back on line?"

"Yes; that equipment was restored through ground based efforts completely independent of my own efforts."

"Then what about the clocks?" Weather Officer Pannin wanted to know. "Didn't they begin to work again too?"

"Oh, yes, everything came back on line when the power was restored," said Weather Officer Leteen. "At first, I tried to bring the clocks back into synchronicity with the Master Schedule but with the power outage, I was forced to spend much of my time monitoring the weather satellites and weather patterns on Earth. Soon, however, I realized that without the clocks functioning, every second that passed, caused me to drift farther and farther away from the parameters set by my mission Schedule. At first, I tried to remain loyal to the station's Schedule but as time went on I began to fall behind. While I was arranging for the Scheduled rainfall in the southern Sahara, temperatures began to rise in Canada and before I could attend to that, they began to fall too early in Patagonia. Suddenly, storms were forming in the Caribbean and ports were remaining ice bound longer than they were supposed to in northern Russia. And while I was getting the weather back on Schedule in England, a monsoon struck Indonesia. But the climactic event for me was when Weather Three detected the first seismic activity on Earth in over one hundred years."

"So what did you then?" asked Weather Officer Pannin, horrified.

"I did the only thing I could," said Weather Officer Leteen. "I made my own Schedule."

There were gasps then by both Astronaut Willins and Weather Officer Pannin.

"You made your own Schedule?" asked Weather Officer Pannin in disbelief. "Is that even possible?"

"At first, I thought so, but after I realized that I'd been making my own decisions right along since the clocks stopped, it became an easy step to arrange what order I would address issues that needed my attention," said Weather Officer Leteen.

"So how did you do it?" asked Astronaut Willins, mesmerized by the Weather Officer's audacity.

"Very simply," said Weather Officer Leteen. "I prioritized. I decided which tasks were the most important and performed them in that order. Of course, it meant that I still didn't have the ability to get to all of them in a timely fashion (no one, after all, can be as efficient in arranging the use of time as the Office of Chrono Scheduling), that was why weather patterns on Earth eventually began to spin out of control. But I only learned just how far events had veered from the Master Schedule after control had reestablished communications with the station."

There was silence for a moment as Astronaut Willins and Weather Officer Pannin absorbed what they had just heard.

"But there's no need for worry," said Leteen, sensing uneasiness on the part of his colleagues. "I've found that adapting to random events is actually an exhilarating process..."

"Exhilarating!" gasped Astronaut Willins.

"Oh, I know what you're thinking," said Weather Officer Leteen. "You're thinking that it would be difficult to operate in a vacuum without direction to which I would reply that yes, there is something to that. But very quickly you adapt to the changed circumstances, or at least I did. In fact, as the days passed, I've found being freed from the Schedule to be an oddly serene exercise. I feel as if a great weight has been lifted from me. If I want, I can eat an hour early or sleep later. I can decide when or even if to monitor the other weather stations. In fact, it was that last realization that inspired me to shut down some of the stations from time to time."

"You allowed them to shut down!" exclaimed Weather Officer Pannin taking a threatening step forward. "You're crazy!"

"No," said Weather Officer Leteen calmly. "The rest of the world is crazy; has been crazy for hundreds of years ever since people permitted themselves to become slaves of a rigid, unbending Master Schedule that has ruled every aspect of their lives until every iota of humanity has been squeezed from them. I came to that realization in the weeks since the power outage. It forced me to recall what we were taught in our psychology courses. Although they were not concerned strictly with history, enough facts were included to make me see what the

Office of Chrono Scheduling had really done. Yes, it had removed the threat of war and famine by eliminating the element of uncertainty, but at what cost? Only by turning men into clockwork machines fearful of the unknown and completely dependent upon a Master Schedule arranged for them by those dead for 200 years!"

"You *are* mad!" said Astronaut Willins, horrified.

"If freedom can be defined as madness, then maybe you're right," conceded Weather Officer Leteen. "But hopefully, as more people are freed, the definition of madness will change and the embracing of randomness and chance can be accepted for the liberating elements that I have discovered them to be."

"Weather Officer Leteen," said Weather Officer Pannin. "By the authority invested in me by ground control, I hereby relieve you of command of Weather One and assume that responsibility for myself. You will confine yourself to quarters until Astronaut Willins has prepared the shuttle for its return to Earth."

"So you still think I'm out of my mind?"

"Absolutely!" said Weather Officer Pannin. "By your own words, you present a threat to this station as well as the world and must be reoriented to the Master Schedule."

"And if I choose not be reoriented?"

"That is impossible. You have no choice."

"Don't I? Haven't you been listening to anything I've said?"

With that, Weather Officer Leteen turned around and exited the guest quarters. Temporarily at a loss for what to do, Astronaut Willins and Weather Officer Pannin could only stare after him.

"Is he headed for his quarters?" asked Weather Officer Pannin.

"It didn't sound as if he were."

"What do we do now?"

Without a mission Schedule, or even a personal Schedule, it was difficult for Astronaut Willins to answer that question. Making a decision on his own was a laborious process and by the time the two men had finished their consultation and followed Weather Officer Leteen out of the guest quarters, their host was nowhere to be seen.

"Where could he have gone?" asked Astronaut Willins.

"I don't know. As long as he refused to follow a Schedule, it's impossible to predict what he'll do."

"What a frustrating turn of affairs!" said Astronaut Willins. "As a weather officer yourself, if you were on Schedule, where would you go under these circumstances?"

It was a strange question and one Weather Officer Pannin had never expected to have confronted. In normal circumstances his every action would have been arranged far in advance by the Master Schedule, but now he found himself adrift in a sea of possibilities that had never existed before. As they crowded in upon him, he felt the first stirrings of panic and quickly determined not to allow himself to be overcome. Taking some deep breaths, he waited for his racing heart to slow before offering a suggestion...not a decision!

"If I were Weather Officer Leteen seeking to escape the consequences of my actions, I think I would try and escape the station," said Weather Officer Pannin in a single explosive breath.

"Then you think we should return to the shuttle?" asked Astronaut Willins seeking confirmation.

"I do."

With a definite purpose in mind, the two men left the guest quarters and retraced their way back to the shuttle dock but when they finally arrived, they found the shuttle safe and no sign of Weather Officer Leteen.

"What now?" asked Astronaut Willins. "I never suspected how difficult it was to decide what to do," mused Weather Officer Pannin. "I'll have more respect for the Office of Chrono Scheduling from now on!"

"Me too, but what do we do in the meantime?"

"Maybe Weather Officer Leteen is attempting to communicate with control in an attempt to explain himself and avoid the consequences of his actions?"

"Then we'll have to go back in the direction of the command pod."

So saying, the two men turned back little realizing that Weather Officer Leteen at that very moment was passing them by one deck below.

On the way to the command pod however, Weather Officer Pannin and Astronaut Willins were required to traverse the part of the station devoted to instruments used in monitoring and controlling the various unmanned weather satellites that ringed the Earth and enabled Weather One to control the planet's weather patterns. There, Weather Officer Pannin's practiced eye noticed something out of the ordinary. On the electronic display units that followed the various activities of the weather satellites, all were flatlined.

"This is not good," said Weather Officer Pannin after he had stopped to study the displays.

"Do these flatlines indicate what I think they do?" asked Astronaut Willins.

"I fear so," said Weather Officer Pannin with mounting concern. Quickly, he threw some switches, pressed some buttons, and flew his fingers over some keyboards. Nothing changed. "This is so extraordinary, I hesitate to even put it into words."

"What's wrong?"

"It appears that Weather Officer Leteen is more disturbed than we thought," said Weather Officer Pannin.

"Is that possible?" wondered Astronaut Willins.

"He has disabled all of the other weather satellites by way of a power surge that overloaded their capacitors and fried their wetware," explained Weather Officer Pannin.

"What!" exclaimed Astronaut Willins. "Why, that would mean control of the weather patterns on Earth would be completely lost."

"Exactly," said Weather Officer Pannin still staring at the flatlines that continued to worm their way across the screens. "By his action, Weather Officer Leteen has condemned many parts of the world to famine and subsequently to disease and war. I surely hope that the Office of Chrono Scheduling can compensate for such radical deviations in the Master Schedule!"

"I can tell you that will be an extremely difficult if not impossible task as it will take years at least to replace all of those satellites and return weather patterns to our control," said Astronaut Willins.

Suddenly, a thought occurred to Weather Officer Pannin.

"The deadline!" he exclaimed. "We were ordered by control to do whatever we could to correct the situation on Weather One as long as we were finished by the time the shuttle was Scheduled to disengage and return to Earth!"

Weather Officer Pannin looked around for the nearest clock but it was off Schedule. Instead, he consulted his personal chrono-piece.

02:12:26 GMT

"We couldn't make the deadline even if we wanted to," said Astronaut Willins with a note of despair.

Suddenly, the full weight of the hopelessness of the situation seemed to bear down on Weather Officer Pannin as he contemplated the consequences of their failure. With the weather satellites disabled, there was no chance at all for restoring the Master Schedule and without a Schedule, was there any accommodation taking into account he and Astronaut Willins' return to Earth?

At that point, a slight shudder seemed to pass through the station beneath their feet.

"Did you feel that?" Weather Officer Pannin asked Astronaut Willins.

"The shuttle!" exclaimed Astronaut Willins rushing from the monitoring room to the command pod.

In the command pod, they were just in time to observe the fiery departure of the shuttle as a blast of its engines nudged it away from Weather One and into Earth orbit which would soon place it along a trajectory for a descent to the surface.

"Weather Officer Leteen has taken the shuttle!" declared Weather Officer Pannin unnecessarily. "What shall we do now?"

Astronaut Willins shrugged. "Wait until a relief vehicle can be launched to take us back to Earth."

"But the Schedule!" insisted Weather Officer Pannin. "Without a Schedule, control will have no means to come to our rescue."

"Unless someone decides independently to take that action," observed Astronaut Willins. "It's ironic that our fate now relies on the very freedom that Weather Officer Leteen vowed to create when he disrupted the weather patterns."

Horrified, Weather Officer Pannin could only stare after the rapidly shrinking shuttle.

"But can they do it? Make a decision outside the Schedule, I mean?"

"For our sakes, let's hope they can..."

07:53:09 GMT

"Can you repeat what you just said?" asked the President of the Supreme Bureau of World Affairs. "I don't think I heard you correctly."

"That's very interesting, Mr. President," said the Vice-President. "Because I don't think I heard him correctly either."

"Well, nothing is wrong with my ears and I'm certain I heard him correctly," admonished the Secretary.

Anxious in spirit and definitely rumpled in his outerwear, the tired looking Chief of the Office of Chrono Scheduling was obviously reluctant to repeat what had cost him a good deal to say the first time.

"I said," sighed the Chief of the Office of Chrono Scheduling, "that the Master Schedule is in a shambles, the direct result of the breakdown in planned weather patterns all over the Earth."

"But surely calculations involved in formulating the Master Schedule have accounted for today's weather?" asked the Treasurer looking out one of the room's big windows as snowflakes drifted down outdoors.

"You don't understand," said the Chief of the Office of Chrono Scheduling. "Although the Master Schedule has called for sunshine today, it is obviously snowing outside. The terrible truth is that the weather no longer has any respect for the demands of the Master Schedule. It is now following nature's course; a random set of occurrences based solely on the chance atmospheric events caused by the movement of the Earth in its revolution around the sun."

"But this is preposterous!" huffed the Vice-President. "Nature must conform to the Master Schedule! I demand that the sun shine today!"

The Chief of the Office of Chrono Scheduling sighed and sank a little lower in his over stuffed chair. "The situation is out of our control. Without the weather satellites, there is no hope of making the sun shine today or any other day that we wanted it to."

"Then what are we to do?" asked the Secretary. "Already, the Planned State is losing control at every level. Citizens are panicking, there are fears over the availability of goods and services, national boundaries are being revived, political committees formed, and worst of all, individualism is breaking out everywhere!"

"I thought we had addressed this problem?" demanded the President. "There was to be an investigation of the weather satellite system and a restoration of its systems."

Instantly, all eyes turned to the Director of the Department of Outer Space Activity who, until that moment, had successfully managed to make himself unnoticed at the big conference table.

"As the Chief of the Office of Chrono Scheduling reported," began the Director, clearing his throat. "Since our last meeting, a shuttle was dispatched to Weather One with our most experienced Weather Officer aboard. But when contact was established with his counterpart aboard Weather One, it was discovered that not only had the station suffered a temporary power outage, but the weather officer in charge had gone mad."

There was a faint stirring around the big table.

"It seemed that Weather Officer Leteen, the officer who had been on watch when the power was cut, found himself loosed, if only temporarily, from the station's mission Schedule and developed the warped understanding that he could make his own decisions."

"Independent of his Schedule?" exclaimed an astonished Vice-President, who was clearly more naïve about such things than the others.

"Going aboard the station, Weather Officer Pannin confirmed the unstable nature of Weather Officer Leteen's mind and as he considered what to do next, Leteen bolted," continued the Director. "You can imagine Weather Officer Pannin's position: without the direction of the mission Schedule, which was disrupted from the outset by a delay in docking procedures as well as Weather Officer Leteen's insistence on ignoring the station's own mission Schedule, Weather Officer Pannin was thrown onto his own resources. The Department of Outer Space Activity considers itself fortunate to have had a man of Weather Officer Pannin's caliber on the scene for what happened next. But even so, no one could have been expected to anticipate the actions of someone operating outside the itinerary of an approved Schedule."

"Certainly not," agreed the Chief of the Office of Chrono Scheduling somewhat self-servingly.

"So what happened then?" the President wanted to know."

"With no chance of guessing what someone operating outside of an approved Schedule would do next, neither Weather Officer Pannin nor his companion, Astronaut Willins, were able to stop Weather Officer Leteen from disabling all twenty-four of the weather satellites needed to control Earth's weather patterns before he escaped in their own shuttle."

"This madman escaped?" said an incredulous Vice-President.

"In a manner of speaking," replied the Director. "He managed to land the shuttle at an aerospace field in North Africa and was immediately killed by a mob fearful that another mouth to feed would put too great a strain on their food supplies. Rather ironic actually."

"In what way?"

"Well, it was Weather Officer Leteen's actions that freed those people from the Master Schedule allowing them to make their own decisions, and one of those decisions was to kill him."

There was silence a moment as those around the big table considered the fate of Weather Officer Leteen.

"So if the key to all this is the weather satellites, how long will it take to bring them back on line?" asked the President at last.

"You have placed your finger on the crux of the problem, Mr. President," said the Director of the Department of Outer Space Activity un-comfortably. "The damage to the satellites is such that they must all be replaced not simply repaired. Doing that will require at least six years."

"But at the rate the spirit of individualism is going, that will be too long!" exclaimed the Vice-President.

"The fact remains," said the Director as the sounds of forced entry could be heard outside the conference room. "That we have no other options."

"But what does the Master Schedule say about all this?" asked the Vice-President in a touching display of faith.

"Don't you understand?" demanded the Chief of the Office of Chrono Scheduling. "The Master Schedule is no more!"

"We must learn to live without the preset direction of the Master Schedule," added the President. "And our first independent decision must be what to do when the people down-stairs burst into this room."

"Don't we have any other choices?" the Vice-President wanted to know.

"None whatever," replied the President with no sense of irony.

08:17:56 GMT

The Boy Who Circumnavigated Venus

"I HATE VENUS!" DECLARED 10-year-old Davey Cescu.

"Now, now, son," said his father, David Cescu. "Venus isn't so bad."

"It really is beautiful," added his mother, Belinda Cescu. "Have another helping of pre-fab potatoes.

The family sat around the tiny, fold-down table that also served as desk and work bench in cubicle #13 that was located in the long west wing of what was grandiosely called Landfall City on the planet Venus.

Cubicle #13 was situated about half way down the west wing, one of four, that were arranged like the spokes of a wheel, or the arms of a cross, radiating from a central hub at the center of Landfall City. On either side of each wing were rows of cubicles where the citizens of the city lived; the standard cubicle was small and cramped and sported an all purpose kitchen/entertainment area, a tiny bathroom stall, and a sleeping alcove. Family cubicles were not much different with the exception of optional fold-down bunks in a second alcove. It was the latter that the Cescu's currently occupied and despite the additional comforts

All around him, for as far as he could see, stretched the limits of an ancient Venusian metropolis.

intended for families, Davey still could not stand every minute spent on the hot, steamy planet.

"I don't want any more potatoes," grumped Davey, holding out his hand to ward off the ladle full of fluffy white stuff that his mother was bringing to his tray.

"Then concentrate on what you have in front of you," said his father.

Davey looked down at the compartmented tray on the table before him. There were greens and tans and blues there but he suddenly realized that he had no idea what he'd been eating. Was it chicken and dumplings? Porterhouse steak with all the trimmings? Bacon and eggs? What? Confused, he found that he no longer had an appetite, if he ever had one in the first place.

"I'm not hungry," Davey said, propping his elbows on the table, resting his chin on his fists, and assuming a sour look on his face.

"Come now, Davey," said his mother. "You know you like fish, it's your favorite."

"Is that what it is?" said Davey testily.

"Are you having trouble tasting your food, son?" asked his father. "Maybe you're coming down with something."

"Oh, dear," said his mother, reaching to the sleeping alcove for the all-purpose cold relief medicine.

"I'm not sick," said Davey hurriedly. "I just can't stand being here. I hate Venus."

Patiently, his father placed his eating utensils on the table beside his nearly empty tray and leaned back in his seat.

"Now Davey, we've been through this before," he said. "We've been on Venus for almost a year now Earth time and you've had every opportunity to acclimate yourself to life here. We had a good two years of prep before ever leaving Earth and you have all kinds of activities here to keep you occupied."

"We never hear of the other children complaining," said his mother not unsympathetically.

"I don't care about the other kids," insisted Davey. "There's nothing to do here and no place to go. I can't ride a bike or climb a tree or picnic in the woods. I can't have a dog or a hamster or even a turtle. All my friends are on Earth and I still have to take a bath every night even though there isn't a speck of dirt anywhere in the City."

"Davey, I'm getting tired of these complaints," said his father sternly. "Sure, you don't have any of those things anymore, but you have other things you could never have on Earth."

"I'm sick of computer simulation games and watching TV shows that are a hundred years old," replied Davey. "And the kids here all think they're brains because their folks are scientists or teachers or technicians."

"We are scientists in case you've forgotten," said his father. "Your mother and I waited many years to qualify for Venus, since before you were born. Being here is vital to my research in xenobiology and chemistry while your mother is doing important work in the food sciences."

"Not so's I can tell," mumbled Davey looking at the remains in his tray.

"And the other children are not stuck up," insisted his mother as she collected the remains of the meal and threw all of it, leftovers, trays, and utensils alike in the dispose-all shute. "I'll admit that they seem to be more conscientious about their school work than you are, but when they're free, they play with you all the time."

"Yeah, but all they want to do is play brain teaser games or jump into the simulators," said Davey. "None of them ever want to do something for real. None of them ever wants to explore or even play a good game of releivio..."

"But you know there's not enough room in Landfall City for that," said his mother. "The central core is off limits for children unless it's for school work and there can't be any running around except in the gym area..."

"Big deal!" exclaimed Davey, throwing himself back in his seat. "Running on the conveyor belt or batting against a sensor screen isn't the same as playing tag or baseball outdoors like on Earth."

"All right," said his father. "I think we've heard enough on that subject. Now, I've got some exciting news. It's only going to be official next week, but since talk about it has been going around the labs pretty freely over the past few days, I'm pretty sure I won't be breaking any rules by telling you that the rocket sled will be ready for its trial run in a couple of weeks!"

"That's wonderful, David," said his wife. "The sled has been under construction for almost ten years now."

"Eleven, but who's counting?" said David. "What a feat it represents though! I have to hand it to the engineers who first dreamed it up; people said it was impossible, that it would cost too much, but they did it and in record time too."

"Is it true that it'll work on magnetic repulsion?" asked Davey, interested despite his funk.

"That's right," said his father. "The track it rides on is actually an electro-magnetically charged band that lifts the rocket sled a few micro-meters off the ground and provides a frictionless ride at incredible rates of speed."

"Allowing travel anywhere on Venus in a matter of a few hours?" asked his mother.

"Right again," replied his father. "When colonization of Venus was first planned decades ago, a rapid transportation system was included in the design and all the early cities were located along the same longitude so that the first length of track could be laid in a giant circle stretching all the way around the planet. If the trial run is successful, we'll be able to visit any of the other cities on Venus with ease."

"No more EV suits or having to plan weeks in advance to catch the supply flyer when it makes its rounds!" said his mother. "Isn't that wonderful, Davey?"

"Yeah, great," said Davey. Although he was as interested in the sled as anybody else, what good did it do him? One city's gym was as good as any other.

"And best of all," said his father, "the trial run is scheduled to start right here, in Landfall City! So don't make any plans that day, we'll all be down at the new entry station to see the sled take off!"

"Wonderful!" said his mother again before she noticed that Davey did not seem to be sharing his parents' enthusiasm for the project.

"Listen, Davey," his mother said, her attitude suddenly grave. "I know things aren't the same here as they were on Earth, but you have to understand that your father and I have very important work to do and that sacrifices have to be made."

"Yes, mom," said Davey quietly, having known how the conversation would end. *But I still hate Venus*

Two weeks later, Davey and his parents were among the crowd standing in the reception area for the new rocket sled station. Outside the big plasteel windows, the hot Venusian sun shone down on the shiny needle nosed sled as it rested on the magno-rails that when charged, would lift it a few inches off the ground and allow its powerful pulse engine to push it with frictionless ease for thousands of miles with the least expenditure of propellant.

Beyond the rocket sled was the thick Venusian jungle that grew in typical fashion, that is, tangled so tightly as to make it impassable for a person without a cutting laser. All along the rail line where it passed through jungle, tiny laser jets kept the fast growing jungle at bay and prevented the rails from becoming swallowed in vegetation in a few days time.

Connecting the rocket sled to the reception area was a short gantry that accordioned out from the side of Landfall City proper to a hatch in the side of the red and white sled.

"Quiet please," called out the mayor of Landfall City, an engineer named Wilson LaFleur. "Can I have everybody's attention?"

Slowly, the crowd of a few thousand people, practically everyone who lived in Landfall, calmed down as adults shushed one another and parents quieted the children. Gradually, the excited tumult died down until the only movement was from the balloons that hung overhead from strings tied to children's fat little fingers. Colored confetti littered the deck and pre-fab pastries and small, crustless sandwiches waited as yet untouched on fold down tables in the rear bulkhead.

"I'm sure I speak for everyone gathered here today when I tell project manager Guy Lorden that Landfall City is honored to have been chosen as the test site for the new rocket sled," said LaFleur, making a small bow in the direction of Lorden and a phalanx of fellow engineers that made up the sled's design team. "I know nobody wants to hear a long speech so I'll just yield the floor to Dr. Lorden."

There was a brief ripple of applause as Lorden stepped forward.

"Thank you for your enthusiastic reception today and on behalf of the design team, I hope that the success of this first launch of the rocket sled will inaugurate an era of increased travel between the various Venusian cities; travel that in turn, will foster a growing sense of community among residents. And since development of the sled would not have been possible without the contribution of your tax dollars..." brief laughter "...the least we can do is to invite you all aboard for a look see before the mayor has the honor of pressing the start button and launching the sled on its first round the world trip."

Lorden stepped over to a hatch that formed the entrance to the gantry and hit a switch. Instantly a red light over the door turned to green and the hatch sprung open with a short hiss of escaping air. Gradually, the reception area was filled with the mumbling of the crowd as people began to move toward the hatch.

"Isn't this exciting?" asked Davey's mother as his family neared the open hatch.

"It sure is," replied his father. "With the use of the sled, we can conduct research in different labs around the planet visiting them all in the same day and still have time to get home for dinner!"

"See, Davey?" said his mother. "This means that neither me or your father need to be away from home for weeks at a time anymore!"

"That's nice," said Davey, not impressed. He still hated Venus; hated the boredom of it; hated the confinement; and though he did not hate them, resented his parents for dragging him across all those millions of miles of space from their real home in San Bosco, California.

Now he and his parents were inside the gantry as it stretched across the short distance of ground to the side of the rocket sled and as they drew near, Davey was able to run his hand over the machine's shiny, smooth surface. The next thing he knew, they were inside the sled and he found himself growing interested in its plush seating, auto-meal servers, and instrumentation whose purpose, for the most part, he did not know.

"As you can see, there's no pilot's cabin at the forward end of the sled because there's no need for a pilot to be physically on board," one of the design engineers was saying. "It operates on much the same principal as our interstate highways back on Earth where traffic flow is regulated from a central control office."

"Where's the bathroom?" asked one of the children in the crowd.

The engineer laughed and pointed over people's heads to a narrow door at about midway along the length of the sled.

"You passed it on the way in," the engineer said. "And don't worry, it works the same way as the ones on the rockets that fly between Earth and Venus!"

Because of the number of people lingering inside the sled, Davey soon found himself separated from his parents as he made his way down to the rear of the vehicle. Tired, he slid onto one of the roomy seats and looked out one of the long windows that stretched across the side of the sled. Only a few feet away, the wall of jungle rose up, its various greens and browns punctuated with huge flowers made up of colors not found on Earth. Somewhere overhead, the sun shone with such brilliance that the top of the jungle wall wavered in the shimmering heat.

The sight of the crowding alien landscape and sunlight too hot to bear without a protective EV suit only reminded Davey of the resentment he harbored toward his parents for coming to Venus in the first place. If only there were a place he could run to but in all of Landfall City, there was no such place. Every inch of the colony held some wire, or computer, or sensor, that was vital to its survival and so constantly monitored by a small army of technicians. In all of the colony's 53.9 acres, there was not a single square foot of excess space. In fact, being on the rocket sled was the first time since arriving on Venus that Davey had found someplace that seemed to be free of monitoring. Looking around, he wondered if there was any place in the sled where a person could go just to be alone.

With the sightseers in the sled thinning out, Davey began to move slowly up the central aisle until he came to the spot where the engineer had indicated the door to the restroom was located. Being so cleverly recessed into the paneling, it took a few seconds for him to find the handle, but he found it eventually and used it to draw open the door.

Peeking inside the restroom, he saw that the tiny stall was much like the bathroom back in his family's cubicle except that there was a small plasteel porthole that let light in from the outside. Stepping in, he let the door click to behind him and as he examined the various fixtures, a plan began to take form in his mind. If he could stow away in here and take off with the sled, for the first time since moving to Venus he could be alone, really alone without his parents, without his teachers, without any technicians. He could be alone with his thoughts and maybe even get off in another city! Sure, his parents would worry, but he could just call them from wherever he dropped off. And besides, a little worrying would serve them right. They were always telling him how lucky he was to live on Venus and maybe his running away, even for a little while, would finally make them believe that he meant it when he said he hated Venus.

With the plan formed in his mind, and imagining what everyone would say when he called from Lincoln Town or New San Francisco, Davey squeezed himself in the narrow space behind the bathroom door. Gradually, the sounds of activity in the sled diminished and for a long time, he heard nothing. Suddenly, there was a knock on the restroom door and a voice asking if anyone was inside.

Davey held his breath.

There was the sound of someone using the handle and then the door opened. Davey could sense someone on the other side as they quickly scanned the restroom and then shut the door again. Then there was another long time with no sound...too long, and Davey began to worry. Carefully, he turned to the door and opened it a crack. Peeking out, he could see right up the center aisle between the seats but no one was in sight. Emboldened, he stepped out of the restroom and took a tentative step into the main cabin. Still no one. Bending low, he peeked out the windows and was shocked to see the landscape on the outside of the sled zooming by at an incredible speed!

———————

Steadying himself on the deck, Davey reached out to a seat back for support and looked at his feet. Nothing was amiss. He felt not the slightest bit of disorientation or imbalance. Relinquishing his hold on the seat, he looked up and began walking along the aisle amazed that he didn't feel at all off balance; in fact, it didn't feel as if the sled were moving at all. And yet, he couldn't doubt the evidence of his own eyes as he saw the jungle outside moving past the windows in a blur of color.

Slowly, the realization came to him that while he remained hidden in the restroom, the test run of the rocket sled had begun; the track's electro-magnetic field had been switched on, the sled had risen on the wave of the invisible pulse, and its engines had ignited, sending it forward at ever increasing speed. Davey didn't know exactly what speed the sled was capable of, but he had heard the engineer say that if all went well, it would take all of six hours to circumnavigate the planet.

Suddenly worried about what his parents would say when they discovered that he was missing and reaching the conclusion that he had hidden away aboard the rocket sled, Davey fell into one of the thickly padded seats and just stared. Only gradually did he come to see that the seat back in front of him contained a visi-phone/satellite television hookup for use by passengers.

Quickly, he reached out for the receiver and barked a command to the computer at the other end.

"Landfall City, Cubicle #13," he said but all he heard was the emptiness of dead air. "Hello? Computer, answer me!"

But there was no reply. Of course, he thought, the rocket sled was not yet operational for passengers and during the test run there would be no need for communications to be open.

He replaced the receiver and tried the satellite television not really expecting a reaction and when none came, he was not disappointed. Well, not much.

Slowly, the realization came to him that he was trapped aboard the sled for the duration of its run and that he would have to face what punishment was sure to come when the machine once again pulled into Landfall station.

Angered at his predicament and blaming his parents for it, Davey convinced himself that if his mother and father had not taken him to Venus, none of it would have happened. Unbidden, his thoughts suddenly found themselves fixed on that last day on Earth when he had seen his friends for the last time.

They had met up in Jack's tree house down the street from where the Cescu family had lived for as long as Davey could remember. He had grown up in that neighborhood and had had adventures of all kinds in the surrounding woods and fields. Now, he was leaving the only home he ever knew or cared to know and the band of friends that he once believed could never have been broken up.

"Man, you are one lucky fella, Davey," he remembered Jack saying on that last day.

"What do you mean, Jack?" Davey said angrily. "If I go, I'll never see you guys again."

"Oh," said Jack, suddenly quiet; clearly, he had not thought through the consequences of Davey's departure. "But still, Venus! Man, what adventures you'll have!"

"Yeah; you'll have to ether-message us every week after you get there," said Dewey. "We'll want to know everything!"

"I want to find out what the Venusians look like," chimed in Marko. "They say they're ten feet tall, have one big eye, and can see in the dark!"

"Aw, there ain't no more Venusians," said Jonny, an agnostic when it came to intelligent life on other planets. "They all died thousands of years ago."

"Just the same, Davey might get a chance to visit one of their old cities and he can tell us all about 'em," insisted Marko.

"Anyway," said Jack. "We all wish we could be going to Venus too!"

"Oh, sure, it's a nifty idea," admitted Davey. "But not by yourself! Who wants to go live in a colony where the living quarters are hardly bigger than a living room on Earth or where you can't go outside any time you please, or where there's no place to go except the gym or the community room if you want to go anywhere?"

"I guess that would get old pretty fast," admitted Jack.

Their conversation was interrupted by a bark from below the tree house and when Davey looked down, he saw his dog Rex making as if he wanted to climb the tree after him.

Getting up, he scrambled down the wooden ladder and gathered up Rex in his arms.

"And I'll have to leave Rex behind," Davey said, his voice muffled in the dog's thick fur.

"Yeah, that is rough," said Dewey as the others came out of the tree after Davey.

Before anyone could say anything else, Davey's mother was heard calling from a few homes up the street. Reluctantly, Davey stood and took one last look at the circle of his friends.

"Well, it's been nice knowin' you fellas," he said. "I'll ether-message you as often as I can...and when I get back, we'll pick up where we left off!"

"Yeah, right!" they all said in ragged unison.

"And Jack," said Davey. "You take good care of Rex, y'hear? He's the best dog in the world."

"You bet I will, Davey."

Then, without further formality, Davey turned and ran in the direction of his home, anxious that his friends did not see the tears that suddenly flooded from his eyes.

Back on the sled, Davey reached up to wipe the tears that had run down his cheeks at the painful memories. Everything he had feared about coming to Venus had come to pass: the tight living conditions, the restriction on his movements, the boredom...and the resentment at his parents for bringing him there.

With a lump in his throat, Davey's mind seemed to shut down for a time and, paying no heed to the alien landscape outside the sled's windows, his thoughts once again fell back on memories of a more recent vintage.

He remembered that first day when his family arrived on Venus; the roar of the rocket engines, the hiss of air as the ship's hatch opened onto the recycled atmosphere of Landfall City, the long walk along the enclosed connector tube from the rocket leading into the central hub. He had expected the roomy reception area of the rocket ports on Earth but as soon as he had stepped from the connector tube his worst fears were realized.

Instead of a wide open reception area with thousands of people coming and going with busy shops and scooting ground cars, he found himself in a tiny room hardly big enough for a dozen people. There was a tiny, upright desk behind which stood a clerk who checked their names against a passenger manifest and around them were a number of thick, steel hatches, all closed, but giving the feeling they led into other rooms just as claustrophobic.

Davey's suspicions were confirmed later as a guide led the new arrivals through the central hub (at a few thousand square feet, the largest open area in Landfall City and naturally off limits to children), into the living area. The west wing was one of four long spokes that radiated out from the central hub with both sides of its long corridor lined with laboratories, storerooms, tech support, maintenance lockers, and finally living units.

His family's new home was cubicle #13 and although his parents had maintained a happy façade trying to convince him that the tiny broom closet that was to be their home for the next six years was just wonderful, they hadn't managed to convince him.

Where on Earth he had had his own room, a space larger than ten cubicles in Landfall City, he now had only a fold down bunk in an alcove that doubled as a computer work station where, in the days to come, Davey would spend a good deal of his time attending school.

Going to school with only a computer for company was bad enough, but when he finally had a chance to get out of the family's cubicle, there was really no place else to go. He met a couple of dozen other children and their parents at an evening social soon after his family had arrived on Venus and though he had made some friends, because there was not much to do in the way of entertainment in the close confines of the city, they did not spend much time all together. No bicycle riding, no tag or releivio, no pets, no hide and seek, and no fun. Oh sure, he and the other children could take turns using the gym equipment or playing video games but even those activities that had seemed so much fun to play on Earth, lost their attraction in the sunless, antiseptic chambers of Landfall City. And so, in a matter of months, Davey had exhausted all of the possibilities for having fun on Venus and each day after that seemed longer than the last.

Making matters worse however, was that his parents seemed oblivious to his travails.

"Good morning, Davey," his mother would say each morning after pulling aside the separator to his parents sleeping alcove.

"What's so good about it?" Davey grumbled, pulling the sheets over his head against the harsh lights inside their cubicle.

"Now, now Davey," chimed in his father. "Every day is a blessing and filled with new things to learn."

"Easy for you to say," Davey replied from under the sheets. "You get to hang around your lab and go out on EV excursions or even go and visit one of the other colonies. I have to stay here and spend all day getting cross eyed looking at that dumb computer screen."

"Is it really hurting your eyes, Davey?" asked his mother suddenly alarmed.

"No, I'm just kiddin' ma," said Davey, throwing off the sheets and jumping down from his bunk. "I just can't stand being cooped up in here all the time."

"But you can go to the gym or visit your friends in their cubicles..."

Davey rolled his eyes. "Ma, that's as bad as staying in here all day. Boy, do I hate Venus! Why did we ever have to leave Earth?"

"You know the answer to that, Davey," said his father, pulling out fresh clothing packages and tossing them to his son. "Your mother and I have vital research that can only be conducted here on Venus. If we're successful, it could mean new kinds of foods and medicines for the people back on Earth."

"I've heard it all before," said Davey tearing open the plastic packages with his teeth and taking out the fresh set of paper-based clothing.

"Davey!" said his mother.

"That's as much as I'm going to take from you young man," declared his father with that tone Davey understood to mean that he was dead serious.

"Sorry, ma, dad," he said with genuine regret. "But I just don't like it here on Venus. It's sooooo boring! There's nothing to do and I miss my friends back on Earth!"

"Well, there's not much we can do about that now," said his father calming down. "Now why don't you get dressed and come to breakfast."

"That's another thing I can't stand," said Davey, folding up his bunk. "I want real food, not that pre-fab junk we have to eat all the time."

"Now that I can understand," said his mother. "This food may be nutritious, but it certainly is not appetizing!"

"Well, finally, there's something we can all agree on!" said his father, laughing.

"I hate Venus," said Davey again, and dragged himself to the table.

The thought of food reminded Davey that he was hungry and even the pre-fab pastries that had been set out in the reception area were beginning to look good to him. But after spending some minutes nosing about the cabin and discovering that the auto meal servers were as inoperable as the visi-phones, he gave up the search for food and fell back into one of the seats.

With his only option to simply wait until the sled had finished its circumnavigation of the planet, all he could do was to stare out the banks of windows that together, allowed for panoramic views of the Venusian landscape.

By now, the thick jungle growth that had crowded close to the track had receded to be replaced by long, sloping uplands that fell away in distance to a shallow valley perhaps hundreds of miles in width. Davey could tell that the valley was carpeted in jungle growth that only gave way near a steaming ribbon of boiling water that drained the depression and disappeared into an impenetrable mist far in the distance.

For a boy like Davey, who had only been allowed out of the city for brief, very circumscribed excursions with his parents, the vista that had opened before his eyes was a revelation that shattered the claustrophobic notions that had compassed his judgment of Venus in the months since his arrival. Suddenly, the planet seized to be the abstract concept forced upon him by the prison of Landfall City or the entrapping walls of its jungle nest; now it was wide open and bursting with the potential for adventure.

With increasing fascination, Davey watched as the huge open valley gave way to foothills that grew quickly into a great mountain range whose peaks were swathed in thick clouds. Then, no sooner had the mountains crowded the view outside the windows, than they were replaced by an inky blackness as the rocket sled vanished from the Venusian surface to plunge into a stretch of tunnel that must have extended for many miles judging from how long it took to reemerge at the speed the sled was traveling.

Suddenly bursting into sunlight again, Davey shaded his eyes against the glare and then marveled at the ocean of molten rock whose thin crust continuously cracked and crashed against a beachfront of solid iron ore. On the horizon, the thick atmosphere was lit in glowing patches where the internal light from numberless volcanoes was reflected against the underside of clouds while along their flanks, streams of lava flowed in sparking rivulets.

Gradually, the molten landscape began to give way and at last the sled plunged thousands of feet before leveling off in a vast and arid plain whose sands radiated and refracted colors Davey had never seen before. Fascinated, he dared not blink for fear of missing some new vista, some new angle on a scene that could reveal unexpected delights. The sled dashed at dizzying speeds across the desert for what seemed like hours before plunging again, this time beneath one of the great Venusian seas that veined the planet's surface and merged into swampy deltas that in turn gave way to the jungles where most of the planet's colonies were located.

Although murky, Davey's fascinated gaze managed to penetrate the sunless gloom of the sea to make out the bulky forms of oceanic leviathans as they drifted just beyond the glow generated by the magno-rails beneath the sled. Drawn by the unnatural light, other denizens of the deep also made themselves visible as schools of exotic fish things flickered in and out of view and at one point, the sled rocketed through a cloud of aquatic sea life made up of organisms no bigger than a cluster of molecules that flashed and sparkled as the creatures drew energy from the electro-magnetism given off by the magno-rails. Then all trace of sea life vanished and the sled seemed to be moving through a jungle again only this time a sunken one; but that lasted only a brief few seconds before the machine emerged into the open air again and Davey found himself surrounded by even more fantastic sights than those he had encountered beneath the sea.

All around him, for as far as he could see, stretched the limits of an ancient Venusian metropolis. He had read about them for school of course, and even seen pictures taken by xenoarcheologists, but he had never expected to see the old ruins personally. His face pressed against the window, Davey stared first at the ruined residential towers that were off limits to Venusian commoners, then at the suggestion of collapsed aero-bridges that had swooped among the taller buildings and along which air cars were thought to have driven, and the vast open spaces that researchers theorized were used either for religious ceremonies or sporting events.

So vast was the city that even at the speed the sled was going, it took minutes for it to reach the suburbs where villas, still elegant in their ruined condition, dotted the hillsides amid a millennia old mass of encroaching moss. Finally, far outside the city and beyond the limits of the suburbs, Davey saw the sprawling cemetery that the vanished Venusians traditionally placed in a ring around their cities. Mostly obscured by a creeping carpet of purple moss, Davey fancied that he could still make out the regular rows of stone monuments that he knew from his studies were marked in an alphabet still largely unknown to Earth linguists. Then, too soon, it was all gone and the sled had carried Davey's vision beyond the great city and back again into desert landscapes mostly hidden under the cover of nightside darkness.

Although he knew it could not have been more than an hour or two, it felt to Davey as if the rocket sled continued on into the starless night for days, time that only seemed longer as he recalled the fantasmic sights of the Venusian city and the flights of fancy that they had inspired in him.

Then it was all over.

As it was when he began his ride aboard the rocket sled, so the end came unexpectedly as the sled slid to a halt at the Landfall City gantry without the slightest warning or suggestion of movement. Without a lurch or even sensation of a lessening of G forces, the surrounding jungle simply reappeared, dim in the suggestion of the coming dawn, and Davey could see the gantry slowly creeping along the ground to make contact with the side of the sled.

The next moment there was a hiss of air as the seal around the entry hatch was broken and the portal swung aside. Immediately, he heard his father shout "Davey! Are you in here?" And his mother asking, "Is he there?"

Suddenly, it seemed as if the empty sled was crowded with people, all pressing around him, hugging and squeezing.

"I'm okay, mom," Davey said as his mother crushed his face to her bosom.

"My baby! We were so worried!"

"I'm sorry, mom, dad," said Davey as his mother finally loosened her hold on him. "I was mad at you, mad at being on Venus and I...I guess I thought somehow, I'd punish you for taking me away from Earth..."

Even as he said it, the excuse sounded weak and contrived, but luckily, his parents were so relieved to have him back safe and sound that they did not seem to notice.

"You gave your parents quite a start, young man," said Dr. Lorden, gentle but stern.

"Yes, sir," replied Davey with equal gravity. "I understand, sir. It won't happen again."

"Oh, Davey!" said his mother, just before scooping him up in her arms again.

"I think we'd better go, now," said his father who did not seem as angry as Davey had expected.

Then, together, the family exited the sled, made their way through the throng of cheering residents, past the tables of pre-fab pastries, through the central hub, and down the west wing to cubicle #13.

———————

Three months later, the family was out again, but this time not for an EV excursion, or a trip to the gym, or the community center, nor even for a ride on the new rocket sled; no, this time it was someplace that they had not visited for almost a year since their arrival on Venus.

Once again, Davey found himself walking along a long gantry but this time it led to a great silvery rocket, poised on its gleaming fins, its nose pointed toward Earth. Through the gantry's plasteel walls, Davey could see clouds of steam beneath the ship as they billowed slowly in the thick Venusian atmosphere and overhead, a few of the brighter stars shone steadily in the sky. Ahead of him, a number of other passengers with luggage trailing behind them, moved in the same direction toward a large hatchway at the base of the rocket where an attendant checked their names against a passenger manifest.

"You know dear," his mother was saying to his father. "I thought I'd be more regretful about going back to Earth and leaving our work behind, but I'm not."

"I know what you mean," replied his father with a sigh. "I thought it would be harder, but I'm actually finding myself looking forward to going back home. Maybe its true what the old timers say, you never get Earth out of your blood."

"Gee, I'm sorry if what I did is making you give up what you really want to do," said a contrite Davey who nevertheless felt as if he had never been as close to his parents as he had in the weeks since he had stowed away aboard the rocket sled.

"Don't worry about it, Davey," said his father. "Your mother and I decided that this is best for all of us. We had plenty of time to talk while you were on the sled and we came to realize finally that it was pretty selfish of us to think more of ourselves and our careers than of what was best for you."

"Yes, even though Venus was the right place for us, it wasn't for you," said his mother. "You were still too young to leave Earth and be forced to live under such restrictive conditions. Landfall City, though a wonderful place for scientists, is no place for a young boy."

"A boy needs open space and room to run around in," continued his father. "A dog and a bike and a pet turtle and like minded friends. Some day, we'll come back to Venus and on that day, you can decide for yourself whether you want to come with us or not."

Davey did not answer. He was happy to return to Earth and his friends and the home he had loved. It was the right thing to do as his parents said but...he stopped suddenly, and looked back at the opening leading into the city and then at the stars overhead and the jungle that hemmed in the gantry and on the other side of that wall of vegetation, the fabulous outlines of the Venusian City beyond the sea...a city he intended to visit again some day.

I...like Venus!" Davey thought as he turned back and entered the rocket for home.

The Disappointed Martian

"How many years?"

EVERY TIME SIRJYL THOUGHT of it he had to do the math: he was 150 years old, his parents were 60 years older than he was and they were born 3 years after the first rocket ship from Earth arrived on Mars... That was as far as he got before giving up trying to figure out how long it had been since the last time he had even seen one of his own kind.

That, however, did not prevent him from hoping it would yet happen. Hoping...*for how many years?* he asked himself again. Smiling at the self-pity he detested, he realized it had been a long time, at least since he was a youth of only a score of seasons.

He remembered the small cluster of traditional Martian dwellings that his family and a number of others had occupied here alongside the canal and how he had played games of hide and seek and chase the soomping with the other children. There were get togethers in the cool winter evenings at neighbors' dwellings and on hot summer afternoons when he and his friends returned from a day in school, parents would take turns sitting in front of each others' dwellings sipping glasses of rare klopel juice waiting for the children to come up the dusty road.

Afternoons were taken up with play exploring the dry canal or looking for klopel fruit or playing competition games. Evenings were given over to homework and quiet time with parents and siblings. Nightfall came early with the thin Martian atmosphere and Sirjyl recalled lying on his cot and staring out the open window of his dwelling at the brilliant galaxy of stars that filled the heavens and listening to the desert winds that sifted red sands across the screening that covered the window openings.

Now, with the passage of well over a hundred Martian years, those times seemed idyllic to Sirjyl. A golden age that he had failed to fully appreciate at the time and one he had tried to preserve in the many years since. But those efforts had become increasingly difficult as one by one all those friends and neighbors and family members had either disappeared or gone on to a happier afterlife.

In his stone dwelling by the canal, the same dwelling he had been born and raised in, he occupied the same room in which he had done so much youthful dreaming and still looked out the same window at the same stars that had not moved or changed in all the years. On shelves in the living section of his home, sat readers collected over a lifetime from the many abandoned dwellings he had explored in the years of searching for companionship. Volumes he had loved in his youth and that he collected now and reread endlessly in an attempt to recapture if only for a little while, that sense of the lost golden age when their stories seemed so important to he and his friends.

Putting away the utensils cleaned after his solitary breakfast, Sirjyl flung a satchel over his shoulder, the same satchel with which he used to carry his readers home from school, and stepped outside his dwelling.

Pausing on the dusty path leading from the front opening of his stone domicile, Sirjyl took a deep breath of the morning air reveling in the fresh scent of the mineral laden sand and fancying that he could taste the suggestion of moisture drifting from the empty canal. But he knew that was only a trick of his mind; wishful thinking, as there had not been moisture on Mars for well over a hundred years...or at least, none worth measuring. With the exception of the specially adapted klopel plant, no other indigenous life form survived on the planet and the great canals that his ancestors had engineered in prehistoric times had run dry centuries before he was born.

Which begged the question: could the golden age of his youth only have been a mirage as seen through the eyes of a child? Although his common sense told him that it was most likely so; that the adults of the time had probably been plagued with many challenging problems the greatest of which was simple survival. But he never could recall any complaints from his parents or other members of the cluster. Were they that strong or had he just never noticed? He chose not to dwell on the subject preferring instead to concentrate on preserving that golden age...without anything to look forward to, no work, no friends, no mate, no family...it was all he had that made life worth living.

Stepping along the path to the unpaved road that ran past his dwelling, Sirjyl noticed that erosion continued to wear away at the thin slabs of slate that formed the roof of his home. He would have to go to the old quarry and chip away a few more to effect repairs. The thick stone walls of the dwelling however, looked as if they had not changed in all the years since he lived there with his parents.

As he did every morning, more out of habit than the expectation of finding anything, Sirjyl checked his message box alongside the road but it was empty...the same as it had been every morning for the last hundred years. Sighing, he took to the road that followed the edge of the canal and led in the direction of the Terran city whose glassite dome glistened distantly in the morning sun.

Once again, Sirjyl wondered at the attitude of the Terrans that kept bringing them to Mars despite the fact that it was in the concluding phase of a death that had gone on longer than any Martian could remember. Sirjyl recalled the stories his parents used to tell him about the time when the first rocket from Earth had arrived on Mars. Of course, they had been too young to have had first hand knowledge of the event themselves, but according to tales that had been handed down to them, the first Terrans to arrive had been friendly and exchanged information with Martians on how to survive on the dying world. Even then, the Martian population was sparse and when the Terrans began to build their first cities, there was no thought of resentment but only consternation about why the newcomers would want to invest so much time and energy on a world that offered them so little.

But Terrans, it seemed, were an adaptable race and many of them claimed to have fallen in love with the planet's barren landscapes and even vowed that in time, they could restore much of it to its former beauty. That idea pleased the Martians who continued their friendly relations with the Terrans and not long after, began referring to the planet and themselves as Mars and Martians. It was only in his old readers that Sirjyl later discovered the planet's original name and the Martians' name for themselves but by then it hardly mattered as the race was obviously dying out.

That too was an unpleasant fact that Sirjyl eventually learned as first his family members died and then the rest of the cluster members began to scatter in search of food supplies that had grown more scarce over the years. In a way, the Martians had the Terrans to thank for the few of their fellows who continued to survive, including Sirjyl himself. If not for the kindly Terrans sharing their food and supplies, the Martian race would have died out soon after their arrival. Looking out over the expansive width of the canal that fell away at the side of the road, Sirjyl saw its sandy emptiness as a symbol of the end of Martian civilization and the ascendancy of the Terran. Some day, the

Earthers said, the canals would once again flow with water and when that happened, Martian civilization would be reborn. But if all the Martians were dead, would it be Martian civilization or simply Terran civilization transplanted to the red planet? Sirjyl suspected the latter, but he had long since stopped worrying about the distant future and preferred to concentrate on his own lifetime and his desperate hope to recreate his golden age that at various times included a mate and family and the bringing together of other families to reform the old neighborhood cluster as he remembered it.

After walking for some little time, the sun had only risen a few fingers above the horizon and the road, having left the canal, veered toward the big air lock that pierced the side of the dome enclosing the Terran city of Arborville. The road itself had gone from a little used trail to one covered with the tracks of many heavy all-terrain vehicles favored by the Terrans in moving about the surface of the planet.

Approaching the base of the dome, Sirjyl passed through a vehicle park where the Terrans left their motorized transports when not in use and, like the over sized air lock that gave entrance to the city, it was unguarded. After all, with everyone from Earth inside the city, who was left to vandalize the equipment? Shifting his satchel, Sirjyl struck a worn knob beside the air lock door and when the portal hissed open, stepped over to the small chamber inside. Behind him, the first door closed and immediately his ears began to pop with the change in atmosphere. Although the air on

Mars was much too thin for Terrans to breath, the oxygen rich environment of the enclosed dome presented no problem to Martians.

In a few moments, the inner lock had swung open and Sirjyl stepped through into the city proper. He shivered slightly in the increased warmth and waved a friendly greeting to the Terran technicians whose duty it was to monitor the dome's seals. They waved back and never gave him a second glance. Long accustomed to each other, Terrans and Martians came and went from the city as they pleased with all of Arborville's facilities available for use by both people...that is, when there used to be more Martians. These days the entire local Martian population consisted only of Sirjyl himself.

Without hesitation, Sirjyl began the long walk up the city's central promenade that stretched for many footpads in either direction giving plenty of room for both pedestrians and the near silent motorized carts that zoomed up and down Arborville's grid of well laid out streets and avenues.

Just as in a city on Earth, Arborville had its suburbs of single unit dwellings (constructed mainly of artificial materials in the peculiar Terran fashion) located on the outer edges of the circular shaped colony while the larger buildings gathered at the center consisted of administrative, manufacturing, and research functions. But to Sirjyl, the most interesting feature of the Terran city was its vast array of plant life.

As much as they claimed to love the harsh landscape of the Martian desert, the Terrans clearly could not be without the lush vegetation that grew wild on their native planet. Everywhere in Arborville, beneath the weak light that filtered down through the pink skies of Mars and through the glassite dome, there were creepers and ivies that crawled over every kind of structure, lawns of grasses that separated buildings in swathes of green, gardens filled with every kind of vegetable and fruit, and everywhere, outside every doorway and window it seemed, were pots of earth that sprouted flowers in a dizzying variety of colors.

Most impressive of all however, were the towering trees that lined the streets and whose branches almost brushed the top of the dome. Over the years, Sirjyl had learned that they represented many different kinds of species from Earth including maple, oak, ash, and pine. Some even included difficult to grow tropical trees whose fronds swayed gently in the controlled atmosphere of the dome.

Sirjyl always enjoyed his walk along "Main Street," gazing admiringly at the patterns of leaves and branches over his head and wondering if Mars had ever been able to support such a profusion of life.

As usual, many of the Terrans walking along the street waved to him in their fashion and sometimes greeted him with a word or two. Very rarely did one express any kind of surprise at seeing him and when one did, it was invariably a very young Terran freshly arrived from Earth. Thus it was with little attention that he finally arrived at what the Terrans called a public media center where computer records, communications to Earth, and even records written physically on a material called paper could be accessed by anyone in the city.

Mounting the stairs, he pushed his way through revolving glassite doors and swiftly went to a drinking fountain that constantly bubbled a clear stream of water that never ceased to amaze Sirjyl. When he was a youngster living in the cluster, moisture could only be had naturally by sucking on the klopel fruit and now that the last of those plants had nearly vanished, he was reliant on what water the Terrans could provide. At first, transported all the way from Earth, water needed to be used only sparingly; but then the Terrans began hauling in chunks of ice as big as asteroids that circled the sun beyond the orbit of Mars and after that, there was enough water to turn Arborville and other cities like it into giant arboretums. Some day, the Terrans insisted, there would be enough to transform the whole ecology of Mars from sandy desert to blooming gardens. Sirjyl, however, was not sure he would like to see such changes, positive as they may have been. It would change the world too much from the golden times he remembered in his youth.

Finished with his drink, Sirjyl passed the information desk saying "hello" in the Terran tongue to the female clerk before entering the hall of computers and finding an empty station. There, he set down his satchel and told the computer his password. When the screen became active, he asked for his personal file and began his search.

Searching the computer files had become a daily routine for Sirjyl over the past several decades; each morning except for the day Terrans called Sunday when the library was closed, he would access his personal files where any report of activity by his people anywhere on Mars would be automatically downloaded from electronically published newspaper articles, professional journals, government reports, privately produced web pages, and even personal correspondences that did not have a privacy lock. All of the data produced over the day before would be collated and collected by the computer and delivered to his address where he could review them himself. In most cases, entries could be deleted safely as they had nothing to do with what he was interested in but in a few cases, they conformed to what he was looking for, namely the companionship of his own kind.

The truth was, that the dying planet had been taking its human population along with the native flora and fauna and leaving people like Sirjyl lonely and isolated and yearning for contact with their own kind. And though Sirjyl had decided long ago that he could live without friends or family if he had to, the desire for the special benefits only a mate could bring had been difficult if not impossible to suppress. In the daytimes, keeping himself occupied with his visits to the city, tending his rock garden, exploring the old byways along the canal, or delving into his old readers, made the absence bearable but the night times were often an agony of longing and loss. It was then that he could no longer deny to himself that he was as human as anyone else and felt that he could not go on without the support only a special female could provide. That was what kept him coming to the library every day; the hope that he would discover somewhere on Mars, a female with whom he could bond. But each day was the same: there was no such person and with each passing day, as the decades stretched on, the possibility of finding such a one became more and more difficult to believe.

Disappointed and angry with himself for allowing his hopes to rise (as they did each day when he entered the library and activated the computer), Sirjyl ordered the computer to shut down, took his satchel, and exited the library with considerably heavier steps than when he had entered.

As he always did, he wondered how he could manage to get through the rest of the day and as usual, he decided to wander through the city a bit before returning to the outside. Somehow, the tree lined streets and neat little rows of dwellings surrounded in green helped sooth his spirits and restore his battered feelings.

He was passing a schoolyard filled with Terran youngsters laughing and running about in a manner not unlike what he recalled doing with his own friends years before when the sound of a voice stopped him.

"Hello, Mr. Martian," said the voice.

Sirjyl turned in the direction of the voice and discovered that it belonged to a Terran female no older than six or seven Terran years.

"Hello, little girl," Sirjyl said. "Shouldn't you be within the enclosure of the schoolyard?"

"It's all right," replied the girl. "I live across the street and they let me go home for lunch."

"I see," said Sirjyl feeling the mood of despondency slipping from him in the presence of the youthful Terran. "My name is Sirjyl; what is yours?"

"Kama," said the girl unhesitatingly. "My mother told me it means 'flower' in Martian. Is that true?"

"It's true," nodded Sirjyl. "But more precisely, the word means 'flower that blossoms in the desert.' When there used to be flowers on Mars, it was of a species that covered the ground like a carpet and whose petals sported colors of every shade from pure white to darkest maroon. It was a very beautiful sight to see miles of surface area covered with the plant...at least, that's what I've been told. I've never seen any flowers on Mars myself."

The girl's expression had gone from delight to disappointment at Sirjyl's final words.

"You never saw a flower?" she asked.

"Well, not outside the city," admitted Sirjyl not without some sadness in his voice. "That's why I enjoy visiting your city so often; to look at the trees and grasses and especially the many varieties of colorful flowers."

"Oh, we have lots of them at my house," said Kama, brightening. "Would you like to see them?"

"I'd be delighted, but what about school?"

"Oh, I have plenty of time," she said, taking his hand and tugging him in the direction of a dwelling across the street.

Finding that being in the little Terran's company raised his spirits greatly, Sirjyl allowed himself to be led into the yard space surrounding the neat dwelling where Kama and her family lived.

Although there were a few flowers planted along the short walkway leading to the front door, Kama did not linger there but instead, continued around the dwelling to the rear of the property. Passing through a squeaky gate and into the small private area behind the living unit, Sirjyl suddenly found himself amidst a veritable bower of blooming plants.

Staring, he noted the crawling species that had been trained to grow along upright trellises and over the roof of the dwelling, beds of vari-colored ground plants that curved along the borders of the yard in elaborate shapes and behind them, rows of flowered plants that grew to different heights, each succeeding the other with the tallest in the back with their giant sunbursts hanging heavily and threatening to snap their stalks with their weight. Overall was the mingled scent of thousands of flowers and even the background hum of Terran insects that were an essential component of the city's vegetation plan.

"It's beautiful!" gasped Sirjyl.

"I knew you'd like it," said Kama in delight. "Me and mother work in the garden nearly every day...but my mother does most of the work."

"How wonderful it must be to come out here to read or simply stare in appreciation that something so rare could be accomplished on Mars," said Sirjyl more to himself than to Kama. Indeed, after seeing such a sight, there was no longer any doubt in his mind that the Terrans could change the planet into a garden again as they insisted.

Suddenly there was a squeaking sound and Sirjyl saw an older female Terran pushing a door open and emerge from the dwelling; no doubt the youngster's mother.

"Kama?" said the older female. "What are you doing back home? And who is that with you?"

"Hi, mom," said Kama. "This is Mr. Sirjyl...he's a Martian. I brought him over to see our garden."

"Good morning, Sirjyl," said the mother, aware of Martian custom that included no salutation of rank or status nor even of surname.

"Good morning, Mrs..."

"Stoneham," said the mother. "But you can call me Helen."

"Good morning, Helen," said Sirjyl extending a hand for the Terran practice of greeting.

Helen shook his hand in the dainty style of Terran women and cocked her head slightly in the direction of the garden.

"What do you think of Kama's handiwork," she said, no doubt exaggerating the little girl's contribution.

"As I was saying to your daughter, I think it's marvelous!" said Sirjyl without reservation.

"Sirjyl said that my name means 'flower that blossoms in the desert,' mom; isn't that beautiful?"

"Very!" said Helen with genuine feeling. "I can imagine how you can appreciate our garden, Sirjyl and of course, you're welcome to come and see it whenever you want."

The invitation did not completely surprise Sirjyl as it was the manner of Terrans to be open and accepting even of strangers until their trust was proven misplaced.

"I'm truly grateful, Helen, and will take advantage of your kind offer," said Sirjyl.

"Yippee!" said Kama literally jumping up and down in her excitement. "We have a real Martian for a friend!"

Thereafter, the daily visits and continuing disappointments of his library search became a good deal lessened when he followed them with time spent in the Stoneham family's garden and in no time, Sirjyl found himself helping Kama and her mother with the plants. Indeed, his visits to their home became those of increasing wonder as he helped to prune the flowers and dig his fingers into the soft loam to pick them clean of old roots and unwanted insects and afterwards planting seeds and bulbs. Later, he was given the chore of watering the plants and over the days that followed, watched as his handiwork grew and eventually bloomed in their own right. At last, he learned the secret of planning ahead, using the little greenhouse attached to the dwelling to pre-grow selected plants and then planting them in the garden in such a way that when they bloomed, colors could be arranged in any order desired: by type or in intricate patterns such as the one Kama surprised him with by writing out his name in purple colored blossoms.

At last, overcoming his reluctance to prune the flowers, he was presented with a handful to take home to his own dwelling. That day, Kama accompanied him home for the first time and helped him choose the perfect location in his dwelling for the stone vase with its spray of flowers.

"There!" said Kama after they had spent some time in serious consideration of the problem.

"I think it looks beautiful!" declared Sirjyl.

"Are you sure there are no flowers anywhere on Mars?" asked Kama for only the hundredth time it seemed.

"I'm sure," replied Sirjyl with the same level of sadness he had answered her all those other times. "The only flowers on Mars these days is in cities like Arborville."

"That's too bad! They look so pretty by the window there."

"They do, don't they?"

"But you're rock garden outside is very pretty too," said Kama hurriedly.

"It is very creative," admitted Sirjyl. "But it's still not as good as a real garden with real flowers."

"From now on, I'll bring you fresh flowers for your house every week!" declared Kama who subsequently did and continued to do so for many years until having married and produced children of her own, came with them as a unit to deliver Sirjyl his flowers.

Over the years, however, Kama had not only grown older, but wiser, eventually coming to realize that her Martian friend was engaged in a constant battle against depression and despondency. Sensing his desperation, she became a good companion to him, little realizing how much Sirjyl had come to rely on her friendship to ease the pain of a loneliness he finally accepted would never be assuaged.

As for Sirjyl himself, for many years he continued to visit the Arborville library and although he occasionally made contact with a few fellow Martians, even female ones, nothing ever came of the effort; it was as if too much time had passed and Martians as a group had forgotten how to be a society. Gradually, his visits became more rare with more of his time spent at the Stonehams' and with little Kama who soon grew into a young woman.

Throughout the years, their mutual love of plants and flowers continued to keep their friendship strong and when Kama had children of her own, Sirjyl once again found his dwelling frequently filled with the laughter of youngsters (albeit through the breather plugs in their little noses). And so, more often than not, he could forget his loneliness as he basked in the love and affection of his Terran "family" who made sure he was regularly seen by a Terran physician and that he received his government benefits.

But not all was undiluted happiness; because of the long lived nature of Martian physiognomy, Sirjyl had outlived many Terrans he had known and Kama, unfortunately, was one. And so, when it came time to bury her in the Terran fashion, Sirjyl was among family members in the little cemetery outside the city and his own sadness at his friend's passing was eased by the little grandchildren who clung to his legs or who wanted to hold his hand. The years that followed were studded with happy moments with the Terran children and their parents, with visits to each other's homes, and celebrations of various Terran holidays but as the years since Kama's death stretched into decades, Sirjyl's own days began to catch up with him. Having learned the Terran language, he spent much of his time writing his "autobiography," a reminiscence of his growing up in the cluster, the rising strength of the Terrans, the beauty of the Martian landscape, his hopes and regrets and shattered dreams with the fitting climax being that the book was rejected by every publisher to whom it was submitted. No one seemed interested.

With the advance of old age and final disappointment regarding his efforts at writing, Sirjyl had learned to accept his fate and retreated behind the walls of the familiar: delving into his favorite readings, gardening in Arborville, tending the little chores around his dwelling, and walking the trails along the canal just as he did as a child. But sometimes, Sirjyl's heart still grew heavy and often he wanted to cry as the Terrans sometimes did and regretted that Martian eyes lacked tear ducts. Instead, he gradually began to give up and stopped coming out of his dwelling and when Kama's great-grand-children came by to bring him fresh flowers, he could barely manage the energy to greet them.

When the children returned home, they asked their parents what they thought was wrong with "grandfather Sirjyl" and was told that the old Martian suffered from the same things Terran elderly did when they reached an age when all they once knew was gone and the world around them had changed beyond recognition.

"It's a natural phenomenon," their elders explained as they watched construction of the new domeless Arborville suburbs made possible with the restoration of a near Earth normal atmosphere on Mars. "Sirjyl has lived almost 300 years. He probably knows that his time has passed and does not wish to live in world he no longer recognizes."

Saddened by the knowledge that they would soon lose their special family friend, the children determined to visit Sirjyl more often but although their comings and goings lifted the old Martian's spirits somewhat, it was clear that his physical condition continued to decline.

At last, having reached the old age he always expected, Sirjyl finally had to admit to himself that he would never find that special Martian companion, the one who would comfort him on lonely nights when the wind swished the red sands against the screening and who would have given him his own children to delight in. Sighing, Sirjyl reached up from his cot and his hand was taken by a Terran child whose face was damp with wasteful tears.

"Don't cry, Vulnoose," he said weakly. "Don't you know your name means "happy face" in the old Martian tongue?"

"I know, grandfather," said the girl. "But I can't help it. I don't want you to die."

"You don't have to cry," replied Sirjyl, looking around at the scores of Terrans who had filled his sleeping chamber and spilled into the rest of his dwelling, all descendents of his old friend Kama. "I have suffered loneliness in my life but my suffering would have been much greater if not for you. I go now to see my Martian family and to never be lonely for them again. Kama, I trust, will be there too and when I see her, I'll say 'hello' just the way we used to and take her hand like I'm doing yours, and tell her all about little Vulnoose and how she cried for my passing."

And with those words, Sirjyl slipped from life and was never lonely nor disappointed again.

No More Eves

SHARA STOPPED WHEN SHE saw the trail.

It was faint, almost invisible, but she was long used to keeping a wary eye out for any sign of unusual activity.

She stood very still, not moving for a good while, listening.

She heard the sound of the ocean of course, as it lapped up onto the narrow stretch of sand that began not twenty feet from where she stood. There was the rustling from the tufts of coarse grasses that covered the land from where the distant line of dead trees ended to where it sloped down almost to the water's edge.

Relaxing her vigilance, Shara crouched close to the ground and parted the grass at her feet. Looking carefully at the sandy soil beneath she found what she was looking for, a narrow band of squibbles that wound its way in the direction of a low rise just ahead.

Fearing the worst, but still hoping for the best, she decided to push on, carefully, to make sure the trail was a fresh one before making a decision to turn back or not. She had been moving north, following the beach but staying off the sandy shore when her senses had warned her of activity in the area.

The tawdry remains of a great civilization, the scattered evidences of a world once populated by billions of
human beings were now merely the elements of a new reality, accepted without question by its new tenants, human
and insect alike.

Although the first rule of survival was to avoid others, turning back would be inconvenient involving a delay of at least three weeks in her migration plan.

Shara hiked up the straps of her small backpack and checked to make sure the hunting knife was still in her belt. She was wearing a pair of camouflaged trousers and a pea green shirt with the sleeves torn off. Slung over one shoulder and with her left hand and finger positioned over the trigger mechanism, she held a small caliber hunting rifle at the ready. If the trail was a fresh one however, her weapons would be useless and if the colony posed a danger her most reliable asset then would be her legs and how fast they could take her away from the colony. But realistically, there was no real reason to doubt that the trail was a fresh one; this close to the ocean, any kind of trail could not have lasted more than a few days.

So it was with extreme caution that she moved up the rise, keeping well away from the trail. That way, even if she was spotted by outlying scouts, she would still have time to realize that she had been discovered and beat a hasty retreat.

Of course, she could have avoided all the bother by just turning back, but there had always been a streak of stubborn pride in her that refused to accept such a sensible course of action. She allowed herself a little smile as she remembered how often her mother had warned her about "pride coming before a fall;" her mother had always been a fount of pre-blast aphorisms.

As she approached the top of the rise she could tell that the trail she was following, which had since been joined by a number of side trails, had become a well beaten stretch of sand. Devoid of beach grass, it crested the hillock and disappeared down the opposite slope. With great experience, she continued to follow it until, late in the afternoon, she spotted the colony.

It was nestled in a small depression between rocky hillocks that gave easy access to the sea at its eastern end. Within the protective confines of the little valley, Shara could make out the telltale living quarters, the hundreds of holes that had been artificially bored among the rocks and the complex maze of inclined planes, stairwells and ledges. There were even a number of cargo elevators operated by a primitive form of steam power. Small plumes of smoke rose here and there among the rocks where foundries were at work and the well maintained roads hosted an impressive variety of steam powered vehicles. Altogether, Shara estimated that the ant colony was composed of about ten thousand individuals. And with a population like that, there was no way she could make her way through such broken terrain without being discovered. And however fast her legs could carry her, she would tire long before she could cross the frontiers of the colony's territory. Frustrated, she turned around and, with the day's light rapidly fading, ran back as far as she could and when she tired, still continued to move for the rest of the night.

A few days later, Shara was making her way steadily through the thin stretch of forest just south of the blasted city. The area further to the west was a mountainous one and so her course was more difficult than it would have been if she had been allowed to continue along the seashore. There was plenty of marching uphill and skidding downhill but now and then she took a chance and walked along the crumbling remains of the old roadways to give herself a rest, but as soon as she felt herself strong enough, she returned unhesitatingly back into the wild area.

At one point, she found herself situated atop a shattered, stony ridge devoid of the stunted, twisted trees that covered its lower slopes. Although it appeared as though the rocky formation had suffered the blow of a terrific explosion it was only the result of some natural catastrophe after all. Resting her rifle against a protruding boulder, Shara unslung her backpack and sat down. Munching on some canned crackers, she took the opportunity to study the city that sat black and gray below her.

Its physicality seemed to spread like a cancer on the landscape from the handful of cracked and crumbling skyscrapers at the center of the blackened area to the irregular, ash-gray fringes of destruction in what remained of the deserted suburbs.

Forty-five years after the atomic bombings, life of a sort still found sustenance in its crystallized, irradiated soil. Great, disfigured plants creeped greenly along the once thronging boulevards and covered the piles of rubble and remaining buildings in a festoon of grotesque verdure. The effect was ugly and dangerous harboring as it did, wild animals, colonies of roaches jealous of their territories and disfigured, imbecilic humans.

But the bombs that had destroyed many of the major cities in the country had not been the primary reason for the landscape's present condition. Many years before, Shara had been told by her mother that the atomic war had come at a time when the world had felt safe from such a fate. Then war came to countries on the other side of the world; atomics were exchanged and when the conflict had come to the point when the combatants realized that victory was impossible, they decided to lash out, irrationally striking at those other nations that had earlier tried to halt their suicidal conflict.

Atomics rained down on the major cities of the world but it was not those direct blasts that had doomed civilization. Lingering radiation from that first wild frenzy of explosions in Asia had already begun to drift across the world and when it was joined by that of the later blasts, a thin blanket of radiation encircled the world killing most of the plant and animal life and driving mankind to near extinction. But although a permanent cloud of dust was left in the atmosphere, the sun continued to offer its life giving warmth as a bright blur in the heavens and so, even though the surface of the earth had been reduced to a wasteland, it did not take long for its dormant plant life to reassert itself. In only a few years, the world was green again. There were many of the old familiar varieties of course, but there were also many unfamiliar ones such as the ground crawling vine that thrived in the dead soil of blasted cities.

Shara shook herself of her unwanted reverie. How often had she imagined those long gone events in her mind? Events that she herself had never witnessed? The world that had existed before her birth, the world of teeming millions, of great forests and green oceans was, as far as she was concerned, a fantasy that had never existed. This was the real world: an empty world of stunted trees, deformed animals, and insect civilizations.

Standing, she scanned the reverse slope of the ridge and began negotiating her way to the bottom.

———————

Shara lay on the roof of a single story ranch house in the midst of what once had been a stylish bedroom community. Even in the worn, dilapidated condition of the houses and the debris strewn streets, it was still possible to make out the contours of the tightly knit neighborhood; the property lines demarcated by broken and twisted fencing, the homes which somehow remained standing and the charred pits of those that had long since been destroyed by fire and blast and the cracked, ruptured streets, avenues and lanes.

But Shara did not really notice all of that. It was part of her world. The tawdry remains of a great civilization, the scattered evidences of a world once populated by billions of human beings were now merely the elements of a new reality, accepted without question by its new tenants, human and insect alike. It had all meant something more to her mother, Shara knew, but whatever her mother had told her of that dead world, however objectively useful some of that information might have been, it was ultimately useless to her daughter. It was of more vital interest to Shara to know how to deal with the ants and roaches and the bees and how to identify the lair of a fellow human than it was to know how a dead race had once lived.

Shara continued to lay on the roof, her rifle at her side and a pair of binoculars against her eyes. She had made her way into the suburbs two days before and, moving by night, managed to identify a likely location to settle in for a week or so while she did some foraging in the neighborhood. It was a two story bungalow, relatively intact, deeply shrouded in wild plant life and across the street. She had had the house under observation for the last 24 hours and having seen no activity around it, only now was beginning to feel sure about it.

Carefully, she inched her way back to the edge of the roof, eased herself down onto an attached garage, and jumped to the ground.

Dusk had fallen as she crossed the street, crouching low. Dashing quickly into a mass of shrubbery surrounding the front of the bungalow, she flattened herself against the warped clapboards. Having studied the building for hours she knew the exact location of every door and window. Swiftly, she bellied herself into one of the windows and slid onto the floor inside. It was dark indoors and her nose wrinkled up with the scent of moldy carpeting and somewhere water was dripping. It did not take her long to search the house and pick out an upstairs room for herself. It came with a good view of both the rear of the building and a good portion of the street out front. Its single doorway also added to her sense of security. Then, feeling somewhat safe, she settled down for her first night's sleep in two and half days.

The next morning, she was up early. She searched the house again by daylight but found nothing of value and so widened her search in the next few days to the rest of the subdivision. She moved by daylight, staying on the broad avenues, and only made her way back to the bungalow after dark.

While on her rooftop perch across the street she had spied the neo-Norman battlements of an old mall closer toward the heart of the city. Early on, her mother had taught her that the amalgamation of stores inside the shopping malls made it easy and convenient to find everything they wanted in the same place, much as it did to her people before the bombs had fallen. The only problem with such a place was that its enclosed area could also be a dangerous trap for the unwary. And Shara had not survived so long without being cautious. She would head for the mall but not go inside; instead, she would rely on the sprawl of minor stores that invariably surrounded it.

Her problem was that the supplies she was looking for were usually the same as those other humans would be searching out. If there was anyplace in the vast emptiness of the country where she would be likely to run into one of her own kind, it would be amidst the lure of plenty. Of course, even that possibility was extremely unlikely, there was more of a chance of trespassing onto the territory of an insect colony than it was of running into a fellow human. In fact, Shara could not remember the last time she had even seen a human being. Her mother had died nearly twenty years before (Shara had lost count) and since then, she had seen only a handful of other people. Most of the time they were imbeciles, the pitiful products of procreation between humans whose genetic makeup had been hopelessly scrambled as a result of the effects of lingering radiation. Even more rare, were the cases of physical deformity. Her mother had once told her that such cases were very few as most of those born that way died in infancy. But not all. Shara had once seen a man with two arms no larger than a child's. The thought made her shudder, even now. But normals, such as she and her mother, were the rarest humans of all. In all her life, she had seen only a single one and in that instance, her mother made sure he never spotted them.

Insects on the other hand, seemed to have had a much easier time of it than human beings. That was because their lives were lived at a much faster metabolic rate her mother had said. A typical insect, in its short life span, lived a hundred human years she claimed. Shara did not know about that, but since her mother had been proved correct about so many other things, she was inclined to believe it. Far from being hurt by the effects of radiation, some insects not only survived, but seemed to enjoy an increase in their intelligence. But it was a soulless intelligence for all that. Shara did not know anything about what insects were like before the bombings and only had her mother's word that there had been nothing remarkable about them, but now there were a number of species such as the roaches and ants who had developed rudimentary civilizations. But the strange thing was that they seemed to still be driven with what her mother had described as instinct because although they boasted such discoveries as steam power and explosives, there was no evidence of art of any kind. Individualism was still unknown to insects and in the meantime, with their blind loyalty to their colony and their faster metabolism, it would not be long before they became the new masters of the earth. Already, Shara had come across whole areas of the countryside devoid of life where she was sure insect wars had been fought with soulless savagery. Someday, she was sure, there would be no place for a human to hide or run and on that day, she firmly hoped she would be long dead!

In the meantime, she needed to gather the supplies she would need to continue her migration northward. It was a pattern begun by her mother years before when she first emerged from the cave she had been visiting when the bombs fell. She stayed in the caves as long as she could, months maybe, surviving on rations deposited there for a spelunking emergency. She eventually emerged into a ravaged, seemingly dead world. But she soon saw the green shoots of stubborn plants begin to poke through the soil again and in the next few years, evolved a survival plan for herself. Luckily, she seemed to be one of the very few people for whom the radiation that blanketed the world had little effect. Oh, she knew it would one day kill her, but not for a long time. As the seasons came and went, she evolved a timetable that brought her north in the summer and back south in the winter, a pattern Shara had continued to follow.

The day had grown warm by the time Shara found what she was looking for. She stood across what was once a multi-laned approach to one of the shopping plazas and took the binoculars from her backpack. Slowly, she scanned her target. Multiple doorways stared back at her across a parking lot filled with the rusting hulks of ancient vehicles and the greens and browns of wild growth. Thick lianas snaked through the open lot, their tendrils ripping up the old tarmac in their search for underground nourishment. Here and there, gnarled trees squatted low amidst the glitter and glisten of glass from shattered windows.

Throughout, there was no other sign of life but the rampant plants. Shara knew that could be deceptive, but her check was the best she could do from where she was. Eventually she would have to draw closer to one of the stores and the army surplus store she had in mind was as good as any other.

Holding her rifle ahead of her, she moved forward, passing through a line of rank grass at the edge of the parking lot before stepping among the piles of rusting metal. She had seen nothing out of the ordinary by the time she reached the first shop and so, with a last survey of the outside, stepped gingerly into the old clothing store. Just inside the doorway she stopped to allow her eyes to adjust to the gloomy interior, constantly alert for any sound of danger. There was none and so, presently, she moved deeper inside. The items closer to the front of the store were always either the most damaged or long since taken so she wasted little time there. Keeping close to one of the walls, she made her way to the rear of the store, clearing herself a safe path by knocking over rusted display racks as she went. At last, she arrived at the entrance to the store room. Its door was ajar so she kicked it in. An opening in the ceiling allowed enough light inside to show her that it was deserted. Still keeping a wall to her back, she began to rip open storage boxes and among the least damaged, found what she was looking for. Keeping one eye on the doorway, she set her rifle down and began tearing at the plastic sheeting whose protection had preserved the clothing almost like new.

Soon, she had two new sets of light, cotton trousers, shirts and undergarments stuffed in her backpack and was moving quickly out of the store. A few doors down, she stepped into a department store. Here she found first aid materials, aspirin, and feminine products. She had kept the store most likely to present danger for last, so moving more slowly, she went to the supermarket which anchored the plaza at the far end.

Ignoring the doors, she stepped into the cashier area through one of the many empty display windows. She stopped there a long while, listening, every sense alert, but detected nothing that seemed to warn of danger. Crossing the row of registers she began to pass along the head of the aisles. With signs long since vanished and unused to how the store was organized, she was forced to look in every aisle for what she wanted. Most of the perishables in the store were long since gone of course, but she learned that these larger stores almost always retained some preserved foods. But the first thing she found turned out to be not food but a very useful flashlight. Delighted, she took it down and ripped it from its protective package which also included batteries. When she inserted them, she found that the instrument still worked. She tucked it in one of the deep pockets of her camouflaged trousers.

At the far end of the third aisle, she found what remained of the canned foods section. Kicking through the scattered debris, she found a couple dozen cans that were still intact and filled a sturdy canvas bag with them that she had brought for the purpose. She moved on, hoping to find some canned juice.

Shara rounded the end of the last aisle and froze.

Near the old refrigerated section she found two skeletons.

They were human and only recently dead. She could tell that because the thousands of roaches covering them were still busily picking the bodies clean of their flesh. Shara had only enough time to notice the column of insects as they moved in the seemingly haphazard fashion of their kind back and forth along a trail that stretched back through what used to be the store's service doors. After that, the alert insects became aware of her presence and immediately detached elements from the column and headed them in her direction. Suddenly, she became aware of noises, the skitterings and scratchings of the insects as, enervated by a new source of fresh food, began to move en masse. Here and there, cans and debris, disturbed by the frenzied movements, began to crash throughout the store and dust dribbled down from cracks in the ceiling as scouts were called in. Still mindful of her belongings, Shara held onto her bags and rifle and backed quickly up the way she had come. Suddenly, all about her, above and below and on all sides, the store seemed to have come alive with a cacophony of sound.

And yet, Shara did not panic. She had been in similar situations before. The one advantage she still had over the insects was her speed and the stride between her long legs. But then again, what separated this instance from past events was that she had been caught inside a building. Her movements were constrained and more immediately, limited between aisles of shelving. Luckily however, the roach civilization was not as advanced as those of the ants or bees due to their inherent laziness. Thus she need not worry about explosive booby traps or mechanized pursuit.

Dashing to the front of the store, Shara had been prepared to continue at top speed through one of the window openings but instead, she stopped short. Great sheets of intricately woven netting had been lowered across the gaping window and door frames preventing escape. She knew from experience just how tough that netting was, having inspected it closely once at the site of an abandoned roach colony.

The frantic noises around her were growing louder now and she was conscious of having to make an effort to control a welling panic. Quickly, she looked around and spied a courtesy booth in the corner of the cashier area with a door in the back. She banged open the swinging doors to the booth and pulled at the knob of the inner door. Locked! Behind her, the skitterings of the converging insects and the sounds of disturbed debris grew more persistent as she brought up her rifle and fired at the lock. Instantly, it vanished as the door blew open. Not waiting, she dashed into the darkened interior as she pulled the flashlight from the pocket in her trousers. As she suspected, the locked door meant little chance that the roaches had occupied the room behind it and as she swept it quickly with the flashlight, she could see it had been an employee rest area. Rusty lockers and broken furniture littered the interior and old vending machines stood in the corners, the hardened contents of their drinks seeping from beneath them like coagulated blood. She found that there was no lock on another, inner door and passed through that, acutely conscious of her pursuit by the roaches which were now literally at her heels. With no time to spare, she flung herself onto an iron ladder that led up to a square hatch in the ceiling. With the horde of roaches temporarily stymied beneath the ladder, she had time to collect her wits and push open the hatch. Immediately, the bright light of the outdoors streamed in, scattering in an instant the milling thousands on the floor below. Enervated by the light and fresh air, Shara lifted herself to the roof of the store and slammed the hatch back into place with an angry shove. Panting hard and sweating profusely, she was not as angry with the voracious roaches as she was with herself for getting in such a predicament. But in reviewing her actions as her mother had taught her to do after every action gone wrong, she could not find anything wrong with her movements. Unless it was entering the store in the first place, but that sometimes needed to be done and she had taken every precaution in doing so. No, this time, the odds had caught up with her. Sometimes it happened. Throwing her groceries over her shoulder, she hefted her rifle and made her way to the fire escape at the corner of the roof.

A few weeks later, Shara found herself in the great fungoid forest north of the blasted city, having passed safely through a recently war-ravaged no man's land between growing insect colonies. Fat, diseased looking mushrooms towered in clumps everywhere and the ground beneath them was matted thick with long grass. Here and there, the desiccated remnants of the hardwood forest that had once stood in its place lay in dry tangles. It was the plentiful supply of this dry timber that had first attracted her mother to the area and her subsequent discovery that much of the fungoidal growth could be consumed. Lying in the thick grass with her head resting on a sunken log, Shara luxuriated in the growing warmth of the morning sun. Beside her the ashes of a cold campfire indicated that she had occupied the site for some time. Twenty feet away, a simple stockade of tree branches made for a simple defense against the occasional rainfall. Shara had decided the night before that it was about time she went back to a nearby town to restock on some supplies but there was no rush in getting there. Closing her eyes, she thought back to her earliest memories of the mushroom forest; of the times, in the company of her mother, that she first learned the ways of the new wild. She smiled to herself. "The new wild" was a phrase her mother had used to describe the post-blast world, a new world in which she had had to learn the rules by trial and error. Many were the nights that she would toss and turn with stomach cramps after sampling the new kinds of foods produced from irradiated farms and gardens. She learned to avoid discovery by other roving humans and studied with fascination the ways of the new insect civilizations. All knowledge she had painstakingly imparted to her daughter, knowledge that had kept Shara alive for the twenty years since her mother's death.

Shara's admiration for her mother knew no bounds and not a day passed that she did not strive to match her courage and intelligence, the kind of courage that had allowed her to survive the trauma of rape and Shara's subsequent birth. In those days apparently, encountering a normal human being was a more frequent occurrence than it was at present and although her mother tried to avoid meeting them, now and then she could not help it. It was as a result of one of those encounters that her mother was attacked.

The man had come upon her in stealth, apparently quite used to woodcraft himself and had asked her mother if they might become a couple and travel together. When her mother declined the offer, she was attacked. When it was over and while the man was less alert, she killed him. Shara never learned how. It was not until some weeks after the event that her mother realized that the dead man had left her with child.

Her mother had once confessed that the idea of inducing an abortion to rid her of the child had crossed her mind, but once she began to consider how congenial it would be to have a child, who would also be a friend, to accompany her in a life that suddenly seemed long and lonely, she could not go through with it. She decided to allow the pregnancy to continue and if the child was born an imbecile or deformed...well, she would decide what to do if that exigency arrived. Luckily however, it never happened. Shara was born on schedule in the seclusion of a fungoidal bower, normal in every way. Someday, perhaps, the subtle effects of radiation poisoning could make themselves apparent, but Shara and her mother had never worried about it. They were too busy surviving and learning to delight in each other's company. Now Shara's heart grew heavy and involuntarily, a lump formed in her throat as she thought back to the day her mother died. It happened somewhere along their migration route back southward. She had suddenly developed internal bleeding and weakened rapidly. Mother and daughter both knew that the radiation sickness had finally caught up with them. Shara buried her mother in an unmarked grave in a forest of poplar and oak and moved on. She had been alone ever since.

Shara rose suddenly, determined to shake off the feelings of melancholy that had crept upon her. Picking up her rifle and back pack, she strode from her campsite and plunged into the depths of the fungoid forest. All that day she spent in the nearby town searching for supplies and by the time she started back, her depression had passed. It was then, after her guard had been lowered somewhat, that she was taken by surprise.

She had been walking up a grassy hillside toward the edge of the forest when she looked up and saw the man at the crest. He was leaning against a low toadstool, apparently waiting for her. He spoke first.

"I saw you moving around in the streets down there and decided to wait for you here," he said. "My name's Morgan."

Shara did not reply, eyeing him instead. He seemed younger than she was and normal with no obvious deformities. But no matter what positive qualities he might have had, no matter how companionable he might have been, there was no escaping the ultimate relationship he was hoping to establish between them. It was the encounter she had been dreading and avoiding her whole life.

"Oh," she said.

"You're the first normal human being I've seen in seven years," he said, straightening. "What about you?"

"I haven't kept count."

Morgan smiled and crossed his arms revealing twin pistols slung at his hips. "You haven't seen many either. Look, we both know that there are precious few of us around. The normals are dying out fast, if we aren't the last after all, we should stick together."

"I'm not interested."

The man was losing patience. Clearly, he had expected a more friendly reception to his sudden appearance.

"Don't you see?," he pleaded. "It would be safer for both of us; we'd have a better chance of staying alive against the imbeciles and the insects. And about the insects? Their colonies are growing and they're getting smarter every day; if we humans don't do something about it, we'll die off and the insects will have the earth for themselves."

"They can have it," said Shara, making as if to move around him.

"Hold it there, we have a duty..."

Shara had brought up her rifle with the muzzle aimed directly at the man's belly. "Keep back or I'll use this."

Morgan raised his hands slightly and took a step back. "I believe you. All right, if that's the way you feel, but your attitude doesn't change the fact that we have an obligation to keep the human race alive..."

"What human race? There's only the two of us here and precious few more," said Shara, still keeping the gun trained on him.

"That's the point, it's our duty to do what we can..."

"There's nothing we can do to change things. Even if we had a child between us, there wouldn't be enough normal human beings around to keep a population growing. The gene pool is too small. The human race has shrunk past the point where it can do anything but produce a few more imbeciles and I'm not in the mood to waste my time. I'm good with this so don't follow me, or I'll have to shoot you."

Shara began to circle around him until she was able to back deeper into the forest. Soon, the man was lost to sight. She stopped behind a thick boled mushroom and peered back. There was no sign that he was following her.

———

He caught up to her that night.

Shara resisted briefly until her wrists were brought together and held in a powerful grip.

"I'm sorry it has to be this way," the man said.

Shara continued to struggle but then apparently resigned herself to the situation. Afterwards, when he had finished, she took her knife from where she had thrust it in the ground for easy access and struck him a powerful blow to the head. He slumped heavily across her. She rolled him over, stood up and went to wash in a nearby stream. When she had cleaned up, she dressed and gathered her things. The man still lay where she had dropped him. She was surprised to find that she did not hate him or even resent him. She understood that he could not help himself, that he had merely been following a biological imperative, a weakness she had turned to her own advantage.

Weeks later, after the alterations of her accustomed bodily rhythms had become too obvious to be explained away, Shara had the satisfaction of knowing that her plan had succeeded. Oh, she could have simply invited the man into her arms, but she had feared that allowing him to do so would pose the danger of the creation of an emotional bond between them, an attachment that would have put an end to her way of life. And most of all, she did not want that; it would have ruined her plans.

She touched her abdomen and smiled in anticipation of the arrival of her daughter who would grow according to the rules dictated by a new world. Rules that did not include such archaic notions as community. She would be a society of one, a world unto herself, and when the time came, she alone would decide whether or not to perpetuate a race, the new, post-blast race that had begun with Shara's mother.

The Future that Used to Be

JOEY IXBEE LAY ON his stomach, his head propped in his hands, as he lay on the carpet in Steve Garabon's TV room. At the moment, it was late on a Saturday afternoon and the two best friends were engrossed in the latest Creature Feature offering: *Earth vs the Flying Saucers*. Although both boys agreed that with stop motion effects by the great Ray Harryhausen the film was a science fiction classic, Joey thought the plot was on the unrealistic side.

Suddenly, the soundtrack swelled and over the smoking ruins of a downed alien flying saucer, the words "The End" appeared on the screen. Instantly, Steve was on his feet and snapped off the television set even before Feep, the show's host, could come on and utter a few concluding inanities in his high pitched voice.

"Great movie!" exclaimed Joey as the picture tube went dark save for a tiny dot of light at the center.

"I'll say!" agreed Steve. "The story was a little too much like *War of the Worlds*, but those force fields and flying saucers crashing into the Capital Building and the Washington Monument were fantastic!"

"The effects were definitely cool, but some of the other stuff was a little too much," said Joey.

"How do you mean?"

"Well, if the aliens were so smart, smart enough to build spaceships and travel all the way to Earth from another world, why didn't they just open diplomatic channels to the UN or something? I mean, that's got to be easier for them than trashing the planet. How's that supposed to help 'em?"

Steve shrugged. "Never thought about that before. I guess it would be easier to just make friends than to start a war."

"Right. And those saucers..."

"What about 'em?"

"In real life, they just wouldn't fly...at least not in Earth's atmosphere," insisted Joey. "They're not aerodynamic enough. In space, their shape wouldn't make a difference, but once in Earth's atmosphere, they'd drop like a rock!"

"You think so?"

"Sure, I think so."

"What if they had anti-gravity?"

"I guess that would work," conceded Joey. "But how likely is that? After all, the laws of physics are the same no matter where you go in the universe. Shucks, Steve, I don't think you've been keeping up with your science fiction reading!"

"Ah, gimme a break!"

"All right, boys," interrupted Steve's mother from where she stood at the entrance to the TV room. "You've been indoors for the last two hours and it's a beautiful sunny day outside. Time for some fresh air before supper."

The boys needed no coaxing from Mrs. Garabon to move on.

Outside, the sun was indeed shining and temperatures must have been hovering in the upper 80s. Across the street, they could hear the splash of water and girlish voices crying in glee behind the Surois' house and overhead, a plane droned somewhere in the deep blue of the sky.

Retreating to the front porch of Steve's house, the two boys began what had become a ritual after viewing an SF film and reenacted to the best of their recollection the scenes they had just finished viewing on television. Notwithstanding the questionable authenticity of *Earth vs the Flying Saucers*, the balance of the afternoon was spent in imaginary war as Joey and Steve saved the world from the evil intentions of space invaders only they could see.

All too soon however, Joey heard his mother's call from down the street signaling the time for supper.

"Five o'clock already?" exclaimed Steve, finishing off an alien saucer.

"Must be, my stomach's grumbling," said Joey tossing a Mattel issue replica of a German Luger to his friend. "See you after supper?"

"Over at Gil's for kick the can," returned Steve heading for the house.

Quickly, Joey ran from behind the Garabon's house to the front yard and hurdled the hedges ringing the property in a single bound. Landing in the street, he barely missed

a step heading down tree lined Maple Road to
his own home at the far end of the neighborhood.

Flying through the front gate, Joey ran
around the house to the back porch letting the
screen door slam shut behind him in way of
announcing his arrival. In the yard outside,
nothing had changed since his parents bought
the property when Joey was still an infant: the
previous owner having been a carpentry con-
tractor, the yard was littered with the debris of
his trade from huge stacks of petrified planking
to sheds and other outbuildings overrun in
weeds and crawling vines. Alongside the house,
a two stall garage stood, still crammed with the
rusting hulks of heavy automated saws and
planers. Everywhere inside the garage were
mounds of old sawdust left uncollected for
years.

Inside the porch, the air was filled with the
aroma of fresh baked muffins so Joey simply
followed his nose into the kitchen. There, the
table was already set and Sally, his younger
sister, sat at her usual place next to the high
chair that baby Cynthia would soon occupy.

"Don't forget to wash up before supper,
Joey," said his mother, tossing the words over
her shoulder as she mashed the potatoes.

"I know," replied Joey heading for the
bathroom.

"Can we hold off on supper for a few minutes?" asked his father stepping into the
kitchen, the late edition newspaper in his
hand. "I'd like to hold a quick family meeting
first."

Mrs. Ixbee blew at a stray lock that had fallen across her face. "It can wait for a few minutes."

"Fine. Let's all step into the family room, shall we?"

A minute later, Joey had joined the others and thrown himself onto one end of the over-stuffed couch that also held Sally at the opposite end and his mother holding baby Cynthia in the center. His father sat in the easy chair across the room from them.

"What's this about, dad?" asked Joey.

"Well, your mother and I have an announcement to make," began his father. "We're expecting company tomorrow and we want you and Sally to be on your best behavior."

"Oh, boy!" exclaimed Sally, clapping her hands. "Company! We never have guests."

"Well, hardly never," said Mrs. Ixbee. "But this one is different."

"How different?" asked Joey, suddenly interested.

"It's my brother," said Mrs. Ixbee. "He's coming over all the way from Xorbid."

"Wow!" said Joey, impressed. "The home-world!"

Mrs. Ixbee turned to her husband then and said something not in English but clearly inflected as a question. Joey's father nodded and replied in the same language.

"What are you saying?" asked Sally, confused.

"Shh," said Joey, listening closely. "They're talking about Uncle Xuxtex."

"Sorry, kids," said Mr. Ixbee. "Sometimes your mother and I forget ourselves."

"Were you talking in French?" asked Sally wide eyed.

"No dear," laughed Mrs. Ixbee. "That was the language of our home planet, Xorbid."

"That's the place we moved from, isn't it?"

"That's right," replied Mrs. Ixbee. "We first moved to Earth from Xorbid many years ago when Joey was only four years old...by Earth standards."

"That's why I still understand some of the language," said Joey proudly.

"Do you remember anything else, Joey?" asked Sally, impressed with her older brother.

"Not much," admitted Joey. "I remember we used to live in a glass house, made like a bunch of soap bubbles jumbled together, and we had a car that could fly."

"Gosh!"

"And I had a pet of some kind; about as big as a dog with red scales..."

"That was called an ozkor," said his father. "A very common creature in the desert regions of Xorbid."

"And didn't we have something like a TV set except you put something on your head and it would be like you were part of the movie?"

His father nodded. "Not like a television at all. Whole different principle. But it was for entertainment sure enough."

"It all sounds so interesting!" said Sally. "Why did we move?"

There was a brief silence then until Mr. Ixbee replied. "Even though we had a lot of nice things on Xorbid, our lives there were not entirely happy so we decided to leave and come to Earth. You were very young at the time so you don't remember. But we've told you how we gave ourselves Earth names and settled here in the United States and how it's really important that you never tell anyone about where we came from."

"I remember that!"

"And you've done a good job keeping our little secret," complimented Mrs. Ixbee.

"Dad, why's Uncle Xuxtex coming to visit now?" asked Joey suddenly suspicious. "Does it have anything to do with us leaving Xorbid and coming to Earth?"

"As a matter of fact it does," said his father truthfully. "Our family back on Xorbid never approved our decision to move to Earth. Although Xuxtex is no doubt coming here to convince us to go back, your mother and I hope that after coming to know Terrans first hand and seeing the way we live here, he'll come to understand our reasons for choosing Earth over the homeworld."

"And why is that exactly?" persisted Joey.

"We've explained our reasons to you before although I admit mostly in general terms," said Mr. Ixbee. "But when it comes right down to it, our lives on Xorbid, though wanting nothing, were yet unfulfilling. In short, we weren't happy there and what we knew of the way Terrans lived on Earth convinced us to come and live among these admirable people."

"No regrets?"

"None. And what about you? Have you been happy here?"

Joey thought about his life on Earth, his friends in the neighborhood and at school.

"Well, yeah, but I could do without having to go to Sunday school," he finally answered. "Why can't I go to regular services with you and mom?"

"You have to learn to crawl before you can walk," said his father wisely.

Everyone laughed then and presently Mrs. Ixbee rose saying that supper was going to get cold if the meeting went on any longer. Together, the family retreated into the kitchen and took their places around the dinner table.

Slipping into his place across from Sally, Joey waited as his mother put baby Cynthia into her high chair and removed the roast from the oven. Shortly, all was ready and his father led the family in a brief prayer of thanks.

"So how was your day, Joey?" asked Mr. Ixbee as he began to cut the roast into handy slices.

"Same as usual, dad," Joey replied, suddenly realizing how hungry he was.

"Watching TV? Riding your bike?"

"Sure. There was an accident down on Sladen Street. A car went off the road and ran down Mrs. Fellows' hedges as neat as you please!"

"Saw the remains when I came up the street. Anyone hurt?"

"Nah."

"You sound disappointed."

"Well it wasn't that exciting."

"It was another gorgeous day to be alive and blessed with such a wonderful world," chimed in his mother. "Never let your days get so routine that you take that for granted."

"Amen," agreed his father. "I count our blessings every day we're here, even during the dullest moments at work."

"That may be easier for you guys," said Joey around a mouthful of asparagus. "At least you have a point of reference. Try that when you're sitting in Miss Faragut's math class!"

"What's so bad about Miss Faragut's class?" Sally wanted to know.

"Only that it's the most boring ever."

"I like her class the best."

"That's 'cause you're not doing fractions yet."

"Fractions come in mighty handy for things like space travel," observed Mr. Ixbee.

"You use 'em a lot at the observatory don't you, dad?"

"Mm, hm. Contrary to what most people believe, an astronomer doesn't just look at pictures of stars. With today's modern radio telescopes, there's a lot of mathematical calculating that's needed. Even with computers to help you."

"Well, I'm finished," declared Joey with a scrape of his chair. "We'll be over Gil Steiner's house."

"You come right home when I call," warned his mother.

"Okay, mom. Sally, you and Polly comin' over later for kick the can?"

"Of course. And Brianna's coming too."

"Great! The more kids, the more fun it is. See you."

"Don't forget what we discussed kids," reminded his father.

"Don't worry," said Joey as the screen door slammed to behind him.

The pink in the western sky had long since faded away as Joey threw himself on the grassy slope that dominated Gil's back yard. He and his friends had been running and hiding for the last hour or so ever since the sun went down and the streetlight in front of Steve's house came on, signaling that it was time to begin playing kick the can. More fun in the dark than in the daylight, the action focused on Gil's back yard due to a pair of spotlights located at the extreme ends of his house. The lights threw just enough glare to pinpoint the coffee can in the center of the lawn while allowing enough darkness for everyone to scatter out of sight. Steve and Joey had their own plan for remaining safe until they were good and ready to run in, one involving a circuitous route through neighboring yards and then popping out of the darkness when least expected to kick the can. That effort often left them exhausted and it was after the latest execution of the plan that Joey joined Steve on the lawn.

Soon, with Polly having finally been caught and the last round finished, the gang was complete and as they sat in a group, small talk ensued.

"Hey, anyone watch that show last night, *Towards the Year 2000?*" Gil wanted to know.

"The one where every week they show something different about how cool things are going to be in the future?" asked Steve.

"Yeah. Last night they were talking about how we won't need cars in the future because there'll be high speed monorails and frictionless trains to get people where they want to go."

"What about flying cars?" asked Joey.

"Nothing about them."

"Rats!"

"You'd probably be disappointed with the show about robots too," said Gil. "That one said we'd have whole factories run by robots but they didn't look anything like Robby the Robot from *Forbidden Planet*. They just looked like regular machines."

"Double rats!" said Joey.

"I have to admit the show's probably showing things the way they really will turn out," mused Steve. "The robots and monorails they have on the show actually exist right now, they just haven't been mass produced yet. I have a feeling that the future isn't going to be as exciting as we thought it was."

The others had to admit that though they would be disappointed if the future held few of the wonders as seen in various science fiction movies, the future as presented on *Towards the Year 2000* certainly looked exciting enough anyway!

"When I grow up, I'm gonna be an engineer so that I can be on the ground floor when those robots start going to work!" declared Gil.

"Not me," said Joey. "I'm gonna work for NASA and build rockets."

"I loved that chemistry set I got last Christmas," said Steve. "Think I'll go into chemistry."

"You have to know German to be a chemist," reminded Gil.

"No foolin'?"

Gil nodded sagely. "We're German; I know."

From there, conversation came around to guessing each other's nationality. It was pointed out that Greeks, French, Germans, and English were represented until it occurred to Gil that no one was able to figure out what nationality Ixbee was.

"What about it, Joey," asked Brianna. "What nationality is it?"

Joey was not disturbed by the question his parents having long since anticipated it.

"Not sure," said Joey shrugging. "I think my parents said it was Eastern European or something. Hungarian or Polish or something."

"Maybe you're a mongrel!" joked Steve.

"Probably."

Just then, Polly's mother called from the darkness that it was time for Polly to come in. As if in signal, Brianna also rose and left with her. Then the porch lights came on behind Gil's house notifying him that it was time to go in. On cue, Joey heard his own mother calling from down the street.

"Must be 9 o'clock already," said Steve getting up.

"Guess we'll see you guys tomorrow morning," said Joey pulling Sally up.

"Right. Hey, Joey, want to go to the movies tomorrow? The Strand is having a double feature including *Billy the Kid Meets Frankenstein!*"

"I'll have to check my piggy bank," replied Joey as he and Sally cut through Polly's yard to Maple Road.

Walking along the darkened street heading for home after a day packed with distractions, Joey thought he liked this time best of all. Breathing deeply of the clean night air, he paused a moment to look up at the star filled sky.

"Which one do you think we come from?" whispered Sally.

Joey considered a moment and pointed.

"See the Big Dipper there? If you follow it to the end of the handle and look to the left...wow!"

He was interrupted by a streak of light across the sky and as it arced down toward the ground, he heard Sally gasp beside him.

"A falling star!" she exclaimed pointing.

"And it's lasting a long time too," noted Joey, as the object disappeared behind a distant tree line. "Usually meteors only last a few seconds coming down. That must have been a big one."

The next morning when Joey came down for breakfast, he was caught by surprise.

Sitting at the table with his father was a stranger. The two were drinking coffee while his mother emptied the dishwasher. Judging by the awkward manner in which the stranger handled his drink, Joey guessed he was unfamiliar with ordinary cups.

"Good morning, Joey," said his father. "Say hello to your Uncle Xuxtex."

"Hello Uncle Xuxtex," said Joey dutifully, sitting at the table and reaching for the box of Wheaties.

"Xylel, how you have grown!" exclaimed his uncle.

"What?"

"Xylel is your birth name," said his father. "When we came to Earth, we decided that our family name wouldn't arouse too much suspicion but that we needed more familiar sounding ones for our personal names. We called you Joseph, a venerable Terran name."

"Oh," said Joey pouring some milk over his cereal. "I'm sure glad you did. I'd hate to have to go to school with a name like Xylel; the other kids would really give me a rough time!"

He said nothing, but Xuxtex looked at his brother-in-law and frowned.

"Uncle Xuxtex hasn't seen you since just before we came to Earth from Xorbid, Joey," said his father clearing his throat.

"I'm sorry Uncle Xuxtex, that I don't remember you..."

"No problem Xy...I mean Joey," replied Xuxtex. "That was a long time ago. But tell me, do you enjoy life here on Earth? I mean, do you miss the homeworld at all?"

"I suppose it's not a fair comparison," said Joey thoughtfully. "After all, I don't remember much from homeworld; just a few things. But I really enjoy living here on Earth. It feels safe and comfortable."

Xuxtex leaned back in his chair and his eyes met those of Mr. Ixbee. Joey's father was smiling, obviously satisfied with his son's answer.

Picking up baby Cynthia, Mrs. Ixbee suggested that since it was such a nice morning, the men should take their coffee and go for a stroll in the yard. Agreeing, Mr. Ixbee and Xuxtex rose and left the house.

Outside, the early morning sun shone down from a cloudless sky suggesting another warm summer day. Morning doves called from somewhere in the tangle of trees at the far end of the back yard and butterflies fluttered about piles of old lumber. A heat bug chirred in the brush.

"You had no trouble with entry last night?" asked Mr. Ixbee presently.

"Nothing," replied Xuxtex. "It was clear over half the northern hemisphere with hardly any atmospherics. I left the ship in stealth mode at the spot you advised. It's still safe isn't it?"

"Yes although there has been talk of some development in that area."

"Where, by the way, do you keep your own rocket?"

"In the garage," replied Mr. Ixbee nonchalantly.

"The garage!" cried Xuxtex, spinning to look back at the old structure with the peeling paint.

"We keep it under a tarp."

"That's all?"

"We tell people it's an antique car."

Xuxtex shook his head.

"It's quite safe there. There are a few pieces of large wood working equipment in there as well and one more covered bulk attracts no attention. I check the instruments now and then to make sure it's still in operating condition."

They said nothing more for a few minutes contenting themselves with their coffee and wading through the tall, uncut grass that covered the yard, chasing grasshoppers from their hiding places. Soon, they had circled behind the garage out of sight of the house.

"I'd forgotten how good this tasted," said Xuxtex presently, sipping at his coffee mug. "Guess it's been too long since I saw you last, when you brought some of this beverage back home with you."

"Thirteen years ago Terran time," said Mr. Ixbee. "When Xaxlee and I returned from our first tour of Earth. You should have come visit us before this, Xuxtex. And the rest of the family too."

"You know why we haven't."

"Yes. But I fail to understand why none of them have become accustomed to the idea yet."

"It's too radical a move, Uxxo," said Xuxtex, using Mr. Ixbee's real name. "People back home just don't understand how you and Xaxlee could just leave your home with all its comforts...its normalcy...to live on this primitive world and among such uncouth natives."

"We've explained that to you all a number of times, Xuxtex," said Mr. Ixbee. "When Xaxlee and I were members of a survey crew assigned to Earth for research purposes, we were impressed not only by the natives' industry and inventiveness, but their sense of optimism and hope. They looked to the future with anticipation and worked hard to make sure that it would be better than what had come before. For that reason, they lavished personal attention on their children and managed to transfer their dreams to following generations.

"At the time, Xaxlee and I weren't the only members of the crew who were impressed with the natives' attitude," Mr. Ixbee said. "Maybe it was because Xaxlee was a sociologist, but she was more sensitive to what made the Terrans a unique and admirable people. Through the long days aboard ship on the way back home she and I talked about her findings and conclusions so that by the time we reached home-world, not only had we fallen love, but shared an admiration for Terran ways.

"When we finally returned to Xorbid, life there only accentuated the superiority of Terran ways and that's when Xaxlee and I really became cognizant of the important differences between the Earthers and our own people," continued Mr. Ixbee. "Where the Terrans were optimistic and industrious, our people were cynical and luxurious; where the Terrans nurtured their young within the family unit, we handed our children over to the state in order to continue our lives of dissipation without interruption. Simply put, our civilization had run its course. The current generations were simply coasting on the great achievements of the past.

And as if to ensure that the creativity of our ancestors could never be recaptured, our people refused to share their lives with offspring having fewer births with every cycle.

"If such trends continue," concluded Mr. Ixbee, "Xaxlee predicts that our race will be extinct in one hundred and thirty-two cycles."

"So?" said Xuxtex, unconcerned. "Where does it say that a race must perpetuate itself? The current generation owes nothing to those that came before it and generations to come can only be better off with fewer people with which to share the resources of homeworld. In time, Xorbid might even return to its nascent condition, clean of the unnatural uses to which our people have put it."

"How wrong you are, Xuxtex," replied Mr. Ixbee. "Children are the glory of the previous generations. Properly nurtured, they can carry on the spirit of exploration and inventiveness bequeathed to them by their forbears while providing a continuum of values that give life meaning and providing it with the momentum needed by succeeding generations. Such is what our own civilization has lost, Xuxtex. The continuum between ourselves and our forebears has been shattered and we have been left like orphans to find our own way in an environment littered with sensual distractions."

"That all sounds good in theory, Uxxo," said Xuxtex gesturing at their surroundings. "But this is the here and now. This is reality. Xaxlee is in that primitive abode right this minute tending to a child herself. Cooking and washing by hand instead of living in a fully automated dwelling..."

"Well, we do have some automation..."

"You know what I mean! It's all such a crude lifestyle leaving little time for personal..."

"On the contrary," said Mr. Ixbee as they came within sight of the house again and Mrs. Ixbee sitting at a picnic table with baby Cynthia in her lap. "We find life here exhilarating and uplifting. And besides, we haven't given up all our ways...what little automation there is still allows Xaxlee plenty of time to continue her research of Terran society."

"But how can she?" Xuxtex wanted to know. "With three children, two more than most women on the homeworld bother with, she must have little time for anything else. What is the role of the state in such circumstances?"

"There is none," said Mrs. Ixbee. "Interference by the state in family life is frowned upon by most Terrans."

"But then how do you explain the need for sending the children to a state institution for their education?"

"There are some things that are more efficiently done as a group than within the family unit," replied Xaxlee. "And even so, parents have a strong voice in how schools are conducted."

Xuxtex shuddered. "And how do you cope with random weather patterns? This planet doesn't employ even minimal weather control. You can never be sure when might be a good day to launch a rocket; how annoying! And then there's the transportation situation: ground vehicles using internal combustion engines! Aren't you afraid the things might blow themselves up at any moment?"

"Oh, they're hardly as dangerous as that," soothed Xaxlee. "Why Uxxo has driven to the observatory every day and has never had any trouble."

"Far more danger is posed by other drivers than the vehicle itself," said Mr. Ixbee. "I'll admit this world is backward in many ways but those ways are all technological. In every other way, I think Terran culture is superior to our own."

"And you agree with that assertion?" Xuxtex asked, turning to his sister.

"I've been trained as a sociologist and have made Terran society my life's work and all my research has convinced me that it is so," said Xaxlee gravely. "For instance, recently in its history, Xorbid found itself threatened by malcontents and when the state asked the young men to step forward and help in the world's defense, not a one did. Too timid to compel the men to do their duty, the state instead submitted to the demands of the malcontents and as soon as the threat was over, all the young men reappeared to resume their lives of indolence and ease. They preferred sacrificing a little bit of their freedoms to defending their heritage. That was many decades ago; since then, the same malcontents have returned a number of times and each time homeworld has given in. Addicted to their lives of ease and plenty, each generation of our people becomes more myopic, refusing to see how much their lives and freedoms have been circumscribed by their own inaction. By contrast, when this nation among others was threatened by powerful outside forces, the state was overwhelmed by the number of young men willing to forego their own pursuits in defense of their way of life."

"So it was you're being impressed by that barbaric display of arms that convinced you to forsake your world and your family to come here and live under these primitive conditions?"

Mrs. Ixbee shook her head. "Don't you understand, Xuxtex? These people still retain the values that give worth to everything they do. They could achieve nothing and still be a great people. Our world mastered nature and even conquered the stars but what did it get us? We are a small minded, self centered people who are rapidly frittering away what's left of our civilization. Some day soon, we'll lose it all but I'm confident that when the time comes that the people of Earth must face the same challenge, it will be the malcontents who'll submit. I want that for my children. I want them to share in the values that will not only give their own lives meaning, but meaning to the entire race of Terrans."

"I understand more and more family units from homeworld are doing as we did; moving themselves to Earth and living anonymously among the Terrans," said Mr. Ixbee, placing a supporting hand on his wife's shoulder. "Already, Xaxlee and I are working to create a support network to help newcomers adjust to life here. Some day our children may decide to return to the homeworld and they'll tell about what they've learned on Earth. If we're lucky, our people will listen and hopefully, heed what they have to say before it's too late."

"You...have given me much to think about," said a chastened Xuxtex. "If you'll excuse me?"

Leaving the couple at the picnic table, Xuxtex wandered from the yard and onto Maple Road where the morning was slowly warming and from somewhere out of sight, the gay voices of children could be heard.

Frustrated and a little angry at his sister and her husband's intransigent attitudes, Xuxtex walked through the neighborhood without paying too much attention to where he was going. It was the raucous warning sound from one of the Terran's smelly internal combustion ground cars that finally roused him from his thoughts and looking up, he saw that he had arrived in the town's commercial district. All about him, Terrans moved briskly to and fro intent on business or pleasure. Females hurried with arms laden in packages and males in formal attire looked to be on serious business. Food markets bustled and proprietors let down awnings to protect their ware from the sun. Coming upon a small park in the center of the town, Xuxtex availed himself of a bench and sat at his ease. Observing the busy Terrans, he found the energy they displayed infectious and yearned to take part in the grand object of all their efforts. But what object was it?

Xuxtex, surprised at his attitude, determined to study the Terrans more closely. He saw how children attached themselves to their parents, how they were allowed to run free to explore their world, to make their own mistakes (one youngster fell and apparently hurt his knee; others traveled in groups independent of adults visiting commercial establishments or eating sweets at their leisure). He observed more than once, the courteous behavior of males toward females, the tipping of hats, or opening of doorways. He saw the orderly manner in which ground cars moved in the streets expressive of large scale community cooperation and broadly accepted rules of behavior. As he watched, Xuxtex soon discovered that the disdain in which he had always held races other than his own, was beginning to ease in regard to the Terrans. He was beginning to enjoy his little sociological excursion and as he watched, he noticed a group of youngsters that included Xilel among them as they approached a sidewalk vender.

"Hello...Joey," called Xuxtex, catching himself at the last moment and using his nephew's Terran name.

The youth turned suddenly at the sound of his name and smiled broadly when he saw Xuxtex.

"Uncle Xuxtex," he said. "What are you doing downtown?"

Xuxtex shrugged. "Just needed to do some thinking so I decided to take a walk. What's that you're eating?"

"Ice cream," said Joey. "Want some?"

"Which item do you recommend?" asked Xuxtex reaching into the pocket of his Terran attire for some legal tender.

"I like the chocolate eclairs," suggested Joey who was nearly half finished with his own.

"I'll have a chocolate éclair," Xuxtex told the white coated vendor and extended some paper currency.

"Whoa there! Too much!" The vendor took only what he needed and returned Xuxtex change. "Have a good day, sir."

After fumbling with the unfamiliar food wrapper, Xuxtex discovered that the frozen treat clung to a wooden stick and after carefully tasting it, found that he enjoyed it.

"This is quite good!" he exclaimed.

"Of course it is," said Joey. "Hey, I'll see you later okay? My friends are waiting for me."

"No problem," replied Xuxtex, relishing his frozen dessert. "Run along and I'll catch up with you back home."

Alone again, Xuxtex moved slowly along the sidewalk. Growing in confidence, he even greeted the occasional female that he passed in the manner he'd seen Terran males do. At last, it seemed that he had wandered away from the commercial district and as the landscape once again became dominated by green lawns and shady trees, a large building attracted his attention and by the cruciform symbol that topped its tall steeple, he recognized it as one of the many places of worship Terrans frequented.

It was one of a number of primitive affectations that Terrans retained that he had never understood and one that he had been disturbed to learn that Xaxlee and her family had taken to on his first visit to Earth many years before. At the time, they told him it had been merely to fit in with their Terran neighbors but in subsequent dispatches, Xaxlee explained that she and Uxxo began to see merit in a certain belief system. As they considered the matter, the notion of an endless, purposeless universe became oddly unsatisfying to them while Earth religion, which gave order to the universe and hope to the individual, gave them comfort. Xuxtex drew his gaze down from that cruciform symbol and recalled the abandon with which the people of his own world lived their lives, careless of others save how their fate would effect their own. When all responsibility had been given over to robots and automatons, what was there left to inspire a sense of belonging or of serving a higher purpose?

His earlier mood of euphoria gone, Xuxtex continued on until he had gone full circle and came upon his sister's home again. It was just coming on to the noon hour when he pushed the screen door open and stepped onto the porch. Somewhere inside the house, his infant niece was fussing and he could hear Xaxlee making cooing sounds to calm her down.

Idly, Xuxtex looked around and spied a scattering of colorful magazines on a table and taking one up at random, thumbed through it. Composed of groups of sequential drawings, it was obviously some reading material belonging to Joey. His attention was arrested by different passages that became increasingly impressive. One of the fictional characters was trapped somehow and yet knowing that death was imminent, his only regret was that he would not be able to continue working to improve the lives of his fellow men.

Noble sentiments! Xuxtex thought as he replaced the magazine on the table. The words seemed to summarize what Xaxlee and Uxxo had been trying to tell him about the Terrans. Had it taken a child's publication to make him finally understand? In a few simple words, the writer of that magazine had encapsulated what it was about the Terrans that so impressed Xaxlee and Uxxo and what it was that their own people so completely lacked or had lost over the years. The Terrans were a young people who still looked to the future with boundless optimism. They had not yet grown so cynical or self absorbed as the people back on the homeworld. Suddenly, it occurred to Xuxtex that the feeling he had enjoyed while observing the Terrans earlier that morning must have been akin to the sense of optimism they all shared and that gave meaning to all that they did.

Eager to confirm his newfound understanding of Terrans and the possibility that he too could share in their beliefs, Xuxtex extended his visit to Earth and in the process reacquainted himself with his sister and her husband. Days were spent reading over Xaxlee's notes regarding her ongoing study of Terran ways and learning about "baseball" from Joey and "hide and seek" from Sally. Evenings were spent lingering over coffee and in long discussions about Terran ways and history. He even took to bouncing baby Cynthia on his knee and surprised himself when he began to wonder if Xaxlee and Uxxo planned to have another child. After all, children here had a future to live for; they would build upon what their forbears had begun and not simply live off its crumbling remains.

Thus it was that Xuxtex had given serious consideration about remaining permanently on Earth but in the end, he felt it was necessary to return home if only to convince himself that his admiration for the Terrans was not unfounded.

It was on the final day of his visit that Xuxtex sat in the living room with the rest of the family when programming on the television set was suddenly interrupted for a news update on the nation's space program. As he watched two cumbersome vehicles draw closer and closer together some 185 miles above the Earth's Pacific Ocean, it occurred to Xuxtex that although the technology was crude, it represented Terrans' first, halting steps beyond the confines of their planet. The significance of these slow motion images assumed new meaning to him and he saw them at last for what they could mean to his own world. Would his people learn to admire the Terrans as he had, or was it already too late for Xorbid? Xuxtex hoped not.

"Is that what your rocket looks like Uncle Xuxtex?" asked Joey, interrupting his uncle's thoughts.

"Pretty much," replied Xuxtex.

"But I've seen our rocket in the garage and it doesn't have boosters or even retros..."

"Those things don't really matter, Joey," said Xuxtex, whose mind was not on the immediate conversation. "It's all the same thing."

"Huh?"

But Xuxtex had nothing more to add.

Later that night, after Sally and the baby had been put to bed, Xuxtex stood outside with Uxxo and Xaxlee and Joey. The four off worlders were looking up at the night sky. Overhead, an untold number of stars glittered coldly in the atmosphere and among them there was movement.

"It's too slow to be a meteor," observed Joey.

"It's one of the Gemini spacecraft," said his father watching the gleaming object make its way slowly above the horizon. "At this rate, it won't be long before the Terrans are moving about space as easily as our own people do."

"Let's hope that they don't repeat our mistakes," said Xaxlee holding her husband's hand. "That they keep their sense of wonder, their yearning to explore and to make things better for their children."

"There's hope for any race who can dream of the stars," said Xuxtex. "Our own race has become jaded and self-centered; so fearful of offending others or violating some social protocol that they have evolved themselves out of dreaming. The future no longer holds any fascination for them, nor does the unknown. They no longer dream of the future and when they bother to think at all, it is to dwell on the past. So long as Terrans maintain their capacity to dream, they'll be all right."

Somewhere, a night bird's cry echoed hollowly through the neighborhood and dimly, there was the sound of a baby crying. A lone light came on in a home down the street.

Tomorrow was another day, the first of many stretching into a future that, for some, no longer held promise and for others, if they were not careful, could still be squandered. But right then, it was 1965, and in the United States of America the future that used to be still shone as brightly as ever...

Somewhere, a night bird's cry echoed hollowly through the neighborhood and dimly, there was the sound of a baby crying. A lone light came on in a home down the street.

Tomorrow was another day, the first of many stretching into a future that, for some, no longer held promise and for others, if they were not careful, could still be squandered. But right then, it was 1965, and in the United States of America the future that used to be still shone as brightly as ever...